# Gentlemen at the Bat

*A Fictional Oral History*

# Gentlemen at the Bat

*A Fictional Oral History of the*
*New York Knickerbockers and*
*the Early Days of Base Ball*

HOWARD BURMAN

McFarland & Company, Inc., Publishers
*Jefferson, North Carolina, and London*

LIBRARY OF CONGRESS CATALOGUING-IN-PUBLICATION DATA

Burman, Howard.
　　Gentlemen at the bat : a fictional oral history of the New York
Knickerbockers and the early days of base ball / Howard Burman.
　　　　p.　　cm.

　　ISBN 978-0-7864-4720-6
　　softcover : 50# alkaline paper ∞

　　1. New York Knickerbockers (Baseball team)—History.
2. Baseball—New York (State)—History.　I. Title.
GV875.N46B87　2010
796.323'64097471—dc22　　　　　　　　　　　　　2009052617

British Library cataloguing data are available

*On the cover:* New York Knickerbockers, 1862. *Left to right, standing:* Duncan
Curry, Walter Avery, Henry Anthony, Charles Birney, William Tucker. *Seated:*
Charles DeBost, Doc Adams, James Whyte Davis, Ebenezer Dupignac,
Fraley Niebuhr (courtesy of Robert Edward Auctions). Background ©2010
Shutterstock

Manufactured in the United States of America

*McFarland & Company, Inc., Publishers
　Box 611, Jefferson, North Carolina 28640
　www.mcfarlandpub.com*

# Table of Contents

## PART FOUR: STRUGGLE FOR SURVIVAL 1847–1849

## PART FIVE: THE NATIONAL GAME 1850–1854

## PART SIX: BASE BALL FEVER 1855–1857

PART THIRTEEN: THE END 1880–1882

# A Note from the Author

*I think that no individual can look at truth. It blinds you. You look at it and you see one phase of it. Someone else looks at it and sees a slightly awry phase of it. But taken all together, the truth is what they saw though nobody saw the truth intact.*
— William Faulkner

This is the story of the New York Knickerbocker Base Ball Club, the first fully organized club and the first with written rules for the game that we have come to know as baseball. Although many details concerning the club and its members are unknown to us today, their influence is undeniable. While they did not invent the game, they stabilized the playing rules and maintained standards of conduct so as to foster the astonishing proliferation of players and clubs that helped shape the development of the game of baseball and profoundly influenced the cultural history of 19th century America.

The story begins with gentlemen players engaged in various informal bat and ball games in and around New York City, and follows them as they organize in 1845 with formal by-laws and playing rules, develop into the most influential club, shepherd the development of important rule changes, see baseball become our national game, lose their influence as the game becomes professional, and finally disband in 1882.

This book has been extensively researched using contemporary newspapers and journals, public records, the Knickerbocker Club Books, the Chadwick Diaries, and previously published baseball and period histories. Still, the Knickerbockers didn't think of themselves as "writing history" and accordingly didn't leave carefully documented records. Hence, the attempt here is to complete the story in a reasonable and consistent way.

I have used first-person narrations, a form of writing that takes advantage of the presentational strategies of fiction but nevertheless retains the truth claim of journalism. It reads as oral history, giving the story a sense of immediacy and freshness it would invariably lack had it been related in the third-person voice. Telling the story from multiple points of view reflect that the characters responded to events according to their perceptions of reality. That is, they acted and reacted according to what they thought to be true.

I have not altered any of the things we know, (or think we know) about the people and events in this story, but rather I have cast the narrative in the voices of those who were involved in the events they describe. Without changing anything for the sake of the narrative, I have filled in the blank spaces using, as playwright Jerome Lawrence used to say, "facts as a springboard for the imagination."

All of the principal figures in the history of the club have their say — Doc Adams, James Whyte Davis, Alexander Cartwright, William Wheaton, Duncan Curry and others.

Whenever practical I have used the actual words of the characters, culled from letters, reminiscences, quotes in newspapers, and other recorded utterances, although sometimes in a slightly edited fashion. In other instances, dialogue has been invented by me. For example, we know of the creation of the "Rules of the Knickerbocker Base Ball Club, Adopted September 23, 1845," as proposed by William Wheaton and William Tucker. What dialogue passed between these two men as they came up with these rules? Since we have no record of this, I have created dialogue that is consistent with the results.

The style of writing and speaking most commonly used at the time often involved long, concatenated sentences. I have tried to simplify these without completely losing the contemporary flavor and color. I have tried, too, to imbue the speakers with characteristics conforming to what we know about them, or at least what might be reasonably deduced given the information at hand. Naturally, the amount of available information varies. In some cases we know occupations, family backgrounds, and other assorted details. In some cases we have only names.

A note about one important character — Ashley Hyde. He is pure fabrication, created to represent the fan, or as they were known at the time, "cranks." I have allowed him to offer observations and insights about the game, the players, and the times that could not reasonably be put in the mouths of anyone else in the book.

A word about terminology. The words used in the early days of the game to describe it underwent many and continual changes, but in most cases it is not possible to put a precise date on when "innings" became "inning," "aces" became "runs," or "the garden" became "the outfield." I have used various terms at various times suggesting the overlapping use of these descriptors. The use of the term "innings" to denote a side's turn at bat is derived directly from cricket in which the team at bat is "in" and one in the field is "out."

In the writing of history, events by themselves are less important than the perception of those events. There are many legitimate ways to write history, but I hope that by offering a first-person approach, I have allowed readers to understand the speakers and events as if firsthand, without the intermediary of an omniscient third-person narrator. The aim is simple — to fill a gap in the story of how and why baseball developed as the game we know today.

# PROLOGUE

## A Real 1893 Letter from Jim Davis to Edward Talcott*

Mr. Edward B. Talcott:

My good friend.

    Referring to our lately conversation on base ball I now comply with your request to write you a letter on the subject then proposed by me and which you so readily and kindly offered to take charge of, after my death, namely, to procure subscriptions to place a Headstone on my grave.

    My wish is that base ball players be invited to subscribe ten cents each and no matter how small a sum is collected, it will be sufficient to place an oak board with an inscription on my resting place, but whatever it may be, I would like it as durable as possible without any ornamentation — simply something that "he who runs may read."

    The Knickerbocker Base Ball Club was formed in 1845. I joined in September, 1850. At that time it was the only organized club in the United States. I was a member for thirty years and the only one claiming so long a membership. My excellent friend Mr. Samuel H. Kissam being next in duration of membership, and who would gladly assist you in your undertaking.

    The cognomens of "Father of Base Ball," "Poor Old Davis" and "Too Late," as applied to me, are well known in the base ball fraternity.

    All relations and immediate friends are well informed that I desire to be buried in my base ball suit, and wrapped in the original flag of the old Knickerbockers 1845, now festooned over my bureau and for the past eighteen years and interred with the least possible cost.

    I suggest the following inscription in wood or in stone:

Wrapped in the Original Flag  
of the  
Knickerbocker Base Ball Club of N.Y.,  
Here Lies the Body of  
JAMES WHYTE DAVIS

*Owner of the New York Giants Base Ball Club.

a member for thirty years.
He was not "Too Late"
Reaching the "Home Plate"
Born March 2, 1826
Died

I should be pleased to show you my Glass Case containing the trophies of my Silver Wedding with the Old Knickerbockers in 1875 and which I intend to bequeath to you, should you so desire as a mark of appreciation of the kindly act which you have undertaken to perform. Kindly acknowledge receipt of this.

And I am yours sincerely and thankfully,

James Whyte Davis.

# 1

## *On Beginnings*

JAMES WHYTE DAVIS   George Washington was our first president and Martha Washington the first First Lady; Thomas Jefferson was the first president to be inaugurated in Washington. Of lesser known facts: Sam Patch was the first person to survive a jump from Niagara Falls, and Virginia Dare was the first child born in what then were the American Colonies. I happen to know these facts.

So who in America played the first game of base ball in some form or other? Probably Virginia Dare's father or brother. Wherever men gather, there resides an instinct for play, and the inclination to throw a ball is inherent in that instinct. Put a ball of yarn in front of a child and he will eventually pick it up and throw it. It's as natural to the child as crawling. Some of us have never lost that instinct, that's all.

There were, however, many shapers of the game just as a child has many shapers in the form of teachers, pastors, friends, and so forth. I count myself among the shapers of base ball even as I now lament its present form and fear for its future.

DOC ADAMS   Every beginning has a cause and every cause a beginning. I have frequently been asked in my dotage if I know who should be considered the true father of base ball? I do indeed. The answer is nobody in the sense of "cause to give birth to." It's like asking Mr. Darwin who was the father of man. You might say the game unrolled as much as anything else.

The story of the early years of base ball is intrinsically tied up with those of us who organized it and played. It lives in our memories, but our memories are seamless with a cohesion that reality lacks. Our lives have plots and narratives only as we impose them. Nevertheless, if we choose to turn our lives into stories we can begin and end where we choose.

JAMES WHYTE DAVIS   Events by themselves lack significance; it is the perception of events that is crucial. None of us can look at the truth because it blinds us. We look at it and see a sliver of it. Someone else sees another piece of it. But taken all together, the truth is in what we see, although none of us sees it intact.

So I couldn't tell you the truth about the game if I wanted to. Where would

I find it? The stories that went around the city for years after? The newspaper account that only tells you who won? I can tell you that: They did.

No, the truth is in the cracks between the realities.

I can tell you how I saw it though, and what it meant to me and what it meant to base ball.

Where to begin? At the beginning, of course. But where is that you, ask? Where is the beginning of anything?

---

# 2

## Meeting Doc and Poor Old Davis

DOC ADAMS   I was born in the rather typical New England rural village of Mount Vernon, in the hills of south-central New Hampshire where Father was a physician.

There were so many Adamses in the area that I lost track of exactly whom I was related to, but I know there was a connection going all the way back to John Adams, our first vice president and second president.

My great-great-great grandfather, Joseph Adams, came from Concord. According to family legend, in 1737 his son, Capt. Daniel Adams, cut a road from Townsend to the Ashuelot River. His son, also Capt. Daniel Adams, held important civil and military offices in Townsend, and my grandfather, another Daniel, was a deacon of the church and justice of the peace.

My father was born in 1773 — yet another Daniel in our family's long line of Daniels that I was to continue. He graduated from Dartmouth College and stayed on to study medicine with Professor Nathan Smith who, because physicians of his day were so poorly educated and unskilled, established the medical department of Dartmouth sometime in the late 1700s. Father's staunch belief in the integrity of medical practice was, I suspect, a direct result of Professor Smith's considerable influence.

While at school, Father married Mother, Nancy Mulliken, daughter of a physician. They spent their first years in Leominster where my brother Darwin and my sister Nancy were born. There was also a baby, Arabella, who died in infancy. To show the regard in which he was held, Father was chosen to deliver the eulogy for George Washington there. A few years later, they moved to Boston, where Father was involved in publishing an agricultural journal. Then in 1813, they moved to Mount Vernon where he practiced as a physician and where I and my sister Nancy Ann were born.

Father was nothing if not a Renaissance man. His book, *The Scholar's Arithmetic, or The Federal Accountant — The Whole in a Form and Method altogether New, for the Ease of the Master and the Greater Progress of the Scholar*, was held in high esteem, frequently reprinted, and used by hundreds of schools for many years.

He wrote and published other pamphlets and journals, too, including *The Medical and Agricultural Register*, containing articles on medicine, agriculture, and such things as recipes for cheap and excellent wine.

He also published a weekly newspaper called *Telescope*, books on oratory, geography, and bookkeeping, and just to make sure he didn't get bored, taught at a private school. Later he was a member of the New Hampshire Senate.

Father was a strict and demanding man with infinite energy and interests. What he wasn't, was a very attentive father. Mind you, I didn't say "bad father," but one who was always so busy with his many projects.

Ever the moralist, he was deeply interested in common schools, an active promoter of improvement in agriculture, an earnest advocate of the temperance cause, and an early decided abolitionist.

He was convinced that strengthening the body was as important as strengthening the mind. There were no discussions about this, just lectures.

"Exercise is a remedy for many of the evils resulting from the immoral associations the boys and young men of this country so often fall prey to. Isn't that right, Mother?"

Mother would nod approval with a little smile. As with all his pronouncements—the nod and the smile were all she ever revealed.

The Massachusetts winters gave me and my brother plenty of opportunities to engage in skating, skiing, sledding, and sliding rocks on the ice, similar to curling, which we did with abandon. Yet it was the summers where we really took advantage of the outdoors.

We filled viewing jars with all manner of interesting specimens. We played with jackstraws and Jacob's Ladders, and somehow Father once even came up with a zoetrope that kept us occupied for days. We played limber jack, hoop and stick, ring toss, and scores of other games we either learned or made up.

But it was games with balls that really caught my fancy. There seemed no end to the variety of games one could play with a homemade ball, many of which included some kind of stick with which to strike it. What we mostly played were variations on the old English game of rounders, but far be it for staunch New Englanders to admit to *anything* old English. We mostly referred to it as goal ball or base ball, or round ball, or more usually, just ball. Later I came to know it as the Massachusetts Game but that was not part of our lexicon then.

Exactly what rules we played is hard to pin down but generally we played on a square infield with four stakes pounded into the ground sticking up maybe three or four feet. To reach the fourth stake was the goal. The strikers stood between first and fourth base facing the thrower who stood in the middle of the square. The thrower delivered the ball to the striker who then attempted to hit it so that it could not be caught either on the fly or on the first bounce else the striker would be out and could not proceed from stake to stake. If it was not caught, the striker became a runner and advanced as many stakes as possible. Fielders could hit the runner with the ball — a practice we called "soaking" or "plugging" — and if he were not on a base he would be out. A runner who reached the fourth stake had achieved a "round" or "tally." How many tallies it took to win a game depended on how soon the first mother called a key player to dinner.

When old enough, I was enrolled at the Mount Pleasant Classical Institution for boys aged 4 through 16. There, in addition to gaining a first-rate classical education, I continued to play games of ball. Henry Ward Beecher, the prominent social reformer, was a classmate of mine, albeit not a ball player.

There I studied the rigorous curriculum offered by that august institution: modern languages, intellectual and moral philosophy, elementary English, *belles lettres*, oratory, Latin, modern and ancient Greek, mathematics, natural philosophy, and drawing.

Also included in the curriculum was a systematic course of physical culture in the gymnasium and, when the weather permitted, out on the field. I might add, we also got healthy doses of moral and religious indoctrination, assets deemed necessary for "gentlemen of higher purposes."

From the body of students came a "Class of Honor" composed of those who were considered to exhibit exceptional deportment, a just sense of right, and an unimpeached moral courage. These were the same virtues we later wanted to instill in the club we came to call the Knickerbockers. The idea of values was paramount. The goal: turn out gentlemen in every sense of that word.

The morning bell woke us at 4:30 after which a half hour was allowed for toilet. At five we assembled on the muster grounds for an hour of exercise and games. We spent from 6 to 7 in the classroom and thence to breakfast, followed by morning devotion in the chapel. From 8 to 12 was given over to recitation and study. From 12 to 1 we were back on the field for more exercise. Dinner was served from 1:30 to 2:30. Study and recitation took up the time between 2:30 and 6:30 after which we returned to exercise and recreation. At 7:30 supper was served followed by evening worship. Depending on your age, it was lights out by either 8 or 9.

I mention this in some detail as it explains my indoctrination into incorporating physical exercise with mental training. One needs the other. This explains a lot about the development of the game of base ball as an exercise worthy of the fully-developed gentleman.

Upon my graduation I entered Amherst College, then after two years, Yale College. While I continued to play some ball during these years, it was rather limited as my academic studies consumed most of my time. I worked hard at my studies and did well, a fact I hoped would please Father.

Since Darwin had chosen to go into the clergy, I think Father had always hoped I would follow him into medical practice. As this was my wish as well I entered Harvard to study medicine.

Harvard was the oldest institution of higher learning in the United States, having been founded just 16 years after the arrival of the Pilgrims at Plymouth with nine students and a single master. As Father reminded me, both presidents John Adams and John Quincy Adams had gone there, as had Samuel Adams of tea-party fame.

"We have an Adams tradition there," he said, "and a fine tradition it is."

The Unitarian clergy had given to the College a character of moderation, balance, judgment, restraint — what the French called *mesure.* Father most definitely approved.

The Medical School had begun accepting students in 1782. A previous college degree was not a prerequisite. Medical education in those days meant attending formal lectures for a semester or two, and being apprenticed to a practicing physician for several years. There were no mandatory written exams. Opening a medical school required only a hall and a group of physicians willing to lecture. Students did not pay tuition but bought tickets admitting them to professors' lectures, producing hefty supplemental incomes for physicians who earned little from patient care. Other routes to becoming a physician included teaching in dispensaries or training as an apprentice and taking private courses. This variability unfortunately led to many unqualified physicians.

My courses generally fell into three categories: basic sciences, which included chemistry, anatomy and physiology; diagnosis; and treatment, which included surgery and *materia medica.* This was real science at a time when too often the diagnosis of illness relied only on pulse, color, character of breathing, and appearance of urine, and when many physicians subscribed to the theories that human disease was an imbalance of the body's four humors (blood, phlegm, black bile and yellow bile) correlated to the ancient Greeks' pathogenic concept of disease based on the four elements — earth, air, fire and water.

When my formal medical education ended, naturally I returned home to Mount Vernon to assist Father who, when he wasn't busy with one of his myriad projects, actually managed to see patients. He was a good and caring man but generally in those days, poor training and the resulting poor quality of care did little to bring much respect to physicians. This bothered me to the extent that I vowed that one day when I had my own practice I would change this — the world through my 24-year-old eyes.

I gradually handled more and more of Father's practice, but eventually, we both knew it was time for me to move on so I went down to Boston to begin my own practice, much of which involved working at a dispensary. Though the first hospital in the United States was created almost a hundred years before, the most common place to treat patients was at dispensaries, or in doctors' homes if they had money, or at almshouses for the poor. The few voluntary and public general hospitals treated mostly infectious diseases, and seldom were operations performed as operating rooms did not become part of hospitals until much later. So it was that dispensaries produced opportunities for medical students and graduates to obtain further education and eventually the experience to enter private practice.

After working in Boston for a few years, the opportunity presented itself to move down to New York. I was able to set up a small practice in my home at 511 Broadway. It was an exciting time for me. I was off on my own, I had started a practice, and I was soon to find other young men with a similar interest — the game of ball.

JAMES WHYTE DAVIS    Men make history, not the other way around. As with anything else, without leadership, the game of base ball would have stood still. The fact that it didn't was due to skillful leadership and no one among the early players was a better leader than Doc Adams.

DOC ADAMS    James Whyte Davis was the most enthusiastic player bar none. He was a true base ball fiend. In fact that was one of our names for him — The Fiend. Nobody, and I do mean nobody with a capital "N," was more committed to the game. He was a long fielder who, if given the chance, would play all day, and had there been a way to illuminate the field he probably would have played all night, too, with nary a pause for food.

His other names were Too Late Davis because he was in the habit of showing up late for the beginning of a game and then demanding that he be allowed to play and, near the end of his playing days, Poor Old Davis, because that's the way he apparently thought of himself.

JAMES WHYTE DAVIS    In 1826 when I was born, New York was growing rapidly and developing into the commercial giant it was shortly to become. Father, who had moved from Connecticut, was 28 when I came along. He was already a shipmaster who, as the nature of his business suggested, spent much of his time away from home. As a youngster, I always looked forward to his returns and I remember them as some of the happiest days in my young life, particularly when he would bring me little presents acquired on his trips. I admired him greatly for the firm command he seemed to have on everything, and he in return gave his considerable attention to my interests. When I got a little older, he tried to interest me in ships and the maritime business, but I suppose the sea is something you either take to or don't. I didn't. Many were the times when he took me aboard a ship and I know he was disappointed when I showed little interest in things maritime, but I also know he wasn't the first father to find his son going in another direction.

Mother, who was 7 years younger than Father, kept a neat and orderly house. My sister, Harriet was 14 years younger than I, and my brother, Samuel, 19, so I didn't really spend much time with them growing up. I did, however, always enjoy being outdoors—just so long as it wasn't on a ship. Even then open spaces around where we lived were scarce, but wherever one was to be found you could find us playing games including many variations of what later we came to call base ball. We also played games like blackman, and three-cornered cat, and bull-pen, and mumble-the-peg. We also wrestled and ran foot races, and tried to see who could go the farthest at hop-step-and-jump. The fun got so exciting sometimes that we didn't hear when called to "books" and got a switching as a punishment for our delinquency.

Although I didn't join Father in working on a boat, I did become interested in the business side of the maritime trade. New York City's economic growth was being made possible by what was widely considered one of the finest natural harbors in the world. Much of this was due to the opening of the Erie Canal in 1819, which gave our city a big advantage over the ports of Philadelphia and Boston. I can remember going down to the harbor with Father and seeing the febrile activity of tall-masted ships coming and going, and all engaged in important commerce. As I came to meet many of those men doing shipping business, I slowly became involved in the business and eventually settled in as a foreign fruit broker.

New York's preeminence as a trading partner with the British Isles made it our country's principal market for the bills of exchange that lay at the heart of international commerce. The cotton trade was particularly important as southern planters relied heavily on our New York markets to convert the receipts they received from exporters into cash. So New York had become the center point in what came to be called the "Cotton Triangle," in which we brokered the exchange of southern cotton and the money from sales of cotton for British manufacturers.

New York was without doubt the heart of the speculation business and the Tontine Exchange, a regular meeting place for business and trading, was always buzzing with activity. It was an exciting place and for the most part I enjoyed the give and take of business and the wheeling and dealing it entailed.

It was with my broker mates that I began playing ball on summer afternoons. We had no formal organization and no agreed-upon rules. Rather we played with whatever rules the first ones on the field decided upon. Nobody kept track of who won or lost or how well the game was played. No one became angry. Does that sound naive? Perhaps, but that's how I remember it. Maybe we all edit our memories to some degree, but we don't make them up out of nothing.

Ball was always a game for professional men. Often we played with men in the insurance business, another area in which New York predominated. The mounting cost of private insurance for ships and cargo prompted more than a few wealthy New York merchants to organize marine insurance companies, and these eventually expanded into companies which covered houses and lives as well as vessels.

Other businessmen, clerks, and merchants sometimes joined us. So, too, did lawyers, and occasionally physicians. We were, indeed, gentlemen at the bat.

---

# 3

# *And a Few Other Early Players*

WILL WHEATON    In the thirties, I lived at the corner of Rutgers Street and East Broadway where William Tucker and I shared an apartment above his father's tobacco shop. Broadway from Bowling Green to the Park was the hub of respectable New York Society. It was here that rich merchants, lawyers, and brokers lived side by side in rows of lofty and well-built town houses. Nearby were blocks of large, commodious shops of every description imaginable — book stores, print and music shops, jewelers, silversmiths, hatters, linen drapers, milliners, pastry shops, coach makers, hotels and coffee houses. Every afternoon, the whole area was the genteel lounge of New York where strolling ladies and gentlemen turned out in the latest European fashions. Few were the adventurous ladies or gentlemen who dared venture much farther north.

I was admitted to the bar in '36 and was very fond of physical exercise. There were at that time two cricket clubs in New York City, the St. George Club and the New York Club, and one in Brooklyn called the Star Club. There was a racket club in Allen Street with an enclosed court.

Before we started playing base ball, regularly, that is, I and intimates— young merchants, lawyers, and physicians—all played cricket. In fact, I was proficient enough that once I won a prize bat and ball with a score of 60 in a match cricket game. But we found cricket too slow and lazy. We couldn't get enough exercise out of it. Only the bowler and batter had anything to do, and the rest of the players might stand around all afternoon without a chance to stretch their legs. The difference between cricket and base ball illustrates the difference between the lively Americans and the phlegmatic English. I never liked cricket as well as ball.

Racket was lively enough, but it was expensive and not in an open field with plenty of fresh air with a chance to roll on the grass.

Three-cornered cat was a boy's game, and it did well enough for slight youngsters, but it was a dangerous game for powerful men because the ball was made of a hard rubber center tightly wrapped with yarn. In the hands of a strong-armed man it was a terrible missile, with sometimes fatal results when it came into contact with a delicate part of the player's anatomy.

Will Tucker, an avid player who had learned the game from his father, and I both belonged to what we called the New York Base Ball Club, although it was really a club in name only. We were just men who agreed to meet at certain times on one open lot or another to play some form of ball.

Many nights we stayed up late talking about the games we played since Will knew little about the law and I little about tobacco other than what kinds I preferred.

William and William sounded like a law firm so mostly he was called Tuck and I, Will. We almost could have made up a side all named William for we also had William O'Brien, who mostly we called Billy, and William Vail. We had a great name for Vail — Stay-Where-You-Am Vail. He earned the name because he was wont to wander away from his assigned playing position. In those days, if the captain assigned you to a base, you damn well stayed on that base. We didn't play off the base as became the tradition later.

How many times do I remember someone shouting, "Stay where you am, Vail." We all laughed and it became something of an ongoing joke. I must say, he laughed, too.

WILLIAM VAIL    I was a successful merchant in the clothing trade when one day I happened on a game of ball being played up in Madison Park. I watched for some time before one of the players asked me if I'd like to play. I didn't know what I was doing exactly, but one of the things about the game was that it was not hard to learn. Anyway, I quickly became addicted and started playing as often as I could.

WILLIAM TUCKER    On Saturday afternoons in the summer, Father and I would ride the stage up to 27th Street to the open field there, which a few years later was turned into Madison Square Park, named after President Madison. I'd watch the older men play base ball there. Despite what Father says, I didn't always want to go, but he was a persuasive man and Mother backed him up by saying, "You boys should spend time together while you still can because the day will come..." She always left the sentence hanging. I didn't know what she meant then; I do now.

Anyway, on my twelfth birthday, Father gave me a bat he had made himself—for in those days all bats were handmade. These bats, as you might imagine, varied greatly from maker to maker. Some were short, some long, some skinny, some fat. Most were basically round, although some had flattened areas.

I know this must have taken considerable effort on Father's part, as he was a tobacco merchant, not a joiner. It was a thing of beauty made from oak and polished to a fine sheen. And it was just right for my size then. I still have it to this day, a most prized possession and lasting memento of the love of my father.

DUNCAN CURRY    All my working life I was an insurance man, first with the City Fire Insurance Company where I eventually worked myself up to the position of secretary of the company, and then later the same position with the Republic Fire Insurance Company. Fire insurance was a particularly big and important business in those days as, given the building materials in use, the danger of fires was always present.

Working in a stuffy office all day made me long for time in the fresh air and sun and so, like others of my mates, it was my habit to engage in friendly games of ball.

I can't remember when I first took up the game, but I know by '35 I was playing with some regularity. I was 23 at that time and during the summers when I wasn't off checking on fire damage, working with books of numbers, or otherwise engaged with my young son and daughter, I could be found with a ball in my hand.

We didn't have any organization. Heck, we didn't even have set rules. We played this way one day, that way the next.

FRALEY NIEBUHR    My parents were German, but I was born in Philadelphia in 1820, and when I was at an early age, we moved to New York. By the time I was fourteen, I was working with a Custom House brokerage firm. Eventually I became a member of the firm of Wood, Niebuhr and Company, Custom House Brokers.

I also became a director of the Gebhard Fire Insurance Company. It was in that capacity that I met Duncan Curry and some others who were enthusiastic players of various games of ball.

I was also good friends with Alick Cartwright and it was he who actually introduced me to the game of base ball, and it didn't take a lot of persuading I must say because I took to the game like ... a broker to money.

We played irregularly, but often. Various players would come by as they could. Jamie Davis, Will Wheaton, Walt Avery, Stay-Where-You-Am Vail, Colonel Lee, Doctor Ransom, the Tuckers—Abe and Tuck—the O'Brien boys, Alick Cartwright, and a number of others were among the most regular. Doc Adams, as I recall, joined us a little later.

ALICK CARTWRIGHT    I suppose it was from my father that I inherited my wanderlust. Born in 1820, I was one of seven children of the merchant sea captain. He was an adventurer all right, who hailed from a long line of like-minded men.

I don't know a lot about the family history except a bit of the infamous Cap'n Edward Cartwright who came to America from England sometime in the 1660s and settled on an island off the coast of New Hampshire from which he sailed up and down the eastern seaboard. According to family lore at least, he was a dashing and courageous seafarer. He captured the heart of Elizabeth Morris, a very proper young lady, and married her. They moved to Nantucket where they settled down so that he could teach fishing and serve as constable. This did not, however, prevent him from being fined for allowing his pigs to run free or from becoming involved in numerous bouts of drunkenness and rowdy behavior. He was certainly a hellion in the true Cartwright spirit.

Another Cartwright — Captain John, who was master of the sloop *Speedwell* — sailed to the British naval headquarters and pleaded for Nantucket neutrality. We also had Cartwrights who served in the Revolutionary navy, survived numerous shipwrecks and at least one who was lost at sea. Cartwrights were also involved in the War of 1812. Father, Alexander Joy Cartwright, Sr., along with other Nantucket men, was captured by the British and imprisoned in a British ship. After the war he settled in New York, a city he had visited on several earlier voyages, on one of which he was fined for illegal berthing and on another occasion, for the illegal landing of passengers. In addition to the financial opportunities offered by the growing city, he was taken by the charms of Esther Rebecca Burlock, a winsome young lady of note and a superb horsewoman. They were soon married and raising a family of three sons and four daughters.

I was born while my parents were living on Lombardy Street. Father was running his successful shipping business. Like most of the young boys in the city I learned to fish, and ride horses, and generally to gambol in the many open fields and farm yards still around in those days. We moved several times while I was still young — over to Rivington Street and then to Cherry Street where we had a great view of the harbor and the village of Brooklyn beyond, and then to Mott Street where cows roamed freely and where fields to play games of ball beckoned.

When I was 16, Father, owing to some unfortunate investments, lost his "fortune." So Levi Coit, an acquaintance of Father's, took me in as a clerk at Coit & Cochrane, a Wall Street brokerage. Father left his shipping business for a position as an inspector for the Marine Insurance Company.

After a few years at the brokerage I moved on and took a position as a clerk for the Union Bank of New York. What was particularly beneficial about this job was that we got off early enough in the afternoon that I had enough leisure time to devote to such things as ball playing. There are real advantages to working in a bank!

My position as a bank clerk was considered quite a respectable position for a young man on the rise, and while I was in that position I met, courted, and married Eliza Ann Gerrits Van Wie, the daughter of a prominent old Dutch family. We set up house on fashionable Clinton Place. It wasn't long before we had four children.

WALTER AVERY　　I graduated from Columbia College in 1836 and first began working as a civil engineer shortly after that. For some time I worked on the original Croton Water Works. I also got interested in base ball at a young age and began playing with other young men with a similar interest.

JAMES WHYTE DAVIS　　We may have had different backgrounds, we may have had different ideas about many things, but there were two things we all shared — we were gentlemen, and we love to play ball — and that was enough to bring us together.

# 4

# Gentlemen Playing All Manner of Games

ALICK CARTWRIGHT　　If the game had a ball and something with which to give it a good thwack, I probably played it at one time or another. Most of us did, for you'd be hard pressed to pass a level open field in good weather without finding some kind of game of ball being played by boys skilled or not. All you needed was a ball, a stout stick, and enough players to agree on the rules.

There were as many ball games as there were players to play them.

WALTER AVERY　　When we couldn't round up enough boys for a proper game, we played O' Cat or Old Cat that you could play with as few as three boys. It wasn't much more than an exercise in striking a ball, but sometimes we'd do it all afternoon until our mothers called us for dinner. See, there's something very satisfying about the very act of striking a ball with a bat. It takes a steady hand, a good eye, and considerable concentration. When you get it right, it just feels good and there's nothing wrong with a ten-year-old feeling good on a warm spring afternoon.

ABRAHAM TUCKER  In the early days there were two very distinct forms of town ball we came to know as base ball. One was known as the Massachusetts game, the other the New York game. The game played by our New England brethren used a smaller ball than we used and the pitcher delivered the ball with an overhand motion. We in New York played a game more closely aligned to cricket because we delivered the ball underhanded.

I was an avid enthusiast and in turn, I instilled a love for it in my son, William, who I must say, was even more rabid about it than I, and certainly a better player. From the time he was maybe ten, we would go to the park near our house and practice throwing and catching. I never had to encourage him for he took to the game naturally. Those practices were a chance for me and my son to be together and I have always been pleased that the game was something I was able to pass on to him. From it, he gained coordination and grace, and learned the principles of sportsmanship so important to a young man growing up amidst the mounting pressures of our hectic city.

JAMES WHYTE DAVIS  There were games with three bases; there were games with four. There were games with posts as bases, and games with rocks as bases. There were fields laid out in squares, in rectangles, in diamond shapes, or where the geography of the space demanded, in irregular shapes. Whoever got to the field first laid it out and those who came later, played on it. Sometimes this would lead to arguments, but eventually a game was played even if it wasn't exactly like the game played there the week before. The game was more important than the rules and we loved playing it regardless of the differences.

FRALEY NIEBUHR  One thing almost all of these games had in common was that there were safe places, be they posts, rocks, stumps, bags of sand, or something else, where a runner could remain without the fear of being put out. Any runner hit by a thrown ball between these safe places was out. Aces, or runs, counted when a runner safely made a complete circuit of the safe places and reached "home," which in those early days was not the same place from which the striker struck the ball. That came later.

WILL WHEATON  In late September of '44, over at the St. George Cricket Club by the East River, a cricket match took place between players from the United States and Canada. The American team was made up of select players from local clubs as well as from clubs as far away as Boston and Washington. By New World standards these were top players.

I went over and watched the match — both days. I tried to get some of my base ball playing mates to come along but my invitation was met with little or no enthusiasm.

"I'm afraid I have family obligations," said Colonel Lee.

"And miss two good days of playing myself?" said Cartwright.

"I'd soon as watch a tree grow as watch a cricket match," said Billy O'Brien.

"You don't know what you're missing," I told him.

"Thank goodness."

My fellow players notwithstanding, thousands of people showed up for the match. The paper claimed 20,000 which was certainly an exaggeration but I can attest to the fact that cricket still had a following in New York.

"How many ever watch us play?" I asked Vail.

"There was someone last week I know."

"Who, your brother?"

"My cousin."

My uncle, a first-rate player, taught me cricket and I can still remember him talking about playing on many a sunny Sunday afternoon in Sussex. Sussex, it was said, was the birthplace of the game sometime in the late 17th century. That's what we were told, and that's what I'll believe, although I know the roots of the game are a little hazy.

As the English continued to colonize, their cricketers took the game to many places around the world, including America, there being games played regularly in and around New York, Boston, and Philadelphia. It is, and was, always a game for refined gentlemen. Those sportsmen with less breeding were more likely to take up rounders or other games of that ilk.

It was seldom difficult to find a cricket match in New York during the summers, and I continued to play occasionally, long after I had taken up base ball. Some old habits die hard.

On the occasional day when a match was not to be found, a good game of wickets might be. I suppose wickets was a variation on cricket with the wickets being shorter and wider and the ball bowled along the ground. The biggest difference, though, was that there were thirty players to a side, which sometimes made getting a match together a difficult proposition. It wasn't the equal of cricket or base ball. Still a game with a ball is just that, and when nothing better was at hand, it filled the bill.

FRALEY NIEBUHR  Some of the old Dutch men of the city still played at bowls under the shade of the trees down on the old Bowling Green. Charlie DeBost, who came from old Dutch stock, his family having settled here from Holland in the 1650s ( he says) to farm over in what was then called Breuckelen (he says), still bowled with the old men although what he saw in the dull game is beyond me.

Charlie lived in a house that was continually filling up with children and I'm sure he was wonderful with them, but it leaves little doubt as to why he spent so much time with us playing ball.

BILLY O'BRIEN  I was born in Boston, having come from sturdy and proud Irish stock. I grew up with minimal connections to the game of cricket, but with great fondness for the game of rounders, an interest I shared with many other Irish youths. Up in Boston sometimes the older cricketers would let us play on their grounds, but when we couldn't arrange that, we played in the park not far from the city center. Maybe the reason why we started playing with just two bases was because we played so much on the cricket grounds. Father would chide me saying that over in the old country they played with 3, 4, or even 5 bases.

"What's the matter," he'd say, "don't you think we're well enough off here to be able to afford the extra bases?"

He'd say this even though he never played cricket at home.

"Don't let him kid you," Mother would say, "he's a rounders man, born and bred. Rounders and stout is what he's about, anything else is pure blarney, and there's plenty of that about him as well."

We had our own words for the players that Father didn't understand. The *feeder* delivered the ball to the *striker* who tried to hit the ball past the *scouts*.

"I don't understand," Father would say, "you can't use the right words? Something's wrong with you youngsters. No respect for the ways of the old world."

"What does it matter? The game's the game."

"Not with feeders and scouts it ain't."

The *striker*, the *batter*, the *hitter*, what's the difference anyway? The game's the thing.

The distance between the stakes again depended on the room available, but generally, it was about twenty paces. Whose paces? Well that, too, was a point to argue about sometimes. Those, like my good friend Tommy Meachem who fancied himself as a good scout, liked as much space between the posts as possible; those of us who fancied ourselves as good strikers liked less.

The first thing we did when we got to a field was to lay out the posts, choose up sides, agree to all the rules because they were always changing and as far as I know, never written down, and then let the game begin.

I'm not sure when, but sometime along the way we began calling the game simply, town ball.

If nothing else, ball took me away from a house rife with rancor. Playing ball, I freely admit, was my way of escaping from the conflicts that embroiled me in my non-playing world.

When the dry goods business in which I had invested so much failed, I decided to get away and start life afresh, so when my brother, Jonathan, invited me to New York to learn the stocks trade, I availed myself of the opportunity and made the move. My wife, unfortunately, didn't then and doesn't now share my enthusiasm for a city removed from her family in Boston. Nor, I might add, does she share my proclivity to spend my leisure time in the parks of our fine city.

CHARLES DEBOST    The O'Brien brothers were always running on about rounders and town ball like they had to defend the New England Irish tradition, but the fact of the matter is that they both took to our form of the game like Irishmen to beer, and soon became two of the best batsmen to be found on any open field in the city.

Town ball, or the Massachusetts game, as it has often been called, was not going to be forced down the throats of us native sons of New York, certainly not by the O'Briens or any of their clan.

"Keep your Mick game," I told them. "You come to New York, you play our game."

Willie wasn't sure if I was kidding or not. "Too complicated for you, is it?"

"Not if an Irishman can learn it."

Willie laughed it off, but by God, there was some truth to it.

As with the number of bases, the number of players varied, too. Mostly we played with 12 defenders, three to cover each base, one in on the field, one out, one player to deliver the ball, one to retrieve it if not struck, and one to play wherever it was felt he was needed.

This we called the New York game.

BILLY O'BRIEN    Down in New York, the more we played, the more the rules became standardized. I'll tell you one thing though that always stayed the same for me. I had an axe haft that Father brought from County Clare that he had carefully shaped into a hitting implement of unbeatable quality. He passed it on to me and my brother, Jonathan. Since we both used it, I attribute our skills as batsmen to that handle and the spirit of our father that resides inside.

For sure, we Irish weren't everybody's idea of what the ideal American should be. Most Irish families, like ours, came here because the conditions at home were terrible, but still the idea of emigrating was difficult and often called the "American Wake" as those leaving knew they wouldn't see the homeland again. They left in droves on ships so crowded and the conditions so terrible that they were known as "Coffin Ships."

As soon as the boats docked greedy men called "runners" grabbed hold of the immigrants and their bags, and for an outrageous fee, took them to a tenement they chose. Most stayed there for the rest of their lives. Many spent their days begging on the streets being spat upon by those who considered themselves part of a higher class, and everyone else considered themselves a higher class. No group was considered lower than an Irishman in the America of the 1840s.

Ads for employment often were followed by "NO IRISH NEED APPLY." We were forced to live in shanties, partly because of poverty but also because we were considered bad for the neighborhood. It was said we were unfamiliar with plumbing and running water. These living conditions bred sickness and early death. I have read that 80 percent of all infants born to Irish immigrants in New York City died. Our brogue and dress provoked ridicule; our poverty and illiteracy provoked scorn.

The only way to survive was to unite and take offense, which sometimes admittedly turned to violence. Solidarity was our strength. We prayed and drank together.

CHARLES DEBOST   They should have said they drank and prayed together — in that order. Mercy, mercy, could they put away the suds!

BILLY O'BRIEN   A few of us managed to dig ourselves out of the shanty towns and make something of our lives.

Of course, we were never completely admitted into "polite society," nor could we ever be admitted into any of the important social clubs of the city. So it was with ballists that we found our company. They were our club. Oh, I know they talked about us behind our backs, but as long as we produced results on the fields of friendly strife, well then we were welcome.

ALICK CARTWRIGHT   Oh, we played ball all right. We played plenty. We also spent a lot of time standing around trying to decide what and how to play. Ah, therein lay a problem. Oftentimes it took more time to decide on the damn rules than it did to play the game.

----

# 5

# *A Connection Is Made Between Volunteer Fire Companies and Base Ball*

JAMES WHYTE DAVIS   Much of my early ball playing was done in connection with and against volunteer fire fighters. This was a fraternity of able gentlemen, of which I happily considered myself a member.

ASHLEY HYDE   My job for the *Bell's Life in London and Sporting Chronicle* was to comment on, and perhaps contrast, life in New York with life as I had known it in London with a particular emphasis on the sporting activities of the Americans.

As a newcomer to New York, one thing of which I quickly became aware was the astounding frequency of fires. Scarcely a day went by when there was not an alarm, a cry of fire, and a ringing of bells. To say the bells were rung and the firemen called out five hundred times a year would not be an exaggeration.

As soon as an alarm was given, bells began in all quarters with great zeal and force, and some continued their clamor for a considerable time after the danger passed, or the alarm determined to be false.

Usually the first to start and the last to quit was the bell of the Middle Dutch Church. Who the ringer of that bell was, I do not know, but he seems to have had a remarkable fondness for pulling the end of a rope.

ALICK CARTWRIGHT    While still a boy, and like many others my age, I became fascinated by the sight of robust men running through the streets pulling shiny engines while trumpets blared and bells rang. Everyone moved aside when these men came running. The city was theirs. You can imagine how truly dashing and romantic these giants seemed. They were champions of right, guardians of probity. They were heroes.

I eagerly awaited the time when I would be old enough to run with the engines as older boys did. Sometimes they would be asked to run errands for this race of heroes; sometimes even help pump or work the bucket brigade. Finally, when I was 15, Father grudgingly gave in to my youthful pleas.

So, for two December nights during the fire of 1835 I followed, gawked, and gazed at the mighty men who were fighting the most terrible fire and greatest catastrophe anyone in New York had ever seen. The fire, which could be seen from a hundred miles away, continued to smolder for four days, destroying most of New York below Canal and east of Broad streets. Almost 700 buildings were destroyed. It was often referred to as the greatest urban tragedy since Pompeii's destruction.

It was so cold that the heat from the fires was the only thing that kept us from freezing to death. Even so, when I finally returned home both exhausted and exhilarated, I went straight to bed where I remained for days. Mother called the doctor, who came and said I was lucky I didn't have pneumonia and told Mother in the sternest of voices that chasing fires was not something "correct" boys should do.

Naturally, neither Mother nor Father was surprised when a few years later I joined the volunteers.

ELIZA CARTWRIGHT    I would have to say Alick was dashing. Definitely dashing. I never told him this, but every time I heard the bell signaling there was a fire nearby I'd run out in the street to watch him come running by, and oh my, what a figure he cut. They all did, really, but Alick particularly so. He was easily the biggest of the boys.

They'd come running by usually in their black pants and boots, and red shirts, all pulling on their pumping engine with its polished brass fittings and shiny lacquered lettering along its sides. Everyone would clear the way for these gallant, brave men on their way to save someone from the clutches of a deadly fire. And did the streets ever clear in a hurry!

It was an incredibly romantic scene and me and my friends, well we didn't miss many fires.

On many Sunday mornings, coming home from church, I would walk over to the park and watch the lads practice climbing ropes and performing calisthenics to keep themselves in top physical condition.

Sometimes during the summers, to help support their companies, they would sponsor picnics attended by many grateful citizens. It was at one of these that I got up my courage enough to talk to Alick for the first time.

WILLIAM VAIL    I first joined the Oceana Hose Company, then a few years later, the Knickerbocker Engine Company. It was there that I made lifelong friends with the likes of Alick Cartwright, Duncan Curry, Jamie Davis, and Walt Avery — ball players all.

ALICK CARTWRIGHT    The Knickerbocker Engine Company had a long history, dating back to 1783.

At the House of Refuge fire in 1838 the company took suction from a mud pond called the "Sunfish Pond," and played into 33 Engine, washing her on that occasion. The 33's folks claimed that the mud from the pond choked their engine. I think they were exaggerating.

I had also belonged to the Oceana Hose Company, the most fun loving group I ever saw. It was always a race with other companies to be the first to a fire. A friendly race to be sure, but a race nevertheless. So you see, we were a competitive group from the start, and a damn good one if I may say. You had to go a stretch to beat Oceana to a fire.

Sometimes some of the boys even slept in the firehouse just so they'd be the first ones to hit the street pulling when the bell sounded. Heck, I even did it a few times myself.

I remember once running the engine through the streets late at night with most of us still in full evening dress since we'd been at a ball when the bell sounded and had no time to change. People shouted and applauded as we ran by and we waved back in appreciation. What a sight we must have been. Dandies off to battle.

WALTER AVERY    I swear Oceana boys would run you over if you got in their way trying to be the first to a fire. More than one person was hurt by a fire race. I know they did good work, but sometimes it was just a little too dangerous.

Someone even got sent a letter down to City hall complaining about the dangers presented by some of these hose companies, but, of course, nothing ever came of it. One of the stuffed-shirt powers-that-be in the city said that since these men were volunteers there needed to be some payoff for their hard work and a little friendly competition was the price the city was willing to pay. That and a few crushed skulls, I guess.

JAMES WHYTE DAVIS    We ran as fast as we could pulling that big old wagon. Some of the lads were better at the pulling part than others. Alick, for example, as big as he was, was a great puller. So was Curry. I could pull my share, but I've got to say, I was the best horn blower we had.

We were pretty particular, too, about who we'd let into the company. You had to be athletic, you had to run fast, and you had to be strong. And, oh yes, you had to want to have fun, too.

ALICK CARTWRIGHT    We were a club as much as anything else and the firehouse, well, that was our clubhouse and we treated it with the same reverence a priest might his church. We kept it immaculate, every inch gone over with spit and spittle and elbow grease. We had a beautiful Persian carpet Colonel Lee donated to the cause. We had a chandelier that would have done any of the best houses in the city proud. Needless to say, we had an ample stash of spirits for evenings when the bell showed enough consideration to remain silent.

In it during the winter months we played various card games and waited for the good weather of spring so that we could play ball and other games of a more physical nature.

Once, a stevedore from down on the docks jumped in and helped us pull the engine down a street that was near impassable due to heavy rains the day before. He was strong as an ox and pulled like one. We just barely beat Hose No. 1 to the fire and probably wouldn't have done so without his considerable help. Later he joined us at the Malvern Tavern and proved to be an amiable man with a great laugh and sparkling blue eyes. None of us thought that we were leading him on, but I guess we were. He stopped by the firehouse a number of times—to visit. Some weeks later, he asked about becoming a member. I'm sure he would have been a good fireman, but, of course, we couldn't let him in. Actually, despite his request, his name was never put forward for membership. A club is a club precisely because its members share certain qualities in common.

JAMES WHYTE DAVIS    We were very careful about who we let into our ranks because we were like brothers. A good example of that was when we elected William Tweed as secretary. You may be more familiar with his nickname, "Boss Tweed."

Tweed eventually became Democratic boss of New York City and proceeded to defraud the city of millions of dollars before being exposed and convicted. Later he escaped and fled to Europe.

How he rose to power was as a volunteer fireman. His interest in fires began as a 12-year-old runner for the Knickerbocker Engine Company No. 12. Later he became an organizer and foreman of the Americus Engine Company No. 6, legendary in fire-fighting lore as the "Big Six."

Give us credit though. It wasn't long after we made him secretary that we became aware of his devious ways and forced him to resign.

The important thing about this story is that it shows how we regarded ourselves. We were gentlemen, and gentlemen behaved according to honorable rules of decorum and behavior in both our public and private lives. This held as true when we were fighting a fire as it did when we were playing ball. The Boss Tweeds and others of their ilk were not welcome.

ALICK CARTWRIGHT   I have to admit on a few rare occasions — and I must emphasize rare — we answered a bell slightly under the influence. I'll never forget the picture of Avery throwing up as we ran down Water Street late one night, and he in his formal attire. It may not have been funny, but we laughed all the way to the scrawny little fire that wasn't worth the cost of a shirt, no less a jacket and waistcoat.

Working one of these machines was no place for weaklings. I say this because it accounts, at least in part, for why so many of the ballists came from the ranks of fire fighters.

We were in a competition with all the other volunteer companies in the city. Although I'm not particularly proud to admit it, sometimes fisticuffs broke out. When we raced each other to fires, some of the good city folk would lay odds on which company would get there first. My brother Ben would always bet on us and as there were often profits, he would give me a share.Once on the scene of a fire, we raced to see who could get a stream playing on the blaze first. Each company had its own supporters and gallery, and onlookers who had money down or otherwise had a strong rooting interest would cheer or boo according to their involvement.

We were, to put it frankly, an amusement attraction.

DUNCAN CURRY   The city eventually established a corps of fire police who assembled at each fire to protect property and suppress tumult.

It was natural that this competitive spirit spilled over into other areas, areas such as sport. We often played games in the late afternoons when most of us got away from work. Of those games, the most popular among us was some form of ball, although if truth be told, we were probably more competitive as fire companies than we ever were as ballists. Nevertheless, many of the early games of base ball were played by and between fire companies.

# 6

# *Playing at Madison Park*

WILL WHEATON   I don't think there was anyone more enthusiastic about the game in those days than Cartwright. He was not only a regular on Saturdays, but frequently during the week, and when he showed up and found there were not enough for a game because not everyone was as fortunate as he to be at leisure in the late afternoon, he would act as if that were an affront to him personally. He would prowl the streets in search of other gentlemen with similar leisure time.

"Now what's a sturdy young man like you have to do on a beautiful day like today that could be more important than a good ball game? Get some exercise, have some fun."

ALICK CARTWRIGHT   This often resulted in recruits with little or no skill, or worse yet, comical skill. Never mind, it allowed us to make a match of an equal number of hands, however many that turned out to be.

The order of business went like this: First, muster a sufficient number of hands, for at least five a side or as many as 15; second, agree in principle on the rules to be followed; third, lay out the field by pacing off the bases; fourth, select captains; fifth, allow the captains to choose their sides; sixth, find an umpire if one were available (often we played without one); seventh, play the match.

The captains were usually the older, or more experienced players. They became the captains for the day either by volunteering or by general assent.

COLONEL LEE   I think we started playing up in Madison Park in the early '40s, or at least that's when I joined in. Cartwright was among the regulars. Doctor Ransom and Abraham Tucker, too. I was already in my late 40s and had been playing some form of ball since the early years of the century, years unknown to anyone else on the field.

So as the reigning graybeard, I was usually tapped as a captain, a role in which I was eminently comfortable. Whoever was the other captain and I would always toss a penny to determine who chose first.

The reason for the penny is simple: My father, to avoid arrest in England for his loud support of the French Revolution, fled to New York and eventually established the firm of Lee & Company, a successful concern that imported almost all the copper tokens used as pennies. These pennies, stamped "Talbot, Allum & Lee," were widely used until the government began coining their own copper coins.

WILLAM VAIL  Most of us thought that Colonel Lee was a bit of a pompous old goat the way he flourished that penny of his as if it were bestowed on him by God, but he showed up almost every time there was a match, so we went along with his act.

He was a colonel in the New York militia. I guess that's where he had learned this annoying "do as I say" attitude but I have to admit, it served the purpose of keeping a match under control when passions became a mite heated.

ALICK CARTWRIGHT  The Colonel wasn't a bad ballist for a man his age, but to play with him was to be forever subjected to his ruminations about the bucolic life of his youth that he either remembered or invented.

"Bowl, Colonel."

"Everything in its time."

"I'll be your age before this match is over."

"You'll never be my age if you're in such a rush all the time."

COLONEL LEE  In the old days, Broadway extended only as far north as 10th Street, but I distinctly remember when the Common Council ordered the opening of 14th Street. It was constant turmoil as streets were paved, ripped up, realigned, widened, paved again.

All of this meant that commerce was rapidly devouring all the open spaces where one could play a good game of ball.

BILLY O'BRIEN  It wasn't all as bad as the Colonel insisted. Not too many years before, the journey by horse from New York to Boston took between four and six days. By the '30s stage coaches covered this route, changing horses frequently, in a day and a half. Then came the railroad and the trip took little more than half a day.

Since my wife was wont to make the trip frequently, this was a boon to me because when she was away I could engage in as many ball games as I could squeeze into my days.

I loved the train. Thank goodness for progress.

ALICK CARTWRIGHT  I took exception to the Colonel's claims that we were being stifled. We weren't being stifled; we were having a whole new world open up before us, a world which we who were businessmen could take advantage of. The changes that were taking place in the city were offering opportunities never even dreamed of by our fathers and grandfathers.

Nevertheless, the Colonel was right when he said that our fields of play were being pushed farther away all the time.

## 7

# Moving to Sunfish Pond

ALICK CARTWRIGHT     We began looking around for a better place to play. I remembered the area around Sunfish Pond hill and suggested that.

"Okay boys," I said. "Let's see how long we can hold out by the pond."

"Until somebody can make a buck by building on it," said the always pessimistic Colonel.

"Well until then..."

"We can probably play all week anyway."

I remember the Sunfish Pond area as a delightful place with fresh breezes, green grass, and clear water.

ASHLEY HYDE     Although born with a withered leg, I had always been interested in the sporting life, even if I couldn't participate in all that it offered. Oh, I learned to shoot reasonably well, and I could put up a fair game of billiards or darts, but for the more athletic needs of games like cricket or base ball, I was content to become an interested observer.

The game that I saw in New York, the game they usually called base ball, intrigued me from the start. It had all the strategy of cricket, but was played at a much faster pace. It was, in that sense, more like the American spirit.

So on many pleasurable summer afternoons, I would sit in the shade and watch the gentlemen play their game. I was not married at the time, and my days were my own just so long as I sent my stories back to London on a regular basis. I must have been, in the parlance of the day, one of the first, if not the first base ball "crank."

I first began to watch them up by Sunfish Pond. It was an idyllic setting, but obviously it couldn't stay that way forever.

By then the population was nearly 400,000. Fifty years earlier it was only about 33,000. Much of the increase came from desperately poor immigrants who were packed into a small area of the city that came to be known as the Five Points. So bad was the situation with prostitutes and thieves, that it was said that there was a murder a night there. Now that was probably an exaggeration, but there was no doubt about the nature of the problem.

WILLIAM VAIL     The city was having its problems due to the mobs of immigrants. We stayed clear of most of them by playing our games up by Sunfish Pond. The area was mostly level, and the trees spaced far enough apart that we could fit in a reasonable playing ground. And too, it was easy to get there by omnibus.

ASHLEY HYDE   How about this for a contrast! Down in the Five Corners amidst the organ grinders and their monkeys, the new 900-man police force struggled to control the adult prowler gangs like the Plug Uglies and Dead Rabbits, the thieves, and the prostitutes, while uptown young gentlemen played healthful games on green grass. Was ever there a more vivid picture of the great distinctions that defined this teeming city?

WILLIAM VAIL   I remember once when a group of us got together on a soggy day near Sunfish Pond, but much to our embarrassment, we discovered that no one thought to bring a ball. We were used to playing without any sort of equipment, of course, but without bat or ball, well, obviously that's not possible

After some useless finger pointing and excuse offering, we got down to the inevitable, "What now?" question.

Colonel Lee came up with a suggestion. "Let's do what we usually do," he said.

"You mean, go and drink?" said Billy.

"I mean, make a ball."

"Oh, you've already been drinking, then?"

"Not a drop."

"How do you propose we make a ball out here?"

"Well," he said looking around, "we could find some ... there, over there, that gentleman still wearing his overshoes. We could use the rubber to fashion a new ball."

"Oh, sure," said Billy looking at him as if he were either stark raving crazy or trying to make a joke, "he's wearing them just for us."

"Hardly likely, but as he looks to be a prosperous gentleman, I'm willing to wager that he would be quite receptive to the idea of making a profit on them."

"You want to buy his overshoes?"

"Whatever gave you that idea?"

"You just said..."

"I was thinking of Mr. Mumford."

J. Paige Mumford was the son of a well-known Manhattan merchant with considerable assets. Later he was to fall on hard times, but at this point he was one of, if not the wealthiest, of any of us.

Mumford smiled. I suspect he liked to be thought of as the top of the financial heap.

"How nice of you, Colonel, to volunteer my money."

"Whatever could be a better use for it than in the service of your friends?"

"I can think of several."

"But not this afternoon, surely."

"I don't barter, dicker, or haggle."

"Certainly not," said the Colonel. "But I do. May I have the honor?"

"Grovel if you must."

Colonel Lee went over to the overshoed man standing off to the side of our field, unaware I'm sure, of the negotiator about to descend on him. From where we were standing, we couldn't hear the conversation, but we could see from the animated gestures, that the workings of higher finance were in operation.

"What do you suppose they're negotiating," said O'Brien, "the purchase of Manhattan?"

"No, that only took Peter Stuvysent a few minutes."

Eventually, the Colonel returned with a big grin on his face. "Well, the details of a complicated financial transaction have been agreed upon."

"How much?" asked Mumford.

Colonel Lee could hardly suppress a big grin when he said, "Ten dollars."

"Ten dollars!" said Mumford. "They couldn't have cost two."

"Well, actually we agreed on five for one shoe since that's all we need, but he argued, and rightfully so, that being left with one overshoe would be a great detriment to his walk home, so we finally reached a compromise and I said we'd buy both for ten."

"That's not a compromise!"

"I know, but it will be a base ball."

Mumford reached into his pocket, and feigning disgust, produced two shiny half eagle coins.

We had our rubber. O'Brien opened the penknife he seemed always to carry for no reason. He proceeded to cut one shoe into strips while I unraveled a woolen stocking. We managed to produce a lumpy ball. It was hardly up to the standard of workmanship that Doc Adams brought to those he would later make, but it sufficed to allow us a game.

Years later, J. Paige Mumford joked that it was the beginning of his financial problems.

WILLIAM TUCKER   For some time we enjoyed the Sunfish Pond area. Then Peter Cooper, the famous inventor who, among other things, designed and built the first locomotive in the United States, the *Tom Thumb*, decided in his infinite wisdom to build a glue factory nearby. Naturally, this polluted the pond and it had to be filled in, making a mess of the area and rendering it totally unfit for ball playing. Too bad, too, because it was a lovely and convenient location.

I never forgave Cooper and years later when he ran for president I made sure not to vote for him. I guess I got even, too, because Rutherford B. Hayes won.

So once again we set out to find a new place to play. But would this just be another stop on the way to losing all the open space in the city? It sure seemed that way.

# 8

## On the Move Again

COLONEL LEE   Ah, progress, isn't it wonderful? Our playing places were disappearing faster than summer memories of snow.

The city was putting up new buildings on every available open space it could find, and where they couldn't find space, they made it by tearing down older buildings, and they did it with little if any respect for memories of the past. The very bones of our ancestors were not permitted to lie quiet a quarter of a century as one generation of men seemed intent on removing all relics of those that came before them. Pitt's statue no longer graced Wall Street, the old Presbyterian Church gave way to a bank, and the Croton River washed away all traces of the old tea-water pump. The city that I knew as a boy was being pulled to pieces, burned down, and rebuilt.

Our beautiful game was as doomed unless we found somewhere to play away from the marble and concrete invasion.

CHARLES BIRNEY   I suggested we move to Brooklyn, if for no other reason than we had a lot more open space, but Duncan and the others wanted to keep the games on Manhattan.

ALICK CARTWRIGHT   We moved to the grounds in the shadows of the magnificent Inclenberg estate on Murray Hill, one of the loveliest spots on the Island. Inclenberg was home to the powerful Murray family, Quaker shipping merchants. The house was a square building surrounded by verandas, gorgeous trees, a wide lawn, and extensive gardens.

This was about as far uptown as you could go before running into the farmlands, and it took a good while to reach by coach or train from where most of us lived.

CHARLES BIRNEY   I worked as secretary of the East River Marine Company so I had to come over from Brooklyn on workdays, but many of our games were on Saturday, so that meant yet another round trip on the South Ferry. For years there had been talk of putting up a bridge between Brooklyn and Manhattan, but it all seemed to be nothing more than that — talk.

I'll tell you this, though. Nothing put a burr under my saddle more than making the trip to find we didn't have enough hands to make a game, particularly when players who said they'd be there didn't show. We usually tried to round up some extra hands, but more than once I had to make the long return trip without having had the benefit of a few hours of beneficial exercise.

WALTER AVERY    Birney was the first to complain anytime we were short of players. But we all grew quickly tired of his bellyaching. Many of us had wives and families and sometimes that meant we had to change our plans for the sake of other interests.

"Birney, move, if it's such a big problem,"

"I like Brooklyn."

"Then stop complaining."

"I'll stop when you show up when you say you will."

"Tell that to my wife."

"Can't you tell her when you've got a game?"

"Only a man who hasn't been married can say that. Anyway, why do you like Brooklyn so much?"

"I'd rather live in the countryside than around all these marble mausoleums."

"You mean you want to have your cake and eat it too?"

"Are you going to play or not?"

"If we have enough players."

And that wasn't all he complained about. He'd complain about the weather, the bad plays, the bad batting. He'll probably complain about the food in heaven. But he was a bear of a man and he knew how to smack a base ball a fair piece.

CHARLES BIRNEY    As I see it, a man is only as good as his word. It may only be a game, but once a man makes a commitment, then he damn well better show up.

FRALEY NIEBUHR    One day I was on my way up to Murray Hill with Alick when an omnibus drawn by 22 gorgeous white horses, splendidly outfitted in silver-mounted harnesses, paraded down Broadway as a publicity stunt to advertise Kipp and Brown's Stage Company. Big crowds lined the street to watch, completely blocking our way. From the nose of the lead horse to the driver's reins it measured 150 feet — or so the papers said.

"Dammed inconsiderate if you ask me," Alick said.

"Damned dangerous if you ask me," I responded watching the driver struggling to control his rambunctious team.

"They'll be waiting for us. I hate to be late."

When Alick had his mind on base ball, that's all that seemed to matter.

Never mind that an accident on such a busy thoroughfare seemed imminent. A far worse fate awaited — delaying a base ball game.

EBENEZER DUPIGNAC   My father, a cabinet maker, came to America from a small village near Rheims, where if the story is correct, his great-grandfather actually built some of the benches used in the magnificent cathedral there. So I come from a long line of cabinetmakers, and according to my father, a long line of ball players.

He told me of a game long played in the little villages of France. The game he called Grande-thèque was played by teams of 10–15 men with sand bags marking the five bases arranged on a pentagon-shaped field. To put players out you had to hit them between bases with the ball. It was played to a score of 40 points in two innings.

I was born in New York and never played that version, but I did play plenty of ball games here. Maybe it was in my blood. A couple of times when we were playing up on Murray Hill, I suggested we play Grande-thèque but all I got were laughs.

"Whoever heard of French ball?"

"My father told me about it."

"And I'm Santa Claus."

ALICK CARTWRIGHT   Life behind a teller's cage at the Union Bank of New York had its rewards: it wasn't difficult work, our workday ended early, and we made a satisfactory living.

What the bank didn't supply was any opportunity to stretch our legs, to exercise, to get out in the clean air. I was always restless in that cage. I suppose I would have been restless regardless of where I worked, but that cage felt like a jail to me. I had the wanderlust of the explorer, but also a family to support.

I worked under a man named Daniel Ebbets, who I tried to enlist for our games but to no avail. The moment I punched the clock on my way out, I looked as if I were rushing to a fire.

"You don't like it here, Alick?"

"Sure you don't want to come along?"

"What's the point in hitting a little ball all afternoon?"

"None whatsoever, that's why I love it."

I did, however, manage to talk his brother into playing with us.

WILL WHEATON   He'd get a little too zealous at times and we'd end up with more players than we needed. Now we could play with 10, or 11, or even twelve men in the field but more than that and a good game was impractical. Still it was better to have too many than too few, even if it did lead to hard feelings when we had to eliminate potential players.

ALICK CARTWRIGHT    When we had too many players, we always made sure to use those who showed up regularly. It was a long trek up to Murray Hill for nothing if you didn't get to play.

CHARLES BIRNEY    There was no question as to whether I was going to get to play or not. If I was going to make the trek from Brooklyn, I was going to play, even if it meant somebody who Cartwright dragged off the street was going to have to watch ... or go home. Some of them didn't even know how to play.

ALICK CARTWRIGHT    Depending on who showed up, we adjusted the rules accordingly. There were always those who voiced their wishes, and those who went along with whatever was decided. I was, for better or worse, a member of the former fraternity.

WILL WHEATON    Sometimes to keep the peace I would moderate between those expressing differing thoughts about how to play. This is not to suggest however, that the rules were infinitely flexible. They weren't, but there were variations within them that had to be agreed upon.

HARRY HART    The indelible memory of one particular game has taken up permanent residence in my mind and shall, I'm sure, remain there for the rest of my days.

It took place on the first beautiful spring day of the year. The snow was gone, the ground was warming, and the air had that apple-blossom crispness that only an early spring day could produce. If there ever was a perfect Saturday to play a game, that was it.

A sometimes player, I was living over on Houston Street with my mother and son, David. My wife had left me a widower a few years earlier.

At any rate, on this particular day I decided to go up to Murray Hill to see if I could find a game. I woke up David and asked him to join me. We had not been getting along very well lately, so I thought the experience of playing in a game together would be good for both of us. Despite my earlier prodding, David had never been keen to play the game. He was then a strapping lad of fifteen, tall and willowy. I suspect, in part at least, because I was so smitten by base ball, he chose to ignore it as a way of saying he was not going to let his father influence him. He was still angry with me. When his mother died, I was off fighting a massive fire. Had I stayed home and attended to the family instead of other people's businesses...

Guilt is voracious. It can slowly consume a man with little bites over a long period. Because I knew this to be true, I found ways to escape its ravenous advance. Drink was not the answer for me as I never had the stomach for it. Base ball, though, provided a few hours a week of welcome respite.

It was only after the intervention of his grandmother with a brazen bribe that David reluctantly agreed to go with me.

"If you two men will get out of the way this morning, I'm sure I can find the fixings for a couple of fresh-baked apple pies."

With the aroma of baking apples almost palpable, David shrugged.

The trip uptown passed with nary a word passing between us. I knew better than to try to engage my son in a conversation when he was in one of these moods.

When we arrived at Murray Hill, a few players were already there. The lure of spring was hard to ignore.

"Glad you could make it, Harry," said Cartwright as we approached. "I see you've brought a real player with you."

"I'm not playing," said David with all the authority he could muster.

"On a day like this?"

David walked away and sat resolutely under a tree.

"Let him be," I said. "He's still angry..."

"A game is good for what ails you."

"So, are we going to have enough to play a full match?"

"I'm counting on it. They'll smell the game in the air I'm quite certain. After the winter we've had they'll smell it."

DOC ADAMS   As the Dionysian festivals of ancient Greece signaled the coming of spring and the resurgence of the "indestructible life," so did a good game of ball. It was a time of unmitigated hope.

HARRY HART   David was a reader. I suppose that was his way of escaping. He was then reading Richard Henry Dana's *Two Years Before the Mast*, a book I had bought him. He unfolded his long legs and settled in for what he assumed would be a peaceful morning of reading and dreaming.

"Enjoying the book?" I asked him.

He simply nodded without looking up.

ALICK CARTWRIGHT   I was sensitive to the problems Hart was having with his son and as players were slow to arrive, I asked David about his book.

It was a story, he said, of a trip to California. We talked about that for a few minutes and then I asked him if he would like to play. He said he wasn't interested in base ball, that he didn't even know the rules, and he didn't know how to play. I told him we'd teach him, but again he refused.

HARRY HART   I saw Alick talking to David and knew what he was doing but I left them alone. If he could talk David into playing, so much the better.

DOC ADAMS   During the course of the late morning, players straggled in. I volunteered to captain one side; Abe Tucker, the other. As always, we alternated choices. Abe took his son, Tuck, Dupignac, Cartwright, Hart, Birney, and Avery. I took the Colonel, Dr. Ransom, Wheaton, Curry, the O'Brien brothers, and Davis.

So, I had eight players; Tucker had seven. Curry asked Cartwright if he wanted to try to recruit a few more.

ALICK CARTWRIGHT    Given that it was our first game of the year, I was more eager to play than spend the day pounding the sidewalks in search of more players. We agreed to play as we were.

DOC ADAMS    Cartwright had already paced out the field before anyone else had arrived — a square marked by burlap bags filled with a little dirt. As usual, the striker's spot was set between home base and fourth base.

HARRRY HART    The O'Brien boys seldom entered into game negotiations or in fact said much about the game at all. They were simply there to play.

While we were settling on the game situation, I saw both of them go over and talk to David. At one point I saw David smile that little crooked smile of his and wondered what the lads had said to him but I wasn't about to ask lest David thought I was prying.

BILLY O'BRIEN    I always preferred it when we played with overhand pitching and usually said so. In Massachusetts we always played that way. Pitchers could make the ball whistle through the air ending with a solid thwack into the catcher's hands. That seemed to be the manly and the right way to play. But for some reason, in New York they always wanted to pitch underhand.

ALICK CARTWRIGHT    Overhand puts too much emphasis on the pitching and doesn't give the scouts enough to do in the field. We get much better exercise with underhand pitching.

WILLIAM TUCKER    Cartwright suggested we play to 25 aces. Dupignac, who had promised his wife that he would be home early to help with spring planting, put forth the idea we play to twelve.

"Hell, she's got all spring to plant," Cartwright laughed.

"Tell her that."

"You can leave whenever you need to," said Birney. "I'm for playing to 30. I didn't come all this way for a paltry twelve."

"We could play two," said Doc. "The first one to 12 after which anyone who needed to leave could and then we could play a second to say 21."

"I can't play a second game unless the first is short." said Avery, "Certainly not if we play one out, all out."

DUNCAN CURRY    I think it was Wheaton who suggested we play three hands out, all out. We had sometimes played this way but it certainly wasn't what was normal.

Mostly we played one hand out, all out. This meant simply that a side lost its at-bat every time an out was recorded. Granted, one way to get a runner out was to hit him with the ball before he reached a base, but this took considerable throwing skill and great aim, something with which not every eager player was blessed. Then too, some runners were very good at dodging thrown balls—those who were agile enough anyway. It was a skill that Dupignac had mastered. He could twist into more shapes than a corkscrew.

Although we hadn't played it for some time, there used to be a time when after a batting side made an out, if one of its players picked up the ball and threw it so that it struck one of the fielding side players before he got completely off the field, his side would retain its batting rights. So, one out all out didn't always end up that way.

Another version was called all out, all out. As the name would suggest, this meant that all hands on a batting side had to make an out in order to end an innings. This was similar to cricket and since patriotic fervor was very much in the minds of many New Yorkers, not everybody wanted our game to be thought of as a variation of anything English. We played all out, all out a little differently though. As we went through the defined batting order, once a player was put out he was finished for that innings, but if he succeeded in reaching a base safely, he could bat again when his turn came around. We would do this until every hand had been retired once. What often resulted is that we ended up playing only one innings. The side that had the biggest tally at the end of the innings was the winner no matter how many aces had been scored.

On this particular day, after considerable discussion we agreed to play one out, all out to 15 aces with the tacit understanding that an equal number of hands had to be played. After that, we'd see who wanted to play a second game.

ALICK CARTWRIGHT   I was always in favor of playing the bounder rule although not everyone agreed. When we played this way, a hand was considered out if a scout caught the ball before it hit the ground or after a single rebound. Of course it went unstated but understood that if a scout could reasonably be expected to catch a ball while in the air, he would do so. Letting it purposely drop and then playing it wasn't the gentlemanly way to go about things.

BILLY O'BRIEN   What playing the bounder rule accomplished was to shorten the length of a game since it was easier to get a hand out. Wasn't pitching underhand making the game easy enough? Why did we have to make it even easier?

EBENEZER DUPIGNAC   Some players didn't seem to have anything else in their lives that needed tending to. I did, so I was always in favor of the bounder rule.

ALICK CARTWRIGHT   The bounder rule simply made the game more appealing to those players who weren't as experienced or who didn't have the best of skills. I always believed that anything we did to encourage others to play the game, the better for all of us. We wanted and needed more players, so making the game more difficult didn't seem like a good idea.

WILL WHEATON    I am told that once upon a time it wasn't even clear in which direction a runner must go. Does he run to the first base and continue in a counter clockwise direction, or fourth base and continue clockwise? I never played the game clockwise but I know some who did. At least that was one variable we didn't need to resolve. We were all headed to the first base with whatever swiftness God endowed us, or in the case of DeBost, cheated us of.

We were out in the sunshine on a beautiful day away from work and family pressures. For my part, I didn't care much one way or the other which rules we played. As far as I was concerned, all the bickering was much ado about nothing.

"Come on, let's play ball."

HARRY HART    The game began shortly before noon with Doc's side at bat. Alick was pitching and Birney catching. Abe was on first with Tuck playing in with Dupignac, and me, and Walter Avery stationed out in the garden. Alick was positioned closer to the striker than we played later, but then the bases were closer together too. How close? I don't know. We never measured the distances but rather we had a sense of how far apart they should be and that's where they were. As always, Doc supplied the ball.

In their first time at bat, both the O'Brien boys reached base safely even though Billy only managed to tip a ball that went safely behind him. We hadn't yet settled on the idea of fair and foul areas although it was not an unknown concept. What Billy did — tip the ball over Birney's head behind the plate — was regarded as a great skill practiced by only the finest batsmen. The innings ended uneventfully, however, when Davis managed nothing more than a high ball which Dupignac easily cradled in his big hands.

Our first attempt at hitting ended quickly enough. Our first striker, Will Tucker, safely reached the second base. Then Dupignac smacked the first delivery he saw deep into the garden past the third base. Duncan Curry scooped up the ball and made a miraculous throw, catching Tucker on the hip just as he was approaching the fourth base. It was such an accurate throw we all stood in awe. Duncan trotted off the field as if it were an everyday occurrence, but I'll tell you, I've never seen him make a throw like that before or since. Tuck was out a scant few inches before he would have tallied a run.

The game was off to a good start: One innings and already a superb act of batting by O'Brien and an incredible throw by Avery. I just hoped that David was watching. This was base ball as it was meant to be played — with skill and daring.

The next few innings were less exciting. Due in part to the one out, all out rule, aces were not easily achieved. A premium was placed on timely batting with the emphasis on not making mistakes because even one meant the end of a side's batting chances for that innings. Nevertheless, within the hour, we managed to tally five aces to the Adams side's eight.

At that point, a slight commotion ensued when Birney refused to swing at any of Adams' offerings.

DOC ADAMS  Walter would sometimes do that. I don't know if he got tired easily or was trying to test the patience of everyone else. I suspect the latter.

"Walter," I said, "something ailing you?"

"Only the way you're throwing the ball."

"Then tell me where you want it."

"I want it where I can hit it."

"Where, pray tell is that?"

"Well it certainly isn't at my ankles."

"Nor did I deliver the ball there."

"You have, Doc, and you can do it all day for all I care. I'm not going to swing at them."

"Show me. Put your hand where you want the ball delivered."

Walter extended his hand indicating he wanted the ball just above his waist. I nodded okay and tried my best to put the ball exactly where he asked. Still he didn't swing.

"Walter," we're going to be here till the snows come again if you don't swing sometime this spring."

"Maybe you need some help," chimed in Billy O'Brien. "Will someone please show Mr. Birney what his bat is for. Colonel, if you would be so kind."

"Maybe Abe should find someone else who can deliver a decent ball."

I don't know what burr got under his saddle, but Walter, he could be an ornery cuss when he got that in his mind. It took me a few minutes to realize that perhaps what was causing the upset was that in the innings before, I had plugged him square in the back with the ball as he was attempting to make it safely to the second base. He may have taken exception to the force of the throw, but I never intentionally plugged anyone harder than necessary. Sometimes in the heat of the moment, though, it's hard to judge. He may have felt otherwise but he would never say so. Ah, but refusing to swing at perfectly acceptable balls, that was something else again and quite within his rights.

I kept throwing the ball where he asked as best as I could, knowing that eventually he would swing or risk serious anger from the others. When he thought he could no longer endure the looks and comments, he swung mightily but managed only a high ball that Harry Hart caught in the garden, although none too easily I might add. It brought sighs of relief and a few muttered "finallys" from everyone.

JAMES WHYTE DAVIS    Naturally we wanted to win each match in which we competed. I say "naturally" because our very basest instincts for survival urge us on to be the competitive animals we are. We played the games to win but that was not the goal. To play is to win regardless of the outcome. We were gentlemen playing a gentleman's game not a group of carmen, omnibus drivers, stevedores, or charcoal vendors playing a scrubby game of football.

I believe that the good Colonel had a talk with Mr. Birney after the match and helped to convince him of this.

DOC ADAMS    The game moved on without incident but with great *joie de vivre* and camaraderie until the match stood at 14 aces each. Then Hart took his turn at bat with no one on the bases. On the first ball he saw he took a hefty swing and smacked the delivery well hit to his left. The ball must have hit a hard patch on the ground, maybe a leftover frozen clump of earth that refused to give up on winter. At any rate, it skidded amongst the trees that bordered the pitch.

In those days the balls we played with were considerably softer than the modern ones and so generally didn't travel that far. Jonathan O'Brien ran to retrieve it at a pace only he among us could have exhibited. Now, Hart was not a very fast runner and on top of that, he slipped to the ground after he swung, but he righted himself and was doing his best to navigate his way around the bases when Jonathan reached the wayward ball, picked it up and threw it all the way to his brother. William gathered it in and in one graceful moment, turned and threw at the struggling Hart. I have no doubt whatsoever that William did not realize just how close he was to the runner for his hard-thrown ball struck Hart flush on his right knee sending him immediately to the ground for the second time within one trip around the bases. He grabbed his knee at the same time as he let out a cry that probably could have been heard in the bowels of the Murray mansion.

I came straightaway to Hart's aid and examined the knee as best I could under the circumstances. Normally our ball would cause scant damage to a runner but as the ball hit Hart his instinct caused him to turn at an awkward angle and thus twist the joint in a manner God had not intended when he created the human skeleton. It appeared that the knee was severely aggravated, but no bones were broken.

The O'Brien boys put their arms around Hart and helped him to the side of the field.

HARRY HART    The initial sharp pain in the knee subsided some within a few minutes, but I was not eager to test it again that day.

"Very sorry, Hart," said Billy O'Brien. "Didn't mean to injure."

"No, I know."

"You'll be okay."

"Sure I will."

The O'Briens were a fiery clan, but not a vicious one.

JAMES WHYTE DAVIS    Since he could not finish the match, it left us in a bit of a fix. Tucker's side was down to six men. We could have given them someone from our side, but Hart suggested a better solution.

HARRY HART    I looked at David who was standing next to the clump of men around me and said, "David, you finish for me, please."

He gave me a look that suggested he felt that I had somehow betrayed him. "I don't know how to play."

Davis smiled broadly and put his hand on David's shoulder. "Come on lad, you've seen us play. You know how it's done and we'll help you out if you need it. You would do us all a great service if you would finish up for your father. We would greatly appreciate your assistance."

I knew Davis, who would later become a widower himself, was doing what he could to come to my aid. I looked directly at David but said nothing

"We could really use your help," added Doc.

David sighed as if he was carrying the weight of the world on his youthful shoulders.

"Thanks, David," said Davis before David could say anything more.

With a gentle tug on the arm, Doc led him to the garden where he was positioned precisely where I had been playing.

DOC ADAMS    I might be wrong about this, but I had the distinct impression that David was not unpleased to be on the pitch. Perhaps since it was someone other than his father who applied the final urging, he was actually eager to test his skills. Perhaps he felt he had something to prove to his father after all.

HARRY HART    I sat with my back against a tree and my knee propped up on a clump of dirt.

I wasn't sure how David would react but I was eager to see.

For some time David had no business to handle in the garden. When hitting, he used my bat and swung with more good intention than skill. At his insistence, I had not practiced with him before, so he was certainly finding his own way.

What he was thinking was impossible to determine because he gave nothing away. His face was as blank as a sheet of unused paper. The other lads encouraged him though, and this made me feel good.

Then, as fate would have it, the first time a ball was hit in his direction, the game was decidedly in the balance.

The score stood at 14 hands each when Adams' side came to hit. Wheaton smacked a ball that Dupignac barely missed catching. Then Curry hit a ball that Cartwright fumbled. It should have been side out, but instead Wheaton was standing on third; and Curry, first. O'Brien — Billy that is — was the next striker and the situation looked dire for us. He was a glorious hitter who loved to produce the important hits for his side.

I suspect he knew where David was stationed, and fully within his rights, decided to take whatever advantage he could find. I also suspect David could sense this. He may not have had any experience with the game, but he was a smart young man with good instincts.

Did I see Billy leak a little smile as he looked out at the inexperienced player in the garden? I can't be certain, but I know what happened next was real.

As was his wont, O'Brien waited for a pitch to his liking and then reared back and unleashed that beautifully coordinated swing of his.

DOC ADAMS　I could see what was in Billy's mind. We all could. But that's part of the greatness of the game. It takes both the physical skill of an athlete and the strategic thinking of a chess player.

HARRY HART　The ball went soaring deep into the garden, passing the first base on its way. Naturally this was David's field to cover. He started running toward where he correctly assumed the ball would eventually approach the ground again. I must say I immediately thought that if he chose to do so, he could one day become a good ballist.

DOC ADAMS　David was much more awkward on his run to the ball than one might believe had he heard the description oft repeated by his father in the days following the game. A father sees these things through the tinted spectacles of paternity, and why not?

HARRY HART　Forgetting my injury for the moment, I instinctively jumped to my feet, only to find my knee did not share in my enthusiasm and I immediately dropped back to the ground.

Getting to the ball was one thing, but catching a high hit ball without ever having done so before was something considerably more difficult.

Without thinking, I shouted to David, "Let it drop, let it drop!"

Remember, we were playing the bounder rule and catching the ball on one hop was as good as catching it in full flight and considerably easier. The ball was coming down from a great height and with great speed. It would be very easy for it to go straight through the cupped hands of even the best scout. Worse still, if one were a little out of position, the ball could catch him flush on the face.

"Let it drop, let it drop."

David and the ball arrived at the landing spot at the same instant. He reached out his hands holding them tightly together as he had seen done. The ball landed directly in his hands and then went straight through them to the ground as if it was angry at having been subjected to the efforts of such a neophyte.

DOC ADAMS   David made a valiant effort in the cause of victory. There's no doubt about that.

HARRY HART   Well, that was that. The game was over, we lost. My first reaction was to be angry that David did not heed my instructions to field the ball as a bounder. I thought he was purposely ignoring me in yet another attempt to show disappointment in his father.

DAVID HART   Yes, I heard Father, and no, I didn't deliberately drop the ball. I was doing exactly what I thought would make him proud. For a long time he'd been telling me that base ball was a gentleman's game played by rules, tacit or otherwise, that gentleman knew to be correct. One of those rules was that you didn't catch the ball on the bound if you could catch it before it hit the ground. I was in position to catch the ball in the air, so that's exactly what I tried to do. I failed and we lost the match, but I did exactly what father had preached.

HARRY HART   When reality set in and I realized what David had done, I couldn't have been prouder of him. It took me a while to tell him that, but when I did ... well, we've been the best of friends since. If truth be told, it didn't matter who won the match, but it did matter what happened to a father and a son on that first beautiful spring day.

Base ball can be a great teacher. I know.

WILLIAM TUCKER   We didn't see much of Harry after that, and I don't know that David ever played again, but I understand what that game meant to them.

# 9

## *Alick Makes a Suggestion*

WILLIAM TUCKER   It was a few days after one of those rather contentious games when we gathered again. Cartwright put forth a suggestion that was to have a dramatic impact on all of us for the rest of our lives.

DUNCAN CURRY   Well do I remember the afternoon when Alex Cartwright came to the Murray Hill field with an organizational scheme for the game.

He had laid out a diamond-shaped field, indicating canvas bags filled with sand or sawdust at three of the base points and an iron plate for the home base. He had jotted down a few other notes as to rules. His plan met with much good-natured derision but he was as ever, persistent.

ALICK CARTWRIGHT    While we had all been playing ball for some time, we had come from different backgrounds, and learned to play in different ways. Some of us had come from rounders, some from cricket, some from town ball. Some were familiar with the Massachusetts game. Some knew none other than the game we played in all its variations. Add to this the fact that it was inevitable that in the not too distant future we would be forced to move yet again as the city was continuing to swallow up all the open spaces. If we had an organized club we could charge reasonable dues and then use that money to rent a permanent place to play. There was some space over in Hoboken across the river that I had in mind.

Other sports had regular organizations—cricket, rowing.

I turned to the fellows and said, "What do you say we get together and agree on some rules?"

"I've got to get home," said Birney.

"You've always got to get home."

"You should try it sometime."

"I don't necessarily mean now. I mean let's set a time, meet, and organize a real club."

"What's the point?" said Walt Avery. "We play now, don't we? What else do we need?"

"Look, if we get organized then we can make it better for all of us."

"That doesn't make it better, only more complicated," Avery said.

"What if we had one set of rules we always went by? One set we all knew and understood. Think of the confusion we could avoid, and we'd have more time to play. We could write them down — the rules. We could have them printed."

"No one else needs printed rules. Why do we?" said Dupignac.

"Good bye, Alick," said Birney as he headed off toward his stage.

"Next Saturday then?" said Billy O'Brien. "Same time?"

"If the weather holds," said his brother as the two of them walked away."

"Anyone join me?" I said.


WILLIAM TUCKER    This was not the first time the idea of organizing had been bandied about. Nor was it the first time some saw no need for it, but Alick didn't give up easily. Some of the lads may have resented him some because he was frequently expressing his opinions about almost anything that was on the table for discussion, and a few that weren't. He was a dreamer — some would say schemer — who was always thinking about what might lie ahead. He had about him, a restless spirit that was unmistakable.

"And another consideration," he said. "If we have to move our games to a space we have to rent, then by having a club, we can assess dues to pay for it."

"Now I would think a bank teller could just help himself," said Dupignac.

"Anyone else want to join us?" said Alick, ignoring the remark.

I had played with what we called the New York Club before this. So had Colonel Lee, and Will Wheaton. It was very loosely organized. Sometimes we went under the name of the Gothams. In those days there was a lot of mixing of players because no one had firmly established set clubs. I played sometimes as a Gotham, sometimes as an Eagle. They were just names for groups who liked to play ball and the groups changed according to who showed up on any given day. Sometimes we'd get together for a convivial evening at a tavern, to talk about playing and enjoy the company of other like-minded men.

"Alick," I said. "We've got clubs."

"Not ones with organized rules," he said.

"Maybe we can organize them."

"Wouldn't it be easier to start from scratch? Form our own club, with our own rules. Play the game the proper way."

ALICK CARTWRIGHT   Some of the fellows didn't see the need, some didn't want to bother, some thought it went counter to the very idea of free play and enjoyment.

"Who needs rules?" said Daniel Carrington. "We play fine just as it is."

"Except we're always arguing about it," I said.

"Look, I got rules at work," said Dan. "If I don't follow them I get fired. I got rules at home laid down by my wife. If I don't follow them, I have to sleep in the front room. I have rules at church. If I don't follow them, I guess I'll be condemned to hell for all eternity. I don't want any more rules. I play ball to have fun not to follow some damn club rules."

"Organization doesn't have to mean no more fun."

"Doesn't look that way to me."

"Let's give it a try. We can always tear up by-laws and disband if it doesn't work out. What do we have to lose?"

"I'm not interested, Alick. I can always find a game when I want to. You form a real club, don't count on me to be a member."

That was the last time I ever saw Carrington. Maybe he continued to play someplace else, I don't know. Maybe he was sleeping in the front room after all or maybe he just skipped it all and went straight to hell.

"Fraley, what about you?"

"Alick, I've got all I can do at home as it is. I can't really find the time, but if you do get organized, I'm more than willing to consider joining."

"Duncan?"

DUNCAN CURRY   As Bartleby the Scrivener said, I am a man who, ever since childhood, has been filled with a profound conviction that the easiest way of life is the best.

Alick was making sense although I knew that some of the resistance was coming because he was the one proposing it. I thought I might be of some help as a more moderate voice — a safe voice.

"It's not a bad idea," I said to those still near. "We've played so many different ways, it wouldn't hurt to decide on one for once and all. I'm for giving it a try. After all, the idea of organized clubs has worked well for our friends of the skull, sail, and wicket. Why not for us?"

Of course, the inclination to form into clubs was prevalent in those days. The volunteer fire organizations served as a kind of club. Formal social clubs were common, most meeting in one of the many taverns where the men would engage in such indoor activities as cards, billiards, and darts.

FRALEY NIEBUHR   The most compelling argument to me was the idea of collecting dues so that we could properly organize matches on a proper field. The problem I saw was that we didn't have enough regulars to form a club big enough to collect sufficient dues to make it worthwhile. When I made my opinion known, Alick, always the optimist, just smiled and said that's how we were going to get more players.

"By charging dues?" I said.

"Exactly."

"How do you reason that?"

"Look, most of us aren't wealthy, but we're not living in poorhouses either. If we assess reasonable dues it will do two things: One, it will keep away the types we don't really want to join us anyway; and two, it will help us get new players who want to be part of a club. You know how it is, men like to have their clubs, like to have the feeling of belonging. Let's give them something to belong to."

"How much? The dues, how much were you thinking about?'

"I hadn't really gotten that far yet. That's for us to determine."

"Ten dollars a year?"

"Maybe."

"That's too much for me. Betsey would have me scalped for less."

"Then five. I don't know, we'll have to figure it out."

"You'll have to limit the number of members. That's for certain. Nobody wants to join a club that anybody can join."

"So, are you in?"

"I'll help if you want."

DUNCAN CURRY   The very idea of social clubs was something that was growing in popularity. As far as I know, the oldest club, the Union Club, was organized in 1836 by (as they called themselves), "gentlemen of social distinction." Many of the city's financial elite belonged — August Belmont, the banker from the House of Rothschild, and Alexander Stewart, the wealthy merchant, among them. Then came the New York Yacht Club. About this time the Century Club was organized to bring artists and writers together with their benefactors. Men such as John Jacob Astor, the incredibly wealthy land speculator, and James Beekman, the famous lawyer and real estate investor, belonged to the Century.

Some of these clubs erected extensive buildings for the exclusive use of their members with sitting parlors, magnificent libraries, billiard, and dining rooms. I was a guest in the Century Club once. Seated among gentlemen capitalists, we ate in a splendid room of carved black walnut paneling, oriental carpets, and immense pictures of wild animals over the fireplaces. It was most dignified.

As I understand it, ancestry played a role in membership admittance, but more importantly I was told, a member must be above all, a gentleman.

Certainly Cartwright wasn't suggesting anything as grand as the Century, but still the idea of belonging to an organization of like-minded men struck a resonant chord.

FRALEY NIEBUHR   The thought of belonging to an exclusive club of merchants, bankers, and professionals, all who had an interest in ball playing grew on me. None of us were wealthy industrialists or land speculators, but we were all successful in our professions and we were all gentlemen.

WILLIAM VAIL   Of course, as my wife later reminded me, most of us already belonged to another type of organization that was similar in some ways to a club. We had the fire houses but also, almost everyone went to church. Most of us were Episcopalians or Presbyterians and I must admit, there was an element of social exclusivity in belonging to certain congregations.

The wealthy mercantile elite tended to belong to the Presbyterian Church, the Episcopal St. Marks Church, or Grace Church where pew rents meant only the wealthy were welcome. Pews there could range from $100 to $800 plus annual dues of $8 to $64.

You just weren't part of New York society if you didn't belong to a good church with a respectable congregation. Even the Jew, August Belmont, attended an Episcopal church.

Now none of us were going to pay $800 for membership in a base ball club, but a more reasonable amount was certainly something to consider.

ALEXANDER CARTWIGHT   "I suggest we get up a group to recruit potential members," I said. "Who'll join me?"

"All right, I'll see what I can do," said Dupignac.

Everyone else stood there as if I were asking them to run naked through the streets.

"How can we ask men to be members of something that doesn't exist?" asked Birney.

"There are plenty of players around. We just need to explain what we're about."

"Well, if you figure out exactly what that is, please let me know."

"That's the point isn't it?"

WILLIAM TUCKER    I looked at Wheaton and he kind of shrugged okay.

WILL WHEATON    "Tuck and I will do what we can," I said.

CHARLES BIRNEY    The way he was carrying on you would have thought he invented the idea of a sporting club. Alick always wanted to be the biggest toad in the puddle. When Alick said "form a club," what he really meant was "form his club." Not that that was necessarily bad, but I thought I'd wait and see before I signed on the dotted line.

"Alick, we've heard this before," I said.

"Well, it's time we acted."

"I don't know."

"What have we got to lose? If it doesn't work, we're right where we are now. No loss."

ALICK CARTWRIGHT    As players were beginning to wander off I said, "All right then, we'll see how many men we can recruit — me, Ebenezer, Will, and Tuck. That sound okay with everyone? We'll go from there."

"I'll see what I can do, too," added Duncan.

Sensing neither great enthusiasm nor outright rejection, I said, "A club, gentlemen. A true base ball club."

---

# 10

## *The Idea of Clubs*

ASHLEY HYDE    It was a time of tremendous social and economic flux. Many men had newly acquired the means of purchasing more and better consumer goods. The "middle class" they called them and they felt they had climbed at least a few rungs on the social ladder. The social norms of the farm and the tenement would no longer do.

Appropriate manners were as necessary as fashionable homes and stylish clothing. Ironically, these rules were largely based upon the norms of the 18th century aristocratic society that the new middle class had supplanted and rendered obsolete.

The men who were to form the Knickerbockers were gentlemen expected to behave according to the manners of polite middle class society. Violations— not raising one's hat gracefully when meeting a lady, for example, or wearing an immoderate quantity of vulgar jewelry, or swearing while on the field of play—were unacceptable.

At the same time, there were many in our fair city who saw the manners of the gentleman as contrary to what they considered the egalitarian nature of America. They considered "highfalutin" manners a product of the decadent Old World. What resulted was often loud, coarse, and rough behavior and downright rudeness, especially from those who were not a part of that class. Anyone wearing a top hat had to be ready to endure the "I'm as good a man as you" reception they might get from the porter, cab driver, sailor or ditch digger.

Clubs had become an important part of the social life of many New Yorkers including the working classes. They had their taverns and saloons, and there were hundreds of them throughout the city and in Brooklyn. Here the laborers met, ate, drank, played, and treated co-workers to the pleasures of the day. Strong spirits were plentiful and in some quarters the cheery greeting, "let's liquor," could be heard more frequently than "good day."

Many of these drinking establishments were unsavory. Once I was lured to one by a casual acquaintance with the prompt, "let's go see how the other half lives." We trekked down to Patsy Hearn's Five Points grogshop across from the Old Brewery. Well, it was like nothing I had ever seen. Around a wooden railed-in sunken pit were rows of rough benches, crammed with men in various stages of stupor. There must have been at least two hundred sweaty men at fever pitch when an escaped slave named Dusty Dustmore released packs of rats. Moments later, trained terriers were dropped in their midst and the carnage began. The dogs ripped the trapped rodents into bloody shreds, while the spectators wagered furiously and loudly on the number of rats the dogs would mangle in the specified time.

We left more stunned than entertained. It remained, however, a vivid example of the class divisions within the city.

COLONEL LEE    I must say I was surprised when on a trip to Philadelphia some years ago my cousin, who is in the furniture business there, told me of their Olympic Town Ball Club. Well, my interest was piqued and we went to watch a Saturday afternoon match. Unfortunately that was a day the skies chose to open up and a game was never played. We did, however, join the lads at a cheerful little tavern near their field. They were a most engaging lot and I have no doubt they would have put on a spirited contest.

Their replies to my queries over a mug of Philadelphia's best draft suggested that the game they played was much closer to what I knew to be the rules of town ball than those of our New York game.

As I was required to leave the next day for militia duties I never got to see them play and more is the pity as I have been curious about it ever since. Nevertheless, fairness demands we credit Philadelphia with the first base ball organization — the Olympics.

WILL WHEATON    When I started playing, it was with a group we called the Gotham Base Ball Club, although sometimes we were just referred to as the New York Club. This was in 1837. Among the members were Dr. John Miller, a successful physician; John Murphy, a well known hotel keeper; and James Lee, president of the New York Chamber of Commerce, and later one of the men who joined us when we created the Knickerbockers.

Lots of players who later joined the Knickerbockers were initially New York Club members — Willie Tucker, Jamie Davis, William Vail, just to name a few.

At first we played mostly on a square with eleven men to a side as in cricket, but later we reduced that number to eight and played on a diamond similar to rounders.

When we started, there were no regular bases, but only such permanent objects as embedded boulders or old stumps and often the field looked strangely like an irregular polygon. Later we laid out our ball ground, we made it into an accurate diamond with a home plate and sand bags for bases.

Now please understand, we weren't organized in a formal way as we were later like what Cartwright wanted, but we did establish rules. The first thing we did was to abolish the rule of throwing the ball at the runner and replace it with throwing the ball to the baseman who then had to touch the runner with it before the runner could reach the base.

We often played with six or seven men on a side, and never with a short stop. I'll leave credit for that with Doc Adams. The scorer kept the game in a book we had made for that purpose and it was he who decided all disputed points. The modern umpire and his tribulations were unknown to us.

Anyway, after our Gotham Club had been in existence a few months, we thought it was necessary to put the rules of our new game down in writing. This work fell to my hands and the code I then formulated is substantially that in use today.

We really didn't stay as a club for very long, and mostly we played amongst ourselves, but in our time we did manage to play two games of ball against the Star Cricket Club of Brooklyn. We beat the Englishmen out of sight, of course.

ALICK CARTWRIGHT    There had been so-called "ball clubs" playing even back in Father's time. Once, after some probing on my part, he averred that various city wards had been known to form clubs for the purpose of playing against other wards. Further probing suggested these were not actual organizations with written laws.

Those early clubs like the New York, the Gotham, the Eagle, and the Washington clubs were clubs in name only. As far as I know, they never set down a constitution, or by-laws, or rules of play. No, they were just names to describe groups of men who shared an interest in sport and talking about their games over libation at neighborhood taverns.

I knew we could do better.

# PART TWO: ORGANIZING THE CLUB 1845

## 11

# *Recruiting Members*

WILL WHEATON   We had an idea. All we needed now were members. Alick, true to his word and his missionary zeal, set out to round up enough gentlemen of the city willing to abide by written rules.

DUNCAN CURRY   Alick wouldn't or couldn't understand one simple point: We were going to have great difficulty as it was attracting enough members to make matches. He seemed to think that every gentleman in the city was going to be knocking down our non-existent doors trying to join and then flock to our matches in such numbers that we were going to have to put up fences to keep them at bay.

He just assumed everyone else shared his passion for the game and would do almost anything to be able to participate. Well, they didn't, and they wouldn't. It's not that many of us didn't love the game, but the reality of our daily lives sometimes impeded. Alick just scoffed at the notion. I guess the romantics don't always see life for what it is but rather what they want it to be.

I reminded him that in the summers, when the weather was best for games, it was also best for taking holidays out of town with groups we called families.

Alick would have none of it. He thought that once we were organized all those men playing cricket would come over to us, and he felt he could recruit others who when they saw a match being played would immediately fall in love with the act of hitting a ball.

In those days we were thinking only of playing matches within our club. There was no sense of a "rivalry" with other so-called clubs.

WILLIAM TUCKER   Alick could sell snow to an Eskimo, arrows to an Indian. He could be the most brazen man in the city. In his efforts to round up enough gentlemen to make up a real club I saw him walk down the street buttonholing any young men who even looked as if he might be capable of swinging a bat at a ball without hurting himself.

EBENEZER DUPIGNAC   Mostly I went to the men who had been playing with us all along — DeBost, the O'Brien brothers, Moncrief, Morgan, Broadhead, et al.

ABRAHAM TUCKER    I owned and operated a tobacco shop down on East Broadway. My son, William, lived above it with the young lawyer William Wheaton.

My tobacco shop afforded me a good living as tobacco was in one form or another a part of most men's lives. Much of what we sold was used for pipe-smoking, chewing, snuff, and, of course, the segar that was becoming more and more popular over recent years. Segarette smoking didn't really catch on until a few years later with the creation of "Bright" tobacco.

Never mind that a couple of years earlier Samuel Green wrote that tobacco was an insecticide, a poison, a filthy habit that could kill a man, the gentlemen of this city will never give up their segars. After a good game of base ball, we would always celebrate by lighting up. I'll have to admit, I assumed any club we might form would be good for my business but the business would also be good for the players because they would know they could always get the segars from me at "the club price."

FRALEY NIEBUHR We were looking for men of character and good will and never did the issue of playing skill come into consideration. We might, on occasion, have checked with fellow workers or acquaintances about someone's background or character; we might have spent some time meeting with them over a drink or dinner; we might have played ball with them, but never for the purpose of evaluating their skills as a prerequisite for membership.

Within short order, we did manage to recruit enough potential members to create a very respectable club. We had several doctors and lawyers, a few clerks and brokers, a marshal, a number of business owners, and a smattering of what for lack of any other terms could be described only as "gentlemen of leisure."

---

# 12

# *Writing Rules*

ALICK CARTWRIGHT    "You're a lawyer, maybe you could use your lawyer language to draw up a constitution and by-laws," I told Wheaton. He seemed the perfect choice to do just that, and since his roommate, Tuck, knew the game well, I thought they'd make a good team.

"I suppose I could," said Wheaton.

Although he feigned some indifference, I think he actually was pleased to be asked. Wheaton liked to feel important. My only concern was that he needed to pay attention to the rules that I had suggested. I knew they would make for a good game if everyone would just agree.

WILLIAM TUCKER   What we did more than anything else was try to bring a sense of order to the disarray that had characterized most of our games. So for several nights after work, Will and I got together in the apartment and worked on organizing rules and by-laws. Mostly Will took charge of the issues relating to club rules, and I worked on the game rules, but we discussed all of it together.

What we came up with was a set of provisional rules and by-laws. We incorporated much of what Cartwright had spelled out, and some ideas of what we thought would work best based on the various ways we had played. Understand, we didn't include every little rule that everybody knew and understood to be inherent in the very nature of the game. Rather what we concentrated on were the parts for which there were many options. So, in reality, what we were trying to do was to reach some agreement on the variables of the game as we then knew them. For example, we didn't specify that a runner had to reach the first base before he went to the second base. We assumed everyone knew that. However, we did specify such things as how many aces constituted a game, how far apart the bases were to be placed, and how a ball was to be delivered to the batsman.

WILL WHEATON   Tuck and I spent several rather enjoyable nights discussing (debating?) the rules that we agreed we would write up and then present at our first organizational meeting. Our aim was simply to make the rules as clear and unambiguous as we could so as to avoid misunderstanding and argument. Also we wanted to adopt rules for the organization of the club itself that would be equally clear. There were plenty of examples around of other gentlemanly clubs, and so we based ours on some of the commonly accepted principles of administration.

Now we knew there would be differences of opinion, but we thought that the more specific we could be, the more likely it was that we could limit the arguing.

---

# 13

## *Gentlemen Inventing a Club*

ALICK CARTWRIGHT   I arranged for a room at the Fijux Hotel over on Murray Street. One of the Fijux boys, while not an avid player, did join us occasionally.

My hope was that by the end of the evening we would have agreed to create a formal organization for the purpose of playing for fun and exercise, that
the organization would operate according to written by-laws, that after due
consideration we would admit only gentlemen of good character, and that in
all matters we would conduct ourselves in accordance with the principles of
good sportsmanship.

Was I expecting too much? The thought did arise.

EBENEZER DUPIGNAC    I wasn't completely convinced the meeting would be
successful. Cartwright was known to carry on about some issue or another, not
all of which amounted to anything. Nevertheless, I was willing to give him the
chance. What did we have to lose but a Wednesday evening?

I also knew that in Tuck and Will we had men who would leaven
Cartwright's excessive zeal with more realistic attitudes.

By the time I arrived they were already there with elaborate notes. We had
rather a better turnout than I might have thought.

We were all sitting around in this little room off the main dining room
under a thick cloud of smoke courtesy of the segars handed out by Tuck as an
apology for the absence of his father. Libations of our choices were offered and
gratefully accepted.

"Well, boys," said Alick. "Let's get to it. What have you come up with?"

"If everyone is in agreement then, we might as well start by settling on
some laws for the club," Will said.

Duncan took a big puff on his segar and blew a friendly circle of smoke
towards Wheaton. "Somebody should write down what we come up with.
Somebody should act as recording secretary."

"Keep your smoke to yourself," said Will. "I've written enough. My hand
has officially retired."

"Then perhaps Dupignac would oblige."

Everyone but me thought this was a wonderful idea.

"I have neither implement nor paper," I protested.

"I'm sure such a fine establishment as the Fijux would oblige us if we
asked," said Duncan.

So as the drinks arrived, we asked for paper and pen and were told that
they would be provided right away.

With me acting as secretary, and Alick Cartwright as major domo, we
began to consider what kind of organization and game we wanted. Not town
ball, not the Massachusetts game, not the game they played in Philadelphia,
but the game as we played it in New York.

WILL WHEATON    I knew that some ideas would be met with doubt or outright rejection, so I began with something I thought everyone would agree
to.

"I think the club should have officers to enforce the club rules, to organize matches, to..."

"You mean to do all the work," said Dupignac.

"That's often the case. I'll grant you that, but it's absolutely necessary. Certainly you don't disagree."

"As long as I'm not one of them, I don't."

"Right then. A president to run the organization, a vice president to act in the absence of a president, and a secretary/treasurer.

"All in favor?" Alick quickly barked.

Alick was getting a little carried away so I reminded him that we didn't need to vote on anything at that point since we had no club rules or by-laws yet. We only needed to come to a consensus.

He seemed a little perturbed at this but nodded his agreement. We had our first item for Ebenezer's list. If only the rest had been that easy.

EBENEZER DUPIGNAC    I can't say it was a contentious meeting, but any gathering with two lawyers has to have its share of arguments, or at least disagreements, and add in others with strong opinions about everything and you've got the makings for an interesting evening.

"What next, Will?"

WILL WHEATON    I proposed that the club president appoint an umpire for each match, the umpire to be one of our members with sufficient knowledge of the rules to assume full responsibility for the match including the levying of fines for violations in conduct or decorum.

"Or the vice president in his absence," said Tuck reading from his notes.

"And that the umpire will keep a record of each club match in a book provided for that purpose."

"Who supplies the book?" asked Ebenezer.

"The club."

"Where does the club get the money for books?"

"From dues."

"What dues?"

"The ones we collect."

"But we didn't agree to that."

"We will."

"Do you want me to put that in here?"

"Maybe when we get to it."

I could see we weren't going to get very far if Ebenezer was going to continue along this line and I'm afraid I might have let my frustration show.

Duncan, ever the conciliator, suggested to the recording secretary that perhaps it would be better if we let Wheaton finish making his point before we opened discussion on it.

"Furthermore," I said, "the Umpire will note any violations in the by-laws and rules during a match."

As soon as I said that, I added quickly, "The by-laws and rules that we have yet to decide on."

We were proceeding under the tacit assumption that most of our matches would be played within the club by members of the club, but in time it might be possible to arrange matches with other yet-to-be-formed clubs. When and if this happened, we could show them our rules and ask the other side to agree to play by those rules. If they didn't? Well then we were back where we started.

"How do we agree on an umpire if we play against another club?" asked Dupignac.

"We'll just have to agree, that's all," I said.

I followed this with the idea that the presiding officer at each match would select two members from those present to serve as captains. The thought was that the captains would retire from the field while they divided the players into sides seeking always to make them as equal as possible. For the sake of the sport, equal sides are always best but it's not possible for the players themselves to decide where they stood in that regard. No, let two men serving as captains do that.

EBENEZER DUPIGNAC    "Who's to say even the captains will divide the men equally?" I asked. "They're each likely to want the best players on their side. It's only natural."

"Why don't we let the captains divide the men as best they can," said Duncan, "then they can toss a coin to see who gets which side. That way when they make up the sides they won't know on which side they are playing."

"Good idea," said Alick.

"They can then toss in a similar manner to see to see which side will be the first in."

Everyone agreed.

"I think we need to set fines," I said. "Real clubs have fines so that everyone has to stick to the rules. I know a fellow at the Union Club and they have fines. Probably all the other clubs do, too."

WILLIAM TUCKER    "We'll get to that," I said. "I think it would be good if we had a name to put on the top of our rules. Rules for the blank club."

Anytime you have a name for something, well then that thing seems real. We'd been talking more about the idea of a club than a real club.

"The Columbia Club," said Ebenezer. "That captures the spirit of the times all right."

Other suggestions included the Murray Hill Club, The Eagle Club, The Manhattan Club, The Pioneer Club, and The First Nine Club.

All the while we were considering names, Cartwright remained quiet. I knew he was a lion just waiting to spring.

"What do you think, Alick?" I said.

"Well, since most of us began playing ball as members of fire companies, and since the Knickerbocker Engine Company was closed down last year, I propose we call our club the Knickerbocker Base Ball Club."

Everyone else thought that made sense. I still preferred The Columbia Club, but I went along and wrote "Knickerbocker" on top of my notes.

CHARLES DEBOST   We were about the first people to settle here — us Dutchman — so you can thank us for the city and the name Knickerbocker. The city was rightly called New Netherlands for a time before some Englishman stole it and gave it to the Duke of York.

As I heard it from my father, a famous Dutchman named Knickerbacker fought in some important battles, and then his name was used by an American writer who wrote under the name of Geoffry Crayon and then Diedrich Knickerbocker. The name stuck to the city like honey on your finger, and so "Knickerbocker" as long as I can remember stood for what New York was and is. Oh yes, the other name that writer used was Washington Irving.

Knickerbockers, or knickers, was also reminiscent of the pants the early settlers wore, the kind that rolled up just below the knees. The figure of Father Knickerbocker in his wig, three-cornered hat, buckled shoes, and his knickers had been synonymous with New York since the early days.

I don't know if this was on purpose or not, but "Knickerbocker" reminded us of the Dutch rather than the British at a time when there still was considerable animosity toward England.

Naming our club after an engine company was anything but unique. Several other ball clubs did the same. The New York Mutuals for example were named after the Mutual Hook and Ladder Company. When the fire houses became club houses, the club houses became the birth-places of teams.

JAMES WHYTE DAVIS   Unlike us ball players, the rowing fraternity was extremely well organized. They kept detailed records, awarded prizes according to set rules, and attracted a large following. In the 20s the first boat club to be fully organized was called the Knickerbocker Club. Whether Alick had this in mind I don't know. I had always meant to ask him that, but for some reason, never did.

EBENEZER DUPIGNAC   After we agreed on the name, I again went back to my idea of setting fines ... and dues.

DUNCAN CURRY   In a manner not too dissimilar to our church congregations, the club set dues as one of the ways to maintain our character.

Setting dues and initiation fees at the right level was critical. Set them too high and the club would eliminate some who would be desirable members. Set them too low and the club would open itself up to undesirable candidates.

Will Wheaton    "I'd suggest an initiation fee of $5 and annual dues of $10," I said.

Ebenezer immediately looked aghast. "My name look like Astor to you?"

"Believe me, Astor pays a lot more than that to belong to the Century Club."

"How much is that?"

"They don't advertise that, but I assure you it's more. A great deal more."

Duncan smiled. "That's because they're trying to keep the likes of us out. Everyone to his own."

"We'll never get enough members at that rate, Will," said Cartwright.

"Only the right ones," I said. I knew the amount I suggested was too steep, but I wanted to make my point.

Cartwright suggested $3 dues and $1 initiation, arguing that the most important thing was to attract enough new potential members so that we could hold matches without having to scramble for players.

After considerable discussion we compromised with a $2 initiation fee and annual dues of $5, and as was our understanding of the policies of other clubs, if a member quit or left for another club, he would forfeit his dues.

Duncan Curry    Permit me to put this into perspective. One could sit in the gallery to see the great Edwin Forrest performing *Othello* at the Broadway Theatre for 12 cents or rent a full box for family and friends for $5. A good strong cup of coffee could be had for 4 cents, or my favorite, a plate of stewed oysters could be found throughout the city for 12 cents.

Will Wheaton    "We'll need to limit the number of members in the club," I said. "No one wants to join a club that's easy to join. Or to put it another way, many men want to join a club that they can't. It's human nature."

Duncan let slip that avuncular smile of his and said, "I most definitely don't want to join a club that admits me."

"Neither do I."

Alick, never the one to let the meeting wander, immediately added the obvious. "We need enough that we won't struggle to field sides for matches, but not so many that members won't get chances to play."

With that, the two lawyers proceeded to determine, through a carefully thought out process of deductive reasoning, exactly how many members our new club was to have.

"How many people live in this city?" asked Duncan.

"Maybe 400,000," I said.

"How many are men?"

"I'd have to say 200,000."

"Of that 200,000, how many are under fifty?"

"I'd guess 130,000."

"Of that 130,000, how many are fit enough to hit a ball and run all the way to the first base without having a heart attack?"

"Exactly 75,282."

"Of those, how many are either single or have understanding wives?"

"Single, 33,552; those with understanding wives, 227."

"Of those, how many are true gentlemen?"

"Forty."

"That's it then, the Knickerbocker Base Ball Club shall now and hereafter be limited to 40 fit single gentlemen or gentlemen with sympathetic wives."

I don't think Alick appreciated the facetious discussion, but in actuality, 40 was a reasonable number — at least for a start.

"I think we should have an explicit rule that members must strictly observe the time agreed upon for games and practices," I said, "and be punctual in their attendance."

"Or else we fine them?" said Ebenezer.

"We tell their wives," said Duncan.

EBENEZER DUPIGNAC   "We could put in a fine for being late," I said.

"There isn't enough money in our bank to cover what some members would owe," said Alick. "I think it would be better if we follow Will's idea and put it in the rules. That way if someone continually violates the rule we could expel them from membership. We do need to set fines, though."

"That's what I've been saying."

WILL WHEATON   Reasonable fines are good for any organization for two reasons: They encourage members to adhere to the club's rules and the revenue they generate helps with the club's operating expenses— expenses like dinners, banquets, and presents to founding members.

"Maybe for profanity," said Ebenezer.

"A dollar for each offense, "I said, "and we'll buy the Murray Mansion within a year."

"Five cents, maybe" said Tucker.

"You planning on doing a lot of swearing are you?" I said.

"Gentlemen don't swear," said Duncan, knowing damn well that in the heat of the game they frequently did.

"Just a suggestion."

"All right, then, 50 cents."

"You'll scare away every potential member this side of Harlem," said Duncan.

"Twenty-five cents."

"This side of 14th Street."

"Twelve cents."

"Tenth street."

"Six cents."

"Shit yes, sounds good to me. After all, we are gentlemen."

"You're damn right we are."

ALICK CARTWRIGHT    We all understood the absolute importance of encouraging those selected as captains to adhere diligently to the highest level of conduct. It was they who had to set the example. If they faltered then the deportment of the entire side could crumble. We agreed that the strongest fine should be levied on them for any breach of responsibility — one dollar for each occurrence. By so doing, we hoped to reinforce the authority, responsibility, and expectations of our captains.

Setting the other fines was a little like bargaining at a Marrakesh market. Wheaton, who was doing well as a lawyer, argued for more. Tucker, who maybe wasn't selling as many segars as he may have liked, kept saying we needed to keep the costs down. Finally we agreed on 50 cents for disobedience (although thank goodness we didn't get into what this word meant exactly), and 25 cents for complaints about an umpire's call.

DUNCAN CURRY    "I think it's important," I said, "that we set a condition that on practice days we don't engage in stump games like one old cat or two old cat."

"Tell me exactly what you want me to write," said Ebenezer.

"Simply, 'no stump match shall be played on a regular day of exercise.'"

EBENEZER DUPIGNAC    I posed the issue of what we would do if not enough club members appeared when we were to play a match. Should we allow non-members to participate?

"That doesn't seem right," said Tuck. "After all, if we have to pay dues in order to play, why should we let somebody else play for nothing?"

"Which is better?" asked Duncan. "Let non-members play or cancel a match because we don't have enough to play a game?"

"How many is enough?"

ALICK CARTWRIGHT    How many indeed? This simple question led to a protracted and somewhat heated discussion.

In the past we had played matches with as many as maybe 28 players equally divided, the "extra" players being positioned across the deep garden as necessary.

I felt we needed at least nine per side to make an honest match and said so with as much authority as I could muster. Anything less and we were playing cat games. Eighteen hands minimum. We could play with more, but not fewer.

Duncan averred that we could make a respectable match with as few as seven a side.

DUNCAN CURRY    Alick said anything less than 18 was out of the question, and he said it with such an imperious attitude that I think he did harm to his own cause.

"If we can play with 18, then let us do so, but if we have 14, 15, 16, then let us not cancel the game for the sake of an arbitrary rule," I said.

"Arbitrary, indeed." he said. "We can't keep changing the game. That's exactly what's hurting it now — no set standards. We need a pitcher, a catcher, three basemen, and four in the garden. By my count that's nine to a side. Anything less and we might as well be playing one old cat, or even seven old cat. That's not base ball. That's a child's game."

WILL WHEATON   "Alick, rules can be changed," I said. "I think, for the sake of efficiency, we should start with fewer players. If we have no trouble attracting enough for a match, then by all means, let's change the rules to nine to a side."

TICE HAMILTON   I might have agreed to join the Knickerbockers as I was invited to do so, but when I was informed that they would play matches with as few as 14 players I decided to look elsewhere for my club affiliation. In my opinion, 14 does not make a game of base ball. Play some other game if that's all you have. I know for a fact, too, that some members who joined the Knickerbockers quit the club for this very same reason. It simply takes 18 men to play a proper game. Why the Knickerbockers didn't understand that, I'll never know.

WILL WHEATON   We eventually agreed that members would always have the first right to play, but if there weren't enough club members present we would let non-members play, and that if members showed up after a game began with non-members on either or both sides, we wouldn't necessarily put the non-members off, but members could be chosen in if mutually agreed upon.

ALICK CARTWRIGHT   We set a few other details of the club's operation and then ordered pretzels and a round of Monongahela.

We had a club: The Knickerbocker Base Ball Club. That was the easy part.

WILL WHEATON   Alick acted like he had ants in his pants. He was so eager to get to the base ball rules that I think he would have agreed to anything just so long as that decided the issue. He was like an impatient kid who couldn't wait to tell his father about what he had learned at school. Sometimes he rubbed people raw because of it, but you have to give him his due, he was out front leading the parade even if not everyone appreciated his strut.

Nevertheless, we were on our way towards forming a real club. Never did we see ourselves as a team. It was not the Knickerbocker base ball team, but the Knickerbocker base ball club, and therein lay a significant distinction between us and the teams that came later.

As we worked out the rules by which we would play, we did so with the tacit understanding that they were not to be etched on a granite monument, but could and would be changed as needed, and so they were.

DUNCAN CURRY   The first issue that arose when we got down to the actual rules was the shape of the playing field, and as with almost everything else, we didn't invent anything new but rather chose from those methods of playing with which we were all familiar.

The shape we most often played on was the four-base square or diamond configuration.

We looked to Tuck who we understood had notes about the rules for the game itself.

"I suggest," said Tuck, "that we set the distance from base to base at forty-two paces."

"And home to second?" I asked.

"The same. Forty-two paces. I've set out the field just that way many times and it seems to work out pretty well."

"Is that better than forty or forty-five?" asked Ebenezer.

"Why, because they're round numbers?"

"I suppose so. Anyway, we used to play shorter."

"Look, we've played lots of times at forty-two, let's keep it at that."

"Except your paces and mine are never going to be the same."

Dupignac had a point. Cartwright was over six feet tall, so his stride was different from just about any of ours.

"A reasonable stride. Everybody can adjust to a reasonable stride length."

"You said you want the game to be the same from day to day, so why don't we measure the distances exactly? How far is forty-two paces anyway?"

"Forty-two paces is forty-two paces. We can't expect someone to have a measuring stick in his pocket every time we want to play a game."

So at Tuck's urging, we agreed on forty-two paces and for many years that's exactly how we, and the many other clubs that came to imitate our rules, played. We walked off exactly forty-two of what we considered standard paces or reasonable strides. Of course, there was bound to be a little difference in the distances between the bases from game to game but it wasn't as much as one might think. We got pretty good at keeping the paces reasonably standard. Now and then someone might complain about the placement after a close call, but mostly we accepted the placement as it was.

Another advantage of this rule was that, when children played, their naturally shorter strides meant the bases were closer together and thus better suited for their games.

The standard of ninety feet wasn't settled on until many years later.

WILLIAM TUCKER   Of critical importance was settling once and for all how long a game was to last. More often than not the tendency was to decide a length based on the availability of players for any given amount of time. If, for example, Birney had to leave early to catch a ferry, he'd argue for 15 or even 12 aces. If it was a particularly nice day and we started early enough, some might put forth as many as 50 aces.

"Twenty-five counts or aces," I suggested.

Duncan thought 21 was a more reasonable number, and as I didn't care so much about the exact number just so long as we had one, I went along with his idea as did the others.

BILLY O'BRIEN   If Cartwright and his cronies had any gumption they would have gone for the manly overhand delivery. I blame Cartwright for this as he probably figured he couldn't hit a fast delivery anyway.

ALICK CARTWRIGHT   Since the primary objective of the game was to offer exercise, the underhanded delivery made all the sense in the world. The ball was to be delivered underhanded as in horseshoes.

WILLIAM TUCKER   The next issue we took up was that of determining where a ball could be fairly hit. For years we had played with the ball being in play no matter where it was hit.

BILLY O'BRIEN   The idea of a ball being foul or out of play was another of the Knickerbocker rules I didn't like. In the Massachusetts game not only were tipped balls in play but skilled batsmen honed their skills to do just that. It was a more skillful game but our rule makers decided that any ball hit outside the range of first and third base would be foul.

ALICK CARTWRIGHT   There was quite a bit of discussion when I first suggested we establish foul lines, but I was adamant. Since we had all played without them it seemed as if I was suggesting a big change, but in reality we had played both ways and the foul lines kept the game much more under control and with underhanded pitching it wasn't as hard to hit the ball into what would be fair territory.

"In cricket, you can hit the ball in any direction," said Ebenezer.

"This isn't cricket, dammit," I said.

"And in some form of rounders, too."

"Exactly! This is base ball and it should be different. It should be better."

"How does that make it better?"

"If you have to hit the damn ball fair, it means you have to hit it where scouts are playing. That makes it more difficult to make aces, and that makes it a better, more competitive game."

To this we added the proviso that no ace or base could be made on a foul ball.

WILL WHEATON    The Knickerbocker fair/foul rule was one of our most important contributions. Although it wasn't always played that way often before we drew up our rules, it was what made our game different.

DUNCAN CURRY    I think adopting the no-soaking rule was singularly important in the game becoming so popular.

   The wording as proposed by Tuck was this: "A player running the bases shall be out if the ball is in the hands of an adversary on the base or the runner is touched with it before he makes his base; it being understood, however, that in no instance is the ball to be thrown at him."

   This single rule established the balance and beauty of the game as we have come to know it. I think without this rule, the game would have remained a game for little boys to play with soft balls on cushy lawns.

   If you want to credit the Knickerbockers with anything important, credit us with this. It became as essential to the rise of base ball as yeast is to the baking of bread.

BILLY O'BRIEN    Throwing the damn ball at a runner was half the fun of playing the game in the first place; dodging a ball thrown at you was the other half.

ALICK CARTWRIGHT    From time immemorial, boys playing all manner of ball and bat games played by throwing the ball at the runner. We all learned it that way, we all played it that way, and we all passed it on to our children that way. The art of hitting a moving target separated the good players from the rest. It was inconceivable to think of the game played any other way — until we changed all that.

   The fact that for years the Massachusetts game continued to include soaking was, I believe, the primary reason it died out.

WILLIAM TUCKER    The night we wrote up the rules, we endorsed the "first bound" proviso. This said simply that a struck ball caught either flying or on the first bound was a hand out.

   Everything we decided that night was aimed at making the game as appealing as possible and that in turn meant making it easier to learn and play. The elimination of soaking, the first bound out, the underhand pitching, all were rules that made this so.

   There was no argument whatsoever, or even discussion, when it came to determining that three balls being struck at and missed would be a hand out. Three strikes and you're out was about as universal a rule as there was in base ball and everybody understood and expected the game to be played that way.

   The issue of how many outs it took to end an inning was a whole different matter. That caused a lot of discussion.

   We talked a little about this before I proposed we play three hands out, all out.

"I always liked all out, all out," said Ebenezer.

"Then go play cricket," snapped Alick.

That pretty much ended the discussion. I didn't care for Alick's imperious attitude, but I did think three out, all out, was the best solution. This is one rule we set that has never changed, and as far as I know has never even been considered for change. It offers a nice balance between offense and defense.

"We also need to add a rule that says all players need to take their turns as striker in regular turn," said Alick.

This seemed obvious if we were going to play three outs, all out, but we put it in the rules anyway. How else could we have played it? Let the best batsmen bat over and over? Obviously, and for good reason, that was never considered.

"I think we need to add a rule," I continued, "that covers balls hit out of bounds."

"We've already settled on the fair/foul line, haven't we?" asked Ebenezer.

"Yes, but we need to account for balls that are unplayable. Balls that hit some obstruction or roll down an embankment or something."

"What embankment?

"I'm thinking of any ball that can no longer be played."

"Let the striker hit again. That's what we usually do."

"I know, but it's not really fair, is it? Say a batsman hits a ball deep into the garden where a scout picks it up and then, trying to get the runner at a base, throws the ball by accident off the field of play where it can't be played."

"Like under a lady's dress?"

"That's not exactly what I had in mind."

"But you wouldn't want to play it."

"I might want to, but I wouldn't. So what happens now?"

"We all fall down laughing?"

"That, too, but I suggest we say that the runner is entitled to only one base."

"And maybe a kiss."

"Maybe we should leave that out of the rules."

ALICK CARTWRIGHT   We added a rule that read, "A runner cannot be put out in making one base when a balk is made on the pitcher."

This is not something we played often, but it made sense and everyone agreed.

DUNCAN CURRY   The hour was getting late and we all had jobs to get to in the morning. Now we didn't account for all the exigencies or variables in the game but we had covered the main ones sufficiently well enough that we could use them as a good starting place and then change or add to them later as needed. We were, after all, writing these rules down for men who already knew how to play the game.

"Shouldn't we specify where the scouts should be positioned on the field?" asked Tucker.

"Or exactly where the pitcher has to be?"

"Later maybe, gentlemen. Or maybe we need a rule about how late these meeting are going to last. But if we do, I'll leave it to you because I'm going home and going to bed."

"It's a good start," said Alick. "We can recruit more members on this."

"We're going to have to."

WILL WHEATON    So it was that the Knickerbocker Base Ball Club came into being on that September night in 1845. At the time we had no idea of the impact our actions would have.

ALICK CARTWRIGHT    I think that as long as we're here, we should go ahead and select officers so that we can go about the business of the club

DUNCAN CURRY    I was chosen as president, Will Wheaton as vice president, and Tuck as secretary/treasurer. I suppose Alick was a logical choice to serve as an officer, and I would have been happy had he been, but he probably served the club better by being its chief recruiter and cheerleader, leaving the routine duties of club business to us more reserved members.

Over the years, so many claims were made on our behalf — that we invented the game, that we gave birth to the modern game. The fact is, we gave form to a game we already knew. The rest is a concoction of hyperbole, fact, misunderstandings, and exaggeration. In what proportions, I'm not sure. Nobody is. We didn't invent, we standardized.

# 14

# A Trip Across the River

WALTER AVERY    One of the biggest dilemmas facing us in the rapidly expanding city was the crisis over water. No longer could we safely draw water for cooking and drinking from our city wells. Those of us who could afford it used water brought in by hogshead barrels from outside the city. Those who couldn't had to make do with well water, often "purified" by adding spirits. Outbreaks of yellow fever and cholera, often brought on by drinking from polluted aquifers, killed thousands of residents each year.

As I was an engineer, I had a chance once to see the new High Bridge up at Harlem close up, and what a magnificent structure it was. Inspired by the old Roman aqueducts, this impressive arched stone structure spanned 1,450 feet and rose more than 100 feet above the Harlem River. Built at a cost of more than a million dollars it was part of the Croton aqueduct system that provided New York City with its first truly reliable public drinking water, and thus allowed it to grow.

The inevitable expansion of the city, I suppose, mirrored the Manifest Destiny of our country. And it was our destiny to find a place outside the city for our fields of play.

It seems that our choice to establish our play grounds over in Hoboken was prescient.

FRALEY NIEBUHR    We had agreed to meet down at the Barclay Street Ferry near the foot of Manhattan and there to embark on the short trip across the river to Hoboken, New Jersey. We were all supposed to be there at 2:30, but, as usual, several people were late so we didn't board for almost a half an hour.

Alick was acting like a shepherd ushering his flock to new feeding grounds.

I think there were about 28 of us, certainly enough to play a spirited game or two. Wheaton and Curry were there, along with Tucker, Dupignac, Birney, Avery and others who would become mainstays of the club. A few who had promised to come apparently discovered the inconveniences of working for a living.

"Hoboken? Isn't that in Europe someplace?" said Charles Birney.

"No, New Jersey," said Avery, "but it's almost the same thing."

"Couldn't we find someplace to play in this country?"

"You'll love it," said Alick. "Wait till you see."

"It's not an overnight trip, is it?"

"Not quite."

Quips aside, we all boarded the big wooden boat for the brisk ride. The sense of excitement was palpable.

Hoboken was a peaceful riverside resort for ladies and gentlemen from Manhattan who, to escape the bustle of the crowded city, wandered along River Walk to the Elysian Field. It was built on one of the very few places along the Jersey shore opposite Manhattan where there was sea-level access to the Hudson River and solid land to build on. Here the Palisade Cliffs, which line the West Bank of the Hudson, move inland just far enough to accommodate an area about twelve by sixteen city blocks.

Colonel John Stevens purchased the property in the late 18th century and named it Hoboken, apparently from a combination of Dutch and Indian words. Stevens had been a great inventor. Among his projects was the first successful steamboat driven by turn screws and a horse-driven paddle boat. He also designed the first steam-driven locomotive which you could ride on a nearby circular track.

The Colonel developed Hoboken, as a resort, beginning with the six-mile River Walk path, later adding a mineral water spa, a tavern, hotel, and a hundred-foot-high contraption called the Observation Tower. Nearby was McCarty's tavern and other suitable locations at which tired base ball players could relax after a game.

The Elysian Fields was a large level greensward area surrounded by lovely trees. To say that it was a gorgeous picture would not do it justice. It was much more than that. It was a shady sylvan glade, a haven a world apart from the busy Manhattan streets.

DUNCAN CURRY    Ah, yes, the magnificent Elysian Fields. They always reminded me of Spenser: "I see thee blessed soul, I see, Walk in Elysian Fields so free." In Greek mythology, Elysium meant "place or state of ideal or perfect happiness."

CHARLES BIRNEY    Pretty? Indeed. Far? Too damn far. I told Alick and the others that Brooklyn had places just as appealing, but to no avail. They had their minds set on New Jersey and no appeal to reason would have any effect.

FRALEY NIEBUHR    We spent a lovely afternoon, exploring the winding paths that surrounded the open areas, laying out a playing field, and playing ball.

Alick beamed with self-satisfied delight. He had led his flock to the Promised Land.

I aver that the games we played there that afternoon were as magnificent and unfettered as any games of base ball ever played. No one kept score, no one argued an umpire's call, no one became angry, no one bet on the outcome, no one was induced to play. Everyone enjoyed the simple and beautiful act of playing a game for fun.

We didn't know it at the time, of course, but this idyllic patch of green would, over the years to come, offer us so very many hours of unbridled joy.

As we rode the ferry back to our more practical worlds on the other side of the river, there was talk of contentment and of engaging with the Stevens family for the use of the space two afternoons a week.

"Maybe they won't go along with that," said Tuck.

Cartwright smiled. "If we pay, they'll agree. I guarantee that."

We all left that night satisfied that we had a club and a home.

WILLIAM TUCKER    Despite some complaints about the distance over to the Elysian Fields and the cost of getting there, it was really only a short ferry ride away and the fare was just 13 cents, round-trip.

It probably wasn't a coincidence that the fields and the ferry were both owned by Mr. Stevens, whose encouragement to play on his fields may have had more to do with profit than sportsmanship.

It didn't hurt either that the Elysian Fields had taverns galore nearby, many of which were visited by us at one time or another. We were first and foremost a social club whose activities centered on base ball but always included agreeable camaraderie, good conversation, a sturdy pint, or glass of bubbly, and a well set table.

WILL WHEATON    The view across the river was quite magnificent. The sprawling city of New York positively glistened in the sunlight. The thing that stood out the most was the 260-foot steeple of the new Trinity Church, easily the highest point in the city.

Informal games had been held on these fields before by a group calling itself the Magnolia Base Ball Club, and probably others. Cricket was played there too by the New York Cricket Club, but we were looking to make it a permanent home, a place of our own, the Knickerbocker grounds.

A few years earlier P.T. Barnum had staged a mock buffalo hunt there. Perhaps that helped fertilize the grounds, but as I understand it, some of the animals got away and went after the 30,000-strong crowd.

We assured Mr. Stevens that our base ball players would do no such things—neither fertilize the grounds nor run after the spectators.

ALICK CARTWRIGHT    Upon agreement of our members, we arranged to rent the Elysian Field and dressing rooms for seventy-five dollars a year. We also agreed to rent a room at the Fijux Hotel for our business meetings. Charles Fijux was one of our members and he was willing to donate the use of the room, but Madame Fijux had other ideas and so to keep peace in the family we agreed to a fee of two dollars a meeting. Fair enough.

---

## 15

# *Playing the First Games as the Knickerbocker Base Ball Club*

ALICK CARTWRIGHT    Since our turnout was not what we had hoped for at our first game as a club, we had to play seven men per side. I captained one side, Duncan Curry the other. Tuck was in that game. So too was Birney, Ebenezer, and Fraley among others who ought to go down as true pioneers of the game.

It took a while for everyone to arrive and get organized, so we only managed to get in three innings, but otherwise we adhered to our new rules.

The game left no doubt that the Knickerbocker rules were a success. Exactly how successful we were soon to find out.

Oh, yes, just for the record, Curry's side prevailed 11 8 on the basis of some timely batting by Fraley and Ebenezer.

WILL WHEATON  As was our wont in those early days, the captains usually arranged their batting order so that the best batsmen came to the bat first, then the next best, and so forth through the lineup. Since Alick and Duncan were thought to be the strongest, they were the first batsmen for their respective sides in that first game. Nevertheless, Tuck and Fraley scored the most runs. Base ball was and is a hard game to figure out sometimes.

In that game, Archie Gurlie made the first involuntary contribution to our treasury when I levied a small fine for complaining too much. Everyone but Archie got a big laugh out of that.

ALICK CARTWRIGHT  We played maybe 14 or 15 games that first fall. I know I was demoted to batting in the second position behind Tuck a few times, but sometimes I batted in front of him, too. No matter, though, because it was the playing that was important, and the camaraderie, both of which abounded.

WILLIAM TUCKER  We played using our new rules, and as far as I was concerned, proved that we were onto something worthwhile. Often the scoring was high — 40, sometimes even 50 runs a game. I remember one game in particular we played in the middle of November when it was downright cold. It was my side against Will's. The score ended up at 51–42 in ten innings. Twenty-one aces were all we needed to win a game, but the coldness of the day didn't help the fielding any, and we ended up with a lot of runs being scored each innings and so a lot of ties. Anyway it was a fun, if frigid, day. I know Alick played in that game, so too did Birney, Fraley, Duncan, DeBost, and the O'Brien brothers. Doc had formally joined us by then and also played in that game.

DOC ADAMS  About a month after the organization of this club, several of us medical fellows joined.

Twice a week we went over to the Elysian Fields. Once there we were free from all restraint and, throwing off our coats, played until it was too dark to see any longer. Eventually people began to take an interest in the game, and sometimes we even had spectators.

WILL WHEATON  I'm not sure why exactly, but in those early days of playing the Knickerbocker rules, I ended up umpiring more than I did playing. Perhaps I had the look of an honest fellow or maybe it was because I had such familiarity with the rules. Or it could have simply been that I was a better adjudicator than a player.

My role then was quite different from what we came to accept later. Rather than placing myself behind the catcher on the field of play, I generally stood either along the third base line or sat at a table placed there. I might don top hat and tails, and never did I interfere or impose judgment on a game unless requested to do so by one or both of the team captains as the result of a controversial play. I always did my best to render a fair decision after, of course, first hearing the appeals of the captains. If I was unsure of the correct decision I might appeal to a spectator with a better view.

WILLIAM TUCKER    Those fields were truly Elysian. The playing ground was fringed with fine shady trees, where we could recline during intervals.

Often our families would come over and look on with much enjoyment. There was none of that hurry and worry so characteristic of the present New York. We enjoyed life and didn't wear out so fast.

I think it's fair to say we turned the Elysian Fields into the first true center of base ball activity in the United States.

Count us among the pioneers, the groundbreakers, the trailblazers. All right, maybe we didn't influence something as important as a new medicine to combat a fatal disease, or a new invention to investigate the heavens. Maybe it was only a game, but what a game!

ALICK CARTWRIGHT    I don't know if there was ever a better time in the long history of the game than those first years at the Elysian Fields. We played the game the way I think it should always be played — for the pure joy of the sport.

I can still smell the newly cut green grass, still see the trees that surrounded the field blowing softly in the wind. Of course, memory is selective, but I'm happy to have kept those from a time and place the likes of which we will never see again.

WILL WHEATON    The game as we knew it and as we defined it in the Knickerbocker rules was a game played out between batsmen and fielders. The pitcher's job was to deliver the ball to the batsman in such a way as to initiate the action of the game. It was never the intention for the pitcher to deceive the batsmen, for what would be the purpose of that other than to minimize the action and thus the exercise the game afforded? What would be the value of the pitcher trying to trick the batsman while everyone else stood by and watched? There was no chicanery, fakery, subterfuge, duplicity, evasion, sleight of hand, indirection, or hocus-pocus. That came later.

Ours was a game of honest and true hitting, running, and throwing. It was an attractive and engaging game of guileless pleasure.

DUNCAN CURRY    At the conclusion of our first short season as an organized club, one big nagging question remained. While we remained contented with what we had accomplished, we weren't at all sure it would last.

Would the Knickerbockers, with our membership rules and our demand for an elevated code of conduct, survive as a club or would we just be the group that wrote down some rules that we and others followed and then disappeared? We didn't know.

# 16

# *Other Clubs, Other Games*

WILL WHEATON   Our rules were proving to be so successful that Tuck and I decided we'd challenge the Union Star Cricket Club of Brooklyn to a game of base ball. Well, Cartwright and the others weren't for it. They said they had enough trouble getting members to show up twice a week as it was. So, instead of playing as Knickerbockers, we set out to organize a game as the New York Base Ball Club.

To that end, Tuck and I talked to Hunt of the Union Star Cricket Club of Brooklyn and suggested that they try a game against our "New York Club" using these new rules. It didn't seem as if we'd have problems getting players together for the match — especially if we were playing a Brooklyn side.

"If it's not cricket, it's not a game old boy," Hunt said.

Now I knew for a fact that a number of their lads had played various forms of base ball, and hitting a ball with a bat is after all ... hitting a ball with a bat.

"Well if you mean standing around in the field all day is a game, I guess you're right, but if you're up for the challenge of real action..."

"It's a bit of an easy game though, isn't it?"

"Try us and find out."

"A boy's game, I believe."

"You'd be surprised."

"I certainly would."

Tuck, who was carrying a ball in his hand, tossed it up in the air, caught it backhanded, and said, "If you don't think you're up for it, then..."

"Well I suppose we could lower our standards."

"Shall we say the Elysian Fields then on Thursday next? We could meet early to go over the rules, and then commence the game say at 2:00."

"I'll have a little chat with the lads and see what we can arrange."

"Yes, do."

WILLIAM TUCKER   When they accepted the challenge, apparently Hunt sent the *New York Herald* notice of the impending match, or so he informed us. As an organized cricket side they were used to playing in front of spectators he said, so we should be prepared for a large crowd.

Either the notice arrived too late or the editors fouled up because on the day of the match, nothing appeared in the paper.

Because he was so familiar with the new rules, we agreed Will would serve as an umpire, leaving us one man short, but as it turned out it was all for the best because the Brooklyn lads showed up with only eight anyway, so there was no argument about playing eight a side.

We had Jamie Davis, Vail, and me along with five others. They had Hunt and Gilmore among their players, and both were quite accomplished cricketers.

"Where are the throngs you said would watch?" asked Vail.

"Ask the *Herald*."

Enough family and friends turned out though, to make a respectable showing.

We spent the better part of half an hour going over the rules, Will presiding.

"First to 21 aces, is it then?" said Hunt.

"Assuming each club has completed the same number of innings," Will replied.

"That should take 15 minutes. Then what shall we do for the rest of the afternoon."

"We'll think of something."

The cricketers were used to games that took hours if not days to complete with scores of hundreds of runs for each side. No doubt 21 seemed puny to them.

"And you're saying, three out, all out?" said Hunt.

"Exactly."

The cricketers were used to playing everyone on the team batted each innings.

"Like I said, a boy's game."

"You boys ready then?"

"As we'll ever be."

It was the New York Ball Club against the Brooklyn Ball Club — or so they were calling themselves. The game started slowly but by the fourth innings we had scored 24 aces. The Brooklyn lads took their final innings with little or no hope of winning the contest, but I must say, they played with undiminished spirit and determination. The final score then ended at 24–4. I managed to score only twice myself, but Jamie did five times without making a single hand out.

"Well done," said Hunt. "Well done, indeed."

The Brooklyn players knew how to play in the field all right, but as they were not as familiar with the underhanded style of pitching, their batting was rather weak.

"You will, of course, honor us with a return match at our home," Hunt said. "But of course."

"It seems even a boy's game takes some getting used to."

"You might say."

WILL WHEATON    One thing was very clear. Although we had to stop the game several times to clarify the rules, the rules worked. The Knickerbocker Rules created an entertaining and energetic game.

JAMES WHYTE DAVIS    At the end of the match we all retreated to McCarty's for a splendid dinner.

"Well, now that you've so kindly showed us how to play the game," said Hunt while hoisting a large tankard of McCarty's finest ale, "we'll be sure to return the favor next time."

"We're glad you enjoyed the lesson."

"Indeed. Even a child's game has to be learned."

"As your humble teachers then, we suggest you do your homework before we meet again."

"You can be sure."

WILLIAM TUCKER    Once again the *Herald* got it wrong. The next morning they ran a notice saying that Brooklyn won the match.

Friday, we took the ferry to Brooklyn.

"I read in the *Herald* that you won the match last weekend."

"Well, you can't believe everything you read now, can you?"

"I didn't know that."

"You wouldn't say a gentleman would stoop to such a level would you?"

"Absolutely not."

"*The Herald*, well, what can I say."

"Good luck to you today."

"And to you."

Once again Will was an umpire, and once again we won the match. This time the Brooklyn boys managed 19 aces, but we tallied 37.

After the match, they treated us to a wonderful dinner at Sharp's during which great *bonhomie* was on display from both sides.

"Still learning are you, boys?"

"With such great teachers, how could we not?"

Much of the joy of the moment came from a general feeling that we had gotten it right with the rules, or if not entirely right, at least we were on the right track.

In November our New York Base Ball Club celebrated our second anniversary with a club game at the Elysian Fields. It was an extremely exciting match. Will and I were on the winning side of a 24–23 win.

At the end of the match, as was our wont, we again gathered at McCarty's for an end of the season dinner. As our guests, we had representatives from the Union Star Cricket Club (aka the Brooklyn Base Ball Club) and the Knickerbockers. Will and I, of course, were members of both.

Doc Adams, Fraley Niebuhr, and Alick Cartwright were there beaming with delight. "Our rules" were working.

THOMAS FANCOTT   Me and my brother and a bunch of other men were playing games of base ball all during the time the Knickerbockers were claiming they were inventing the damn game. We played by our own rules, not those of the Knickerbockers, and we didn't organize the way they did, but we played good games. I have to admit though, little by little we began to look to the Knickerbocker rules for our use. In fact Will Wheaton acted as umpire for some of our games, and he recommended the Knickerbocker rules to us.

COLONEL LEE   My cousin (the one from Philadelphia), knowing how interested I was in base ball, sent me a copy of the constitution of their Olympic Ball Club which they had formally drafted in 1837.

They set Club days for practice as the second Thursday of each month. The first thing they did was call the roll and anyone absent or appearing with a soiled uniform was noted. After the selection of captains, they proceeded to agree on the rules they would follow that day and then commence the game. As I understood it, they never formally adopted a set of playing rules. They did, however, agree on a long list of fines.

What amazes me is that with a constitution so specific and detailed, and with so many specified fines for violations of club rules, they didn't bother to specify the rules of the games they were to play. Perhaps they thought they were too well known, or perhaps they enjoyed variety in the games and therefore found no need to codify them. Either way, they were no match for the Knickerbockers when it came to standardizing the game. They may, however, have been more than our equal in making money for the club.

DOC ADAMS   Sure, we had our own internecine squabbles about the rules.

Every winter, among those of us interested in playing the game, the "Knickerbocker Rules" was a hot topic of conversation.

Not everyone, myself included, was completely convinced about the bounder rule.

Some didn't like the loss of soaking.

Some wanted overhand pitching.

Not everyone was convinced that three out, all out, was best.

Not everyone was convinced the rules would last.

The biggest concern, though, was could we attract enough players for the game to survive as we were playing it? The answer was far from certain.

# 17

# *Can They Carry On?*

WILL WHEATON    We had a club, we had members, we had by-laws, we had rules, and we had a place to play. There was no question about this. What we did have a question about, however, was whether we could sustain the club. Would the members continue to show up on game days? Would they maintain their interest in the club over time? Would we still have a club when the next summer came around?

WILLIAM TUCKER    The fact is, for the first few years we seldom played with nine men to a side. We might play with as few as five, or if we had a particularly good turnout, as many as eleven or twelve.

     More than once I went to the field to find only two or three members present. Despite our previous agreement, we were obliged to take our exercise in the form of "old cat." Some of us had to employ all our rhetoric to induce attendance. Sometimes I thought it useless but my love for the game and my happy hours spent on the fields of play led me to persevere.

ALICK CARTWRIGHT    It seemed as if the idea of a permanent club was going to take time to percolate though the thick brains of some members. I was sure, though, that if we could keep the membership engaged for the first year or so, we could grow from that. I kept looking for new members, but I wasn't about to sacrifice our standards.

EZRA KIMBALL    The Knickerbockers needed members but you wouldn't know it from the way they went about their business. They had this rule where they had secret votes on applications for membership, so if one or two members didn't like you for any reason at all, they could keep you out. I mean even if they didn't like where you worked or maybe the way you wore your clothes, or how you talked, or anything like that they could stop you from joining even if you already knew how to play the game and would have made a good player for them.

     I didn't want to join a club that didn't want me anyway so I stayed in Brooklyn and played with fellows who did. The Knickerbockers thought they were big bugs anyway.

DUNCAN CURRY    First of all, to become a member you had either to be above needing to work for a living or you had to be employed in a capacity that allowed you to devote two afternoons a week to base ball. You also had to be able to afford the dues and later to buy uniforms. Then too, when the club's treasury ran desperately low, as it did occasionally, we issued assessments to our members, so a potential member would have to be able to cover those expenses as well.

I know some to whom we denied membership were bitter and that's natural, but that's the way private clubs work.

GEORGE HENDRICKSON   Look, Hoboken was just too damn far to travel for games, no less for practices. I wasn't about to take the seasick-making ferry any more often than I had to, so I gave up the idea of playing for the Knickerbockers and played instead for the New York Club that may not have been as good, but at least we didn't have to go to another damn state a couple of times a week.

DUNCAN CURRY   We were a decidedly conservative and temperate group of gentlemen who enjoyed mixing our games with good conversation, wit, food, and, of course, drink. That our non-playing friends didn't understand this is probably natural.

I had a good friend with whom I shared many a convivial evening, mostly discussing politics, a subject into which he poured considerable opinion.

We were dining together one night in our favorite tavern enjoying a nice pepperpot stew with pan-dowdy and washing it down with apple jack when I asked him if he would like to join us for a game of ball.

"Now why would I possibly want to do something as foolish as that?" he asked with appropriately raised eyebrows.

"Take you pick," I said. "Exercise, fun, fresh air, good companionship."

"My dear old friend, I am afraid you demean yourself by engaging in idle sports like base ball for it is nothing more than childish amusement."

He was, of course, right to call it that, but very wrong in assuming it was without its compensating virtues.

"Not like politics, is that it?" I asked.

"Nothing like."

Many a friend and wife expressed this and similar concerns, and so some who joined us early on left the fraternity of ballists for more "adult" entertainments. I say those who believed that were welcome to their sedentary lives.

# PART THREE: THE FIRST FULL SEASON 1846

## 18

# *An Important Decision*

ALICK CARTWRIGHT We determined that there was no such thing as a perfect time for all the members to meet as work schedules and family commitments varied, but eventually we agreed to meet regularly on Tuesday and Friday afternoons.

So it was on a Friday in '46 — a Good Friday — that we began our first full season. We had been able to attract a few new members, so things were looking up.

For some reason that I can't remember, I agreed to be the umpire. There was still a hint of winter chill hanging in the air which may have had something to do with the sloppy fielding that unfolded. The score ended up 40–35.

On days when a team reached 21 aces quickly, someone usually suggested we play on and if enough people agreed, that's what we did.

I remember one game in particular where we didn't stop until the score reached 71 to 46 — and that was in only five innings. Clearly our batsmen held the upper hand in these early matches. Because of this, I made a suggestion that we require a batsman to swing at any delivery clearly within his reach.

"We can't keep changing the rules all the time, Alick, you said so yourself. That's why we wrote the damn things down in the first place," said Fraley.

"But if the game is so out of balance..."

"The more hitting, the more exercise," said Vail.

"Let's consider it, that's all."

It wasn't an argument I was to win.

DUNCAN CURRY Although he never said so, it seemed to me that Alick, having been left off the Board the previous year, might have been offended by the slight, so at out annual meeting, I suggested we split the position of secretary/treasurer into two. I had already spoken to Tuck about this since he had been serving in that position and he agreed although he made sure it wasn't because I thought he hadn't been doing a good job. I assured him that wasn't the case.

EBENEZER DUPIGNAC   I couldn't see any reason why we shouldn't re-elect
Duncan Curry as president. He was a sober and rational man, particularly good
at calming passions when necessary. In fact, all the officers had done a good
job and I thought continuity was important, so I moved to nominate the same
slate, adding Alick as club secretary.

CHARLES BIRNEY   Frankly, I would have liked to have been on the Board
but I speak my mind and this always works against anyone considering leadership.

ALICK CARTWRIGHT   "I propose," I said, "that we grant Colonel Lee and
Abraham Tucker status as honorary members for life of the Knickerbocker Base
Ball Club."

    Colonel Lee was as genial a gentleman as ever I had known and Abraham
Tucker was a true sportsman. Both were beginning to limit their physical activities.

    We had a good turnout for the meeting — about twenty of our members —
and all agreed to the proposal.

COLONEL LEE "I appreciate the honor, Gentlemen," I said, "but don't think
that means I'm ready to be put out to pasture quite yet."

    I pledged to continue my interest in promoting the game and in promot-
ing the Club. I may not have been the player I once was, but that was hardly
the point.

DOC ADAMS   I made the suggestion that started a rather lengthy contentious
discussion.

    "I would like to propose that we organize a match against another side
and that the president select a nine to represent us."

    As we often proclaimed, we were a club, not a team and some of our mem-
bers wanted to keep it that way. This was an issue that was to come up again
and again.

    My feeling was that a friendly match against outsiders would help bring
our members together in support of our club and would in the long run do
much to help recruit new members.

    "What club?" asked Birney. "Who the hell would we play?"

    "There are certainly enough other players around to get up a decent side."

    "Are we sure we want to do this?" asked Walter Avery. "Why change a
good thing? We're having a fine time playing amongst ourselves. Why not leave
it at that?"

    "Nothing in life stands still, Walt," I said.

    He laughed. "Why not?"

    "Damned if I know."

    "What have we got to lose?" said Duncan.

"The game," said Walt.

"How could we lose?" I argued. "It's our game."

"It changes everything," said Birney. "It's not why we organized, is it? It's not what I pay my dues for and here's what it can lead to: We start playing games outside our club and then pretty soon we'll be trying to find better and better players so that we can win. Where will that leave the members who aren't good enough to represent the club as one of the best players? As second class members, that's where. We shouldn't have different membership classes, that's what I think. We should all be equal, all have the same chance to play in matches. That's why I think most of us are here."

At this point, Alick stood up. "I think it's a grand idea" he said. "I understand your concern, Charles, but in the long run, games against others will create more interest in base ball, and that's good for all of us."

"I don't see how it's good for me," said Birney.

And therein lay the heart of the issue. Some, like Alick, cared about the future of the game he had helped shape; others like Birney saw the club solely as a means to achieve his personal exercise aims.

After a protracted discussion, Duncan, ever the diplomat, said: "Gentlemen, I think there's merit to both positions, so I suggest we try to organize one or two matches against an outside group as a test, and then meet again to consider whether we continue the practice or not. Let's not close ourselves off to possibilities without giving them a chance. We can always change our direction if we think it's best."

As usual, Duncan won the day.

"I move we form a committee to investigate the possibility and practicality of an outside match," said Will Wheaton.

The motion carried, although not unanimously.

"The important thing, though, is that whoever we play needs to abide by our rules," said Alick.

"That's why we wrote them," said Duncan.

"Here, here," said Tuck.

---

# 19

# *The First Match Game*

DUNCAN CURRY    What a surprise awaited us!

Franklin Ransom, who was a member but who wasn't at the annual meeting, approached me at the intermission of Christy's "Ethiopian Minstrels" show that we were both attending at Palmo's Opera House.

"I hear the club wants to get up a match with another side."

"Well, we do under certain conditions."

"Such as?"

"They agree to play by our rules."

"I think I could get some of the boys together who would agree to that."

We met again a week later at the Tontine Coffee House down at the foot of Wall Street.

"How did you come out, I asked?"

"It depends on when the game is scheduled for, of course," he said. "I can get a few of the boys if the day is right."

"But not nine?"

"We might have to play with Knicks on both sides."

We discussed a few possibilities and then settled on Friday, June 19th.

DOC ADAMS    Ebenezer Dupignac I know particularly wanted to participate but he couldn't manage to get the afternoon off. Neither could Will Wheaton or Duncan Curry who was in Philadelphia on business. Nevertheless, we had enough to make up a good side. We had me, Tuck, Birney, Avery, both Anthonys, Tryon, Paulding, Turney, Davis, and Ransom.

The side we agreed to play called themselves the New York Base Ball Club, but as expected they didn't show up with enough players.

DOCTOR RANSOM    I agreed to play on the New York Ball Club side made up of several players like Al Winslow who joined our club later.

CHARLES BIRNEY    I have to admit, the ferry ride over to the Elysian Fields was accompanied by a smidgen of apprehension. Now normally I looked forward to the trip and the pleasures to follow but this was a little different. We would be playing against some men I didn't know and in front of some spectators I didn't know either. I wasn't sure I liked the change but I agreed to play and play I would.

WALTER AVERY    It was one of those perfect June afternoons— warm but not hot, sunny but not so glaring that you couldn't see a ball in the sky.

"Suppose they know we're the Knickerbockers?" Birney said jokingly.

"If they don't now, they will soon," said Tuck.

DOC ADAMS    When I got to the field, I saw the canopy from which the ladies could watch the game safely shielded from the sun. This was going to be a different game, that was for sure. Just how different we were about to find out.

DUNCAN CURRY    Of course, Alick would like to have played, but given his knowledge of the rules, I asked him to serve as umpire. He reluctantly agreed.

ALICK CARTWRIGHT   When everyone got there, we spent some minutes going over the rules. The last thing we wanted was an argument during the game.

MICHAEL LALOR   We agreed to play by the Knickerbocker rules but some of us didn't like the one that said you couldn't throw the ball at a runner. Hell, that was half the fun of the game.

DAVID COPELAND   I'll tell you this; I lost interest in the game when they took out throwing at the runners. Those of us who liked the old game were churned up by the new rule and never got used to it. I missed the excitement of the old days when runners dodged and ducked to get out of the way of a thrown ball.

When just about everybody started playing the new rules, I gave up the game for good.

ASHLEY HYDE   Despite some complaints, there is no doubt in my mind that the Knickerbocker rule eliminating soaking was the most important of their rules for the advancement of the game. It was, in base ball terms, a stroke of genius.

ALICK CARTWRIGHT   When it came time to start the game, the New York Club was still short one player. Naturally enough, someone shouted out, "Don't worry, Too Late will be here in five minutes."

There wasn't a person on the field who didn't laugh when, as predicted, a few minutes later over the rise came Too Late himself, bat in hand, ready as always to play.

Davis had a big smile on his face. "Haven't started without me, have you?" he said.

"Wouldn't matter if we did," I said. "You'd figure out a way to wheedle your way in anyway."

"As long as I'm playing."

Jamie wasn't yet a member of the Knickerbockers, but he was an avid player. I figured it was just a matter of time.

DOC ADAMS   The coin flip sent us up to bat first.

Turney took his place and patiently waited through four Winslow deliveries before he swung hard and hit a ball wide of the first base. Once upon a time it would have gone for a hit, but now it was only a foul ball. He hit two more foul balls bringing looks of dismay from both players and onlookers. Perhaps some thought this kind of rule would add up to long and boring games where everyone stood around and waited while foul balls flew. Nevertheless, on his next swing, he managed to hit the ball fair. Unfortunately, it looped straight into the hands of Case who, being a proficient cricketer, was very adept at holding onto weak drives such as this.

So the Knickerbockers began life as a competitive club with a limpid out. There was nothing to worry about, I thought, as I picked up my bat.

I put my hand out waist high, indicating to Case just where I wanted the ball delivered. Case was extremely accurate with his first pitch to me, but for some reason, I let it go by. This brought a look from Case as if to say, "What are you waiting for, the Second Coming?"

With a gesture of exasperation, Case delivered what I finally thought to be an acceptable delivery and I swung hard, hitting it over the second base for what I was certain would mean a safe trip to the first base. I don't know who was more surprised, me or Case, when Trenchard came racing in and with his left hand, grabbed the ball on the first bound just as it was to land a second time. Two hands out.

Tuck followed with a weak ball to Doc Ransom playing by the first base. The good Doc, who might in other times have simply thrown the ball at the running Tucker, had to scoop up the ball and outrace the runner to the base. They both appeared to arrive at the same instant, so everyone looked over to Cartwright who now had his first opportunity to make a decision.

"I got him. Didn't I, Alick?"

It took Alick a moment to say anything. Finally, he said, "The runner is out. The New York Club will now come in."

I thought Tuck was safe, but Cartwright, probably wanting to demonstrate his impartiality, sided against his own club.

"Too Late" batted first for them and promptly took the first delivery he saw and smacked it into the left garden. It rolled far enough that he was standing safely on the second base before Birney could pick it up and return it.

Al Winslow followed on the very next pitch with a similar hit and the first ace was recorded. Winslow, Ransom, Murphy the hotel-keeper, and Case also scored before we finally managed to get three hands out.

So we were down by five aces before we took our turns hitting again. This was dispiriting, to say the least. We had naturally assumed that by playing "our game," we would have a great advantage over the put-together side. We knew we didn't have some of our best players, such as DeBost and the O'Brien brothers, and Cartwright was the umpire, but we really hadn't thought they would be necessary.

"We've plenty of opportunities to win the game, don't you worry," said Birney just before he was put out on a bounder to the right garden.

James Whyte Davis    It's a funny thing, competition. It can get under your skin no matter how much you try to keep it at bay. Here we were playing a game amongst friends. The results didn't matter in any meaningful way, yet passions were unusually high. Was this a good thing? I'm not sure, but I know it infected me too.

ALICK CARTWRIGHT    It was during the Knickerbockers' second round of batting that Too Late Davis, aka The Fiend, showed why he earned that moniker. Instead of waiting for a bounder on a ball hit by Walt Avery, he came running in and attempted to grab it with his reaching hand just as it was about to land. Did he catch it, or not? That was difficult to answer as it all happened so quickly. Avery, not the swiftest of runners even in his younger days, made it to the first base looking as if he intended to stay there for awhile.

Davis, as he stopped his forward momentum, held the ball high for all to see, including presumably me as umpire. As I couldn't really tell what had happened, I said nothing.

"I caught the ball," cried Davis. "The batsman is out. Mr. Avery is a hand out."

Avery didn't budge, but said, "I saw the ball hit the ground."

"You didn't see any such thing. I caught it."

Avery turned to me, "Mr. Cartwright?"

Since I wasn't sure, I looked behind me to see if any help might be forthcoming from a spectator in a better place to see the play than I. A gentleman with whom I was not familiar was standing near the first base, nattily attired, I might add, in top hat and tails.

"Mr. Cartwright, I believe the ball touched ground," he said with his booming bass voice.

Hearing no opinions to the contrary, I said, "The runner is safely on the first base."

Well, you would have thought I had just insulted his parentage, the way The Fiend came toward me.

"Goddamn it, Alick, can't you make up your own mind!"

There it was, out in the open for all to hear. Given our rules, I had no choice but to issue a fine for swearing.

Suppressed grins all around accompanied my announcement — including one from Mr. Davis, himself.

Just for the record, let it be known that I myself had been fined earlier in the year during one of our club games when I was caught wandering away from the field with Billy O'Brien. The fine was for delaying the game. I plead guilty.

JAMES WHYTE DAVIS    I was wrong, of course, and Alick right — about the fine I mean, not the play. With my dying breath I will assert I made that catch.

Swearing on the field is wrong, particularly since ladies were present, but dammit, the passion of the moment just got the better of me. I apologized to our umpire immediately.

"The fine will be six cents Mr. Davis," said Cartwright.

"All right," I said.

"Payable now."

"Now?"

"It's in our by-laws."

"Surely you can wait until our next meeting?"

"I'm afraid not."

"But I'm not playing for your club."

"Nevertheless, we all agreed to abide by Knickerbocker rules."

And so I dug into my pocket and came up with the required mulct, accompanied by the good-natured applause of our members.

Arguing with an umpire's decision would also bring a fine, so I suppose I got off lucky, albeit a few cents poorer.

DOC ADAMS    When the game continued I think we all anticipated a change in fortunes for our side. However, it was not to be. Avery made it as far as the third base but we left him standing there while we went three hands out.

By the time the New York Club went three out in their next turn at bat, they had added another seven aces to their tally.

Our turn at bat came and went without much better luck although Birney did manage to score an ace for us when Avery sent a ball deep into the right garden where no one could catch up to it until he had made it to the third base. Not being content with that, however, he tried to make it home, but Austen Thompson made a deft throw from the garden and he was tagged (not soaked) by Lalor for the final out.

To put it mildly, it was not going well for the Knickerbockers. The New York side may have lacked the experience we had, but several of their players were Knickerbockers, and several others were highly skilled cricketers.

By the time the score reached 17 aces to one at the end of their third turn batting, the inevitable outcome was clear. The club that made the rules would lose by those rules.

"Hey, Jamie," I said to Davis as we were coming in for what would be our last turn at the bat, "take it easy on us old boys, won't you?"

He laughed. "We are."

"You've already scored three runs yourself. That's more than our whole side. Don't be such a hog."

"Well, that's up to you."

To add insult to injury, I came to bat with two hands already down, but with Turney and Paulding on the bases. It was an opportunity to get back a little of our pride.

I watched several deliveries go by without swinging.

"Maybe sometime today, Doc?" called Davis.

I watched several more.

"Grass grows faster than you hit," he said.

Now the onus was on me.

"Winter's coming."

I finally picked out a delivery, swung with what I deemed was enough control to smack the ball between the scouts on the left side. Instead the ball went straight to Davis who easily caught it in the air. Game over.

"The final score," announced Alick, "stands at 23 aces for the New York Club, one ace for the Knickerbockers."

DOCTOR RANSOM   The moment the game was over the conviviality of friends immediately showed itself. There was much back-slapping, laughing, and good will. The result of the game was of no matter. What mattered is that we had a good time, engaged in healthy exercise, and passed an engaging hour or two with friends.

I do point out, however, for the record, that I scored three aces.

DOC ADAMS   As was our custom, the losing side paid for a gala post-game dinner. McCarty's was filled with the laughter and *bonhomie* of all the players (except Ransom who had to go home early to see to an ailing mother).

Al Winslow offered the first toast. "Here's to the Knickerbockers, our gracious hosts. May they have many opportunities to be so again."

Many toasts followed, until still flush with drink, food, and good humor, we all made our way back to the ferry.

JAMES WHYTE DAVIS   Despite the outcome, the game was a success. That being said, it should be noted that we were not to play a match against another club for five years. During that time, however, amazing things happened to the game of base ball.

---

## 20

# *Returning to Club Games*

DUNCAN CURRY   Since games against others meant most of our members couldn't engage in any given contest, with nary a whimper of dissent we returned to our schedule of playing games amongst ourselves.

ALICK CARTWRIGHT   I wasn't sure we should eliminate all games against others. I understood the argument, but the reality is, at times we struggled to attract enough members to allow us to mount a reasonable contest.

I offered this argument at several meetings but was always voted down.

CHARLES DEBOST   One afternoon we ended up with just enough for two good sides of eight each, but no one to serve as umpire unless we wanted to play eight against seven.

"That's all right with me," said Charles Birney, "as long as we're the eight."

"That's all right," I said, "as long as Birney's the umpire."

"We could play without one," Dupignac said.

"Then who'd stop you from cheating?"

"My well-known sense of honor."

"I'll repeat. Then who'd stop you from cheating?"

"I don't give a damn."

"Or swearing."

"I have an idea," said Mumford.

"No, we can't buy an umpire, Mumf," I said.

"A better idea."

He looked out beyond the right garden, where several spectators had spread blankets on the grass and were enjoying a light repast.

"Mrs. Doolittle," he said.

"Surely you jest," said Dupignac.

"Why not? She's watched enough games to understand the rules, and she'd be a lot better to look at than Birney."

"I won't argue that point," said Birney.

Mrs. Doolittle, a married woman of some standing, was known to watch games from time to time. If truth be told, it was widely understood that she was not there so much to watch the game but to watch a particular player. Since a gentleman does not talk of these things in public, I shall reluctantly refrain from identifying the player.

"Yes, but what if Ebenezer says 'damn' again. Or worse?" asked Colonel Lee. "We can't stoop to swearing in front of the ladies. Not even Davis would do that."

"I'll be a son-of-a-bitch if I won't," Davis said.

"We'll have to be on our best behavior," Mumford said.

"What's the fun in that?" said Billy O'Brien.

"Shall I ask her, then?" said Mumford.

"Might as well," I said. "Davis will be left speechless for a change."

While Mumf ran over to where Mrs. Doolittle was seated, we began, rather childishly I must admit, to cataloguing words we couldn't or wouldn't say.

"'Fuck' is definitely out," said Billy. "And 'shit.'"

"So is 'pussy,'" said his brother.

"What about 'tarnation'?" asked Davis.

"Or 'lick-spittle,'" added Dupignac.

What followed was a virtual catalogue of contemporary swear words— "crap, devil, whoremonger, breast."

"Can we say, 'bosom'?" asked Tuck.

"Only if you're talking about a chicken," I said.

Someone added "fart" and "French pox" before Mumford and Mrs. Doolittle began walking toward us. By the time they got within earshot, we were all laughing like little children.

Mrs. Doolittle smiled graciously and said, "Good afternoon, Gentlemen."

By that time we were anything but. Nevertheless, we all greeted her politely.

We did play eight against eight, and she did act as umpire. Davis' team won 21–13, but what characterized that game like none other is that every time a close play occurred, you could see those involved mouthing swear words without any sound coming out. It was one of the funniest games we ever played, and if you count all the unvoiced swear words, it was probably the most profane game ever played. Astor would have had trouble coming up with enough money to cover the fines had they been assessed.

WALT AVERY    Although I was never as good at it as Charlie DeBost, I occasionally played as a behind. What a job that was! I never liked it. Because we wore no protection in those days. Not even gloves. We stood well back from the hitter and caught the ball on the bound. That was okay until a foul ball came screaming back at your head. I was mighty glad when DeBost joined us.

He actually enjoyed it back there and it wasn't long before he was considered our best player.

CHARLES BIRNEY    I remember once when Billy O'Brien took a pitch from Doc Adams and swung so hard the ball sailed high into the cloudless sky. It didn't come down until it had gone over the embankment leading down to the river. The result: one smiling batsman, one lost ball, and lots of angry players. We usually came with only one ball and if it was lost, so was the game.

We spent some minutes looking for the ball before realizing it now belonged to Davey Jones. We could, and often did, play balls off trees. That was an expected part of the game. But out of the water? O'Brien's show-off stunt may have impressed some, but it was uncalled for, although not untypical of the O'Briens, who thought they were better players than the rest of us. They were, but that was hardly the point. We were out for an afternoon of exercise and good fun. So because of O'Brien's stunt that day we had neither.

JAMES WHYTE DAVIS    An inadvertent result of one particular rule adopted by our club helped ultimately to change the game in ways we had neither seen nor advocated. By drawing foul lines out from the home base, we had created an area close to the action where spectators could gather to watch without interfering with the action. We didn't have a lot of spectators to be sure, but wives, family members, and friends sometimes took advantage of the opportunity to enjoy the beautiful scenery and lovely perch of our field.

The idea of creating an area for spectators was never the intention, but eventually it led to base ball becoming a great spectator sport, and with it the opportunity to turn the amateur sport into a professional one. Had we anticipated this, maybe we would have re-thought the rule.

# PART FOUR: STRUGGLE FOR SURVIVAL 1847–1849

## 21

# *The Winters Between*

ALICK CARTWRIGHT  The winter months are, and I assume always will be, difficult for the true ballist. Some of us got together anyway for an occasional dinner or outing.

I remember one late winter Saturday when the weather hinted at the spring blooms soon to come, Doc Adams, Avery, Davis, Birney, and I took a side-wheeler steamer from Manhattan to a small pier jutting out into Gravesend Bay on the western point of the Coney Island beach. Two enterprising business-men I knew, Eddy and Hart, had just built a pavilion there with the idea of developing the area for day tourists.

We had the foresight to bring a bat and ball with us and had a brisk prac-tice on the sand. We giggled like little kids as we toppled on the soft surface, chased the ball trying to keep it out of the surf (we failed), and teased each other mercilessly.

"Walter, you're even slower on sand than you are on grass."

"Even you can't hit the ball into the trees here as you usually do."

We played for maybe an hour before Birney sprained his ankle slightly trying to turn quickly in the soft sand. He wasn't hurt badly, but he limped off the beach as if nothing short of amputation would help him. By the time he got to the pavilion he acted as if he had just come back from Lourdes.

"Anyone want to go see Tom Thumb with me tonight?" he said. "He and Barnum are back from Europe."

He was answered with a rousing chorus of "no."

Eliza would sometimes chide me for the amount of time I spent with my club friends, but I think she understood the necessity for a man to share his interests with other men — just so long as I didn't neglect her. Once when we played three days in a row she said that was too much. For the sake of peace in the family, I said I'd limit my playing to two days a week.

DUNCAN CURRY  One Christmas day Will Wheaton, Alick, and I took our wives to see *The Count of Monte Cristo*, a play that we were led to believe was based on a real story. It was during the intermission that talk first turned to the fire that only days before had destroyed the magnificent Park Theatre (we were at heart still volunteer fire fighters and talk of fires always engaged us), and then to the report that John Jacob Astor, who had died early that year, left $350,000 to found a public library. After several facetious comments about how he should have left the money to a struggling base ball club so that it could build a magnificent club house on Park Avenue complete with statues of its founders, Alick made the first mention that I can remember from him about being as rich as Astor and about how he had read that gold had been discovered in California.

Little did I realize how serious he was and how much of an impact that would have on the Knickerbocker Base Ball Club.

CHARLES BIRNEY    Although base ball was our chief form of diversion, it certainly wasn't the only game we played. We were known to retire to a local tavern to play billiards with, of course, a few bets being wagered along the way. Occasionally we played Nine Pins. Chess, checkers, and chuck-a-luck were not unknown to us, nor were any variety of card games such as monte, faro, and draw poker.

DOCTOR RANSOM    One night, Doc Adams and I took a number of the boys to an extraordinary exhibition.

As physicians, Adams and I had both watched and participated in horrific surgeries. In the early days of our practices, there was no such thing as anesthesia other than perhaps opium or a stout shot of whiskey. Sometimes patients sang hymns, bit a bullet, or got stinking drunk to distract themselves from the dreadful but inevitable pain of surgery. The agony could be so intense that sometimes surgeons worked too fast and mistakes were made.

Then dentists determined that nitrous oxide was effective. It was also determined that it was a great entertainment.

So on this night Adams, Cartwright, Tuck, Avery, Birney, and I went off to "A demonstration of the effects produced by inhaling Exhilarating Nitrous Oxide, or Laughing Gas." According to the handbill, "The gas will be administered only to gentlemen of the first respectability. The object is to make the entertainment in every respect a genteel affair. Eight strong men are engaged to occupy the front seats to protect those under the influence of the gas from injuring themselves or others."

We decided that since we all considered ourselves "gentlemen of the first respectability," we would put forth one of us as a volunteer.

"So who is the most adventurous?" asked Adams.

With nary a pause, we all looked at Alick.

"That settles it then," said Tuck.

Alick put up no protest. Being the center of attention came naturally to him.

Well, when he and the other volunteers sniffed the gas, they stood upon the stage laughing and acting silly. I don't know who had more fun, Alick acting stupid, or us laughing so hard at him that we could barely remain in our seats.

A few of the sniffers fell hard to the floor, but Alick fought to maintain what little composure he had left. Two got sick to their stomach, but of course, not Alick.

When the effect of the drug came to its abrupt end, they all stood around in total confusion.

It was one of the most enjoyable times we spent together off the field of play.

WILLIAM TUCKER   To show you how avid we could be, on a few occasions neither rain, nor sleet, nor snow could stop us from a good game. When it got cold enough to freeze over some of the ponds, we actually played ball on the Washington Pond ice over in Brooklyn.

Me and Dupignac were good enough skaters to play a pretty decent game. DeBost, too, joined us a few times.

The game was played pretty much like regular base ball except, of course, the impossibility of obtaining a good footing made for a few good laughs. In running the bases on ice skates, all you had to do was cross the line of the base, since it was near impossible to stop on it. You couldn't be put out until you returned to the base and then left again.

Some years later on a cold and blustery day in February some of us went over to Litchfield's Pond in South Brooklyn to watch two clubs play on ice. What was so interesting is that not only were we foolish enough to want to see the contest, but so were about 12,000 other people.

"At least they're playing by the Slickerbocker rules," DeBost said with a none too straight face.

As ridiculous as it sounds, the game actually became popular with some who apparently could find little else to keep them entertained in the dark days of winter.

WILLIAM VAIL   This was another bad year for fires in the city. One in particular will forever stay in my mind — a huge fire in a saltpeter warehouse just north of Bowling Green. I watched the building collapse with firemen standing on the roof riding it to the ground.

Another fire that year swept through downtown destroying three hundred buildings and taking thirty lives with it.

In July when a fire took the Union Bank where Alick Cartwright had been working, he went into the book-selling business with his brother. Now he had even more time for base ball.

WALTER AVERY    I remember Charles Birney was going on about a new movement pushing for changing the name of the United States to the Republic of
Allegania.

"What's more inappropriate than 'United States'? I mean what do we call
ourselves, 'United Statesers'? How clumsy can you get? It rhymes only with
'late, sir' and 'fate, sir.' Besides, there are five other United Stateses in the hemi-
sphere. So the New-York Historical Society, to which I belong, has looked for
a name in our mountains, or our lakes, or our rivers, or someplace like that.
The Rockies, they thought too far away; the northern lakes too linked with
Canada; the great Mississippi and its tributaries have already given names to
six states. Ah, but the Alleghany Mountains are the grandest natural feature of
the country, one that is common to north and south, the backbone of the original thirteen states. So they've take the cue from Washington Irving and come
up with 'Allegania' to be pronounced 'Algania' for poetical reasons."

"Poetical reasons?" I said. "What the hell is it supposed to rhyme with,
'mania'?"

"Maybe 'Mauritania,'" said Alick."

"Or that's vain o' ya," added Duncan.

"At least you could keep the USA monogram," said Wheaton.

"Cynics!" said Birney.

I bring this story up only because it's typical of the after-game banter into
which we all entered. We were first and foremost a social club. I'm not sure the
after-game get-togethers weren't more important to us than the games themselves.

"Sneer all you want," said Birney, "but the name brings up images of colo-
nial adventure and revolutionary heroism; its Indian derivation gives it a native
quality and it's a hell of a lot better than the corruption of the idiot Italian
explorer Vespucci's forename."

"I think we should just call it 'Yankee Doodle,' and be done with it,"
DeBost said, hoisting his tankard.

And so it went until our next game and dinner.


JAMES WHYTE DAVIS    In December of '47, I married Maria Harwood, a
young lady I had been seeing for a while. A few years older than I, she came
from a good family in Maryland. We planned to raise a family and settle into
a comfortable life in the growing metropolis. Maria particularly liked the city
and all that it had to offer in terms of fashion and culture and, to top it off,
didn't seem to mind my afternoon excursions to play ball. She knew nothing
of the game, but vowed to learn.

Although I was playing some ball, I hadn't yet officially joined the Knickerbockers. The fruit brokerage business was taking up much of my time while
not yet providing the income I needed to support a family. Nevertheless, it

was clear to everyone that the Knicks were the guardians at the gates of the base ball firmament. I knew that one day soon I would be in a position to join them.

# 22

# *Struggles for Survival*

DOC ADAMS    Colonel Lee came up to me one particularly demoralizing afternoon when only a few members showed up to play.

"Doc," he said, "I think it's time we had a little chat about this club of yours."

"'Ours,' you mean. Our club."

We spent a couple of hours at McCarty's with his "little chat."

"I'm not sure we shouldn't give up the idea," Colonel Lee said. "Call it a well-intentioned experiment that just didn't work out the way we hoped."

"What are you talking about?"

"Too many times I've made the trip across the river to find four, five, six members here ready to play."

"It's not easy for everyone to make it twice a week, what with family and jobs."

"Then they shouldn't have become members."

"Maybe we should increase the membership size."

"Or play other sides."

"Do you know how many men are out there playing by our rules?"

"That's just it. We wrote the rules. Maybe we should leave it at that."

"I'm not ready to give up."

"I think we should bring it up at our next meeting. Put on the floor the idea of disbanding unless more members show up more often. Maybe that will drive the point across that we're not a club unless the membership takes more responsibility for maintaining our... I suppose we could put in a by-law or something that says a member has to show up at a certain percentage of play days or they're automatically dropped from membership, or put under review, or something like that."

This and several discussions like it came up more often than any of us would have liked. The idea of disbanding the club hung over our heads like the Sword of Damocles. More than once, it looked as if we would have to take that drastic step.

JOHN CLANCY    I got almighty tired of Doc and his cronies complaining that I didn't show up for enough play days, not to mention club meetings. Well, for one I ran a stationery business, and for two I had a demanding wife, and for three, I had a trick knee that sometimes acted up. I paid my dues on time, played when I could, turned out for scores of meetings—some of which were a complete waste of time—and always behaved as a gentleman. Well, almost always.

DUNCAN CURRY    Business pressures were mounting on me, and although I maintained my interest in the Club and in the game, it was time for me to step down as president and leave the duties to someone with similar interests but with more free time.

Doc Adams, one of our staunchest members, readily accepted the nomination.

---

## 23

# *On Operating a Gentlemen's Club*

DOC ADAMS    I had been serving for a year as vice president so the business of the club wasn't new to me.

I didn't necessarily want the position, but at Duncan's urging I accepted. As a matter of course, it should have gone to our vice president, Will Wheaton, but he also was no longer available. Cartwright was elected vice president; Drummond, secretary; and Birney, treasurer.

We were now an established organization with a stable membership ... well, reasonably stable, anyway. As with any volunteer organization, there was always some membership turnover, but we had a strong base of active and eager members.

ALICK CARTWRIGHT    When Doc became president, I moved up to vice president. Doc ran a tight ship and not everybody always appreciated that, but Doc did what it took to see that things ran smoothly.

Among our duties as officers was to choose the players and team captains for each game. Needless to say, this could at times provoke antagonisms.

Some days we didn't have enough players, some days we had too many. Some naturally were better than others, but in the interest of fairness, we tried to reward those who came to most of the practices and showed up at the meetings.

Birney complained a few times about being left out of sides, but what could we do? You can't always keep everyone happy.

Of course, Doc wasn't married at the time, so that automatically gave him more time than those of us who were. It seemed it was up to the medical men, book sellers, bank clerks, and lawyers to run the club.

CHARLES BIRNEY    I suppose in every organization there are those few who do the lion's share of the work and the rest of us who go along with the will of the group for whatever value we get from belonging to it. Well, Doc was one of those who was willing and to do his share and a lot more. He liked to be out front waving the flag just so long as everyone noticed and saluted as he went by.

I'll have to say, he did put in a lot of time on Knickerbocker club business. I'm not sure how busy he was in his practice, but judging by his club work, I'd have to guess, not very.

ABRAHAM TUCKER    Give Doc his due. He always wanted to be the one in charge, but he "bought" that right by working harder for the club than anyone else. I wouldn't have been surprised had I seen him sweeping the floor before meetings and pouring the beer during it. And he did buy boxes of segars— mostly the expensive Cuban ones.

ALICK CARTWRIGHT    We were, like the other clubs of the city, an organization in which the members of the club had complete say over who could or could not be a member and who could or could not continue as a member.

Once when we were playing a game amongst ourselves one of our members—whom I shall refer to only as Mr. Q because his family is still an important name in the world of New York entrepreneurship—became extremely agitated when, going into the second base, Billy O'Brien applied the ball to him with more force than Q thought necessary.

Q spun like a dervish and started for O'Brien, calling him names associated with the lower class of Irish immigrants. Now Billy had heard these before and usually just turned his back. Besides, he was anything but lower class. Billy started moving away toward the long field, but Q followed him spewing the invectives. Billy immediately grabbed hold of Q and an unsightly wrestling match ensued, broken up only by the efforts of Duncan and Tuck.

Naturally at the next regular meeting, the issue came before the members and stirred a very lively debate.

"He nearly put my eye out," claimed Q.

"I was trying to put a runner out, that's all," responded Billy. "There was nothing personal in it."

Q's actions were clearly unacceptable. You might get away with an invective or two under your breath, but shouted curses about one's ancestry was something else again.

Some members argued for a fine for Q and nothing more. Others like Doc argued for expulsion in that he provoked the ensuing fight. In the final vote, Doc's position won, and Q was dropped from club membership. Later he played for the Eagles and this provoked an awkward situation when we played them although it never came to anything.

In the end, though, despite some calls for expulsion from our more zealous defenders of the sportsmanship code, O'Brien was simply fined and invited to continue his membership.

If truth be told, the monies collected for these fines were important for the operation of the club, so while no one wanted to encourage actions like profanity, I don't know what we would have done without it.

WALTER AVERY    Sometimes when the competitive instincts got the upper hand on sportsmanship, things got a little out of hand, but when they did, cooler heads always prevailed. Always.

DAVID AYERS    The Knickerbockers sometimes acted as if they were God's greatest gift to the world of sport and the only real club around. I can't be certain about the first claim, but about the second all I can say is "bunk." I belonged to a group we called simply the Brooklyn Base Ball Club. We didn't at that time have a constitution or by-laws but we met occasionally at the Star Cricket Club on Myrtle Avenue.

Shortly after the Knickerbockers wrote down their playing rules, we got a copy and played two games that fall against the New York Base Ball Club, another group who met sometimes in Manhattan. Mostly we played by the Knickerbocker rules. In fact, several of the New York Ball Club's players, including Tucker and Vail, were Knickerbockers. This was not unusual as players often played outside their own club.

---

# 24

# *Games Amongst Members*

MARIA DAVIS    Let me see if I have this straight. In base ball one fellow tries to knock another down with the ball, but he strikes it with a big club (similar to an Indian war club); if he hits it, he has to run around the square, but he has three places called bases to stop for breath. Then there are fellows outside the square who get the ball, and in the old days they too tried to hit him (in such cases, he had to drop but was sure to fall on a cushioned bag placed there for his accommodation). If he gets through all right and of course out of breath, he gets a little black stroke on a piece of white paper for it which anyone would consider a sufficient recompense. In this manner all have a chance of getting these little strokes until one side gets 21 of them, then they all go out and drink.

JAMES WHYTE DAVIS   I remember once some scamp ran off with our ball. Well, I tell you, you never saw someone run as fast as O'Brien did on that day. He chased the little scallywag across the field into God knows where. Anyway, he returned with the ball and a grin. What happened to the offender we never knew. The only thing Billy ever said was, "He wants you to know he's pleased to give the ball back."

The ball was a bit misshapen. How it got that way, nobody asked. Doc managed to squeeze it back into a reasonable semblance of its intended shape.

We never had what you would call "regular" positions. That is, I wasn't considered a first base man or a right fielder, or a behind, because we all moved around the field, often from one turn in the field to the next. Our captains had the right to ask us to play a certain position, but they seldom did, rather letting us run out to any position we chose. Some players had preferences, such as DeBost at behind because he was so good there, but sometimes he played in the field, too.

Had the emphasis been solely on winning, I suspect we would always have positioned players where they played best, but at what cost? I suggest by playing all over the field we got better and more varied exercise. It was also more fun.

WILL WHEATON   We played the last game of our first season as a club on a cold and dank November day with clouds hanging low.

We had enough members for two full sides so we all warmed up by Doc Adams throwing the ball up in front of him, striking it before it touched the ground, and hitting it out to the rest of us. This was our typical pre-game practice, and given the chill in the air, we needed all the warming we could get.

Playing with the Knickerbocker rules meant we would play to 21 aces—usually something like three or four innings, but this one was quite an exception. Probably the cold weather had a lot to do with it.

Thanks to cold hands and stiff joints, the score stood at 21 aces each after three innings. An apple brandy and a warm fire at McCarty's seemed imminent.

Then an amazing thing happened. Inning after frosty inning we matched each other ace for ace. By the ninth inning we had scored 42 aces each and a wet snow began to fall.

"What do you say we call it a draw for now, go get warm, and resume it next spring," said a shivering Duncan Curry.

"Let's finish what we started," said Billy O'Brien.

Duncan looked at him as if he was a lunatic and I'm not sure he wasn't right. "Sure, in April," he said.

"Why is that, don't you think you can win now?"

"Will, it's too cold to think."

We took a straw vote and by a narrow margin decided to play on and see what happened. I don't think everyone wanted to continue playing so much as they didn't want to be seen to be giving up. We were always saying winning didn't matter but that wasn't completely true. I suppose it was more a matter of degree than anything else.

So with the game still knotted at 42, my side came to bat in the bottom of the ninth innings. With Talman, Turney, Dupignac, and Jones all making big hits, we ended up making nine aces.

In the tenth innings, they managed to load the bases with two outs and, as fate would have it, Billy O'Brien at the bat. Our scouts all moved back a few paces. I was pitching and delivered a ball chest high as requested. He took his usual mighty swing and sent a ball deep into the left garden. Dupignac raced toward it, but after the ball hit the hard ground, it skidded straight ahead. Ebenezer slid on the now wet grass and miracle of miracles, grabbed the speeding ball with his outstretched left hand. Given the conditions, it was one of the best bounder catches I ever saw.

O'Brien was furious but we all gratefully headed to the warmth of McCarty's lounge to hail the wet hero. Even O'Brien had to admit the catch was superb, and when he calmed a bit even offered a heartfelt toast to Ebenezer. Billy, despite all his bluster, was a true sportsman. It was a wonderful ending to our first full season as a club.

Led by Cartwright, we toasted well into the evening — to the Knickerbockers, to base ball, to New York, and to extend the evening to just about anything and everything we could think of.

The reason we were toasting amongst ourselves was a practical consideration, not a philosophical one. We simply didn't have enough damn players showing up often enough to organize anything as complicated as games against others. If I'm painting a picture of a club on the teetering on the edge of survival, it's not accidental.

## 25

# *Doc Invents a New Position*

DOC ADAMS   One day we were playing a game with our usual eight men a side. As always, our basemen played on, or at least very near, the base they were covering. By the end of the game I was playing the left field. The quick game ended with us beating Cartwright's team 21–4 but much time was taken up by fielders running a long way after balls and then trying to get them to the basemen. Batsmen had been hitting the ball farther in recent days due at least in part to the fact that I had developed ways to wind the balls tighter with the result that they were more resilient and therefore flew farther.

As there was still plenty of light when the game ended, I suggested we play another. McCarty wouldn't be expecting us for at least an hour anyway.

"I'm all for another," said Alick. "And another after that if the light holds."

All agreed, even Birney who was usually the first to leave.

"Same teams, or should we chose new ones?" asked Alick.

"Since Cooper and Mumford have arrived, I propose we play with nine to a side."

"All right," he said. "Your choice."

"I defer to you as the losing side."

"Then we'll play with Mr. Mumford, and you with Mr. Cooper."

"More than acceptable," I said. "Come join our winning side, Mr. Cooper, if you please."

"I do indeed," he said.

The coin flip determined that Cartwright's team would be at bat first, so I told Cooper to take my place in the left field while I took up a position mid way between the second and third basemen.

"What's the matter, Doc, can't you find a base to cover?" called Will.

On the very first delivery from Ebenezer, Billy O'Brien found it to his liking and sent it just fair but far into the left garden. Our new fielder, Cooper, ran after it, stopped it with his foot, picked it up, and turned ready for the long heave back toward the third base. As he turned, he saw me standing half way between him and Avery perched on the third base.

"To me, Dan," I called. "Just throw it to me."

And that's what he did, it being an easy throw from where he was. I took the ball with both hands, then shifted it to my right hand as I turned and threw it to Avery who tagged the surprised O'Brien who stared at me as if I had just broken some law. Seldom did he ever see a ball he hit that far returned that quickly.

The idea took hold and we started regularly playing that way. The fielders liked the easier throw and it made the game more scientific for the batsmen. Now they had to work harder to place the ball out of a fielder's reach.

And so the position of short fielder, which we came to call shortstop, was born.

JAMES WHYTE DAVIS   I'm sure Doc wasn't really the first man ever to play what we now call the shortstop position. At times in earlier years we played with many more men than eight, but certainly after we came up with our set rules he was the first and by far the greatest champion of that position.

As he often claimed, the idea of playing "scientific" base ball was what the game was all about.

# 26

# *Sporting New Uniforms*

WILLIAM TUCKER   It was at an April club meeting that Ebenezer again brought up an issue that we had talked about from time to time but had never taken any action on.

"I think it's time," he said, "that we adopt a club uniform. One that every-one wears on play days. It would make us more ... official."

"What would make us more official," I said, "would be if more people turned out on play days."

"That's my point. If we had real uniforms, more men would turn out because it would seem ... well, more official."

"I'm not sure I see the connection, but it might not be a bad idea."

"Except it will mean more money will have to be put out by everyone. I don't see how that's going to help membership," said Birney.

"You make enough," I said, "maybe you could buy uniforms for everybody."

"Just as soon as Zachary Taylor makes me Secretary of the Treasury."

"You never know."

"I know."

Doc Adams, who had recently been re–elected president, averred that he thought uniforms might be a good idea. "I think," he said, "that good uniforms would help convey that what we play is an adult game, worthy of serious con-sideration. Clubs that take pride in their uniforms always command respect. But they have to be uniforms that suggest that respect. They need to be neat, and clean, and well designed."

Allusions were made to the uniforms of the military and of fire fighters. It was suggested that the club uniform include the fire fighters bib used to stop flying cinders.

After a lively discussion about uniforms good and bad, it was agreed we would come up with suitable uniforms and give them a try.

Walter Avery said he knew someone he thought could make them for us. With the invention of Elias Howe's machine for sewing just a couple of years earlier, there were women in the city who had taken to making clothes at home and there was a burgeoning business in mass producing clothing. What once would have been a difficult task — to get forty matching uniforms made — was now a simple reality.

What followed was a ridiculously protracted discussion about uniform colors, choice of materials, and fines for showing up on play days without the requisite attire. You would have thought, given the fervor and length of the discussion, that we were debating the presidential elections. Some members seemed more interested in the uniforms in which to play the games than in the games themselves.

Without going into the details, here is what we came up with: blue woolen pantaloons, white flannel shirts, and chip hats with flat brims to shield our eyes from the sun. These straw chip hats were important because they suggested the wearers were men of the respectable class.

It wasn't until many years later that some teams began wearing knickers as part of their uniforms, and although some people still think the Knicker-bockers started the trend to knickers, it's not so.

DOC ADAMS   The consideration of color was an interesting one. Blue was eventually chosen because it seemed to most of us to be a dignified color, representing the gentlemanly class. When someone suggested red, the idea was immediately derided as "too garish," and "too common." It seems the sentiment was that gentleman would never wear red.

Some years later we were playing a lower class club when they came onto the field wearing bright red pants with dark red belts.

"That figures," said Jamie Davis.

I knew what he was talking about without another word being said.

Similar thinking went into the choice of material.

"Cotton would surely be the least expensive and the most comfortable material," said Birney.

It was if he had just uttered a profanity in front of the ladies.

"Never," said Mumford. "Wool is the only possible material."

What he was implying, of course, is that wool set us apart from working class cotton. Enough said.

---

# 27

# On Crowds and Riots

WILLIAM TUCKER   One day in early May, coming back from a particularly long match, we ran into a riot near Astor Place.

It seems the eminent English tragedian, William Charles Macready, and the American, Edwin Forest, were engaged in a professional feud which apparently began over a public disagreement about the interpretation of Hamlet, which then spilled over to their supporters.

On this night, both were playing *Macbeth,* and the fight was on.

A man running by handed us a broadside: "Workingmen! Shall Americans or English rule this country?"

As we approached, we could see both the police and military running toward the melee.

We pressed ourselves against the wall of a nearby shop so as to avoid the crush of the rioters. Just at the moment the crowd seemed to be reaching peak frenzy, shots rang out, and we beat a hasty retreat.

"See," said Alick, "this is what can happen when there are no good outlets for one's stronger emotions. Thank God for base ball."

You know, I think he actually believed that.

The papers the next day claimed that 10,000 rioters, including Five Points gangs, were involved. I think that's an exaggeration typical of the sensationalist press, but no doubt there were several thousand. Various reports had anywhere from 20 to 30 people killed. Apparently it was easier to count the number of rioters than the number of dead.

ALICK CARTWRIGHT   Martial law was imposed on the city for three days, meaning among other things, no base ball games. One paper I saw suggested renaming Astor Place "Dis-Astor Place." Not a bad idea.

JAMES WHYTE DAVIS   When the Swedish singer Jenny Lind, "the Swedish Nightingale," made her American debut promoted by P.T. Barnum, 30,000 people greeted her on her arrival. When she performed at Castle Garden, 6,000 people attended the event. According to published reports, she earned an incredible $1,000 a concert plus expenses, while Barnum supposedly took in almost $27,000.

These seemed to be astronomical figures. In our wildest dreams we never imagined that base ball was headed in the same direction.

---

# 28

# *Of Bats and Balls*

DOC ADAMS   Making a good ball posed its own challenges. First you had to find the right yarn — lots of it. Naturally, raiding the wife's or mother's sewing basket was an act both fraught with danger and ripe with possibilities.

However, if enough of the purloined material could be found, what you did was wrap it as carefully and as tightly as you could around a rounded lump of cork or a nice gummy ball of caoutchouc, or as it is more commonly known, India rubber. The cork was easy to find as all one had to do was to finish off a good bottle of one's favorite cork-stopped beverage. India rubber from a lump meant for erasing pencil marks could be worked into a ball. If one were very careful, it could also be extruded from certain adhesive bindings used in some illustrated table books. Naturally this would render the books into piles of single sheets, but in the cause of the game, this might be considered justifiable sacrilege. Old rubber overshoes, too, could be a good source.

The process of tightly winding the yarn had to be undertaken with great attention to detail as each winding had to lay correctly against the others or the result would be an unsatisfactory lump. I was fortunate to have piped-in gas from a central factory so that the light in my study was steady and up to the inevitable late night task of ball winding.

Once a ball of a suitable diameter was created, the end of the yarn was glued down so as to avoid having to tie a knot which again would have resulted in an unwanted lump. There was no way to determine an exact diameter. If the ball felt right in your hand when you threw it, it was the right size. Some things in life don't need to be scientifically arrived at. When they're right, they're right. A good base ball is like that. It is a perfect sphere that fits a man's hand and flies through the air with the grace of an eagle in flight. No other determination of its correctness need be applied.

Now came the hard part — covering the sphere with smooth calf skin. This might be obtained from a cordwainer or cobbler or direct from a tannery. At first I had some difficulty with the hides, but eventually I found a Scotch saddler who was able to show me a good way to apply horsehide, such as was used for whip lashes. The skin had to be fashioned into quarters, wet, and then carefully stitched around the yarn ball, working to keep it taught and snugly closed so as not to leave protruding seams.

Sometimes some of the lads would make balls with seams that weren't completely flat and this resulted in blisters on thrower's hands.

Making a good ball was an art. At one point I scoured the city in search of craftsmen to make the balls for us, but finding no suitable takers, I ended up making most of the ones we played with myself. For that matter, eventually I made many for other clubs as well.

CHARLES DEBOST   In addition to making balls, Doc Adams also made some of our bats, but mostly we made them ourselves. Many happy hours were spent selecting and whittling these beautiful objects. Since there were no rules as to what could be used, there were bats as much as five feet long and nearly as thick as wagon tongues.

Since pitchers were still delivering the ball as in horseshoes—that is, with an underhand motion—there was no need for a lighter instrument. However, in time I discovered, as did many others, that a lighter bat could better be put to use in scientific hitting.

Doc Adams    Early on, a stout rake or a pitchfork handle worked perfectly if cut to a suitable length and with the edges nicely rounded with a file or rasp. Again, we didn't measure the bats; we just knew how long they should be for each hitter's likes. Most were probably three to three and a half feet long, although I know the O'Brien brothers used slightly longer ones. They could be fat or skinny, or as heavy or light as one wished.

Later we found some skilled wood craftsmen who turned bats beautifully.

As time went on, ash became the preferred wood, but you could also find batsmen using such woods as white pine, spruce, cherry, chestnut, and hickory. Also popular among those who favored a lighter bat was English willow, hence the expression often heard around the game, "to use the willow."

At one point, too, there were some experiments with using hollow bats. Needless to say, they were a complete failure; nevertheless, it shows that some batsmen were beginning to go to any length short of using metal to try to gain a little advantage.

---

# 29

## Printing the Rules

Alick Cartwright    On numerous occasions, other gentlemen interested either in learning the game for their own amusement or because they wanted to form their own club came to our club matches. Some asked for copies of our rules.

One of our members was a printer, so one day I asked him if he would print up the Knickerbocker Rules and By-Laws.

By making them available to anyone who wished to read them, we were spreading the gospel of base ball. And why not? We couldn't conceive of any red-blooded American man of decent standing who couldn't benefit from playing the game.

Doc Adams    What an incredible impact publishing our rules had. Once, to learn a game, you had to watch it being played. Now, no matter where in the country you were, you could learn it by reading our rules.

HENRY STARKEY    I was living in Detroit, Michigan. There was an old fiddler in the city named Page. He used to take a New York paper, and one day he showed me a copy in which there was quite a lengthy description of the new game of base ball. Since there were a fair number of us who had an interest in the game, we came to the conclusion that the new way must be an improvement over the old. Anyway, we decided to try it, so I wrote for a copy of the new rules, and paid $1 for it. After we got the rules we organized a club — the first in Detroit.

WILLIAM TUCKER    Once our rules were published it led to clubs being formed in many distant cities. I know this because in time people began send us copies of reports in various papers around the country as if they were showing off to their parents what they had done.

DOC ADAMS    According to some, we regarded our rules as Holy Scripture. That didn't mean though, that we weren't constantly trying to improve them.

In 1848, I was asked by the membership to head a "Committee to Revise the Constitution and By-Laws." Although Cartwright was wont to resist changes, he reluctantly served as a member. The intention was to review our rules, and where we deemed it necessary for the good of the game, to make alterations.

Up until then we played that a runner could be put out at any of the four bases if an opposing player was holding the ball on the base to which the runner was going. This was so even if the base behind him was unoccupied. As this was very untidy, I suggested that we rewrite the rule to state that except at first base, that if not forced, a runner could only be put out if tagged by a fielder with the ball in his tagging hand.

This was the first of many changes to come as we refined the game rule by rule.

WILL WHEATON    The Marylebone Cricket Club was founded in London in 1787 as a private members' club and thereafter established itself as the governing body for all cricket. They were the framers and copyright holders of the Laws of Cricket.

Sometimes the Knickerbocker Base Ball Club (or simply the KBC), was thought to hold a similar function. In some respects we did, although not in such an official way.

ABNER CALDWELL    In Massachusetts we played the fly rule, we played with overhand pitching, we played with soaking, and we played without a foul territory — a man's game. The Knickerbocker game was simply indolent, sickly, puerile, effeminate and disgusting.

Had not the damn rules been printed up, the game never would have caught on.

# 30

# *Going for the Gold*

ALICK CARTWRIGHT    In all the city's papers and coffee houses, the talk was of Manifest Destiny, spurred on largely by Polk's presidential campaign. I agreed with Polk and those who argued that the expansion of our country was a virtuous reflection of the American people and our institutions, and that our mission was to spread these institutions. By doing so we would redeem and remake the world in the image of America. It was our destiny under God to accomplish this work.

DUNCAN CURRY    I don't know if Alick's ever-increasing discourses on expansionism were meant to convince us or him, but I know he had the seeds of the born-wanderer in him. Alexander Joy Cartwright was a true romantic.

ALICK CARTWRIGHT    Ever since I can remember, I always loved those places over the hill. What's around the next corner? I had to go and see.

DOC ADAMS    One day after a wholly satisfying game, I was sitting with Alick and Will Wheaton drinking coffee at the Tontine when Alick excitedly moved the conversation from the game to his latest fixation.

ALICK CARTWRIGHT    Our book and stationery shop was down near Trinity Church. I enjoyed the book business and the convivial conversation it generated.

Books were a good business in New York as the literary scene was flourishing and books by such local writers as Edgar Allan Poe, Washington Irving, Walt Whitman, Herman Melville, James Fenimore Cooper, and William Cullen Bryant were in constant demand. Together with the emerging women's literature they were pushing books sales to unimaginable heights. Then too there were always the new Charles Dickens works which sold better than just about anything this side of Tontine coffee.

The shop was reasonably profitable for me and my brother, Alfie, but Eliza and I were in the early stage of raising a sizeable family. Our oldest son, DeWitt, was named after an old Knickerbocker friend, Peter DeWitt; the next we named Bruce. Our third child was a girl named Kathleen Lee after Colonel Lee; our fourth, Alexander Joy Cartwright, III.

We had friends, a good business, and we were in New York City with all the benefits that bustling place offered. Still, I was cursed by a streak of restlessness that forever has been a part of who I am.

DOC ADAMS   The Tontine Coffee House seemed always to be filled with underwriters, brokers, merchants, traders, and politicians. Everything was in motion at the Tontine — all bustle and activity. Here was a place to tell stories and hatch plans. It was there that the NY Stock Exchange was organized and where Alexander Hamilton and his Federalist friends met to talk about dueling. It was also where Alick brandished a copy of the *New York Herald* with a story of the California gold rush.

It seems that it had started at a place known as Sutter's Mill and places like the Tontine were abuzz with excited would-be adventurers. Count Alick among those so roused.

"Listen to this," he said, his voice raising a good octave as he read from the paper. "The gold discovered in December on the south branch of the American Fork is only three feet below the surface."

"Don't believe everything you read," I said.

"Why would they make something like that up?"

"Maybe they just want to lure immigrant workers out there. To work on the railroads maybe."

"Yeah, and maybe they found gold."

"Maybe."

"A man could set himself up pretty good if he got a pocketful or two of that stuff."

"You're not thinking about going out there, are you?"

"I'm thinking about a lot of things."

"Do you have any idea what it's like — the trip to California?"

"I know it's a long way."

"And it's filled with Indians and wilderness the likes of which none of us have ever seen. Either that or it's a long unbearable trip around Cape Horn."

"I get seasick easily."

"Avoid boats."

At the time I couldn't tell if Alick was being serious or puckish. Will didn't say much, but I could see that logical mind of his sifting through the gold fever beginning to rise in Alick.

"Alick," I said. "You've got a lovely wife who's not used to anything more rustic than a muddy sidewalk in spring."

Eliza, his lovely wife, was the daughter of Pieter Gerrit Van Wie. As I understand it, the Gerrit Van Wies were a prominent Dutch family with an immense estate overlooking the Hudson River. It was hard to picture her working the reins of a Conestoga wagon through Indian Territory.

"She's got relatives going back to Bonnie Prince Charles," he said.

"What is that supposed to mean?"

Alick laughed. "I don't know, exactly."

"You've got four little kids."

"Who are just itching for an adventure."

"You've got a going business."

"But I've also got the itch."

"And you've got the Knickerbockers. You wouldn't give that up, would you? Base ball, you love it."

"I was thinking I could teach the game to young men everywhere I went. Spread the gospel a little bit."

"A regular Johnny Appleseed of base ball, are you?"

"Why not? I could be an ambassador for the game."

Once he got an idea into his head Alick was not one to give up easily.

"You're serious, aren't you?" I said.

"I think I am."

"How long do you figure it will take you?" asked Wheaton. "To get to San Francisco, I mean."

Cartwright laughed again. "Damned if I know."

WILL WHEATON　　We all heard rumors about egg-size nuggets lying about for the taking. In some circles nothing else was talked about but the quick and easy fortunes to be made in California. Walking down by the docks you could see thousands of people lined up to book passage on anything that would float.

As we later learned, within a span of about four years, the population of California ballooned from 20,000 to 223,000.

The thought came to me that I might try my hand at wielding pick and shovel, and if that didn't work out, there would always be an opportunity (you might say golden opportunity) for a young lawyer to do well in such a situation.

I talked it over with Alick a few times and the more we talked, the more the idea seemed appealing.

WILLIAM TUCKER　　This was the first time in history that this most precious metal was available for the taking by anyone and everyone. The gold was sitting there free for anyone willing to travel out there to pick up and stuff into bulging pockets.

Well, I talked a lot with Will about this and soon I too was burning with the fever.

DOC ADAMS　　Will and Tuck tried to enlist me as well, but I was an easterner who considered myself a cultured man, an identity rooted in education, not labor or wealth.

When Cartwright, Wheaton, and Tucker decided to try their hands in California the Knickerbockers were about to lose three of our founding members and three stalwart defenders of the base ball faith.

We organized a farewell gathering at Schwartz's Hotel. Many of the old group were there: Charles Birney, Walter Avery, Colonel Lee, Ebenezer Dupignac, Duncan Curry, the O'Briens.

We had a good time talking of games past where reality became embroidered with wishes and the more the pints emptied, the more elaborate became the embroidery. Scratch hits became blistering drives and routine catches became acrobatic marvels. And why not? The game brought us joy and if we exaggerated that joy a little what was the damage?

FRALEY NIEBUHR   It wasn't going to be the same without Alick, Tuck, and Will, but there is a time for everything and their time with the Knickerbockers was over. I offered a toast.

> Here's to three of the best
> Who give up the city to head out west.
> They're looking for gold
> And if they're not already too old
> They may even find a nugget or two
> To stick in their pocket or jam in their shoe.
> So now the game we love so much
> Will lose the expert touch
> Of two who made it so
> And that is something we all know.
> So this is what we have to say
> Good luck in Cal-ee-for-nee-ay!

DOC ADAMS   Fraley was a better player than he was a poet but we all laughed and applauded.

I then presented to Alick, Tuck, and Will the original balls we used in our first games four years earlier. Alick wasn't the most emotional man I ever knew, but I thought I saw a little tear in his eye.

ALICK CARTWRIGHT   "Thank you, boys," I said. "I will keep this forever and always remember the great times with the Knickerbockers. There's not a better group of gentlemen in this city, or in any other I dare venture. It is my intention to spread the gospel according to the Knickerbockers as far as San Francisco and I promise to write and let you know how it is in the West."

Of course, they wouldn't let me off without the obligatory hazing.

"If you find any pitchers better than you, send them our way," said Birney. "And that shouldn't be too hard."

"Maybe the Indians can teach you how to run the bases like they run after buffalo," said Avery.

"What do you know about running after buffalo?" I responded.

"About as much as you do about running the bases."

"You can't find third base, so how do you expect to find San Francisco?"

DOC ADAMS   A few days later I walked with Alick and his family down to the ferry for Jersey City and Newark. From Newark they were to board a train to Philadelphia and then on to Pittsburgh where it was to be a Conestoga wagon all the way to the coast.

He did write eventually saying it took them 156 days to make it to San Francisco. According to his letters, whenever they stopped long enough and could find enough men, they played base ball. At least that's what he wrote.

He was a missionary for the game, no doubt about that. Nor did I have any doubt that before long he would have the prospectors cutting off handles from their shovels for bats.

He wrote that under the expert guidance of Colonel Russell, a company of 110 men with 32 wagons followed the Santa Fe route. He told of his encounters with Indian tribes, Mormon settlers, Baptist missionaries, trappers, and soldiers. When he arrived in San Francisco, he joined up with his younger brother who had preceded him there by boat around Cape Horn. Along with Alfred (who played some with us and also served as umpire), they bought an interest in a gold mining enterprise. Apparently they found some gold, but as it was not enough to his liking, within days he set sail for Hawaii. Although he wrote that it was so he could regain his health after bouts with dysentery, it was typical of Alick's adventurous spirit.

As we might have expected, he became the inspiration for the spread of base ball across the islands.

He never returned to New York, but the legacy he left continued with the Knickerbockers.

WALTER AVERY   It wasn't long before I too bid farewell to my mates, boarded the steamer *Columbus* and headed for California and all the bounties it offered. I knew I would miss the club (and I did) but the West promised a new life and I was eager for the experience. I couldn't see why those of us who understood the game couldn't teach it to the Californians.

WILLIAM TUCKER   Since Alick was subject to seasickness, he went overland, but most of us went by sea. It was a long and hard journey, much more difficult than the romantic pictures I had imagined. Alick may have been smarter because soon, for many of us, seasickness replaced gold fever. Inadequate food and water, rampant disease, and overcrowding made the journey miserable. Then when we landed in California, we discovered we were still 150 miles from the closest gold fields, and almost all of the easy placer gold had already been picked up.

Gold folly might have been more like it. A harsh reality quickly set in — loneliness, homesickness, physical dangers, and damn hard work.

It wasn't long before I longed for a return to the peaceful life of a New York tobacco merchant and gentleman ballist.

# PART FIVE: THE NATIONAL
# GAME 1850–1854

## 31

# *Members Old and New*

FRALEY NIEBUHR   We were starting to lose some of the "old guard." Cartwright, Wheaton, Tucker, Avery, the DeWitt brothers, Frank Turk, Charles Case, Edward Ebbetts—Knickerbockers all—were off chasing their golden dreams.

Opinions differed on how or whether the club would survive.

JAMES WHYTE DAVIS   I had been playing ball for some time with and against the Knicks.

"Don't you think it's about time you joined?" said Duncan after a particularly spirited game.

"You mean pay dues?"

"Precisely."

I didn't have the money that some of the members did, and by then we had a young son, James, Jr. (Fearing complications, Maria and I had gone back to her family in Maryland for the birth, but everything worked out fine and we returned to New York.) We talked about it and agreed we could manage.

"You might as well," Maria said in a teasing way. "You're an addict anyway, so you might as well feed your habit. We'll get by."

DUNCAN CURRY   Some members found Jamie a mite aggressive and at times when he became frustrated, downright profane. Nevertheless he was a committed player, and a pretty good one at that. He was a straight talker who might sometimes act as if he had a chip on his shoulder, but he was also a man who could get things done and the club certainly needed that.

JAMES WHYTE DAVIS   I wasn't one for sitting around and watching others do the work, so as soon as I joined, I began pitching in wherever I could. My aim was to stay actively involved with the club's operations. Little did I know at the time just what that would mean.

DOC ADAMS   I was glad when Jamie came aboard. He quickly became one of our leaders. Although he always insisted otherwise, I think he liked to be in control. He aspired to leadership responsibilities and relished the power even

113

if he might have overdone it a little once in a while. Still, we were very fortunate indeed to have him.

SAM KISSAM    In May 1854, I was elected to membership. I had known Jamie Davis from the brokerage business, and it was he who got me interested in the club. At the time Fraley Niebuhr was president, Jamie was secretary, Doc Adams and Charlie DeBost were directors. These men were to become my lifelong friends.

DOC ADAMS    Sam was a great addition to the club. He came from old New York stock. His father was a pastor and he had a sister who married William H. Vanderbilt — yes, that Vanderbilt.

JAMES WHYTE DAVIS    Sam was a much more important broker than I was. In fact, he was one of the best known men in the financial life of the city. He became a member of the Board of Governors of the Stock Exchange, and one of the trustees of the important Gratuity Fund. It was his brokerage firm, Kissam, Whitney & Co., that handled much of Vanderbilt's business. See, it definitely pays to have a smart and rich sister.

He was, though, a dedicated member of the club for a long time. Maybe he wasn't one of the better players on the field, but he was one of the best members we ever had. He knew the meaning of loyalty, sportsmanship, and commitment.

SAM KISSAM    If anyone was worried about the future of the club, they shouldn't have been. Doc and Jamie had easily taken up the leadership vacuum left by Alick, Will, Tuck, and the others.

JAMES WHYTE DAVIS    Being a Knickerbocker meant among other things that you had additional social responsibilities ... and pleasures.

Most of us went over to Fraley's wedding to Julia. She was a lovely girl, as I recall from Pennsylvania. After the ceremony, the couple and their families left on their nuptial journey.

"Hurry back, Fraley," I said. "We need you for a game next week."

Fraley laughed. I think he thought I was kidding.

Of the older members, Doc was one of the few still not married. He was always quiet about his courting activities but I knew he was keeping company.

"You ought to try it, Doc," said Fraley. "You might like it."

"I have no doubt."

"Once you taste the happiness of the marriage union, you'll curse yourself a fool that you lived so long without it."

"Well, I wouldn't be the first to call me that."

DOC ADAMS    A letter came from Will Wheaton. He wrote that after a time in San Francisco, he had moved on to Sacramento where he opened a wholesale grocery business. He also informed us that Walt Avery was then in Stockton where he was a partner in the firm of Avery and Hewlett, Wholesale Dealers in Groceries, Dry Goods, and Produce. For all the world it appeared that selling groceries paid better than digging for gold. I suspected that we would eventually see both back in New York, but only Walt returned. Will settled down there and made California his permanent home.

I did note, however, that a new base ball club had been formed in California — the Knickerbocker Base Ball Club of San Francisco.

The other man who came back to us and re-joined the club was Tuck.

WILLIAM TUCKER    The only gold I saw was in the front teeth of Chinamen.

I was happy to be home and happy to return to the club. I hadn't played a game in over two years and I missed both the game and the members.

---

## 32

# *Base Ball, Base Ball, Base Ball*

CHARLES DEBOST    Base ball, base ball, base ball. Suddenly it was everywhere.

DUNCAN CURRY    This proliferation in clubs coincided with the great shift in our population from farm to city, made possible, at least in part, by the expansion of the railroads.

JAMES WHYTE DAVIS    One aspect of the game that made it so immediately appealing is that it didn't take much to play — a bat, a ball, and open space. Compared to the needs say, of horse racing or yachting, base ball made only the simplest of demands. Even cricket, to which our game is often compared, required meticulously manicured grounds well beyond what we needed. Then too, base ball was easy to learn, and for those so inclined and physically equipped, easy to master.

Really there was no secret to why it became so popular so quickly.

DOC ADAMS    I was occasionally asked for suggestions on how other groups might organize.

The first was the Washington Base Ball Club, made up, as we were, of several men who had once played for the informal New York Base Ball Club. They began playing games on the field of the St. George Cricket Club up in Harlem. A few years later they changed their name to the Gotham Club and became one of the most successful organizations in the city.

The Eckfords came next. They were a Brooklyn working men's club.

Then along came the Eagles. I received an invitation asking for a committee to join them in arranging a set of playing rules, so I, Duncan, and Tuck obliged. We met with their committee and went over our rules in considerable detail. In short order they had adopted them and began playing accordingly.

Along the way we did make a few rule changes, although they were mostly for the sake of clarification and did little to alter the basic structure of our game. We had noticed that in some games, pitchers were inching forward so as to gain an advantage over the batsmen, so we set the distance between the batter and the pitcher at no less than 15 paces.

We also included the rule that players must take their strike in regular rotation; and after the first inning is played the turn commences at the player who stands on the list next to the one who lost the third hand.

We clarified the wording on a few other rules as well.

A player who intentionally prevented an adversary from catching the ball was a hand out.

If two hands are already out, a player running home at the time a ball was struck could not make an ace if the striker was caught out.

We also agreed that we would all adopt the rule that balls must weigh between five and five and a half ounces and be between two and three-quarters and three and a half inches in diameter.

DOC ADAMS    All clubs in the area basically followed our rules but not all followed them to the letter. Some varied the number of players on a side and the number of aces necessary to win. For a while, the Putnams incorporated some of the old Massachusetts game rules including playing to 62 runs.

Eventually though, those variations dropped by the wayside and our rules became more and more the standard.

When we originally selected the Fields for our meetings, we had no thoughts whatsoever of having to share the space, but such was the burgeoning expansion of the game.

JAMES WHYTE DAVIS    By 1854 we had four well organized clubs playing regularly in New York. Brooklyn, which was then still a separate city, also had four — the Atlantics, the Excelsiors, the Putnams, and the Eckfords. For some reason, Brooklyn seemed to be an area which took to the game even more passionately than anywhere else. Maybe the inhabitants over there believed that they were in some manner of competition with New York. I don't know if that's right, but it certainly looked that way.

The formation of the Eckfords brought a whole new identity to the game. They were not from what was generally considered the "gentlemanly class," but mostly laborers from the Brooklyn docks. Some sentiment was expressed by our membership that we shouldn't play matches against them. (Actually there was some sentiment that to maintain our status as the game's founders we shouldn't play matches against any other clubs period.) Others felt that as long as they acted appropriately on the field of play, it shouldn't matter from which class they came. Wall Street brokers, bankers, and physicians playing against shipwrights? The idea was going to take some getting used to.

Of course, too, the Eckfords were named for Henry Eckford, a Scots-Irish immigrant who had worked his way to becoming the richest shipbuilder in the city, so while the club members may have been laborers, they certainly wanted to have their names associated with a higher class.

FRANK PIDGEON    Being shipwrights and mechanics, it wasn't convenient to practice more than once a week. Still, we had some merry times among ourselves; on Tuesday afternoons we would forget work, go out in the green fields, don our ball suits, and go at it with a perfect rush. At such times we were boys again. Sport brightens a man up and improves him, both in mind and body.

FRALEY NIEBUHR    After a while, it seemed as if every time I opened a paper, I read about a new club — the Independents, the Charter Oaks, and others.

Clubs were formed in New Jersey and out on Long Island and, according to reports, springing up in Philadelphia and Boston.

JOHN H. SUYDAM    One balmy November day, for reasons I have long since forgotten, I stopped to see a base ball game being played by the Eagles. Watching the enjoyment the men were obviously experiencing, it occurred to me and my mates that it might be a valuable idea to get up our own base ball club. A few days later, with only a rudimentary idea how to play the game, we met for practice. By even the most liberal of standards, the game we played might best be described as "a shambles." We laughingly called ourselves the "J. Y. B. B. B. C.," otherwise known as the Jolly Young Bachelors' Base Ball Club.

Later we decided officially to name the club the Excelsiors, from the Latin *excelsus* which, according to Richard Wetherington, our self-professed most erudite member, means "of a high standard."

We adopted a constitution modeled after the Knickerbocker constitution. Our published objective was to "improve, foster, and perpetuate the American game of Base Ball, and advance morally, socially and physically the interests of the members."

Another objective, which went unpublished, was to create a superior club of players. Simply put, we wanted to beat the stuffing out of the Knicks or any other club for that matter. To that end, we sought members with exceptional athletic skills.

DOC ADAMS    With neither reservation nor undue modesty, I can say that for at least our first ten years, the Knickerbocker Base Ball Club was the benchmark against which all other clubs were measured.

So much in demand were our constitution and by-laws that we had to have hundreds of more copies printed and even resorted to publishing a notice to that effect in the *Mercury*.

The very term "base ball" was fast becoming synonymous with "the New York game," which in turn was becoming synonymous with "the Knickerbocker game."

JAMES WHYTE DAVIS   Our rules became the rules by which most teams played, our club structure was the structure most new clubs adopted. Even our uniforms were copied, albeit always with some small alteration in design. The Eclectics wore dark blue flannel pants, blue-trimmed white shirts, and white caps adorned with blue stars. At least they didn't use "Knickerbocker blue" but a slightly darker shade. The Charter Oaks had the audacity to be seen in white pants with pink stripes, held up by black belts with the words "Charter Oaks" inscribed on them.

Perhaps this was another example of the direction in which the game was headed, for I can assure you, no Knickerbocker would have been seen on the field with such attire. Frankly, we considered ourselves above such displays of ostentation.

ALBERT TRAYO   I was a charter member of the Social Base Ball Club when we organized according to the Knickerbocker rules. Why not use them as a model? We aspired to organize ourselves according to their high principles of sportsmanship and genial conviviality.

JAMES WHYTE DAVIS   Clubs like the Socials may have claimed they were organized according to our principles and to some extent they were, but if you look more closely at their constitution, you can see little tell-tale signs of their true nature. For example, their fine schedule was similar to ours with one major exception: they included a huge one dollar fine for being inebriated at a meeting or in the field. We never felt the need for such a fine. Don't get me wrong, I'm not saying no one on our club ever drank a little too much before a meeting or after a game, but we handled the matter as gentlemen should. Embarrassment can be a strong motivator.

I wondered what Alick would have thought about all this.

I'm afraid that as new clubs were formed, some of the values of sportsmanship and good character that we so assiduously cultivated with the Knicks were being passed over in favor of other values, most notably those related to playing ability. I suppose we shouldn't have been surprised, and maybe we weren't, but I for one lamented the change.

The Putnams had a song they often sang:

> And should any club by their cunning and trick
> Dishonor the game that it plays,

> Let them take my advice and go to "Old Knick,"
> And there learn to better their ways.

Need I say more?

---

33

---

# *Return to Playing Other Clubs*

JAMES WHYTE DAVIS   With the advent of so many new clubs, the old debate as to whether we should play games against them came up again and to no one's surprise, the "let's play other clubs" group won. We hadn't engaged another club since that drubbing we took from the New York Club in 1846.

The next intra-club game we played was in 1851 against the Washington Club at the Red House Grounds in Harlem which we won 21–11.

The return match was played at Elysian Fields. It was a much better game and went back and forth for quite some time before we finally won in ten innings, 22–20. I had a particularly good game as I accounted for only one out while scoring three runs, including the run that proved to be the winning tally.

So we were a happy group when we gathered at McCarty's Hotel after the game for our usual entertainment.

Anderson was president of the Washington Club, and after dinner he stood up and offered a toast I thought summed up our situation very well.

"Here's to our very good friends, the Knickerbockers, to whom we all owe a debt of gratitude for the splendid work they have done to bring order and structure to the game we love. Maybe we should honor them by changing the name 'base ball' to 'Knick ball,' for such is their importance."

There was a general nodding of agreement before DeBost popped up and said, "I think there's something very important that we need to discuss."

He sat there not saying any more until Doc took the obvious bait, "And what might that be Mr. DeBost?"

"I would have scored two more runs today had my hat not flown off my head hindering my running."

"Is that so?" said Doc, willing to play the straight man.

"And had I scored those two runs we would have finished the game after eight innings and, had we finished after eight innings, we would have been drinking at least an hour earlier, and that I consider to be of the utmost importance."

"I suggest then, that you tie it on with a ribbon next time, Mr. Debost," said Mr. Anderson.

"No proper gentleman would be seen with ribbon holding down a chip hat, Mr. Anderson."

"Then it shouldn't be a problem, for you, Mr. DeBost," laughed Mr. Talman.

"Speak for yourself, Mr. Talman. As for me, I suggest we take the matter up at the first opportunity."

"This would appear to be that opportunity, Mr. DeBost," said Doc. "What would you suggest in lieu of a ribbon?"

"I'm so pleased you asked. I have given this matter considerable thought and have come to the conclusion that the problem lies with the hat itself. I propose we replace them with proper caps."

"Caps, Mr. DeBost?" said Talman.

"Mohair caps."

"You mean something like cricket caps?" said Doc.

"I mean exactly like cricket caps."

"I say, old chap, do you want us to copy the wacky English?"

"I put to you that they are more practical, will stay on heads better, cost less, and look very ... sporty."

"And very English," said Talman.

"No more so than straw hats."

He had a point.

"Do gentlemen wear mohair caps, Mr. DeBost?" asked Doc.

"They will soon."

And he was right. We traded in our straw hats for mohair caps shortly afterwards.

WILLIAM TUCKER    As we began to play more games against other clubs, we started designating a "first nine," a side made up of our better players. Naturally, the composition of this group was a matter of some contention and I understood why — it was simply not compatible with our aim of playing the game for its inherent values. We had entered a new phase in the organization of the Club. Rather than all members being on equal footing, we now had categories, or, if you will, rankings. Our first nine was like a club within a club. They were acknowledged to possess the best skills but it elevated them to a higher status. Then came a second nine. Our so-called "muffin" teams were made up of those not skillful enough to make the first or second nines.

I never liked the distinction but had to acknowledge that the creeping competitive urge made it inevitable.

DOC ADAMS    To those who argued that all we cared about was the outcome of games with the first and second nines, permit me to say that our muffin games were as organized and supported as any others. I can remember several particularly exciting matches with the Excelsior Muffins followed by splendid collations.

JAMES WHYTE DAVIS    At any rate, while we continued to play most of our games within our own membership, more and more matches were being organized between clubs. Although we eschewed competition as the essence of the game, it was natural for any player to want his club to be seen as the best, and so with the coming of all these new clubs, rivalries were being sown.

CHARLES DEBOST    One game I would like to forget was a Friday afternoon game against the Gothams up at the Red House. It was a return match for a game played earlier that took two days to complete because of a storm and was one of the most exciting games played between clubs to that point. The Gothams went ahead early in the contest and we were left desperately trying to catch up. With the score at 14 runs for the Gothams and ten for us, we came to bat again.

Led by Jamie, Doc, and Fraley, we mounted a staunch comeback, finally winning 21 to 14.

Here's what I added to our great triumph: I made six outs, all on fly balls or bounders, and I was the only one of our side who didn't score a single run.

Several days later, the *Spirit of the Times* had a story about "The Base Ball Match," in which my dismal effort was printed for all the world to see. At our next dinner, the article was prominently placed in front of me at the table.

"This was the finest, and at one time the closest, match that has ever been played between the two clubs. All the Gothamites want is a little more practice at the bat; then the Knicks will have to stir themselves to retain the laurels which they have worn so long."

Above this someone had underlined, "DeBost, 0 runs, 6 outs."

Of course, no one would take credit for putting it there and I knew it was meant in the spirit of good fun, so when I feigned raging anger, everyone burst out into laughter which stopped only when I said, "All right, all right, the beer is on me."

"At least you've done something for the club this month," said Jamie.

The next time we played the Gothams, I managed to score two runs although we lost 21 to 16. As predicted by the *Spirit*, the Gothamites were indeed getting better.

When the opportunity arose at our next dinner, I put the *Spirit* note about the game on the table in front of Mr. Murray and underlined "Murray 0 runs."

"Mr. Murray," I said. "May I assume the champagne is on you tonight?"

He laughed. "It is indeed, Mr. DeBost. It's the least I can do."

"And it's the least you have done," said Jamie.

All of this, of course, in the spirit of good natured fun.

FRALEY NIEBUHR   We had planned a club match for May 1st, forgetting that it was the traditional moving day for tenants in the city who each year tried to improve their housing. Stores shut down that day because the streets were so clogged with carts loaded with belongings that shoppers couldn't get around. Nor could base ball players heading for the ferry.

After being stifled by the crowds, Duncan Curry said, "I think an organized withdrawal is called for."

To which Jamie Davis replied, "What! Lose a perfectly good day for a game because of this rabble?"

We all looked at him waiting for what was to come next.

We didn't have to wait long. "Make way, make way!" he shouted. "Police coming through."

The fact that policemen had that year been put into uniforms seemed to have no effect on either Davis or the parting crowds.

## 34

# *On Matters Political*

BILLY O'BRIEN   Mostly at our gatherings we tried to stay clear of politics. But at one postgame dinner, the issue of "the Cathedral" came up. Archbishop Hughes had just announced that he wanted to build a magnificent new cathedral at 50th Street and Fifth Avenue. Well, it seemed that some of the Protestants on the club (and that meant most everyone else) started talking against it. Now I couldn't sit still for that and said so—maybe a little too loudly. Anyway, the argument got a mite heated. It was probably the biggest argument I can remember at any of those dinners.

CHARLES DEBOST   My objection wasn't anti–Catholic, it was anti-building on every open lot in the city. I'd have been just as annoyed had A. T. Stewart said he was putting another dry goods store there, and I'm not anti-store.

FRALEY NIEBUHR   When cholera broke out in Brooklyn killing nearly 700 people, there was a lot of concern about people traveling from there to Manhattan for fear of spreading the terrible disease.

Several of the members suggested all of us Brooklynites should be uninvited to join them for awhile.

Nevertheless, to the displeasure of some, I continued to play when I could and in times the scourge died down and so did the panic.

DOC ADAMS   One of our members, whom I shall not name, had gone to a rally of some 5,000 people to celebrate the return of a former slave, James Hamlet.

I averred that the act of sending slaves back to their southern masters was immoral.

Our narrow-minded member responded that the law was on his side.

"Then the law is wrong," I said.

"I'm a law abiding citizen, Doctor Adams."

"And I'm a moral one."

The argument continued to escalate until I'm embarrassed to admit that I stormed away without even finishing my dinner. I'm normally more prudent than that but I couldn't abide such sentiments.

Normally our dinners were civil and filled with convivial spirit. This was quite the exception.

Whether this had anything to do with this particular member being denied re-election to the club I do not know, but although I did not use my black ball, I was not unhappy to see him gone. The Knicks were not political as a club, but we did seek members who were upstanding and moral.

# 35

# *Dinners and Diversions*

DUNCAN CURRY   Occasionally we would get together with our families for some group activity. I remember some of us went to the opening of *Uncle Tom's Cabin,* and several of us went as a group with our wives to the first American World's Fair in Bryant Park. They had erected a spectacular iron-and-glass exhibition hall called the Crystal Palace and in it we saw a demonstration of Mr. Otis' steam-powered passenger elevator. DeBost and Davis volunteered to ride the contraption. The rest of us, possessing more sense, stayed our distance.

Much to our amazement, the machine went up and down smoothly, if somewhat noisily. Our two stalwart volunteers drew great applause as it did.

Little did we realize at the time the impact the elevator would have on the rapid development of our city.

FRALEY NIEBUHR   When the A. B. Taylor steam boiler exploded, it caused the greatest loss of life the city had ever seen. More than 60 people were killed and many others injured.

"It kind of makes base ball seem trivial, doesn't it?" I said to Jamie as we were waiting for a Club meeting to begin.

"It just reminds me that life is too damn short not to play."

JAMES WHYTE DAVIS After gentle, but persistent, pressure from Maria, I skipped a game one beautiful summer afternoon and instead accompanied her on a walk along the public promenade at the Battery. A more delightful scene could not be found in our city. It was a lovely landscaped park full of fashionable strollers enjoying a glorious view of New York Harbor. On the way home, with a twinkle in her eye, she said, "See, now wasn't that better than an old base ball game?"

She was teasing me, and I knew it. "Absolutely dear," I said. "We should do it more often."

"Next week then?"

"Maybe next year."

"So soon?"

"All right, in two years."

The thing is, all afternoon I was actually wondering how the game was going.

"Do you ever think you might be a trifle shallow in your interests?" she said.

"All the time."

DOC ADAMS   On June 8, 1854, Father died up in Keene. He was 90. I was gone from the city for a few weeks to attend to family business.

Naturally, one is not surprised when someone passes at 90, nevertheless it was a difficult time for the family. Father had been such a strong force in our lives.

# 36

# *The National Game*

JAMES WHYTE DAVIS   A writer in the *Spirit of the Times* called base ball "our national game." Had anyone told me just a few years earlier that base ball, not cricket, would earn this title, I would have called him stark raving mad.

What a testament to the organizers of the Knickerbockers!

Whether we wanted it or not, the sporting press was beginning to take interest in us.

The *Spirit* and a few of the daily papers sometimes provided short comments of three or four lines on games, usually noting the number of aces scored and the number of outs made by individual players. They also commented on the formation of new clubs.

The *Spirit* claimed, "The interest in the game of Base Ball appears to be on the rise, and it bids fair to become our most popular game."

I doubt if even the writer of those sentiments knew how accurate that prediction was.

JOE DECKER   I didn't understand all the commotion about base ball becoming the new "American national pastime" when we already had a perfectly good game that didn't need all the fiddling with rules that base ball started doing every year. It was called cricket.

When I made my position known one day to Charlie DeBost, he responded by saying, "Blimey old boy, it's an English game. I thought we got rid of those things nearly a hundred years ago."

The fact is, base ball is a fine game, but no one in his right mind who has ever played both games could disagree with the conclusion that playing base ball requires less skill than cricket. Perhaps that's why it was gaining in popularity — Americans just didn't want to work hard enough to develop the skills of top notch cricket players.

JAMES HUTCHINSON   As an Englishman from old York exiled to New York, and a devoted player of the noble game known as cricket, permit me to point out a few relevant observations on the two games.

It may be that the love of invention which belongs to a new people led to the raising of base ball above all other games. Yet in the essence of base ball there is nothing new. As long ago as 1748, a game called base ball was played by Frederick, Prince of Wales. It is very possible that the resemblance between this and the American game extends further than the name.

Without difficulty, the origins of base ball may be traced back to the club ball of the fourteenth century. I have seen a representation from that time of two men engaged in this amusement. One is delivering a ball to the other, who stands ready to receive it with a crude kind of club, and in it the germ of both cricket and base ball is easily recognized. It is curious that the attitude of the two figures is closer to base ball than cricket. This may either be taken as an indication that the American game was an intermediate step between club ball and cricket, or that the base ball players employed a conservative wisdom to reject the branches to get at the root of the tree. The former interpretation is likely to find general acceptance among English men who as schoolboys played a game which was held to be quite inferior to cricket — rounders. Base ball is, in fact, little more than glorified rounders.

Runs are scored in precisely the same way as rounders. The bat used is precisely the same as used by the schoolboys in rounders and may be said to come between it and the cricket bat much as the German student's *schlager* does between the small sword and the saber.

Some of the chief beauties of cricket are absent from base ball. There are none of those pretty cuts and well-judged drives. Granted, most of the niceties of cricket batting are lost on spectators without special knowledge, but on the other hand, the hard hitting which appears to be the object of the base ball batsman appeals to all who see it, however ignorant they may be of the game.

The absence of a wicket to be attacked and defended is another serious disadvantage to base ball. In the matter of bowling, too, the American game seems far inferior to cricket. The variety of English bowling contrasts favorably with the apparent monotony of base ball pitching. There is undoubtedly some skill involved in pitching a base ball but the constant employment of the same action by all the bowlers strikes these eyes as wearisome.

One curious circumstance of base ball is the waste of force which is brought about by the need to hit a ball within certain limits. This means that all the fine hits in the direction of square leg go for nothing.

As I said, base ball is but schoolboy rounders grown up a bit.

JAMES WHYTE DAVIS    Yeah, I've heard Hutchinson ramble on about the supposed superiority of cricket, but I don't buy it. Look, I've played both sports and I find base ball far more exciting and interesting. Cricket is slow, long, and made for fat Englishmen who drink their lager, smoke their pipes and shout "pip, pip, old boy" while sitting on their ample asses all day watching the game from the smoke-filled clubhouse.

Base ball is free from the boredom of waiting hours for something more exciting than bowlers changing at the end of each over. Base ball action is continuous and rapid and the fielding of the American players is singularly more accurate. The certainty with which catches are made, the judgment and quickness with which fielders back one another up, the neatness and rapidity with which balls are stopped and thrown in have no similarity in the English game. And the runner in base ball is simply more graceful, if for no other reason than he is not encumbered with the luggage of a bat.

Leave cricket, I say, to John Bull.

CHARLES DEBOST    Someone wrote in one of the papers that of all the games played in this country, the two that would become the most popular were base ball and coits. Coits? Apparently the St. Andrews Coit Club and the New York Coit Club were going at it full tilt. Maybe the writer hadn't looked out his window recently. Base ball was everywhere. Thank you, Knickerbockers.

Another paper kept campaigning for lacrosse to become the American pastime. Tell that to the Indians. You don't make a game the national pastime by editorials. Base ball was becoming more and more popular because people liked playing it and watching it. It's that simple.

Look, the Greeks had their Olympic games; the Spaniards, the bull fight; the French, fencing; the English their much-loved cricket. We'll take base ball any day.

## 37

# *Healthy Bodies, Healthy Minds*

COLONEL LEE    I read in the papers that in 1850 the population of New York, which then meant Manhattan, was 515,547. I read in the same issue that there were 6,000 gaming houses in the city, and that as much as a twentieth of the city's inhabitants gambled in order to make ends meet.

I can honestly say, though, that I never knew one Knickerbocker who frequented these houses. We had other and better outlets for our spare time.

DOC ADAMS    Cholera epidemics were fairly frequent in those days. In some instances, within hours of death the corpse would be so swollen that it wouldn't fit into any available coffin. In other cases, the flesh would fall to pieces in a putrefied mass giving off the most terrible stench.

Now I have no science to either prove or disprove this, but it is my observation that significant physical activity such as playing base ball strengthened the body against such scourges. As far as I know, no Knickerbocker died of cholera.

An important element necessary to pursue a happy and fruitful life is bodily health. Not simply freedom from disease, but the mental and physical supremeness which results from judiciously alternating periods of activity and repose for every part of the human system. But exercises such as riding, rowing, running, jumping, calisthenics, etc., all have a radical defect when the stimulus of competition is not present.

Something more than mere exercise is needed. Exertion needs to be made such that the sense of labor is lost and pleasure gained. The mind must be disengaged from all its cares and anxieties if it is to derive all the possible benefits.

Dr. Franklin prescribed walking up and down stairs as one of the best exercises and I have heard others recommend wood cutting as combining utility with pleasure, but I fail to see the pleasure in either activity. Rowing is a pleasurable exercise but does little for the legs. The gymnasium stimulates the blood, builds up the muscles and expands the lungs, but that is all. It is all about physique and it is taken like a physic. Farm work in the open air is invigorating, but it is all work and does not exhilarate.

Base ball contains all the elements calculated to produce that state of health necessary to life's complete enjoyment — strengthening the arms by batting, opening the doors of the lungs to the entrance of invigorating air by running the bases, adding suppleness and strength by chasing speeding balls, stimulating the flowing tide of life by catching the ball on the fly, giving pliability to the vertebral column by pitching or catching.

Throughout the game each period of severe action is followed by an interlude of rest thus preventing excessive fatigue and affording the opportunity to recuperate.

Not only the body, but the best powers of the mind are needed. The game requires judgment in running; discrimination in throwing; watchfulness in pitching; carefulness in catching; resolution in batting; and throughout, perseverance, determination, and presence of mind.

The outpouring of emotions also plays its healthy part. Witness the exultation that accompanies the well knocked ball, the mortification of a tip, the self-complacency of a good catch, the chagrin at a miss, the delight of making the home base, the despondency of being put out. And the joyous abandonment of care makes the game a most pleasing recreation.

"It does not pay," says the businessman. But it does pay to have the brain occasionally washed, as it were, from the muddle that constant attention to labor produces.

"Too trivial," exclaims the indolent hoarder of wealth who prefers the prospect of having his declining years embellished with sciatica, or rheumatism, whereas he might have had a hale and hearty old age and modest means.

"Aw! weally! not my stoile," gasps the votary of fashion, with undeveloped form and listless brains, dawdling through a life of selfishness and sensuality.

"No time to spare," says the hard-working mechanic. Three hours a week devoted to an enjoyable diversion will give him more than three years of additional life in which to prosecute his labors.

Pitch me a good ball!

JAMES WHYTE DAVIS    According to a friend traveling to London, a paper read before the British Association asserted that the Anglo-American races in the New World are degenerating physically and before long "would utterly disappear by their own default to be replaced by a mighty Republic of pig-tailed Chinamen."

All I can say is come and watch the ball players!

SAM KISSAM    Father being a pastor, the question of whether amusements such as base ball should be countenanced or not by true Christians was sometimes put to him. Is it right then for Christians to seek amusement? To this Father always argued that healthy amusement was not only acceptable, but beneficial.

When the famous speaker, Rev. Henry Beecher Ward, came to New York to deliver a lecture on "Amusements" at the Lexington Avenue Opera House, many of the city's leading politicians as well as clergymen including Father turned out for the speech.

What particularly pleased me were his comments to the effect that it is the duty of every man to have plenary health, and should he fall short of that he fails to perform perfectly the duties of life. He then specifically recommended the ball field.

He referred often to the idea of "muscular Christianity" which can and should control our games.

Father was pleased.

HENRY CHADWICK   As a schoolboy growing up in England I learned and played both rounders and cricket. After emigrating with my parents to Brooklyn when I was thirteen, I witnessed my first game of base ball and even played a little but I remained rather apathetic toward the game. It seemed to me then an inferior game to both those I played in England. Then I watched a wonderful match between the Knickerbockers and the Gothams. The playing was positively mesmerizing, with players displaying skill and daring the likes of which I had never seen before.

It was during that magical match that I decided to promote base ball. At the time I was a cricket reporter for the *New York Times* (as well as an occasional contributor to other papers) so I approached my editor with the idea of my covering base ball.

"Who would possibly want to watch and cover all those games?" asked the editor.

"I for one."

"Do you really think anyone will care?"

"I do indeed."

And so I began my long career covering a game I came to love. I suppose it would be fair to say that I became the first base ball sportswriter.

I thought it perfectly suited to the character of the American people. One aspect that commends it greatly to popular favor is that it is a game which the fair sex can patronize without the risk of encountering any of the objectionable features found in other sports previously in vogue.

Here's how I saw the model ballist:

He comported himself like a gentleman on all occasions, especially on match days. He abstained from profanity, leaving that vice to the graduates of our penitentiaries.

He controlled his temper and took everything in good humor, or if angered, kept silent.

He never criticized errors made by others, fully understanding that fault-finding never leads to improvement.

He never disputed the decisions of the umpire, nor implied that his judgment was weak, or his character doubtful. He was particularly careful not to question the decision of the umpire by his actions which in many instances could be as expressive as words.

He never took an ungenerous advantage of his opponents, but acted toward them as he would wish them to act towards him.

He played the game solely for the pleasure it afforded him. If his side won the game, well and good. If they lost he applauded the victors and by so doing robbed defeat of half its sting.

He arrived for a match on time, readily obeyed the instructions of the presiding officer of the day, whether winning or losing always played the game to the best of his ability, and left the field content with the results whatever they might be.

He abided by every rule of the game.

As to the physical qualities of the model player: He was able to throw a ball with accuracy up to a hundred yards. He was fearless in facing a swiftly batted or thrown ball. He was able to catch a ball on the fly or bound either within an inch from the ground or ten feet from it, and he could do it with either hand or both. He was able to run swiftly and pick up a ball while running. He was able to hit a swiftly pitched ball or a slow twister with equal skill and to whichever field the occasion required.

JAMES WHYTE DAVIS    I remember once when a boy was killed in an upstate game. Apparently he was in the field hurrying to catch a ball when he was struck in the head by the knee of a runner. He died sometime later as the result of a crushed skull. Once again cries rang out that base ball was too dangerous to let young boys play. By all means let's not let them out of the house, for crossing the street is even more dangerous.

The values of the game were as clear to me as the water in a Catskill brook. It promoted good health, and energy, and a positive attitude to life

Anyone who said otherwise was a donkey's ass.

DOC ADAMS    We played the game for all it offered us, and we played it seriously. Well, most of the time. Once when I was playing at the second base, I happened to turn around, and there was DeBost, who for some reason that day was playing in the deep field. He was stretched out on the ground smoking a big old segar. What of it? It didn't seem to matter much as long as he didn't do it all the time. He could still get up and chase after a ball whenever he needed to.

Leaving the field I said to him. "You wouldn't do that if Jamie were playing today."

"What?"

"Smoke."

"I wouldn't even sit if Jamie were here."

It must be said not all the members had the same commitment to the practices as others. Many belonged to other social clubs or societies as well. Some wanted to spend some of their spare time hunting, or fishing, or rowing, or swimming and often this presented a problem for us.

"God dammit, Doc, what the hell do they think this is?" asked Jamie on more than one occasion.

"A voluntary club."

"Voluntary, hell! Where does it say, 'the Knickerbocker Volunteer Base Ball Club'?"

## 38

# *Good Players*

JAMES WHYTE DAVIS    When we were voting on new members, among the qualities we looked for were civility, manners, desire, compatibility, availability on play days, and the means with which to meet the financial demands of the organization. Athletic ability beyond the reasonable ability to play the game at any level was not a requisite. That being said, we did have a few men whose skills were clearly better than those of most.

We generally considered the behind, or catcher, to be the most important position. He had to have a good throwing arm and the flexibility to stop wild deliveries. So naturally, as our best athlete, Charlie DeBost mostly played there.

We didn't rely on "stars." We relied on committed members no matter their abilities. Charlie may have been our best player, but that didn't give him any advantages in the club.

CHARLES DEBOST    Had I been born a few years later, undoubtedly I could have made a good living playing a game at which I was good, but I subscribed completely to the Knickerbocker principles of fair play and sportsmanship and don't regret for a moment my years with the club.

SAM YATES    Despite all their "sportsmanship first" proclamations, the Knicks did have a "first nine" and it was usually led by Charlie DeBost.

It was in the spirit of healthy competition that matches between clubs were held, although I have to admit that when I was a pitcher for the Empires, beating the Knicks was always a little better than beating any other club. I wouldn't exactly say we didn't like them, but the lofty attitude in which they held themselves made for an inviting target.

LOUIS WADSWORTH    As a young boy growing up in Connecticut, I was attracted to bat and ball games, particularly a game we called wicket. The game died out after organized base ball came, but in those days, it was a popular game among us Nutmeggers.

I was able to do well enough in school that I could go to Washington College. After graduating with a law degree in 1844, I went to Michigan where my father owned some land. But I was restless and yearned for someplace more exciting. So in 1848 I moved to New York where I was able to secure a position as an attorney with the Custom House.

It was while there that I made the acquaintance of Duncan Curry who introduced me to the game of base ball, a game to which I took immediately. In short order, I joined the Gotham Club and for several years participated in their activities with great vigor.

We had quite a good club, but after playing with them for three or four years, I had a falling out with some of the members and switched my allegiances to the Knickerbockers.

THOMAS VAN COTT    Louis Wadsworth played with us for a while before he left to join the Knicks. I heard the Knicks offered him money to join their club as they needed a good first baseman, and he was that.

Even if they didn't offer him an inducement to join them, it shows that despite their claims to the contrary, they were as competitive as any of us. How else could you explain their putting up with him? He'd argue with Saint Peter at the Pearly Gates if given the chance.

JAMES WHYTE DAVIS    I know it was whispered about in some quarters that we had "lured" Wadsworth away from the Gothams. That charge was so ridiculous it doesn't even need denial.

Look, Wadsworth could be a charming and witty fellow who excelled at after dinner toasts and speeches. I don't doubt he could have been an entertainer had he set his mind to it. Granted he was a big-bug lawyer who had an opinion on just about everything and it was usually a different opinion than that held by everyone else, but as long as he was with us, he was a constant source of inspiration at our dinners and meetings.

True, when he was in one of his contentious moods, if someone said "the sky is blue," he might say "it's not really blue, it only looks that way because of the dust in the air." Say "that was a great catch," and he'd say "it wasn't as difficult as it looked."

The fact is, three times he resigned from our club because of disagreements with other members.

We didn't "lure" him away so much as tolerate him.

# 39

# *Spectators*

DOC ADAMS    Unlike cricket and the Massachusetts game, the Knickerbocker game's V-shaped field invited spectators to the center — the batter's position.

This is a by-product of how we played. We wrote our rules so that we could have a better experience playing the game. The rules were for us, not for spectators.

In those days, many sporting events were used to attracting spectators. Horse and foot races sometimes had thousands. The same for boat races.

Now with the creation of so many new clubs playing against each other, spectators began turning up at ball fields — first by the tens, then hundreds, and eventually by the thousands.

While we never envisioned it as a spectator sport, obviously the spectators did.

ASHLEY HYDE    I dare say it would not be an exaggeration to claim that the number of spectators was increasing exponentially as new clubs came into existence. Why would someone want to watch exercise? That's how the Knicks thought of the game. However, there is something absolutely elemental in wanting to watch a competitive struggle between relative equals. Choose one side for your emotional investment and the struggle takes on personal meaning — not exactly good against evil, right against wrong, but the outcome matters.

With all these new clubs, many of which carried the identities of a particular job or profession, cranks could care about the outcome of "their" club. Fueled by newspaper stories, barkeeps followed the exploits of the Phantoms; policemen, the Manhattans; shipwrights, the Eckfords.

I think in those days profession or status-related loyalties counted for more than geographic loyalties.

Maybe I couldn't play, but I could and did invest considerably in the outcome of Knickerbocker games. They represented to me all that was good in the game and I took pleasure in their victories and dismay in their defeats.

I can remember matches so popular that cranks had to climb to rooftops to get good views of the game. I don't suppose Cartwright ever envisioned this. Or did he?

CHARLES BIRNEY    When they finally got around to putting streetcars in Brooklyn, the fare of 5 cents certainly didn't stop many people from using them. One of the results was that more and more people were making the journey to games. As more people were watching, the emphasis on winning was becoming more predominant. I blame the streetcars for what was happening to our game. Well, maybe that's an exaggeration, but they didn't help.

DOC ADAMS     The growing number of spectators at matches spawned a number of significant changes in the way the game was being played. Slowly, but assuredly, the pitchers were beginning to find ways to "trick" the batter, to try to gain the upper hand. I guess the change was inevitable.

Perhaps the pitchers felt slighted, or as was more likely, spectator interest was increased when a game of cat and mouse between pitcher and batter unfolded.

Either way, pitchers were beginning to throw with more pace. Some were learning to bend their elbows so as to put more movement on the delivery.

HENRY CHADWICK     As the pitchers began to find ways to deceive the batsmen, the batsmen became more scientific and intelligent at placing the ball where it could not be caught. The inevitable battle between pitcher and batter had begun.

JAMES WHYTE DAVIS     Of one particular match, I have nothing but uncomfortable memories. Doc and I went over to New Jersey to witness a match game between the Washington and Columbia clubs. It was a day of brooding clouds, and, as it turned out, brooding spectators.

It was a particularly ugly game with many blunders committed by both clubs. The first baseman for the Washingtons dropped five balls thrown directly to him, and the judgment of many runners was highly questionable.

None of this would have mattered, however, had not the large group of spectators become so vociferous in their shouts and calls that it caused the players to adopt a similarly aggressive attitude. Playing ungainly ball is one thing, but playing with such belligerence is quite another. The competitive fires that burned that day were out of proportion to the importance of the match. Where were the friendly feelings so vital to the spirit of the game? Why was there such envy and ill-feeling among the spectators?

Let me be clear about this. It was not the players who initiated the antagonism, it was the spectators who shouted verbal abuse at the umpire, as well as at sloppy players. The situation was only made worse when some of the players joined in the verbal assaults.

I looked at Doc during one particularly offensive verbal exchange. He returned my look but neither of us said a word. We didn't need to.

One can only hope that during the post-game dinner the antagonisms were put aside in favor of expressions of good will.

On the way home Doc said, "We've got to do something."

"It's their club, Doc."

"But it's our game."

MARIA DAVIS     We had all heard of The Brewery in the Five Points. It was the worst tenement in the Five Points, but no one I knew had ever dared go down there.

Then one day I read in the *New York Evening Post* that they would shortly be tearing it down to replace it with a modern building. According to the *Post*, those who had a desire to see "the abode of the most wretched poverty" should not miss the last opportunity to visit it. Prospective visitors were reassured that to better accommodate them, the building, which was still partially occupied, would be well-lit at night.

"Let's go see it," I said.

"A slum?"

"The Ladies Home Missionary Society of the Methodist Episcopal Church says that its destruction will be a red letter day in the annals of our city's history."

"You want to go to the Five Points at night? Are you mad?"

"It will be interesting."

"Interesting? The people down there are the people we go out of our way to avoid. They're not interesting, they're dangerous."

"Then I'll go by myself."

"No, you won't."

"Come with me. Lots of New Yorkers will be there. It will be perfectly safe."

JAMES WHYTE DAVIS     There were 20,000 people who went down to see the last days of the Old Brewery, Maria and I among them.

I guess people will turn out for anything they think interesting — a fire, a riot, a slum, or a base ball game.

---

# 40

# *The Umpire Issue*

JAMES WHYTE DAVIS     I'm not saying we never got angry or upset with decisions or talked back to umpires, but it seems with some clubs it was becoming the rule rather than the occasional occurrence. Fault finding with umpires was becoming a popular pastime.

When we began, we played with an umpire appointed by the president. Then when we started playing against other clubs, we had two umpires, one supplied by each team. More often than not, there were no problems with this arrangement, but once in a while, things got a little argumentative.

Once in a friendly match against the Eagles, Duncan Curry was our umpire; Marvin Gelston was theirs. The close game was moving along smoothly when Charlie DeBost came up to bat with Fraley Niebuhr on third base.

The pitcher for the Eagles, Andrew Bixby, was delivering the ball from the extreme end of the 12-foot-long pitcher's line which was certainly within his rights.

Since DeBost was batting right-handed, their right fielder, Charlie Place, moved in and positioned himself between the first and second bases where he was really a fifth short fielder. What the Eagles were trying to do, of course, was to get DeBost to hit the ball to the left side of the field. Ah, but DeBost was a very scientific hitter and was not about to play into their hands. He let several pitches go by that he might otherwise have swung at, waiting rather for a ball he could hit to the right side. He finally selected a pitch to his liking and swung so as to hit the ball high over first base. It landed well out of reach of Place and by the time he retrieved it, both Niebuhr and DeBost had scored.

Now the argument began. Mr. Gelston averred that the ball landed in foul territory and ordered DeBost to take his turn at bat again. Duncan said that in his opinion the ball was not only fair but that Bixby had delivered the ball from a position beyond the pitcher's line.

Duncan was a man most level in temperament and as fair and honest a man as you would ever want to meet. Although loud arguments were inconsistent with his character, this time he became outwardly agitated — not because he was trying to influence the game in favor of the Knicks, but because he honestly thought his decision was correct. I am quite sure about this, for Duncan would no sooner cheat than he would cut off his arm.

"Mr. Gelston, I assure you, sir, that I was in a very good position to see that the ball landed fairly in the field."

"And I assure you, Mr. Curry, that I was in just as good a position to see that it was not a fair ball."

"I would suggest to you, Mr. Gelston, that as you were standing to the right of the batter, and I to the left, that my angle to see down the first base line gave me an advantage over your position."

"That is an incorrect suggestion, Mr. Curry. I moved along the line as the ball was hit and therefore was in fact on the same angle as you, but closer to where the ball landed."

This went on for some time, with neither man offering or willing to change his stand. Then it got even more contentious when the argument turned to the position of the pitcher.

"I was watching Mr. Bixby closely," said Duncan, "and saw him move some inches off the end of the line."

"Are you saying that he cheated?"

"Perhaps in the excitement of the moment, he did not notice the end of the line."

"Perhaps in your excitement, you saw what you wanted to see rather than what was real."

"Mr. Gelston, I take exception to your defamatory statements."

"And I to your insinuations."

I had never seen Duncan so agitated, but I am sure it was more because his integrity was being questioned than because of his opinions about calls.

Doc and I had to step in to take charge of the situation by asking if any neutral spectators could proffer an opinion. This only made matters worse as both the situations under question were so close as to engender opinions as contrary as those of the umpires.

We eventually agreed to repeat DeBost's turn at bat which turned out not to be in our favor since he then hit a ball that put him out on a bounder. We ended up winning the game, but the altercation left a sour taste in my mouth.

At dinner, when the passions had calmed and more rational thoughts offered, Duncan suggested that in the future we solicit the services of a referee from a club not involved in the match to serve as the deciding voice when the two umpires disagreed.

For the most part, that's how we played for a time — two umpires, one referee, and 18 argumentative players.

CHARLES DEBOST   The idea of two umpires and one referee was really ridiculous. The umpires became little more than advocates for their respective sides. Every time an appeal was made you could expect one umpire to call "not out," and the other "out." So the issue went to the referee who was forced to make a decision. The result was that there might as well not have been any umpires in the first place.

DUNCAN CURRY   For the sake of the sport it was imperative that those of us who were capable of doing so took our turns as arbiters. It was considered an honor to be asked to officiate an important match and a testament to the respect in which we were held.

It wasn't always easy though and I learned early on that you couldn't let a partisan crowd intimidate you. In fact, I would say — although not the first to do so — that the most important trait of a good umpire is moral courage, for once you let the spectators see that you are fearless in discharging your duties you found that the respectable portion were with you and it is they whose opinions one should respect.

When the "roughs" got on the umpire, I learned that the best way to handle them was to treat their remarks with contemptuous silence as if they were so many yelping curs.

In one particular match where I served as umpire (for the sake of propriety I shall refrain from naming the sides although I will affirm that the Knickerbockers were not involved) several of the players were guilty of the most unsavory behavior and took to complaining about every decision. They were in effect calling into question my integrity. I took the only honorable course: I resigned. This of course ended the game for no true ball player would dare act as umpire after another had resigned under such circumstances.

Only by such acts could the decorum of the game be maintained. Despite the grumbling, I hoped I had made a point worth making.

GEORGE BLISS   Once upon a time in the land of base ball, the umpire was a revered and respected figure, above whom no one on the field stood. I recall when clubs vied with each other to engage the most respected men in the community to umpire. These deities, often top-hatted and in formal attire, sat in plush armchairs, usually along the first base some twenty feet from the home base. Too hot? Provide them with a fan. Too sunny? Provide them with an umbrella. Hungry? Provide them with sandwiches, cakes, or other victuals as they desired. Thirsty? Provide them with beer if that be their choice, or other potables as requested. The home club always provided these because authority needed to be respected.

At game's end, after three cheers were given for each side, the umpire was given three, six, or even nine.

I know these things because I once belonged to this race of men. Once, I said.

One day I was called upon to serve as umpire in a match between the Rochester Live Oaks and the Rochester Olympics. With the score tied at 16, I was called upon to render a decision on a close play at the home base. From my vantage point (I had risen and moved a few feet towards the base), it appeared to me that the runner had been cleanly put out by the catcher and I stated that loudly and unequivocally. In the old days that would have been the end of it. The runner was out. Let the game proceed.

However, the Rochester captain shouted a few epithets in my direction that I shall not repeat here, heaved the ball in the air, and he and his team walked off the field. I left the umpire's chair never to return. There was enough stress in the world those days without base ball adding to it.

JAMES WHYTE DAVIS   Oh my, oh my, what changes had we wrought?

## 41

# *The Fever Spreads*

ASHLEY HYDE   I have the distinct impression that by attempting to limit the game to those of their social class, the Knickerbockers did exactly the opposite. That is, by putting their imprimatur on the game, others wished to copy them. By doing so they felt as if they were on the Knickerbocker's level. For them the Knicks were a model of upward mobility.

And did the game ever spread fast! By 1856, new clubs were complaining that they couldn't find suitable space since all the good open grounds were taken.

In that year alone the papers reported on 53 games played between clubs in the New York area. Some clubs even added junior sides in order to develop younger players who would eventually graduate to the senior sides. Several grounds were given over completely to base ball.

I can't think of anything that demonstrated the growing popularity of the game better than this: some clubs stretched the length of the playing season to ridiculous extremes. I went to a game played so late in November and in such cold weather that I think Santa Claus might have turned back. The Atlantics, who were mostly composed of men used to working outdoors, challenged the Excelsiors, made up mostly of clerks and merchants. Why the Excelsiors agreed to the match I have no idea. Nor do I know why I decided to watch. I suppose such is the folly of the true base ball crank. Anyway, I arrived at the game after it had started and much to my amazement, there were several hundred shivering spectators already there, including, I might add, a few hearty (or foolish?) women.

The Atlantics easily won the game and as far as I know, after the Excelsiors thawed out, they never played that late in the year again.

JAMES WHYTE DAVIS   As much as we were surprised by the incredible speed at which the game had been expanding, it was nothing compared with what happened starting in 1855. We quickly went from about a dozen clubs to something like 125. Brooklyn was particularly active in forming new clubs. In fact, known for many years as the "City of Churches," it was now often referred to as the "City of Base Ball Clubs."

The big difference between these clubs and the KBBC was that they contained members from all walks of life — professional men, shopkeepers, factory and dockworkers, students.

I doubt if it was in his professional capacity as a physician, but Doc Adams took to calling it "base ball fever," and so it was.

DOC ADAMS    I was walking with Jamie one afternoon when we passed a large open lot dotted with boys all playing base ball, or at least trying to.

"Are we responsible for all of this?" I asked.

"I suppose we are, but you know what? If we hadn't done what we did, somebody else would have."

"Do you really think so?"

"It's basic. Put a ball and a boy together on an open field and you'll end up with something akin to what we now have."

"I can't image where all this will end. So many clubs, so many players. In my office some of the keen lads practice before work, during their lunchtime, and then again after work."

"Well, we've just more clubs to play, that's all."

"Just so long as they remember we're the Knicks."

"And if they don't I'm sure you'll remind them."

PETER COBES    I found all this new interest in forming base ball clubs a hindrance to the proper work of a sober man and a tremendous waste of valuable time. It was not the game itself that was the problem, but the demands on one's time that came from club membership.

I ran a small but profitable business making ladies' hats, and as we were expanding I was always looking for industrious young men who wanted to learn the business and, by so doing, make a successful life for themselves. But when a promising applicant appeared before me, one of the questions I always put before him was, "Are you a member of a base ball club?" If they said they were, I politely informed them that their services would not be needed. Club members were just too inclined to ask for time off for what they always called "important" matches. Either that or they were getting hurt on the playing field and that affected their productivity.

I took this position, not out of a meanness of spirit, but because I had seen the problems base ball had brought in the past, and because I believed it important to teach young men the values of hard work and discipline. These values would pay dividends in later life; hitting a ball with a stick wouldn't.

DOC ADAMS    There was even a song about this:

> Our merchants have to close their stores.
> Their clerks away are staying.
> Contractors too, can do no work.
> Their hands are all out playing.

JAMES WHYTE DAVIS   On some days you could pick up a newspaper and read about as many as five clubs having been formed that week.

One, the Columbias, whose members were principally merchants and clerks from New York who reside in Brooklyn's Eastern District, claimed they played their games at 5 A.M.

I'll have to take their word for that.

ASHER COLE   I never took to the game — yachting, horse racing, polo, tennis, yes. A man wishing to rise on the social ladder was well advised to choose a sport that was more appropriate for such purposes. The Astors and Vanderbilts simply didn't play base ball.

When offered the chance to join the Knickerbockers, I chose instead to join the Meadowbrook Polo Club where, along with the likes of Thomas Hitchcock Sr., and August Belmont, we first played our matches on the infield of the race track of the Mineola Fair Grounds, and then eventually on our own grounds.

Belmont was a powerful man in New York politics, and as chairman of the Democratic Committee, he was invaluable in helping me to secure my position with the mayor's office. Base ball could never have done this for me.

---

# 42

# *Club Squabbles*

LOUIS WADSWORTH   At one of our meetings, I brought up an issue that had been a source of contention for years.

"I move that for the sake of maintaining the integrity of our intraclub games, when we have fewer than 18 members present, we adopt a formal policy that allows us to use other players who may be available."

It's not as if we had never done this in the past, rather that it almost always led to bickering between those who agreed it was a good idea, and those who, for whatever reason, didn't. I thought it was time to settle the matter once and for all.

"I think it's a good idea," said Doc, "so I'll second the motion. It's always better to play with a full side whenever possible. It makes for a better game."

Duncan Curry, usually the conciliator in club squabbles, this time put forth a counter-argument. "I'm afraid I can't agree. Our club members pay dues for the right to participate. Since others don't, I don't think they should be granted the same privileges as members."

DUNCAN CURRY   Mr. Wadsworth had a way about him that often brought forth my ire.

"My dear Mr. Curry," he said in a rather patronizing tone, "don't you see that our members are best served by playing full-side matches?"

"No, Mr. Wadsworth, I most decidedly do not. We are best served by maintaining our membership standards. We are, after all, a club, not a gang."

"Thank you for clarifying that."

"If you'd rather go down to the Five Points and recruit players..."

"Sarcasm aside, even you must agree that our vaunted position as guardians of the gates of base ball propriety will survive even if we admit lesser beings into our firmament."

"You all know we have encountered problems when we have permitted those with whom we were not familiar to join us."

"And what problems might that have been? Perhaps playing without the proper caps?"

Choosing not to escalate the conflict by saying that perhaps Mr. Wadsworth himself was the problem, I said instead, "I am quite willing to agree that if 14 members are available we play the game shorthanded at seven a side and admit no outsiders. Fewer than that, we admit others."

Jamie Davis immediately seconded my motion and the debate was on. Often our motions were unanimously agreed upon, but on this issue the membership was divided between those of us wishing to protect the character of the club and those wishing to put the game above club considerations.

When the vote was finally taken, my motion backed by Davis and others, prevailed 13–11.

I then put another motion to the membership. "I move that we play all our matches to seven innings."

LOUIS WADSWORTH   We had always played our games to 21 runs—or "aces" as we once called them—and other than Duncan being obstinate and full of himself because he had just won a close vote, I could see no reason to change this.

"The game is, and has always been, decided at 21 runs. This is base ball."

"But it doesn't have to be," said Curry.

"Are you suggesting that a side could win a game by scoring only one run?"

"Precisely."

"And how is this supposed to make it a better game?"

"Twenty-one is just an arbitrary number."

"So is seven."

DUNCAN CURRY   I felt there was purity in playing the game to a set number of innings rather than a set number of runs. A three to two game was just as exciting—perhaps more so—than a 21–20 game. We had sometimes played this way anyway, and I knew there would be some support for the idea and indeed there was, but again we were divided.

"I think it's an excellent idea," said Jamie, again coming to my support. "It adds an extra dimension to the game. No matter how far behind a side might be, as long as it has outs left it will always have the potential to come back and win. I like it. I like it very much."

DOC ADAMS    I could see the value in Duncan and Jamie's position and thought it had merit, but for me the issue was the number of innings. Seven was too short. It squeezed the game too much. Base ball should be at once a leisurely activity befitting a fine summer afternoon and a balanced struggle of strategies and skills. It is a game better played without a clock, a time limit, or a run limit, but only seven innings?

"I agree on an innings count, but I would rather see nine than seven."

"Why not 21 then?" said DeBost facetiously.

"Give it breathing room."

"Twenty-one is a good breathing number."

"Except we'll all be old men before the game is finished."

"You're already an old man, Doc."

I was 42, but I suppose in sporting terms I was old. Nevertheless, the remark brought a smattering of laughter.

"But what's so magical about nine?" continued DeBost. "Why not eight or 11, or 12."

"Three outs an inning. Nine men, nine innings. There's a nice symmetry about it."

"And you think that matters?"

"I wouldn't say 'matters' exactly, but I wouldn't say it's a bad idea exactly."

"Well, if we have to change the rule at all," said Wadsworth, "I'm with Doc and the nine innings game. Definitely nine."

DUNCAN CURRY    When it came time for the vote, seven innings won. I suspect that sentiments against Wadsworth might have had something to do with it but I doubt if that was the sole cause. It must be said the nine-man-nine-inning idea wasn't very persuasive and seven innings seemed reasonable. Many of us had other pressing demands in our lives that made the idea of a shorter game more appealing. We could always play two games if time permitted which was a better alternative than cutting short a nine-inning game.

In all the years I was with the Knickerbockers, this was probably the most contentious meeting I can remember. We had always been a particularly affable group. I did not like for one moment setting myself against Doc, for he had done as much if not more than any of us in giving direction to the club and the game. I made sure to go out with him for a drink after the meeting and let him know that.

LOUIS WADSWORTH   It wasn't long after our debate over the inning limitation that I met with Van Cott of my old club, the Mutuals. He suggested they too were amenable to adopting an inning-limited game. I told him that we had just settled on a seven-inning game, but that in my opinion it was a mistake and that nine innings would make it more interesting. He didn't say much about that but shortly afterwards they set their games at nine innings.

I don't know for a fact that Doc spoke to others, but I suspect he did, because all the other important clubs in the city also went for nine.

So for a while it was our habit to play our club matches at seven innings, but nine against other clubs. For the first time that I know, the lead of the KBBC was not followed by the other clubs. Were we losing a grip on the influence we had wielded with so much authority for so long?

# 43

# *Time to Organize*

JUDGE VAN COTT   The rapid increase in the number of organized clubs argued for some sort of governing organization. On several occasions, I talked with Doc Adams and a few other Knickerbockers and urged them, as the senior club, to call the meeting. While Doc didn't exactly say "no," it was quite apparent to me that they were not especially eager. The Knicks were "settled" in their ways and rather complacent in their position as the first and most influential club. I don't think they wanted to surrender their influence which would certainly happen to some extent if they were one of many. Could there be a first among equals?

"Doc, I'm sure you'll agree it's time to organize," I gently argued.

"Actually I think it's time for tea."

So over tea we had a rather lengthy discussion about the idea.

"Only then can it become a truly national sport," I said.

"I do think some of the rules need to be looked at with an eye towards change."

"Such as?"

"Well, the fly rule for one."

"Then that's the place to do it."

"We've been experimenting you know. Played a few games that way."

When it came to proposing ideas for improving the game, Doc took second place to no one and no one in the history of the game ever did more to influence the rules than he did."Doc, it's going to happen sooner or later whether we want it or not. Someday there will be an organization, a governing body, so wouldn't it be better if the Knicks spearheaded that? Shouldn't you be the convening club?"

Doc agreed to bring it up with his membership. He was at heart a very reasonable and thoughtful man and I suspected he could and would convince his club.

DOC ADAMS    I met with officers from the Gothams and the Eagles to talk about setting up a meeting of all the clubs to go over the rules. We agreed it would be a good idea, but there were so many new clubs that the attempt to reach all of them proved daunting. We decided to put the idea aside for the time being, agreeing we would call a meeting at a later date.

JAMES WHYTE DAVIS    When the spectators began showing up we lost a few club members. Some just didn't want to be the entertainment for these big crowds; some didn't like the inevitable pressure it brought.

So popular was the game becoming, that we, like most of the other clubs, started requiring our members to attend two practice sessions per week if they wanted to play on our first nine. Some members complained, some went over to other clubs that were more lax in their operations, some quit.

Things were getting messy enough that the calling of a convention seemed wise.

---

## 44

# To Plan a Convention

DOC ADAMS    So we decided to call a convention of ballplayers having as its purpose the reviewing of all rules and revising as appropriate. It would also provide an excellent opportunity for players to socialize with other club members and to schedule matches.

JAMES WHYTE DAVIS    I moved that Adams, Grenelle, and Wadsworth be appointed a committee to arrange a convention of the various local ball clubs.

Doc was the obvious choice, Grenelle was particularly good with details, and Wadsworth volunteered.

Porter's Spirit of the Times and the Sunday Mercury carried this:

"Pursuant to the above resolution the various Base Ball Clubs of this city and vicinity are requested each to select three representatives to meet at 462

Broome street, in the city of New York, on Thursday the 22d day of January next, at half-past seven o-clock P.M."

The game of base ball was about to take a giant step — whether it was a forward step or a backward step remained to be seen.

DOC ADAMS   The idea met with general approval although a few clubs declined the invitation, citing the distance or the impossibility of returning home that night.

CHARLES DEBOST   When the call went out, the sporting press heartily endorsed the idea. One suggested that young New Yorkers should join base ball or cricket clubs and quit the "bar rooms, and other night amusements."

I thought that was taking things a little too far. Play base ball, yes; give up the bar rooms and night amusements, never.

NATHANIEL LAW   Yes, I know they were the "grand old men of the game," but the fact is, many of us saw the need modify the old Knickerbocker rules. There were just too many arguments about this, that, and the other thing. We were happy to let the Knicks call the meeting, but we had no intention of letting them dominate the revisions.

You might say it was "thank you Knicks, now let's move on."

COLONEL LEE   We had a pretty good game in the old days, and as the old philosopher said, "If it ain't broke don't fix it." Nevertheless, when Doc went to that first base ball convention, what he did was to open the door to all those other clubs to put in their two cents.

I always thought the game needed the leadership of the Knicks more than it needed ... well, the rule of the majority. It is somewhat like the military. It is run by leaders (enlightened leaders in the best of worlds), not the collective opinions of the troops.

By the time of the convention I was no longer playing, but I still cared and I still kept in touch with some of the boys.

# 45

# *The First Meeting*

DOC ADAMS   The meeting was set for a day during which *The New York Times* carried a story about the shooting of two runaway slaves in nearby Pennsylvania. This commanded the conversation of those who arrived early.

By the time the meeting began, fourteen clubs were there with three representatives each. The atmosphere was convivial and I think most everyone was eager to see just what, if anything, we could accomplish.

As president of the convening club it was my duty to start the proceedings. I called the assembled to order and then offered a short prepared speech in which I briefly outlined the development of the game to that point and then opined about the benefits that would accrue to the game, if a proper revision of the rules were to be had, and a new code established by which all of us could be governed.

I know that not all of my fellow Knickerbockers agreed with this, but I always felt that rules were not chiseled in stone but rather were there to be evaluated and modified as the demands of the game and the skills of the players changed.

The first order of business then was the electing of officers.

JOHN MOTT   There was no debate about who to elect as president. Doc had called the meeting, Doc represented the senior club, Doc was respected for his commitment to the game. So, Doc for president. Reuben Cudlip of the Gothams was elected as one vice president, and I the other. James Andrews of Excelsior was secretary. Walter Scott of Empire was assistant secretary, and E.H. Brown was treasurer.

All of this assumed that we would end up with a stable organization, something that was far from certain.

DOC ADAMS   I proposed that we select a committee charged with preparing a code of laws to which all the clubs would adhere. The motion passed unanimously. Mr. Tassie then moved that the committee be composed of twenty members.

"That's too many," countered Grenelle. "Committees of twenty do nothing but spend their time arguing. I think we'd be better off with one from each club. That's enough. Everyone's voice could be heard that way."

"I think it's too important for that," said Mr. Tassie. "Nothing's more important than the rules."

"I don't think there should be a committee at all," said John Silsby of the Continentals. "I think we should handle the rules as a committee of the whole."

"John, there are more than 40 of us here," said Grenelle. "It would be chaos."

"No, it would be democracy."

"Same thing."

After a lively debate it was decided that the Committee to Draft a Code of Laws be composed of one member from each club present and that the recommendations of this committee be submitted to the Convention as a whole for approval.

We then each met with the delegates from our own clubs in order to determine who our representative would be. This was an important step and the delegates took it seriously. Much buzzing came from the huddled delegations.

As president of the Convention, I excused myself from consideration. Louis Wadsworth immediately volunteered. I think Grenelle would have been the better choice, but neither he nor I made an issue of it and we agreed Wadsworth would represent us.

When we re-assembled, Robert Cornell put three specimens of balls on his table. The first he said weighed 6⅓ ounces; the second, 6½; the third 6¾. "I'll pass these around, gentlemen, for your inspection," he said. "See what you think. Eventually we'll have to decide on one as the official ball."

For the rest of the meeting, men were tossing these balls from one hand to another. It was a bit distracting so I asked if they wouldn't mind stopping until we adjourned.

We eventually decided on a ball that weighed between 6 and 6.25 ounces, with a circumference of not less than 10 and not more than 10.25 inches.

A motion then carried which said that each club was to pay the Treasurer $2 in order to defray incidental expenses, to which our new treasurer, Mr. Brown responded, "I must of necessity notify you that I don't take Spanish quarters." Mr. Andrews, our secretary, then read off the names of all the clubs in attendance and the delegates dug into pockets to come up with the Spanish-less dues.

As we had accomplished what we had set out to do in our first meeting, I adjourned the convention at about 9:30.

Some delegates had to leave immediately, but those who didn't remained as we partook of the best of Smith's liquid hospitality.

---

# 46

# *The Rules Committee*

LOUIS WADSWORTH    The day after our meeting, the *Spirit of the Times* wrote an article suggesting that "the gentlemen assembled last evening at Smith's Hotel were engaged in work not of that trifling importance which a casual observer might suppose. *Mens sana in corpore sano* is a maxim worthy of notice in this age, when young men are forsaking the fields and outdoor exercise for the fumes of cellars and the dissipation of the gaming table. Let us have base ball clubs organized by the spring all over the country, rivaling in their beneficent effects of the Roman and Grecian republics."

Roman and Grecian republics?

JAMES WHYTE DAVIS    I talked to Doc about proposing to the rules committee that we adopt the fly rule for all games. He wholeheartedly agreed but wasn't sure he could convince the others.

"It's not easy to get people to change once they've gotten comfortable with something," he said.

"But you will try?"

"As forcefully as I can, but you know Wadsworth is on the committee and you know how obstreperous he can be."

"Appeal to his vanity."

Doc smiled broadly. "You mean to say he has any?"

"It's been rumored. Tell him with the fly rule and his obvious base ball skills he could be the best player on the field."

"He thinks he already is."

"Tell him he'd be the best player in the country."

"He thinks he's already that, too."

"In the whole world?"

"I'll try."

DOC ADAMS    It fell to me to meet with the rules committee at Smith's Hotel. It was quickly agreed that there was no sense in starting from scratch and that we would start with the Knickerbocker rules as the basis and then discuss any alterations or additions we wished to make to those rules.

I began the discussion about changes which I knew to be less controversial than the fly rule.

"I think we need to set the distances to the bases and to the pitcher's line."

"We already have that," said Francis Pidgeon. "Forty-two paces."

"Your paces or Dickey Pearce's?"

"It all sort of evens out over time."

"That's just it. If it evens out it means it's not always the same and for the sake of the game wouldn't it be better if we all played on fields set the same distances? We all have our own fields, don't we? Measure once, set a marker in the ground and we'll be done with it. That shouldn't be too hard."

"What about all the players who don't have permanent fields?"

"Our concern should be our clubs and having a consistent sized field seems to me to be essential if we're to play matches against each other."

There seemed to be general consensus about this, but, of course, the question remained, what distance?

"I've actually looked at this rather carefully," I said. "I've been out to our field with Mr. Davis when we marked out several possibilities—all pretty close to what we normally consider to be 42 paces—and we've practiced with these variables. It appears that 30 yards is a perfect distance."

"Because it's a round number, or because it's the right distance?" asked Constant.

"Both really. Thirty yards, ninety feet sets a good distance and is pretty close to what we've been playing."

Van Cott slammed his hand down on the table as if he had just discovered the secret to living forever. "I say we trust Doc's experiments and accept 90 feet! All those in favor?"

There were ayes all around although how many were enthusiastic ayes I don't know.

"What about the pitching line?" asked Pidgeon. "If we set the bases, shouldn't we set that, too?"

"Forty-five feet," I said. "We worked that out, too."

"Don't tell me because it's exactly half of 90," said Constant.

"Is it really?" I said. "I was never good at arithmetic."

"I've spent hours checking my calculations," he said, "and I can now conclusively confirm the fact."

"I'll take your word for it."

That was indicative of the spirit of cooperation with which the meeting began. I think we all realized we were in on something important for the future of our game. Of course, as with any committee, disagreements were inevitable and it didn't take long before they began to show up.

JAMES WHYTE DAVIS    It was as inevitable as the sunrise that at some point the dimensions of the infield would be standardized. As far as I'm concerned, when the committee accepted our suggestions it really marked the beginning of the game as a national institution. Everybody playing on the same size field meant that the results from one game could be equitably compared with the results from another, and this included statistics like batting results.

DOC ADAMS    On to the more difficult issues.

"Our club has endorsed the idea of games being played to seven innings rather than 21 aces and I suggest we do the same."

Once again, this proved to be contentious just as it had when we debated it within our own membership. Oddly quiet on the subject was Wadsworth, who had argued so strongly for a nine-inning version. I was to find out later, why.

Van Cott led the charge for nine, but in the end the committee agreed with me that seven made the most sense and so voted.

Then came the big debate.

Base ball had come under attack in some quarters as not being as manly a game as cricket and football. I did not hold with this view, but nevertheless felt that it was time to do away with the bounder rule and replace it with the fly rule.

"I feel very strongly," I said, "that in order to make the game more manly and scientific, I propose that the ball must be caught in the air or the player is not out."

This was not a new idea, as it had been considered before and we even played that way sometimes, but I knew there would be objections. At one point, there was even a proposal that we play with six outs per inning with a ball caught on the bounce counting for one out, and one caught on the fly, for two. Obviously, this idea never got very far.

"I don't agree at all," said Dr. Charles Cooper of the Baltics, "not at all. As a physician I can assure you that real damage can be done to the hand that way. Real damage."

"With all due respect Dr. Cooper," I said, "as a physician I can assure you that real damage can be done by running into a tree, too."

"I have seen fingers broken by trying to catch balls in the air that could just as easily have been caught on the bound."

"No doubt you have. There is some risk to any sporting event, wouldn't you agree?"

"But we need not add any that is unnecessary."

"I suggest, Gentlemen, it makes for a much better game, a more difficult game to be sure, but a more challenging one is welcome."

"I think Doc's right," said Van Cott. "Doc Adams, that is. Too many people see base ball as a child's game. The fly rule would go a long way toward changing that."

"It'll make the game too much like cricket, and the last thing we want to do is align ourselves with the British game," said the Putnams' Thomas Jackson.

"Why is that the last thing?" I said. "Let's not reject a rule that will make it a better game just because of nationalistic considerations. That's simply foolish. Anyway, what any Englishman can do, we can do better."

That was one of a score of similar speeches I made on behalf of the fly game, but it came to naught. When the motion was finally put to the vote, the fly rule lost 9 to 4 with one abstention.

LOUIS WADSWORTH   I could clearly see during the rest of the meeting that Doc was still smarting from losing that vote. Maybe even sulking a little. No, definitely sulking. I'll admit to a modest degree of satisfaction at his pique.

We made a few other small changes to the rules like forbidding fielders to stop the ball with their caps and re-confirming that a full side is nine men. Since cricketers used a nearly flat bat we said that the bat needed to be round and no more than 2½ inches in diameter, which was pretty much what everybody used anyway.

I remember reading about a championship game played up in Massachusetts using their rules that lasted a day and a half with 101 innings necessary to provide a winner. Needless to say, this sort of thing would have killed our game. Nevertheless, 7 innings was just too damn short and I vowed to do something about it.

# 47

# *Recommendations*

JAMES WHYTE DAVIS     We met in March in order to consider the recommendations of the Base Ball Convention Committee. Doc read the rules they had agreed to and after a brief discussion, I moved that "we accept the report of the committee, and that we also accept the rules of the game as adopted by that body only so far as to govern this club in playing matches with other clubs." The motion carried.

I was extremely disappointed that the fly game was not a part of the recommendations, but we played some of our club games that way and we vowed to keep arguing for its implementation.

LOUIS WADSWORTH     When the delegates met to approve the rules committee's recommendations, I proposed that we adopt the nine inning standard, with five necessary for a complete game should a match have to be shortened because of bad weather or the like. After the obligatory argument, the motion carried. Our game was nine innings as it should be.

Maybe as a result of our convention, the Massachusetts players called their own convention up in Dedham. They, too, adopted their own rules for the Massachusetts game including the use of 4 foot high stakes for bases, soaking runners with the ball, 100 runs necessary to win, and sides of 10 to 14 men. No wonder their game died out!

CHARLES DEBOST     Wadsworth always got his way. Either that or he sulked off. The thing is, he could be witty, charming, and when the spirit moved him, even inspirational. Give him the stage and he lit up like a lantern. He was also the most avid reader I knew. He'd always have a book with him, usually the newest one out.

"What are you reading?" I asked him once on the ferry.

"It's called *Moby-Dick*."

"What's it about?"

"A whale against a man."

"Who wins?"

"Well I'm only up to the sixth inning, but I'm betting on the whale."

"Any spicy sections."

"Not a woman in sight unless the whale's a woman, but I doubt it."

Despite his charm, he could be the most argumentative son-of-a-bitch in the world.

After one meeting in which he argued with just about everything that was said by anyone, I lost my patience and said, "Louis, for christsake, will you please stop arguing with everybody about everything."

"The only time I ever argue about anything is when I'm right."

"Why do you even want to belong to this club if you think everybody's so damn wrong?"

"Actually, it's mostly you I find wrong."

"Yeah, and why is that?"

"Well, for one..."

At that point, Doc called an end to the confrontation. The next day, Wadsworth resigned from the club. A few weeks later he joined the Gothams. And they were welcome to him and he to them.

JAMES WHYTE DAVIS   Wadsworth ended up resigning and then rejoining the club three times. The thing is, despite his contentious attitude, he was a fine ball player.

---

## 48

# *Playing the Fly Rule*

DOC ADAMS   I was absolutely convinced that our initial insistence on under-handed pitching, bound outs, and a clearly identified foul territory added greatly to the adaptability of the game to men of varying ages and abilities and thus its growing popularity. Despite the Convention's refusal to go along, I was also absolutely convinced that the time had come to abandon the bound rule for the fly game, and so, in many of our club games, that is exactly what we did.

ASHLEY HYDE   Watching the Knicks play a fly game one afternoon, I was taken by the quickness in which the game was completed — under two hours. It was a taut, controlled match completely devoid of the boyish rule of the catch on the bound. The superiority of the game was so obvious, the play so much more brilliant, even with some wild throwing and otherwise muffin-like play, that it seemed inconceivable to me that the other clubs wouldn't adopt the same rule.

Yet as much as I admired the Knickerbockers for their adoption of the fly rule, I have to admit that they were no longer among the best nines in the city. It was generally believed, and I suspect rightfully so, that other clubs took it easy on the Knickerbockers as soon as they had a substantial lead. Of course as more people came to watch the games, more emphasis was placed on winning — except to the Knicks.

SAM KISSAM   When, for a while, I played with the Excelsiors, we too started playing intra-club games using the fly rule, and I know that some of the other clubs did the same. While nobody wanted to admit it, the fact is that most of the weaker clubs argued for the bound rule, and most of the stronger clubs favored the fly rule. The one major exception was the Knicks, whose support for the fly rule was unflagging due in large measure to the efforts of Doc and Jamie.

# 49

# *On Maintaining Standards*

ASHLEY HYDE   The biggest change happening to base ball in the mid-'50s was not the creation of so many new clubs, but rather the makeup of those clubs. The idea that membership would come solely from men who earned annual or at least monthly salaries was giving way to the clubs that were made up of men who were working for hourly wages.

Some clubs didn't change much if at all. The Knickerbockers, for example, remained one of the great bastions of the old system.

Other clubs though, particularly the newer ones, were much less exclusive in their membership roles. A lot of this had to do with the great waves of immigrants who found a game that required a minimal financial investment to play. Joining a base ball club was one way of assimilating into the culture of their adopted country.

Associating the clubs with the various trades also increased the spectator interest. What German butcher wouldn't pull for the Atlantics over the Knickerbockers?

JAMES WHYTE DAVIS   One might think that with more clubs, the competition for membership would become more extreme, but the reality was that many players looked up to us as the premier club and so aspired to membership with us. But our standards remained in place and we admitted only those of the highest character.

THOMAS VAN COTT   The Knicks may have talked about character as the *sine qua non* for membership, but they were like the rest of us: character is good, but character with playing ability is better.

DUNCAN CURRY   Once we interviewed a man who showed great enthusiasm for joining our club. He had practiced with us a few times as a guest and evinced considerable skills in hitting a base ball. During his interview he talked loudly about having recently gone down to Norris's livery stable to watch a boxing match between two women.
   "Two women, really?' I asked him.
   "Stripped nude above the waist, they were."
   "That's incredible."
   "You could come next time," he said. "They're having another one next month. Women with great big breasts."
   I probably don't need to add that he never became a Knick.

---

## 50

# *First Nine Matches*

WALTER HESS   I was secretary of the Atlantic Base Ball Club when I approached the Knickerbockers to see about arranging a two-game series. Playing that august club would have brought instant recognition to our organization, but I was turned down — rudely, I might add. They said they only played against clubs using the Elysian Fields. What they meant was that they only wanted to play clubs who could afford the fees for the Fields.
   I went back to our officers. "We don't need the Knickerbockers," I said. "We've plenty of teams to play." And so we did. Where once they were the high and the mighty club, they were now just one of many.

JAMES WHYTE DAVIS   Since we were receiving challenges from clubs all over the city, we simply decided not to travel to Brooklyn or anywhere else for that matter. We could find all the games we needed right on our own fields.

Naturally this decision drew criticism from some other clubs and from the press, who opined that by restricting our games we were shying away from the competitive aspect of the game in favor of a strictly social one. In a way they were right, but the criticism came with the tacit assumption that as the senior club we should exert more of a leadership role.

Sometimes, rather than choosing sides we would set up games according to some distinction like the bachelors against the married members.

I remember one particularly spirited match, and a close one at that, when the bachelors won 23 to 21.

The dinner following the game was full of good-natured jousting.

"Marriage is a great institution."

"I know, but I'm not ready for an institution yet."

"Nothing in life is as good as a marriage of true minds between a man and a woman."

"The only good marriage I can think of would be between a blind man and a deaf woman."

We did engage in a few interesting matches against other clubs though. I can recall two against the Empire Club, both of which we intended to be seven innings, but in the first game, after more than three hours and eight innings, we had to stop due to darkness at 21 runs each. The other game we won in seven innings by a score of 21 to 12.

We played a few games against the Eagles on our field. We also played a seven inning game against the Gothams. Of this game, one paper wrote: "Yesterday the cars of the Second and Third Avenue Railroads were crowded for hours with the lovers of ball playing, going out to witness the long-talked-of match between the Gotham and Knickerbocker Clubs. We think the interest to see this game was greater than any other match ever played."

One or two of our members suggested that we play games up at the Red House in Harlem, the home of the Gothams. The Red House was a very active place, not only for base ball, but also for cricket, pigeon shooting, and trotting with specific days allocated to each of these activities. It was also easier to get to than the Elysian Fields as the Second Avenue cars passed there every ten minutes to the delightful fragrance of the country — six miles for ten cents.

SAM KISSAM   We did play a game against the Gothams at the Red House. Now a major issue within the club was who was going to play as our "first nine" or, as it was sometimes called, our "picked nine." It was up to the club president to choose the side, but he usually consulted the other officers first. This way he could avoid some of the criticism that might have come his way for his choices by saying, "Well, it's what our officers thought best."

The problem was that the officers were among our best players. So should they appoint themselves for the good of the club, or choose others for the sake of good will? Well, after discussing the issue, we concluded that we should select whomever we thought would produce the best results on the field.

I remember at one point Alex Drummond was president; I was vice president; Jamie Davis was secretary; George Brown, treasurer. Doc Adams, Charles DeBost, and William Eager were the club's directors.

Certainly DeBost, Doc, and Davis had to be on the field. We considered others, too, but of course, not everybody was available on the scheduled date. Both Brotherson and Niebuhr, for example, were to be out of town, their wives apparently believing that family vacations should take precedence over ball games. As a result, we added Eager, Stevens, Conover, and me.

This meant that four of the nine were officers, not the best situation for club morale, but it was what we came up with. A few complaints came our way, but none too vociferously.

William Ladd agreed to be our umpire; John Hone for the Gothams. After several requests, we finally managed to get a referee from the Eagles: Mr. Armfield.

A large crowd turned out for the match, which we ended up losing.

Several comments from members let us know we hadn't selected the best nine. Perhaps.

We did, though, win the return match with pretty much the same side. I'll let the *Spirit of the Times* tell the story.

> These two Clubs, who rank foremost in the beautiful and healthy game of Base Ball, met on Thursday at the Elysian Fields to play the return match. The Gothams having won the first match this season, fully expected to beat their opponents on this occasion, but they were sadly disappointed. The Knickerbockers came upon the ground with a determination to maintain the first rank among their Ball Clubs, and they won the match handsomely, by superior playing, beating their opponents by 15 runs.
>
> There were about 1000 spectators present, including many ladies, who manifested the utmost excitement, but kept admirable order."

For the record, here's the results of the matches we played against the Gothams.

|  | Knickerbocker Runs | Gotham Runs |
| --- | --- | --- |
| Elysian Fields, July 14, 1853 | 21 | 12 |
| Red House, Oct. 14, 1853 | 21 | 14 |
| Red House, June 30, 1854 | 16 | 21 |
| Elysian Fields, Sept. 20, 1854 | 24 | 13 |
| Red House, Oct. 26, 1854 | 12 | 12 |
| Elysian Fields, Sept. 13, 1855 | 22 | 7 |
| Totals: | 128 | 100 |

That season of '55 we also played two matches against the Eagles. We won the first in double quick time as we scored 11 runs in the first inning, 1 in the second, 6 in the third, and 9 in the fourth. We also won our second match against them. As in most of our first nine matches that year, William Talman was our pitcher and DeBost our excellent man behind.

We had little doubt that when we played our first nine, whoever they may be, we were still a top club.

---

# 51

# *Challenges*

JAMES WHYTE DAVIS    There was no such thing as a "schedule" of games between clubs. If one club wanted a match game against another, they would issue a written challenge. We received scores of challenges, and had we wanted, could have played match games almost every week during the summer. We didn't, however. For example, during the summer of 1857 we accepted challenges from only the Eagles and the Empires.

As far as I remember, we didn't challenge anyone. They challenged us. We were, after all, the Knickerbockers and had a position to maintain.

That season, Brooklyn's Atlantics showed themselves to be the best nine in the area by winning seven of their nine matches against other clubs. The only matches they didn't win were a tie with the Continentals and a late season loss to the Gothams. In this match, the New York club jumped out to a 20–6 lead after six innings only to witness the Brooklynites chop eleven runs off the lead in the seventh and eighth. The Gotham club put away the match with four more in the ninth to win 24–19.

The next day *The New York Clipper* was effusive in its praise of the teams, especially the fielding of the Gotham's Wadsworth, singling him out for a most brilliant catch.

They beat the Eckfords to take the best of a three-game match and claim what some were calling the championship of 1857.

It seems that where once a club was accorded high honors for the character of its membership, now it was shifting to winning the most games.

EDWARD SALTZMAN    I had played a few years for the Gothams before I moved up to Boston to work as a watch case maker. I soon joined the newly created Tri-Mountains Club. After some cajoling I was able to convince the members of the value of the Knickerbocker rules. The president of the club, B.F. Gould, even took a trip down to New York to meet with Doc Adams and watch games played by their rules. These were, of course, quite different from the rules of the Massachusetts game that they knew, but in short order they understood the advantages of the game and that's how we played.

Naturally, at first we had no other clubs to play because they were all playing the Massachusetts game, but eventually we convinced the Portland Club of Maine to join us for a match on Boston Common. A lot of spectators saw us play this beautiful version of the game and in no time the New York Knickerbocker game spread throughout New England.

# 52

# *Women at the Games*

MARIA DAVIS   I was certainly not alone among the women who frequently attended the better base ball contests. They were most pleasurable occasions—sunshine, green grass, athletic grace. The clubs liked to have us there. They claimed our presence helped keep the men's behavior within acceptable boundaries. Perhaps so, for it is generally recognized that women control their tempers better than men. I'm not talking so much about the players, but the spectators. Few would deem to be so rowdy with women present.

I went to the games, though, for no other reason than I enjoyed them. Isn't that enough?

I remember cutting an article out of the *Clipper* once and keeping it around in case Jamie ever forgot. "Let our American ladies visit the ballfield and the most rough or rude among the spectators would acknowledge their magic sway, thus conferring a double favor upon the sports they countenance, because the members of our sporting organizations are usually gentlemen and always lovers of order, but they can no more control the bystanders than they can any other passengers along a public highway. When ladies are present, we are proud to be able to say that no class of our population can be found so debased as not to change their external behavior immediately, and that change is always for the better."

Some clubs went so far as to erect special seats for us while the male spectators sat on the ground. Some put up tents or parasols to protect us from the summer's sun. The Eckfords come to mind in this regard. We were always welcomed and treated with respect. Maybe they should have paid us.

Often, too, we were invited to year-ending balls and dinners. These were splendid affairs where we would wear our best dresses and dance with the men in their formal attire.

So you see, no true history of base ball can be told without considering our influence. The same, I suppose, could be said about many things.

Going to base ball games with Jamie was one thing, but when Susan B. Anthony presided over the two-day National Women's Rights Convention in the Mozart Hall, I told him I was going to the convention and not his game. I think he understood, but I can't say the same thing for everyone else since the meeting was disrupted by rowdy men.

Afterwards I said to Jamie, "We support men's games, why can't you do the same for our activities?"

He laughed. "Who won?"

"We women."

COLONEL LEE   Once in the early days, I sometimes escorted a young lady of considerable grace and refinement. Mattilda was her name.

In return, she asked me to join her in her area of passion — music, particularly the Philharmonic organization. They were raising funds to build a new music hall.

We went together and met Duncan Curry and several other club members.

The concert featured the American premiere of Beethoven's *Ninth Symphony*. More than 400 instrumental and vocal performers filled the stage. It was a wonderful, but odd performance as the singers were kept at bay until the end of the piece.

Unfortunately the high ticket prices of $2.00 and an uptown war rally that same night kept the hoped-for audience rather small and the plans for the new hall had to be put on hold.

Mattilda asked me to talk to the Knickerbockers about making donations to the fund. I did on an individual basis and some members made contributions, but I couldn't make it a club issue as it would have been outside the bounds of our concerns.

# 53

# *Papers Taking Note*

HENRY CHADWICK   I came to realize that it would be the game's advantage, as well as to mine as its chronicler if I could develop more interesting ways to convey the details of the game — that is, something more than the score and a comment on the level of play. I tried various methods, eventually adopting from the practices of cricket reporting the ideas of box scores and batting averages.

At the same time, the terms used to describe the game were in transition. Both "aces" as well as "runs" were in use, although, of course, "runs" was becoming more popular. For balls hit out into the field, both "outfield" and "long field," were replacing "garden," and the "inning" was coming to replace the cricket-inspired "innings" to refer to a side's turn at batting.

As with everything regarding the game, these changes didn't just happen one day as if by decree, but rather they edged their way into the sport little by little until they became the accepted standards.

JAMES WHYTE DAVIS   Since newspaper writers often worked for more than one paper, it was not unusual to find essentially the same coverage of a game in several papers. Sometimes these were short reports and at other times, when the reporter considered it an "important" game, a longer story might follow. They also occasionally published stories about our meetings, end-of-season banquets, or other social events. Letters, too, from spectators were sometimes published, as were announcements put out by clubs. They also held mail for some clubs and players.

No one was as important to the reporting of base ball as Henry Chadwick. He was by far the most prolific writer as well as the game's most passionate supporter. A typical Chadwick article would include a description of the weather, the crowd, and a recap of each inning. I think it would not be an exaggeration to say that much of the mushrooming popularity of the game was due directly to the coverage it received from Mr. Chadwick. I don't know whether to thank him or damn him for that.

DOC ADAMS   Chadwick always promoted "his" game. By that I mean he had an idea of how the game should be played, organized, and administered, and had no qualms about letting his readers know what they were.

He frequently and loudly defended the game as a "scientific" and "manly" sport worthy of being labeled a "national sport for America." For this praise I gladly applauded his efforts.

But he could be a cantankerous stubborn mule whenever criticism of his ideas arose. He believed in the game of base ball as he saw it, and woe be to those who disagreed.

For example, at one point he argued that the ball we were using was too lively and thus affecting the game in ways that weren't scientific. Challenge him on that and you were likely to be subjected to a lengthy screed informing you of the errors of your ways.

Another time he campaigned for the addition of a tenth player, a right shortstop. He let anyone who disagreed know that there was no possible reasonable objection to the idea, implying that only a fool would disagree. Years later he called the Players League a "terrorist organization" because of the tactics he claimed they used to "persuade" players to join.

He could be equally lavish in doling out approbation or castigation.

He was a real promoter of change in the game, both by his writings and by his active membership on various rules committees, particularly when he campaigned for a more balanced game between pitching and batting.

He may have written about yachting, cricket, billiards, and even chess, but it was base ball that was his passion. He could also play the piano, write songs and drama criticism. He was quite an accomplished man.

HENRY CHADWICK   I suppose my most important mission was to fight the inroads being made into the game by those either unwilling or unable to play good scientific base ball, intelligent base ball, and play it with character and integrity. I give the Knickerbockers full credit. That character was slowly eroding away certainly wasn't their fault.

WILLIAM TUCKER   I took to spending many an afternoon at Richardson's & McLeod's English Restaurant down on Maiden Lane where they kept a book recording the results of all the base ball games played in the New York area. As Henry Chadwick continued to develop the art of recording the activities of a base ball game, I became more and more interested in the statistics.

It was a wonderful club-like place where I pored over the game results with a concentration I seldom demonstrated in other ways. There was a little corner table where I would sit, eat, and read. Sometimes some of the Knicks would come in and join me — Jamie Davis in particular.

"So who's the best batsman?" he might say.

"Well, Gelston of the Eagles has scored the most runs."

"In total, or per game?"

"Total. I'll have to do some figuring on the per game question."

---

## 54

# The Changing Game

WILLIAM TUCKER   I'll tell you one thing that was changing, and fast — pitching.

We were playing a club game one afternoon and I came to bat against

Richard Stevens. He had been a member of our club for a while, having been influenced by watching our games at the Elysian Fields that were owned by his family. As I came to bat, I surveyed the positions of the fielders and judged that I would try to put the first ball to me between the first base and the second. It was a particularly important moment in a very close game. The bases were full and there were already two hands out. So it was my chance to be the hero of the day.

I settled into my batting position, looked towards Stevens, acknowledging that I was ready. Stevens took a deep breath and delivered the ball with such pace and I, having already made up my mind that I would swing, lunged badly at the ball and hit it weakly in the air right back to Stevens. Game over.

I suppose I might have said something about the deceptive delivery but I didn't want to appear to be a sore loser. Nobody else said anything either as far as I know, but I'm sure everybody was thinking the same thing.

The very nature of the game, the balance of the game, was changing.

DOC ADAMS   When we played the Atlantics I took particular note of their little chubby shortstop. Dickey Pearce looked like a fire plug but he displayed great skill and cunning.

"Look at that," Charlie DeBost said to me. "He plays the position like it's supposed to be played."

"How would you know?"

"I know good playing when I see it."

"And you've never seen it, is that it?"

"Not until today."

The next time we played an intra-club game, I was a captain so I put Charlie at the shortstop position. Well, as good an athlete as he was, he made a complete hash of several balls hit his way.

"You give a whole new dimension to the position, Charlie," I said.

"I give up," he said, laughing. "Put me back at catcher."

Little Dickey Pearce was one heck of a player though, I'll grant you that, and a devil to play against — as cunning and devious as the rules would allow. At shortstop he moved all over the place so that you could never be sure where he was going to be next. At bat, he was even trickier.

TOM DEVYR   One day I was playing at shortstop for the Mutuals when Pearce came to bat for the Atlantics. What he proceeded to do was to take a little half swing and push the ball in the general direction of third base, but he hit it such a way as to cause the ball to bounce first in fair territory and then into foul territory. He was on first base long before I could track down the ball. This was similar to the technique that a lot of cricketers used.

The rules of the day specified that any ball was considered fair if it first struck in fair territory. In time this became known as the "fair-foul" hit. When well executed by someone as skillful with the bat as Dickey Pearce, it became a valuable strategy because since foul balls did not count as strikes, there was no penalty for attempting the "fair-foul."

It wasn't long before others began using this trick maneuver as well as the technique (again like in cricket) of just blocking the ball down in front of them and then running like the dickens to first base. Remember, the catcher was then stationed well behind the batter and wasn't to move closer until years later when the catcher's mask made its appearance. Anyway, these two plays—the "fair-foul" hit and what came to be called the bunt—were, depending on your views, either brilliant batting ploys or examples of poor sportsmanship.

CHARLES DEBOST    I hated these little baby hits. I hated Dickey Pearce for starting them, and I hated everyone who thought they were funny.

DOC ADAMS    "Bad Dickey Pearce," as he was sometimes called, often brought derisive cheers, cat calls, hisses, and groans when he attempted the "dark art" of fair-foul hitting or when he blocked little bunt hits in front of home base. As frustrating as it was trying to play against the likes of Pearce and Tommy Barlow, who employed the same tricks with his little miniature bat, I had to give them grudging admiration. After all, the object of the batsman is to reach base. No, to me the real baby hits were those which gave easy chances for fly catches.

DICKEY PEARCE    Look, if I had been able to hit the ball consistently to the long field, don't you think I would have done that? But that's one of the great things about base ball. You don't have to be big and strong, you just have to be good. I know not everybody liked the way I played and some of them let me know it.

"Little Dickey, is that as far as you can hit a ball?"

"When you grow up will you be able to hit the ball as far as the pitcher?"

"My little boy can hit the ball farther than that—and he's four!"

At least they knew who I was.

HENRY CHADWICK    Many spectators and some players thought fair-foul hits and bunts demeaned the game. I believed to the contrary that they required the most skillful handling of the bat, and a quick eye and a steady nerve besides. Base ball is, after all, a test of character. Nevertheless, the fair-foul caused difficulties for the umpires in determining if a ball first hit fair or foul.

A number of years later, a proposal was put forward to make any ball foul that didn't reach the pitcher's line. When this didn't get anywhere, it was finally decided to eliminate the fair-foul altogether.

Like all games, base ball changed as the players became better, and no mistake about it, the players were getting better—a lot better.

# 55

# *New Equipment*

DOC ADAMS   One of the reasons for the spiraling number of base ball clubs was simply that it was a reasonably inexpensive recreation. All that was absolutely necessary was a ball, a bat and canvas bases which the clubs provided. Of course, the players had to provide for their own uniforms but these weren't too difficult to make at home by any wife with the inclination and the time.

The only other item that many players desired, although not absolutely necessary, was a good pair of spiked shoes. We frequently wore buckskin shoes with one, two, or even three long spikes in the sole to prevent slipping while running. They were particularly effective on wet or dewy grass, especially when attempting a quick stop. To get these made you had to go to a blacksmith who fashioned the spikes, and then take the spikes and shoes to a cobbler who set the spikes into the heels.

At first we had no problems with these because runners generally stayed on their feet as they approached the bases. But then, some players like Wadsworth began diving head first when they thought it offered them some advantage although I'm not exactly sure what that was. Anyway, a few players then tried diving to the base feet first. That's when the problems began.

Fraley was playing at third one day when Johnny Boyle went into him leading with his feet. His right foot, complete with spike, went into Fraley's shin, ripping his pant leg and causing considerable bleeding. He wasn't able to play again for several months.

A few years later after other players were severely lacerated by these spikes, a call went out to outlaw them. When so many players balked at giving up their spikes, Henry Chadwick suggested that players use four short spikes rather than the more common, three long spikes, which is what a lot of players did.

SAM KISSAM   In a game amongst our members one afternoon, Charlie DeBost, never the swiftest of runners under the best of circumstances, chose a pitch to his liking and sent it swiftly to the right field. With head down, he chugged around the first base and headed directly for the second. What happened next varies depending on who you ask. From my vantage point waiting to bat next, it appeared that he tripped and made a headfirst and awkward lunge landing just short of the base but his momentum, such as it was, carried him right to the base where he stopped safely.

"Enjoy the trip, Your Grace?" I called out to him.

"Trip my ass, that's what we call a beautifully executed slide," he said getting up and dusting himself off.

"Are you pretending you did that on purpose?"

"Ain't no pretense, Sonny. Watch next time and maybe you could learn something."

"Like how to break your neck?"

"Does it look broken?"

"No more so than usual."

It wasn't customary to slide into a base, but when it did occasionally happen, it was usually headfirst.

It was some days before we learned that he had broken a finger on that slide.

CHARLES DEBOST   I broke that finger moving some furniture at home, and I'm sticking to that story. Besides, had I broken it sliding as little Sammy claimed, I never would have admitted it anyway.

For a while there was talk of allowing runners to overrun the bases without the possibility of being put out, but it never came to anything other than for allowing it at the first base.

HENRY CHADWICK   Most of the balls in use at that time were being commercially made by either Harvey Ross or John Van Horn. Ross was a member of the Atlantics and a sail-maker by trade. He made the balls in his home. Van Horn, a member of the Union Club, made his in a little boot and shoe store on Second Avenue.

The clubs bought these balls and then protected them as if they were the Holy Grail.

Bats too were highly prized instruments of play. They were generally the same diameter from end to end, or if they had any taper it was very slight. The reason for this was simply that the more tapered bats broke more easily and had to be replaced at considerable cost. At some point, the players started painting the bats with rings in the club's colors.

# 56

# *The Pennant*

JAMES WHYTE DAVIS   In the middle of August '55 we specified new uniforms of blue woolen pants, white flannel shirt with a narrow blue braid, a mohair cap, and a belt of patent leather. With the exception of changes to the cap over the years, this remained our "official" KBC uniform.

Then in honor of our tenth anniversary as a club we created a Knickerbocker banner — a triangular pennant with a "K" in a circle on red and blue panels.

This pennant flew on a tall pole at the Elysian Fields during every game.

Ah, that pennant! What a great symbol it was! The image of this pennant is indelibly etched in my mind and always brings back memories of those wonderfully idyllic days. Maybe some days weren't so perfect after all, but memory is selective and that's how I choose to remember them.

Ten years on and the game had grown so much. I remember wondering where the next ten years would take us.

DUNCAN CURRY   I was in my eleventh season of continuous activity with the club and had given it my best years as a player and I think some good service as an officer. I had seen the sport grow from a disorganized series of bat and ball games to a carefully codified national game played by thousands of men and boys. It was time to say goodbye to the club, but I knew I would always at heart be a base ball player.

DOC ADAMS   Duncan deserves a lot of credit for his contributions to the game. His leadership, especially in the early years, was critical. Without his moderating voice, I'm not sure we would have made it. Would the club have survived those first critical seasons if Alick, or Jamie, or the O'Briens, or any number of other members (me included) had held sway without his mitigating presence? I doubt it. He certainly wasn't our best player, but in our early years maybe he was our best leader.

I think I told him how much he meant to the club, but perhaps I didn't.

FRALEY NIEBUHR   At times Duncan might have appeared a bit humorless but he was so damned level headed that people just naturally listened to him — well, most of the time, anyway. He was a real avuncular figure, a stickler for protocol and decorum, and he always ran a tight meeting. To Duncan there was a time to play and a time to conduct business, and never the twain should meet.

WALTER AVERY   I couldn't resist watching when a steam fire-engine from Cincinnati challenged a local company using the old hand-engine No. 42. I gathered some of the old Knicks to watch. There was still something that roused our blood about a good old fire fighters competition.

How pleased we were when old No. 42 beat the Ohio machine! The men on 42, though, were so exhausted by the experience that they could barely breathe, move, or talk when it was over.

"Hey, Duncan," I said. "Let's take them to a big dinner."

We took up a collection from our members and did just that. Old loyalties die hard.

That was the last time I saw Duncan because like so many of us from the early days, he was moving on to other things in his life. For most of us, base ball playing was a phase of our life eventually to be replaced by other things.

# 57

# *An Impediment?*

DOC ADAMS     There was considerable speculation in base ball circles as to whether the Knickerbockers were an impediment to progress. Had we become a useless appendage on the corpus of the game? Or were we the last bastions of integrity?

Perhaps the reality was that we were like parents who, once we raise our offspring with all the good manners, intentions, and morals of which we are capable, take pride as we watch that which we brought to life assume its own unique life. Like all parents, we may not approve of everything it does, but we rest assured that it was brought up with the proper values and that in the end those will out.

Base ball is a part of us and we of it. We are justifiably proud of it and the part that we played and while it may occasionally err and perhaps stray from the straight path, we will love it all the more.

Base ball was moving away from the game we had created, but we remained proud parents still.

GEORGE GRUM     Yeah, the old Knickerbockers waved the flag of sportsmanship like they invented the idea. They presented themselves as the saintly guardians of probity. I for one found it tedious and pretentious, and I know I wasn't the only one.

"Bow down, boys, here come the Knickerbockers."

"Kiss their rings and then kiss something else."

They gave the impression that they, and only they, understood the higher values of the game and the rest of us were to look to them for guidance when floundering in our sinful ways. They were the starched-shirt elite; we the work boot rabble. We who worked with our hands were unworthy to mix with those who worked sitting on their behinds, or who didn't work at all.

What were they afraid of? Despite their protestations to the contrary, they were afraid of losing to us. They thought of it as the humiliation of the royalty by the plebeians. "What, m' Lord, play a game against the rabble? What if we lost? We'd be the laughing stock."

So mostly they remained on the royal grounds playing amongst themselves and holding lofty banquets where they told each other just how much better they were than the rest of us and drank away the evening oblivious to what was happening in the sport.

It looked to me like the high and mighty Knickerbocker Base Ball Club for Gentlemen of Means had become a detriment to the game. They were like over-protective parents who would broach no criticism of their precocious nipper nor would they allow any anyone else to discipline him. They would set the rules for behavior. They would chastise when necessary, praise when appropriate.

They were, in a word, "jealous" of anyone who aspired to influence or gain the confidence of their offspring. They soaked up praise that came their way but avoided situations that might suggest fault.

The Knickerbockers had become an anachronism, an artifact that belonged in another time. I have no doubt they were good men, but in base ball terms they had become little more than an afterthought.

As far as I'm concerned, they surrendered their leadership position when they no longer had the full respect of the other clubs.

JAMES WHYTE DAVIS   We were beginning to read more and more in the press about how we had become a dinosaur on the way to extinction because somehow we were an impediment to progress. As far as I was concerned, this was a complete mis-reading of the situation. If what was meant was that we were an impediment to the degradation of the game, I might have agreed. That we were guilty of maintaining standards I will admit to.

On the one hand we were criticized for wanting to control the development of the game, and on the other we were criticized for abdicating the mantle of leadership we had worn for years.

I fully understand that some players on other clubs resented us, but isn't it always the case that those with principles are maligned by those without?

THOMAS TASSIE   I can't tell you how many times we challenged the Knickerbockers, only to be rebuffed. After a while we just gave up. To tell the truth, though, had we played them it wouldn't have been much of a contest.

Our club, the Atlantics, had a trophy case full of inscribed game balls, those being the prizes for winning and winning is what we did best. After each match it was the custom that the losing captain would present the game ball to the winning captain accompanied by a short speech praising the winners, which would then be followed by the losing captain saying a few words praising the losers. Then it was on to a tavern, restaurant, or hotel for the after-game festivities.

I dare say the Knicks didn't need a very big trophy case.

HENRY CHADWICK   It's true the Knickerbockers were still held in high esteem for the leadership they had brought and as upholders of the traditional values the game prized, but their skills as players were no longer up to the level played by many other clubs.

CHARLES DEBOST   One day thousands of unemployed men — the papers said 15,000 — gathered in Tompkins Square Park and paraded all the way down to Wall Street.

"The next thing you know, they'll be forming their own base ball club," said Norm Welling.

"The Unemployed Base Ball Club of Manhattan."

"And then they'll want to play us as they all do, and when we refuse, we'll be called snobs."

"We are snobs."

"Oh yeah, I forgot."

ASHLEY HYDE   One aspect of the game that was quite noticeable is that first generation immigrants were absent from most club rosters. There were probably a number of reasons for this. Most worked in labor intensive jobs which limited the available time for activities such as base ball and most, not having played it in their youth, knew little of it. There were a few Irishman in a couple of the clubs and maybe a few Germans. This was not necessarily so in the prisons, as I read someplace that half of those arrested that year were Irish. But then almost 30 percent of the policemen were born in Ireland, too.

JAMES WHYTE DAVIS   I can honestly say that we made no effort to keep immigrants out of our club, but in all honesty, few if any were interested in us.

Incidentally, the O'Brien boys were both very successful brokers who went on to become quite wealthy.

PADRIG RYAN   Join the big bugs at the Knickerbockers? You must be joking. To become a member you had to be proposed by another member and they always proposed their own. Even if you were proposed by a member, you would have to be voted on by the Membership Committee. Who was the Membership Committee? The Board of Directors, the biggest of the big bugs. To each his own. That's the way it worked and that's the way it always will work.

DOC ADAMS   At the end of the '57 season, the presidents of the four most senior clubs— Knickerbocker, Gotham, Eagle, and Empire — put out a call for another convention to be held the following March. It was at that meeting that the next giant step in the progress of our great game was made.

GEORGE GRUM   Like it or not, the Mighty Knicks were about to put up their child for adoption.

# PART SEVEN: THE GREAT BASE BALL MATCH 1858

## 58

# *The Second Convention*

WILLIAM GRENELLE   At a January club meeting Jamie Davis read a letter from the Empire Club requesting that we call another meeting of all regular organized base ball clubs.

After meeting with the presidents of the other older clubs, Doc reported back on the inevitability of the meeting and although we weren't thrilled with the prospects, we realized that if we didn't organize it, another club would. Doc and I were to be our delegates.

DOC ADAMS   We held our second convention on the 10th of March at the Gothams' headquarters. According to the best estimates, there were something like 50 organized clubs now in the area. Twenty-two clubs responded to our announcement, each sending two delegates.

As president of the previous convention, it was my duty to call the proceedings to order. I said that the goal of the meeting was to create a fixed and permanent plan of representation, and, if necessary, to amend the playing rules. Immediately after that, I nominated Anthony Bixby of the Eagle Club as interim president. He had been a delegate to the earlier convention and was familiar with most of the men present. My nomination was accepted without debate. We then chose Sears of the Baltics and Voorhis of the Empires as secretaries and re-elected Brown of the Metropolitans as treasurer.

As a number of new clubs were present, we needed to review their credentials in order to assure that each was regularly organized. These included the Columbia, Stuyvesant, St. Nicholas, and a few others.

The Committee on Credentials that we had previously set up recommended that six clubs that had sent delegates appeared to belong to a class commonly known as junior clubs, and therefore should not be admitted to the convention. I immediately averred that I thought all the delegates should be admitted.

ALFRED KEITH   I represented the Ashland Club, one of those under question.

"Boys of eighteen, who make up most of our club, are as qualified as

171

anyone else to contribute to any discussion about the rules of the game," I said. "What does age have to do with it? We play the game as well as anyone else."

"I sincerely doubt that," said Mr. Wadsworth of the Gothams.

"We are prepared to put that to the test any time you deem fit, Mr. Wadsworth."

"We're not about to play a junior club."

"Perhaps for good reason."

This ludicrous situation came about as a result of an elitist clique of men with plenty of money but little energy and spirit who wished to make the game a means of showing off their fancy dress and wealth. They were more concerned with their own money, status, and fitness than the health of the game they claimed to encourage.

Just look at who their leaders were — doctors, lawyers, and a judge!

LOUIS WADSWORTH   I argued that any club composed chiefly of mere boys should, if they so desire, form their own association and leave ours to the senior clubs. Let them play by all means, encourage them to play even, but the rules should be determined by those of us with maturity and experience.

Eventually a compromise motion was proposed saying that junior clubs would have a seat but without voting privileges. I voted against this wishy-washy compromise but it carried nevertheless, so we were forced to put up with the children.

DOC ADAMS   A committee was established to draft a constitution and by-laws for the government of the convention. They were to report back at the next meeting. Another committee was to review and revise as necessary the playing rules. I was on that committee.

Mr. Brown, the treasurer, moved to assess each member three dollars for expenses of the convention. Interestingly enough, this was approved without discussion. I think that shows how important the delegates thought this convention.

We agreed to meet again in two weeks hence.

GEORGE GRUM   The Knickerbocker influence was obvious here as they wished to continue to exert their smothering influence over the game.

DOC ADAMS   We came under some criticism in the press and from individuals after the convention voted against admitting the junior clubs. What does not seem to have been recognized is that I, as a representative of the Knickerbockers, argued assiduously in favor of the admission of all teams.

We were not the ones blocking the progress of the game. Quite the contrary.

# 59

# *The National Association*

WILLIAM GRENELLE    I was a member of the five-man committee charged with drafting a constitution and by-laws. After the reading of this document, it was agreed that we would formally organize as the National Association of Base Ball Players, with Judge Van Cott as our first president, Doctor Jones and Thomas Dakin as vice presidents.

That being said, in reality Doc Adams, who was president of the Convention the year before, was actually our first president.

JAMES WHYTE DAVIS    No one from our club was represented in leadership of the Association, nor did we desire representation. We were happy to continue playing our games for the recreational and social advantages they provided. Let the other clubs move forward in their competitive zeal if that is what they desired. Van Cott was a very capable man and I had no doubt that he would provide strong and effective leadership.

Still, Doc was chairman of the Rules Committee and that was certainly the most important and influential part of the organization anyway.

JUDGE VAN COTT    It was my responsibility to oversee the organization as it tried to bring stability and cohesion to the disparate goals, constitutions, and rules of the various clubs.

JAMES MURTHA    A National Association? The hell it was. It was anything but national. Look, by the time they anointed themselves as the governing potentates of the game there were already clubs in cities from Buffalo to New Orleans and scores of cities in between. I know because I played for the New Orleans Pelicans.

It wasn't even regional. It should have been called the New York Association of Spoiled Base Ball Clubs. It was nothing more than a small group of dictators who were trying to mold the group into an elitist organization along the lines of the New York Yacht Club. Truth is, a few individuals wormed their way into power and tried to mould men and things to suit their views. They weren't even really representative of all the local clubs because they didn't fully admit anyone under the age of 21.

JUDGE VAN COTT    I might point out that although we started with clubs exclusively from the area, within a few years we had 60 members representing clubs from all over — New Haven, Detroit, Philadelphia, Baltimore, Washington, D.C.

In order to join the Association a club needed to be organized with at least 18 members. So that we could evaluate the character and standing of the club, an application was required at least thirty days before our annual convention. A two-thirds affirmative vote from the membership was required for a club to be admitted, at which time the club was entitled to send two delegates to the convention, each with one vote.

Many regulations we were to pass had to do with players' activities. So as to prohibit clubs from recruiting players for some important match game, we included a provision stating that in order to play in a match game, a player had to have been a member of that club for at least 30 days, and if he did change clubs, the club he was leaving had to declare that he owed no money to that club and that all his club affairs were in order.

Of course, no member of any club was to receive compensation of any kind.

JAMES WHYTE DAVIS    As a consequence of this new Association, the administration of the game was passing from the players themselves to a central organization. Where once we had set the game rules and club regulations amongst ourselves, now that right was ceded to a central organization and the club officers were forced to serve as the "police" of a host of rules and regulations, assuring that everyone adhered to the same damn ones.

As clubs began competing in more match games with other member clubs, they became more particular about their "first nines," and began accepting non-playing members (or seldom-playing members), all of whom were dues-paying, however. So now, since all the clubs were voting members, the game was being administered in part by those who didn't even play base ball!

As an indication of the direction in which the game of base ball was heading, the Association set up by-laws to deal with serious issues. A nine-man Judiciary Committee was created to handle disputes and violations. Charges against either player or club were submitted in writing to the Association's secretary, who was then to pass them on to the Committee to make a decision within ten days. However, should there be an appeal, this would be taken up by the convention delegates at the end of the year.

Can you imagine the likes of Cartwright, Duncan, and Wheaton foreseeing the need for a Judiciary Committee? To do what? Gentlemen settle their own disputes in a ... gentlemanly manner. To establish a judiciary process presupposes serious violations. And, of course, the framers of the Association were prescient. They would, in time, need a committee and more.

Included in the Association laws were prohibitions against players, umpires, and scorers from betting on contests. Now why in the world would anyone put that in their laws if they didn't think it either had already happened or would soon happen?

Perhaps more importantly though, with the advent of the Association something new had entered the game — politics.

HENRY CHADWICK   Without any doubt, the creation of the National Association was a crucial event in the long history of base ball. It was at once the end of one stage in its development and the beginning of another. An organization which began as a local entity quickly became a national one, setting the rules of the game, determining eligibility, and overseeing its development, eventually leading to organized base ball as we came to know it. It also, for all practical purposes, ended the Knickerbockers' authority as its chief arbiter and rule-maker. They had done so much to shepherd the game to that point that, in hindsight, it's a shame more acknowledgment wasn't given to them.

60

## *Another Rules Committee*

DOC ADAMS   I met with the members of the rules committee and upon their recommendation assumed the leadership of that group. The committee was made up of nine members representing not only the older clubs — the Knickerbockers, Atlantics, Putnams, Eagles, Baltics, Excelsiors, and Continentals, but it also had representatives from two of the newer clubs — William Brower from the Stuyvesants and Sam Clark from the St. Nicholas Club.

So any criticism that the Knickerbockers were shoving our rules down the throats of the other clubs was simply wrong. Yes, I came to our meeting with written suggestions for rules changes, but they were discussed at length before being put to the vote.

The first thing we did was to look at the playing rules of all the clubs and found very little variation. We agreed that they would be the basis from which we would then proceed to make any revisions we thought valuable.

We clarified a few things: The pitcher's line was 12 feet long, the center of which was marked by a fixed iron plate. Home base was place entirely in fair ground. The batsmen were to stand behind a six foot line crossing home base.

The committee put forth no arguments against these distances. Some of my other suggestions, however, I had to argue for.

Once again I brought forth the idea of the fly rule and made arguments for it similar to those I had previously proposed.

"Doc, we've been all through this," said Tassie of the Atlantics. "It's not practical, that's all."

"But do you agree it's a good idea?"

"Good or bad, our clubs are not going to accept it, that's all that matters."

"Well, we for one would," said Leggett, the Excelsior catcher. "We already play our games with the Knicks that way."

"Maybe, but when you play us you're going to have to play without it."

Tassie threw up his hands. "And it turns young players away from the game."

The debate continued but it was obvious that once again I would lose the argument.

Most of the press agreed that the fly rule made for a better game, often lauding the fly catch with words like, "He caught the ball in superb style, having judged the flight of the ball beautifully."

"All right," I said, "...for now. Let's look at some of the other rules. Now what slows the game down more than anything else?"

"Your batting?" said Phillip Weeks.

"Well, besides that?"

"Your base running?"

"Leaving me out of it."

"Batsmen waiting all day for a pitch to their liking."

"Exactly."

Thomas Dakin of the Putnams feigned sleep as he said: "Ever see Bixby at the bat? Last summer I watched him take 14 balls before deigning to swing. Erosion is faster. No wonder so many clubs want to keep the bounder rule. Why take the chance that he might bat again? Hey, maybe we should add a two-bounder rule just for him."

Tassie turned to me. "What are you suggesting, Doc?"

"That the umpire deems if a batsman doesn't swing at a pitch that he should, it will be considered that he did and missed. In cricket if the batsman doesn't swing at a good ball and it knocks the bails off behind him, then he is out. For us there is no penalty for letting good pitches go by and that just adds time without any action."

This was not a new idea that suddenly sprang into my head but rather something that some of us had considered from time to time.

"To strike or not to strike, that is the question. Whether 'tis nobler in the mind to swing at a ball properly delivered or to ponder the nature of reality..."

"Thank you, Mr. Tassie."

"Don't mention it."

"Do you really think that's going to solve anything? Don't you think there's already enough pressure on the umpires as it is without having to decide on every pitch whether the striker should have swung or not?"

"Not on every delivery."

"What, every other delivery? Every third delivery? Fourth?"

"At the umpire's discretion."

"His discretion? You must be joking."

"Not at all. I propose a rule that gives the umpire the discretion to warn a player who is not swinging at perfectly good pitches by calling a strike.

"You mean any time he feels like it?"

"I think we have to give our umpires the credit they deserve. They're all reasonable men. Let them decide."

"What's the result? So they're given a strike. So what?"

"Well, after they're given so many warnings, if they still don't swing they're declared out. It will keep the game moving along."

"How many warnings?"

"I was thinking two. Then on the third they're out."

Considerable discussion ensued on how many warnings would be proper, with the arguments ranging from one to four. There was general agreement though, that the idea had merit. I suggested that if it didn't work out, we could always change it.

This was something of a compromise because the umpire was required to warn the player before calling the first strike. After three strikes were called, the batter was bound to make his run to first base if the last called strike was not caught by the catcher on the fly or first bound.

"While we're talking about the umpires," I said, "the use of two with a referee making the final call is not working. The umpires have become little more than litigants for their side. I suggest we go back to one umpire who has the authority to make all calls."

Everyone, even the argumentative Mr. Tassie, thought this a good idea.

ASHLEY HYDE  As a result of the decision to allow the umpire to call strikes as he saw fit and thus penalize the batter, but no penalties for the pitcher if he didn't consistently throw the ball where the batsman could hit it, the pitchers began to throw harder but wilder. So this didn't end up quickening the pace of a game very much if at all.

Although they returned to one umpire, the reality remained that he still made few calls until and unless he was appealed to. So when a player was dissatisfied he would call out "judgment" or similar to cricket, "how's that," at which time the umpire rendered a decision. Other than that or to call out foul balls, they kept their mouths shut.

DOC ADAMS  Before we finished we had sifted through many of the playing rules and made a few recommendations. These included adding a three-foot boundary line allowing the pitcher to take a short run before delivering the ball just so long as he didn't overstep the line, and adding a declaration that it was the duty of the challenging team to provide the game ball.

WILLIAM GRENELLE    When we reassembled to hear the results of the recommendations of the Rules Committee, Doc presented their report in such a controlled and reasonable manner that the Committee's report was quickly accepted.

Say what you will about Doc, but he worked tirelessly on behalf of the game and was undoubtedly the single most influential figure with regard to formulating the rules which became the standards of the modern game.

# 61

# A Symbol

ASHLEY HYDE    The three biggest events in the city during 1858: Construction began on St. Patty's Cathedral, a Nantucket Quaker named R.H. Macy gave up whaling and opened his store here on 14th Street, and the Great Match of '58 was played. I was interested primarily in the last.

JUDGE VAN COTT    It was at an Association meeting when Dr. Jones stood, declared he was speaking on behalf of all the Brooklyn clubs, and laid down the challenge:

"We, the Brooklyn clubs of the National Association of Base Ball Players, hereby challenge the esteemed clubs of New York to a series of base ball matches, each side being composed of the finest players from their respective clubs. The games will decide whether Brooklyn or New York fields the best clubs. We propose a three-game series to be played this summer, the location and details of which to be worked out by this Association."

ASHLEY HYDE    Brooklyn and New York were rivals in almost everything. They competed economically for shipping and manufacturing businesses, and now in base ball. If ever a natural rivalry existed, this was it.

They were, however, very different areas and not as they later became, one city. The area known as Brooklyn was made up of two cities on the East River waterfront, across from New York City: the City of Brooklyn and the City of Williamsburgh. Beyond them was a series of villages including Bedford, Greenpoint, and Bushwick.

New York was one teeming city then stretching as far north as cross streets in the mid-forties. Above that it was mostly farmland.

When I read that Brooklyn and New York were going to play a series of base ball games, all I could think was, "perfect."

JUDGE VAN COTT     At first the New York clubs were a little chary about the idea. After all, New York was the birthplace of the game and the home of the oldest, most esteemed clubs. The Brooklyn clubs had a large number of working class members, had not played the game for as long, and certainly were not recognized in the same way as the New York clubs.

Had there been an honorable way out, I think the New York clubs would have taken it, but as the challenge was made known to the public, the feeling was that it would be better to go through with it.

An "All New York Nine" against an "All Brooklyn Nine" certainly would bring attention to the game.

# 62

# *Laying Plans*

JUDGE VAN COTT     The first thought was that we would play one game in Brooklyn and then one in New York, with the third to be...? Therein lay the problem. We could play four games but that allowed for the possibility of a 2–2 split and that didn't sound like the best solution. Then too, many of us felt that three games were about all that could be expected to hold the interest of the spectators and players.

"Simple," said Louis Wadsworth. "We'll have to find a neutral field."

"And just where might that be?" asked Dr. Jones. "The moon? Every other field worth playing on belongs to one club or another. I suppose we could play in Boston but that would defeat the purpose, wouldn't it?"

"Nah, the game's too difficult for the Bostons to figure out. Don't they still play the soaking rule?"

"Some do."

"I was thinking of Long Island — maybe someplace like the Fashion Race Course."

"The fastest team around the track wins, is that it?"

"It could be set up for base ball. Why not? It's big enough to get in lots of spectators. We want that, right? It's on neutral ground. The railroad runs right to it."

"It's a mud hole."

"We can fill it in. We can make it work."

Further discussion about the Fashion Course led to the conclusion that it could hold up to perhaps 50,000 spectators with enough seating for maybe 10,000. Provisions for ladies could be handled by setting up a large awning with seating for several thousand.

When we agreed that the idea had merit, a couple of us took the train out there to meet with the proprietor.

"One important point, though," I told him. We can't have intoxicating liquors sold on the course."

"Judge, this is a race course, not a church."

"And we're playing base ball, not racing horses."

"Perhaps just beer then. Look, I got four kids to feed."

"Perhaps."

"And one other thing," I said. "No gambling on or about the grounds."

"You're joking, right?"

"We simply can't have it."

"Then I'm afraid we can't strike a deal, Gentlemen. Anyone coming to a race course is expecting to gamble. That's why they're here in the first place — to gamble on the damn horses. Hell, they were probably betting on the chariot races in old Rome. The sport of kings is about gambling."

"We're not horses or chariots."

"Won't stop them. Don't be naive, Judge. People will bet on just about anything if they get the chance. They'll bet on horses, prize fighters, rowers, the weather. You can't stop them. Thank goodness, too, or we'd be out of business."

JAMES WHYTE DAVIS   Talk of gambling on base ball made my blood boil. The point is that only when the game takes on great importance does gambling enter into it. Should a game be that important?

JUDGE VAN COTT   Since we had to insist on no gambling, it appeared that the Fashion Course was out of the consideration.

"Let's look at it from another perspective," said the proprietor. "Let's talk about the gate split."

"The gate?"

"You're going to need considerable money to turn this place into a base ball field, and I ain't no charity, so if the gate split is sufficient, I'll agree that we won't officially allow gambling. I hope you're not foolish enough, though, to think that if men want to place bets with each other, they won't, for as sure as we're smelling horse dung now, they will."

"Then you'll agree not to have your gambling windows open."

"Let's talk about the gate split first."

"Gate? What gate? We don't charge admission to base ball games. Who'd pay that?"

"You kept telling me how popular your sport is."

"Yes, but..."

"No 'buts.' You want the Fashion Course, you come up with the money, and that means either a gate split that makes it worthwhile to me, or you fine gentlemen dig deep into your silk pockets."

"We've never talked about things like 'gate receipts.' Even if we wanted to, I wouldn't even know how much we could charge."

"Well, I'd suggest if you want a hoity-toity crowd, you charge a hoity fee. Maybe 75 cents."

"Seventy-five cents? I mean we'd never ... why, that's probably more than half a day's wages for most working men."

"But not for a judge."

"That's hardly the point."

"Maybe you should look someplace else for a playground. I don't think we're what you're looking for. Now if you'll excuse me, I've got horses that want lunch. Lunch that I got to buy and pay for."

So it was back to New York and the Planning Committee.

We looked at other possible locations, and while all had something to recommend them, none could match what the Fashion Course had to offer. So while the idea of charging admission was unappealing, it seemed more and more like something we'd have to accept.

After giving thought to what it would take to turn the course into a reasonable base ball playing field (it was in pretty poor shape if truth be told), we came up with the idea of charging 50 cents admission. If we attracted enough spectators we would be all right. But could we? It would be, if you'll pardon the expression, a huge gamble.

We went back to the Fashion Course and after more negotiations, finally agreed on a deal.

That we could charge any admission was possible only because the race course was completely enclosed. That way we could control the entrance of spectators.

JAMES WHYTE DAVIS   There it was— the first admission charges for a base ball match. For better or worse, the game took a step — albeit a tiny one — towards becoming a commercial enterprise.

JUDGE VAN COTT   We all agreed that if we were successful in attracting large enough crowds, we would use the money to cover the costs of putting the Fashion Course in proper order for the games, and then if we had money left over we would donate it to New York area fire department's funds for widows and orphans. So you see, the admission charge made the matches charity events.

The biggest concern, however, was whether or not there were enough cranks willing to part with 50 cents for the privilege of watching other men play a game. There was a considerable faction of our membership that thought not.

JAMES WHYTE DAVIS   We could call our matches anything we wanted, and although there was no thought whatsoever of the players getting any money from the games, we were really seeing the first hints of the looming professional game. Pandora's Box had been opened and once opened, the lid was thrown away forever.

ASHLEY HYDE   As soon as the press made the announcement, I knew that regardless of what else might be happening on the days of the matches, I would have to be there. Just the thought of the finest players of the day competing against each other was enough to get juices flowing; then to add that it would be New York against Brooklyn just made it that much more enticing. Newspaper coverage was so heavy that I was worried that I might not be able to get into the Course, so I vowed to get there early.

The papers said that the Brooklyn Nine would be composed of players from the Atlantic, Excelsior, Putnam, and Eckford clubs; the New York Nine, of players from the Gotham, Eagle, Empire, Harlem, Union, and Knickerbocker clubs. Some people argued that the Knicks, who played their games on the other side of the river, were actually a New Jersey club, but as far as I was concerned, that was just heresy.

I wondered who would represent the Knicks, however, as with all us Manhattanese cranks, I would be there to cheer for the New York Nine regardless.

JUDGE VAN COTT   The task of arranging the details of the game was placed in the hands of our Management Committee, and a difficult task it was. Some clubs were more diligent than others in putting forth names for consideration. Naturally this was contentious as some players who thought they should have been selected weren't and a few clubs thought they should have had more representatives. Making the selection more difficult was the simple fact that since all the men under consideration held jobs, not all were available on potential dates. So we came up with a list long enough to include alternates.

In the meantime, we nervously worked on putting the Fashion Course in order for the games. I say "nervously" because we weren't at all certain that we would attract enough spectators to cover our costs, much less make the charitable donations we had promised.

Preferring to err on the safe side, we made arrangements with the Flushing Railroad to be prepared to run special cars out to the Course if necessary. We did the same with the stage company and plans were made for the steamer,

*Iolas*, to depart the Fulton Market slip connecting at Hunter's Point with the railroad.

Again, hoping for the best, we asked each club to furnish ten members, giving us a special force of more than 200 to attend to guests and to preserve order. They were to be issued special badges for the occasion and were to be under the immediate charge and direction of the sheriff of the county.

In the stands normally occupied by the Course judges, we arranged seating for the mayors and common councilmen of New York and Brooklyn along with other specially invited guests. An appropriate place was reserved for any who might wish to remain in their vehicles.

We eventually adjusted the gate charges so that there was a more nominal charge of ten cents for entrance to the grounds, with additional fees of 20 cents for each one-horse carriage, and 40 cents for each two-horse vehicle.

We had lots of volunteers help get the playing field ready.

The first game was scheduled for 2 o'clock on the 13th of July.

Given the fact that this had never been done before, we thought we were about as prepared as we could be.

---

## 63

# *To Play or Not*

JAMES WHYTE DAVIS   We had a long discussion about whether or not to participate in the "Great Match." I must say I, myself, was conflicted. On the one hand we were members of the Association and had an obligation to support its activities. On the other hand, we were the Knickerbockers, and the thought was expressed that perhaps we should stand apart from such stunts.

In the end, largely due to the prodding of Doc, we agreed to participate.

But who should represent us? Who among us deserved to be part of an "All New York Nine?" Even the act of considering this was a radical departure from our club's essence. We weren't used to taking into account such thing as "good," "better," and "best."

So who were our best players? Well, Doc for one was still an excellent fielder at short stop or second, a good scientific batsman, and certainly our most influential member, so I nominated him.

"I appreciate the thought, Jamie," he said, "but I'm 44. I think we should leave this to the young bucks."

Someone threw my name into the ring. I was flattered but while I was a good player, I knew I wasn't among the best. I was then 32. I didn't know if that counted as a "young buck" or not but I'm sure I was nominated for my years of service to the club, not my batting.

Louis Wadsworth certainly would have qualified as one of the best, but he had bolted to the Gothams.

We discussed Harry Wright, too, who wasn't there for the meeting. He could catch, pitch, or play the field with the best of them and he was young, too. I think 23. But as he was new to the club he was not yet really known by many of us and we wanted to send someone who had been with the club for a while and who would represent what we stood for.

For us, there really was only one choice. A man who was one of the best at his position, a true gentleman, and a longtime member of the club. We unanimously nominated Charlie DeBost as our sole representative. Later, when they needed more, we added Wright.

CHARLES DEBOST    It was nice to be nominated and yes, I was honored, but there was also a lot of pressure and I'll have to admit to some nervousness. I was to be the Knickerbocker player and that meant ... not making a damn fool of myself.

## 64

# *The Day Approaches*

ASHLEY HYDE    As the date for the first game approached, almost everyone I knew felt Brooklyn would be the victors. The *New York Clipper* even came out with a statement that the odds were 100 to 75 in favor of Brooklyn, and the *Brooklyn Eagle* claimed odds of 15 to 20 were on offer but found no takers.

JAMES WHYTE DAVIS    The very fact that the press was posting odds meant that gamblers were taking an interest. It turned my stomach.

HORACE DODGE    Anybody who didn't think there'd be gambling on the games was either plumb crazy or a complete coot. We've always had the gambling urge and always will. Hell, the Puritans were probably laying bets on when they would sight land — 6 to 1 on Thursday. The Colonies — and I mean all of them — had lotteries to raise money. How do you think places like Harvard, Yale and Columbia got built? By some geniuses? Nope, by us gamblers playing the lotteries.

Prize fighting always had gambling but horse racing has always been the home of those of us who like to take our chances with chance. Hell, the first race course in America was built on Long Island and goes way back to the 17th century sometime. I know these sorts of things.

Of course, there has always been a lot of cheating going on in horse racing. Sometimes the odds and payouts were faked. Sometimes the bookmakers themselves owned the horses so they could make races come out the way they wanted. There were ringers that pretended to be another horse but were really slower or faster than the horse they were supposed to be.

One year they put on a great match race between the fastest horse in the north, Eclipse, and the southern challenger, Henry. The *Evening Post* said that 20,000 spectators showed up and wagered a million dollars. By the way, Eclipse won.

Base ball was better. It took 18 men to play, not one fixed horse.

Anyway, why in the dickens were the base ball men going on about gambling on the game? Didn't they put on their big show on a race course? Of course there was going to be gambling. Why the hell not?

The Fashion Course I knew well. The track was very wide and a half mile around. All around it had a brick wall, maybe six feet high. The entrance was real ornamental and fancy and inside the fenced-in area on a beautiful green lawn was the Colton Mansion where they held important events and meetings. It was a real nice place if you want to know.

DOC ADAMS   A few days before the scheduled first game, Jamie and I rode the train out to the race course to take a look at the preparations. They had laid out the ball field on the infield of the course but the entire area had been stripped of the last blade of grass. So what they had was a lumpy dirt surface that didn't look very good for ground balls, and even worse for trying to catch the ball on the bound.

We had taken a ball with us which we threw around on the ground to get a test.

"This isn't going to be easy," Jamie said after taking a thrown ball on the right shin. They should have mowed and rolled it."

"Try a couple of bounders," I said.

I threw a couple of balls into the air so that they would come down near where he was standing. Although he managed to corral a few, the bounces were erratic at best.

"I've got an idea," I said. "Let's do away with the bounder rule."

"You're preaching to the choir, Doc."

"Maybe if enough people see these games, I'll be able to press my point."

"You think there will be lots of people here?"

"That's the rumor."

## 65

# The First Fashion Course Game

ASHLEY HYDE    The day dawned bright but as the morning wore on, clouds began rolling in. I feared the worst. Nevertheless, neither Mother Nature nor my reportorial duties could have prevented me from heading out to Long Island. I took the special train to the Fashion Course with a lot of others who apparently reported in sick that day. I'm not sure how the commerce of the city was operating. Maybe it wasn't.

When I arrived at the Fashion Course, I found every street in the area jammed with carriages, both private and public. There were wagons, too. Even people riding milk carts. With all the energy, rushing, and bustle, you might have thought we were back in Manhattan.

I bought an admission ticket for 10 cents, but before going in I watched the clubs arrive in all their splendor. The crowds parted as first the Excelsior Club drove up in a magnificent stage drawn by fourteen beautifully caparisoned gray horses topped with feathers in their head gear. All cheered as the formally attired members stepped out with big smiles and waves. Within minutes I heard the sound of an approaching band. Everyone turned to look as the band drew near followed by a magnificent eight-horse team pulling the carriage of the Jersey City Eagle Club. Next came the Empire Club with two stages each drawn by six horses. Each club's arrival brought forth cheers from the crowds.

As wonderful as the spectacle was, I thought it prudent to go inside so as to get a good viewing point.

Inside I could see the course was ringed with omnibuses adorned with the colorful banners and flags of all the clubs.

There were thousands of us there when at about noon the skies opened up with a torrential downpour.

When a man came out and announced through a megaphone that the game had been canceled you could feel the collective disappointment. The man said he didn't know when the game would be rescheduled but that we should check the newspapers.

I headed back to the city understanding that whatever ailed so many men would strike again soon.

The first thing the next morning I read that the game would be played the following Tuesday, July 20th. I had hoped for a delay of only a day or two, but a week was better than a month.

That Tuesday was a beautiful July base ball day.

JAMES WHYTE DAVIS   Having decided to eschew the coach party, Doc and I took the train. When we got to the Fashion Course we noticed several three-card monte games had been set up to fleece the gullible. Of course, the dealers had placed their confederates in the crowd. When these men were allowed to win their bets, the naïve spectator was induced to try his luck. Well, actually "luck" wouldn't be the right word here since the games were fixed.

"Who's putting on these matches," I asked Doc, "the Association or P.T. Barnum?"

We watched a burly man quickly run out of "luck" and lose $30.

"I hereby inform you," he said to the dealer as he produced a police badge, "that games of this sort are illegal in this county."

With that the dealer handed the officer his $30 and moved on, presumably to set up business again around the corner.

I hated to see this kind of carnival but there was no question about attracting spectators. As we later learned, some 7,800 paid the admission fee. How many others were there as invited guests, or club members, it's hard to know, but I would imagine that easily 10,000 people were there that day.

ASHLEY HYDE   I secured a good seat near the first base. By the time the game was ready to begin, the grandstands were crammed with people and hundreds of carriages were parked so as to offer their occupants the opportunity to watch the game in comfort. Many had brought picnic lunches and beverages. Scores of people sat on the racetrack's infield grass.

Out in the Ladies' Stand, the players' wives, sweethearts, daughters, and sisters sat protected from the summer's sun. Altogether there had to be 400 or 500 ladies all dressed in their finest. The men, too, were dressed well in suits and ties, and almost all wore hats.

Given so many people, I suppose it was a good thing that only lager-bier and water were the beverages to be had on the grounds.

Now certainly most of the gathering was made up of respectable citizens. I, however, managed to sit next to one who wasn't. I suppose I should have suspected something when he slid close to me and asked if I thought that was Smith warming up on the far side of the field. "Smith? Smith? Oh, you mean Charles Smith of the Atlantics." I said. "I don't think he's playing, though."

"You sure? Look closely. That sure looks like Charles Smith to me. It surely does. Charles Smith as I ever seen him."

I shaded my eyes with my hand and looked to where he was pointing. "No, I do believe that's Frank Pidgeon. Yep, that's Frank for sure."

When I turned back he was gone. I looked around and saw him running through the crowd faster than Dicky Pearce going to first base after one of his little chop hits. Before I realized what had happened, I saw a man rush over to

him and grab him by the arm and pry my wallet loose from his hand. I immediately went up to them.

"That's my wallet," I said.

"Take better care of it next time, will you."

He handed me my wallet and turned back to his catch. "Now be a good
lad and give me your name or I'll have to beat it out of you."

"William Jackson," said the knuck.

Because I was later asked to press charges, I found out that the man doing
the catching was a Brooklyn detective named Van Wagner, who for the afternoon, managed to catch and arrest three such knucks. Jackson turned out to
be one of a long list of aliases used by Squib Dixon, a dodgy Englishman with
a long record.

Slightly shaken, but not deterred, I returned to my seat just as the game
was about to begin.

ASHLEY HYDE   The New York Nine took to the field first and I immediately
checked to see who was playing. Sure enough, DeBost was at catcher and Harry
Wright in the middle field. So the Knickerbockers had two very good representatives. The Gothams also had two: Wadsworth at first, and Thomas Van
Cott, the judge's brother, pitching. The Eagles had Bixby at third and Gelston
at shortstop; the Empires, Hoyt in left, Benson in right. At second was Pinkney
from Morrisania (later known as the Bronx), which wasn't exactly a New York
club, but I don't suppose that mattered. Brown from the New York Metropolitan Club was the umpire.

The Brooklyn Nine was a strong team with Frank Pidgeon pitching and
Dicky Pearce, who some would hail as the greatest shortstop ever, at his favored
position. They were expected to win so it wasn't a surprise when they scored
three runs in their first time batting. With every hit and fine play in the field,
the crowd let out loud cheers and shouts of encouragement. It was truly an
exciting event.

DeBost was, as usual, solid behind. Those six balls that managed to get
by him I dare say couldn't have been stopped by anybody else. In the long fields,
no one made better catches on the fly than Wright. Although I thought
Wadsworth a traitor, I have to admit he was as fine a fielder at first as one was
likely to find.

By the end of the third inning, the score stood at 7 runs for Brooklyn and
3 runs for New York. It looked as if the odds makers were right and although
all the New York cranks continued to cheer at every good turn of play, I must
say our spirits were drooping. Then in the fourth innings, our fortunes turned
as Brooklyn went out without scoring, thanks to some good catches on the
bound. When the New Yorks scored four runs in their fourth inning, the game
was tied and our high spirits returned.

By the end of the eighth innings, the score stood at Brooklyn, 18 runs, and New York, 22. Nothing changed in Brooklyn's ninth inning which gave the game to New York.

Despite the score, several of the Brooklyn boys insisted that New York take their final turn at bat, which they did to the mighty cheer of the crowd. New York went out for no runs so the result stood as it had at the end of the eighth.

A robust cheer was sent skyward by the spectators as the defeated side led the victors off the field for the final time. If anyone in the crowd felt that they hadn't gotten their money's worth, I certainly didn't hear them.

I saw Doc, Jamie, and some of the other Knickerbocker lads go out on the field and congratulate DeBost and Wright. DeBost had scored two runs. While Wright was excellent in the field with several good catches, he had not particularly distinguished himself at the bat. In fact he was responsible for four hands out and was the only player on the New York side not to have scored a run. His time was to come, though.

To me the entire day was a splendid example of the game at its very best, but I suppose if I had to choose just one high point it would have been the long home strike of John Holder, the second baseman from the Excelsiors. He got hold of a delivery to his liking and sent it clear out in the middle garden where Harry Wright simply had no chance to catch the ball either on the fly or on the bound, nor to retrieve it in time to send it back, allowing Holder to race all the way to the home base accompanied by the most lusty applause.

In great spirits and with the sounds of the enthusiastic crowd still circling, I, along with about 9000 others, simultaneously began making tracks for the same exit gate made even more difficult by the three miles of carriages also maneuvering through this passage. It was truly every one for himself, and the devil take the hindmost. The result was not kind to my pressed suit but eventually I made it outside and back to the crowded train station.

---

# 66

# *Aftermath of the Game*

JAMES WHYTE DAVIS    As the game was ending, I couldn't help noticing one man I didn't know furtively passing money to another.

HENRY CHADWICK    Two Brooklyn cranks had made a wager of $100 a side on John Holder's making a home run. One was an Atlantic rooter, the other an

Excelsior crank. In this game I noticed Holder was very particular in selecting his bat. It appears that the man who had bet on him said that he would give him $25 of his bet if he made the hit; so Jack was very anxious. When he found a ball to suit him, he sent it flying over Harry Wright's head, thus winning the $25.

DOC ADAMS   During the contest, I took careful notes concerning the number of hands out recorded by fly catches and those by bound catches. New York retired batters 11 times by making bound catches; Brooklyn seven. Interestingly enough, the teams made an identical number of fly catches—six. Had we played under the fly rule perhaps several more base hits would have been made. Certainly not all the bound catches would have dropped for hits, as on several occasions players let balls drop that otherwise they might have caught with a little more effort. This was still an unsavory aspect of the game.

HENRY CHADWICK   I wanted to use statistics to allow the reader to be able to play a game in his mind's eye. Some statistics of note from that game: Matty O'Brien, pitching for Brooklyn, made 264 pitches in all with 69 being the most he threw in any innings; Van Cott for the New Yorks threw 198 balls, 55 in one innings. Leggett, the catcher for Brooklyn, let 12 balls get by him; DeBost only 6. The game took almost exactly three hours to play.

I also think it's important to note that at all times the game was played in the finest spirit of sportsmanship and good manners.

JUDGE VAN COTT   The game, not without its problems, was nevertheless a great success. After the match ended, the players and invited guests were ushered up to the Committee rooms where refreshments were provided.

When glasses were filled, I offered the first toast: "Health, success, and prosperity to the members of the Brooklyn Base Ball Clubs."

This was received with all the honors and three times three and a tiger.

Dr. Jones, president of the Excelsior Club, responded in like terms and with much good taste, hoping that the return match might favor Brooklyn. This too, was followed by three times three and a tiger.

Since representatives of the club from Buffalo had made the long trip, I offered a toast to "the health and success of the members of the Niagra Base Ball Club of Buffalo," which was enthusiastically received and responded to by Mr. Williams of that club.

I think everyone involved with our noble and invigorating game was thrilled by the success of The Great Base Ball Match.

JAMES WHYTE DAVIS   Along with three other members of the Association, I made a trip over to the New York City Fire Department to deliver half the proceeds from the first game. (The other half went to the Brooklyn Department.) They were pleased to accept $35.55 for the Widows and Orphans Fund of the Fire Department of New York City.

I guess that was the first profit ever made for a game of base ball and I was glad it was going to a worthy cause. It certainly wasn't the last profit ever made.

CHARLES DEBOST   It's fair to say those favoring us went home happy but we all knew Brooklyn had a good side and that they would come to the second match looking to get even. So, we got together to practice.

---

## 67

# *Getting Even*

ASHLEY HYDE   I was nervous about the second game because I knew Brooklyn would do everything they could to even the series and they had good players. Why did this bother me so when there was so much more to be concerned about? The issue of slavery was a real concern. The question of whether Kansas would be admitted to the Union as a slave or free state was a concern. John Brown's bloody raids were a concern. The Supreme Court's Dred Scott decision stating that slavery in the Midwest was lawful was a concern. I'd like to say the issue of slavery was uppermost in my mind that summer, but in all honesty, it wasn't. New York's batting was.

This time I left earlier to avoid the crowds, but while there were plenty of spectators making the trip again, there were not as many as for the first game. The skies threatened to let loose at any moment, so this may have led some potential spectators to stay home. What I did notice, however, was that there were more carriages parked around the course. Certainly the wealthier cranks were turning out. Maybe they thought sitting in their carriages would protect them in case of rain.

Just as the game was about to begin, the skies became very dark and it looked as if the match might again have to be put off. Nevertheless, with upward glances, the players came out to begin the match.

I took particular note of the changes each side had made. I was delighted to see Jamie Davis in at center field. He was replacing Harry Wright. DeBost was back in at catcher, so the Knicks again had two representatives.

Bixby had moved from third to first base. Where was Wadsworth?

"I heard he's sick," said the big man next to me.

It was the Brooklyn side, though, that made the most changes. The Atlantics turned out in full force with five players. It was clear: they weren't interested in giving all the Brooklyn clubs a chance to have someone on the field. The odd thing was that Johnny Holder, who hit that home run in the first game, wasn't in the lineup. Nevertheless, it looked as if we might be in trouble — and so we were.

Throughout the afternoon, rain fell as sporadically as New York runs. Neither DeBost nor Davis managed to score and the entire side managed only eight against Frank Pidgeon's tricky delivery.

In the first inning, they scored six runs and we came back with two. When they went three out for no runs in the second inning I thought maybe we had a chance to come back, but they wound up winning the game by the embarrassing score of 29 to 8.

I wish it had rained.

# 68

# *Rubber Match*

JAMES WHYTE DAVIS   The third game was scheduled for September 10, and as it turned out, a beautiful, warm Friday afternoon. The decision by the committee was that I would be replaced in center field by Benson. After what I did (or didn't) do in the second game, I couldn't argue. DeBost was still going to be out there at catcher carrying the colors of the Knickerbockers. Anyway, I agreed to be a scorer and Doc, the umpire.

HORACE DODGE   After the second game slaughter, Brooklyn was now the heavy favorite to take the series. We weren't finding many takers on New York. Lopsided scores ain't good for gamblers.

HENRY CHADWICK   The fight for supremacy was bitter. Both teams were on their mettle, every player feeling that the future welfare of the city represented by him depended upon the result. The crowd at the Fashion Course was huge. I dare say it was the largest crowd that had as yet ever attended a game of base ball, and, of course, that meant the punters were out in full force.

ASHLEY HYDE   So great were the crowds that finding a seat proved to be the most difficult task of the day.

JAMES WHYTE DAVIS   Any thoughts of a gentleman's game played on bucolic fields solely for the pleasure of play were long ago put on the shelf. The Course was teeming with people filled with the intoxication of competition.

I took my place at the scorers' table with Mr. Dakin from the Putnam Club. Surveying the crowd he said, "Ever see anything in your life like it?"

"Not for a base ball game anyway."

"Maybe for a hanging."

ASHLEY HYDE   A quick check of the players coming out for the start of the game showed that the Brooklyns had again made some changes in their picked nine. Masten, the Putman catcher, who had allowed 5 runs to score by his failure to block pitches, was replaced by the Atlantic's Polkert Boerum. So now players from the mighty Atlantic and Eckford Clubs comprised the entire Brooklyn side. So much for the idea of democracy.

The New York side, having been thoroughly trounced in the last game, made a number of changes, including Dick Thorn at pitcher. I was particularly pleased to see Wadsworth back at first base and, of course, DeBost again back as catcher.

One other big difference in this game was that Doc Adams was the umpire.

DOC ADAMS   It was my intention to enforce rules upon which we had agreed but were seldom enforced.

The New York enthusiasts responded loudly as a Gelston home run put them up 1–0 before everyone had settled in. Before the inning was over the New Yorks had quickly established a 7-run lead, a lead they were never to relinquish. They won by a score of 29–18.

What the gamblers made of this I have no idea, but I know the New York supporters were ecstatic. The first great inter-city rivalry had been established and New York had come out on top. Brooklyn, the bastion of base ball, was smarting.

Would this hot rivalry be good for the game of base ball, or would the emphasis on winning ultimately destroy it? That was the question for which none of us who truly cared about the game had an answer.

CLARENCE BROSS   I was a Brooklyn crank, then, now, and always, and I'll tell you three reasons why we lost that third game: Doc Adams, Doc Adams, Doc Adams.

Doc, as everybody knows, was a Knickerbocker through and through. The Knickerbockers, as everybody knows, was a New York Club.

Three of our best batsmen were called struck out by Adams. It was a cowardly way to umpire a game and not what base ball is about. Base ball is hitting and fielding, not walking back to the sidelines because some umpire didn't like the way you were waiting for a good pitch.

Oh, yes, I might add, he didn't call out one player on his New York side that way.

It put our other batters off, that's all. It's just crap, all crap.

Doc thought he was God of the great game, and that anything he said came from on high. That's crap, too.

DOC ADAMS    Standing with a bat in your hands and waiting, seemingly all day, for a pitch to your liking is simply not in the best interests of the game. Perhaps an example from that game will suffice to make my point. In the first innings alone, Frank Pidgeon made 87 pitches. For the game he made 436. Thorn added 297 pitches for his side. This totaled 733 pitches. Now if we had been playing cricket, maybe that would have been acceptable to an English Lord sipping his brandy on a long, uneventful summer's afternoon. But this was base ball, and we were in New York. We also had a big audience so I thought this would be a good time to show how the new rule should come into play.

Matty O'Brien was the first to feel the effects of the rule. He came to bat in the third inning with his side already behind 7–3. Men were on second and third with one out. Thorn delivered several pitches which Matty might have swung at, but he kept looking out at the arrangement of the fielders. I guess since he was a good scientific hitter, he thought that they might eventually shift positions so as to give him a better opening to place the ball.

I heard a few murmurs from the crowd of "come on, ya bum, swing!"

"Mr. O'Brien," I said quietly so as not to cause him embarrassment, "it is my duty to give you fair warning that in the opinion of this umpire you have already refused to swing at no fewer than two pitches that were well within your reach."

"Is that so," he said more as a statement than as a question.

Matty was a sure fielder who sometimes pitched, so he knew both sides of the coin. He was also the cockiest little player on the field.

"That is so," I told him in my most assured tone.

I suppose now he was set up to challenge my authority. He stood, stared, and again watched a good pitch go by.

"Mr. O'Brien, having forewarned you, you now have one strike against you."

I don't know if his look was intended as a sneer or not, but that is how I took it. I was now determined more than ever to enforce the rule in its strictest sense.

"That's strike two," I called after several more pitches went by with no action.

I could hear the murmur of the crowd. Again came the look. I think now he was as determined not to swing as I was to penalize him for his inaction. I don't know if he actually thought I would call him out on the third strike or not, but I could tell by his resolute stubbornness that he would continue to challenge me.

MATTY O'BRIEN    Although he always claimed he didn't, I think Adams really loved to umpire. He thought he was an all-fired rules czar.

When he laid the third on me, it was more a matter of him showing that he was in charge. Emperor Adams was putting on a show for the paying customers, except what he forgot was that they had come to see the players, not the umpire. Anyway, if he had been good enough to play in the game, he would have been out there, but since he wasn't, he probably was angry about that. That's why he made such a big deal about the pitches.

Hell, I'd let millions of pitches go by better than the one he said was strike three. That had always been part of the game — waiting for one you liked.

DOC ADAMS   He wanted to argue with me. I could see that. But he didn't. He just stared and walked away. Probably had there not been so many people watching he would have put up a fuss.

The O'Briens stick together, I'll say that about them. Later in the game, Pete O'Brien pulled the same stunt and with the same result. The next batter, Polky Boerum, was subjected to the same fate. I couldn't tell from the rustling of the crowd whether they were on my side or the batter's side but nobody said anything to me. After that, players swung when they should have and that was the end of it. I hoped it was lesson learned for the betterment of the game.

Now if I could just make the same point about the bounder catch rule!

JAMES WHYTE DAVIS   Doc and I had talked it over before the game and both agreed we needed to enforce the strike rule and we figured the New York–Brooklyn match was the best place to make the point. This, of course, changed the game some because from then on pitchers began to look for ways to deliver the ball so that the batters wouldn't swing but the umpires would call for a strike.

I can't say all the umpires followed suit right away because most of them were also players and they didn't want to say another player was out that way, but the precedence was in place and little by little it caught on.

At Doc's request, I carried a notebook and a pencil with me to the game and finished keeping track of the bound outs that he had begun in the first two games. For the three games, 33 bound outs were recorded. This amounted to a little more than 20 percent of all outs in the series. Neither one of us had thought to take note of the missed catches on fly balls in the first game, but we did for the next two. There were 17 of these where the balls were dropped on attempted catches.

Doc was a stubborn son-of-a-gun when it came to his ideas for rule changes, so I knew he'd press for the fly rule again.

# 69

# *Praise and Complaints*

HENRY CHADWICK    From all quarters came praise for the matches—the spectators, particularly those supporters of the New York Nine, enjoyed the contests; the press was generous in its approbation; the Association was pleased with its organization and ability to manage the game; the Fashion Course made money; and the fire departments were happy with the donations.

There was no question that these matches helped make the game even more popular than it had been. One could honestly say that the product delivered to the public was an appealing one. Of course, the very use of the word "product" indicates the direction in which the game was moving.

My only real complaint was that they did not play with the fly rule. Despite Doc's lobbying efforts, and my pleading in the papers, the clubs continued to resist. It was a pity really.

Another issue I really felt needed attending to was the habit some batsman had of waiting at the bat until a passed or overthrown ball enabled the base runner to leave the first base. The addition of called strikes was intended to put a stop to this but, unlike Doc, many umpires were simply not enforcing the rule. How often did we see the striker stand still at the home base waiting for the moment when a runner on the first base could take advantage of the first failure of the pitcher and catcher to hold the ball while tossing it to one another.

I talked to Doc about this, too, and he agreed something needed to be done.

JAMES WHYTE DAVIS    It was time for the other popular sports of the day to move over to make room for base ball. Cock fighting; boxing matches; horse, yacht, and scull racing, walking and running races; pigeon shooting; cricket contests, all were now relegated to the back pages. Base ball was king. But for how long, I wondered. As long as people were willing to pay to watch, money would control the game. Of this I was pretty sure.

The Fashion Race Course itself was a perfect example of this. That summer, the manager was accused of not delivering the advertised race programs and a scandal followed with the result that many punters lost faith in the honesty of the races and the attendance dropped dramatically. I could see the same thing happening to base ball if we were not careful.

The game had taken on a seriousness we never intended. Players were becoming more specialized because that helped win games. Many clubs were recruiting laborers in various fields who were more accustomed to physical labor than the professional men.

I could see a coarseness creeping in, too. Once I was invited to a post-game celebration of one of our best Brooklyn clubs that I shall refrain from naming here. Anyway, the celebration was exceedingly boisterous with much that was of dubious taste, including indecent anecdotes and off-color songs. I am neither a prude nor a preacher, but I contrived an excuse for an early exit.

# 70

# *Season's Play*

ASHLEY HYDE    The rivalry was on. New York versus Brooklyn was to become a staple of the competitive scene for ... seemingly forever.

SAM KISSAM    Although a member of the Knicks, I found myself, as a matter of local convenience, playing for the Excelsiors in '58. The next year I was fully back with the Knicks. Anyway, in '58 we (the Excelsiors) played the Knicks. The club was then four years old but this was the first time these two clubs had met.

I assured the fellows that the long-established Knicks would put up a strong side since they were clearly the older and more powerful club.

As we were assembling, I saw Charlie DeBost walking towards me. "Hello, Ben," he said.

"Ben?" I answered.

"You are Benedict Arnold, aren't you?"

"Not today."

He let out that big belly laugh of his. "I could have sworn..."

"You could be fined for that, Mr. DeBost."

"Oh, it's you, Sam. I didn't recognize you in that uniform. It's a little big for you, don't you think? And those God-awful colors, they don't do much for your pasty complexion."

"Put on a little weight, have you?"

"Pure muscle."

And so it was. Charlie was a muscular sportsman, a little shorter than I was, but stockier. He usually wore a full bushy beard, above which his blue eyes sparkled with good humor.

"I'm not sure why you bothered," he said. "You know we're the Knicker-bockers, don't you? We invented the game."

"So I've heard."

"Why, if I'm not mistaken you used to belong to the club way back when the bases were posts."

"Not quite."

Well, for all the ribbing I took before and during the game I might add it was with some gratification that we won by a score of 31–13.

After the game Charlie came over to me. "Maybe you should think about coming back."

ASHLEY HYDE    The return match with the Excelsiors was a topic of consid-erable interest among us cranks. We were all surprised at the results of the first one and the thinking was that the Knicks would make amends in the second. There were more spectators at that game than I had seen at a club match in some time. I suppose that's why they moved the game to another place at the Elysian Fields—so they could accommodate the bigger crowd.

Perhaps there was a decided want of judgment by the Kickerbockers in playing the return match on ground with which they were unaccustomed since the positions of the fielders were exactly reversed from that in which they were used to. The sun being brought in front of the short field, third base, and left field reduced the advantage they would have had when surrounded by the dark foliage on their own ground. The two missed catches by Harry Wright might be attributed to this somerset of position.

The Knickerbockers went first to the bat, with Charlie DeBost who took his position like Ajax defying the lightning—and for that matter, the Excel-siors. DeBost's appearances were usually accompanied either by applause or hilarity. In this game the applause came as he hit a ball over the center field which brought him clear home. The hilarity was produced by his humorous temerity in attempting to make third base and dodging and ducking the fielder who had attempted to run him in.

Despite the new field, Dr. Adams made a splendid fly catch with his left hand of a high ball. The batting of Davis was, as usual, quite good. Although he missed two balls rather widely thrown, he did make two good catches on the fly and two on the bound, all meeting due applause.

Oh, lest I forget, the final score was 15–14 in favor of the Excelsiors.

If there was one thing that was most apparent during the match it was the gentlemanly and good-humored courtesy which was displayed by both sides. In fact, it seemed anything but a contest for the superiority between two rival clubs.

JAMES WHYTE DAVIS    At the conclusion of the match, we escorted the Excel-siors to the Odd Fellows Hall in Hoboken where we were met by delegations from numerous other area clubs. There were close to 200 of us who sat down that night to a most sumptuous dinner.

As president of the club it was my honor and pleasure to present the game ball to Dr. Jones, president of the Excelsior Club.

> To Dr. Jones, members of the Excelsior Base Ball Club, their family and friends, as President of the Knickerbocker Base Ball Club I warmly welcome you as our honored guests.
>> May there always be games for your boys to play.
>> May the rain stay away on every game day.
>> May your throws always be straight and strong
>> May the ground always be firm where you run along.
>> May the hand of a friend always be near you,
>> And may God fill your heart with gladness to cheer you.
> Here's to the health and success of the Excelsior Club.

This was followed by three times three, after which Dr. Jones raised his glass.

>> Here's to these old men in their wooden rockers
>> Who play ball as the Knickerbockers.
>> Here's to the men so ancient and old
>> Who show us at play they still are bold.
>> Here's to their success and health
>> That's all they need as they already have wealth.
> So now I propose three times three for the parent of base ball clubs, the Knickerbockers.

Doc Adams then took the floor and "on behalf of the 'old' men," thanked the company for the good feeling exhibited by the Excelsiors. He then proceeded to refer to notes he had prepared in advance with statistics showing the great advantage of the present system of playing games of nine innings as we were then doing. He also went on some, waxing philosophical about the advantage of the game for Americans both young and old. He was, of course, preaching to the choir, but this seldom stopped him.

It seems speeches and toasts were the order of the day. First came Judge Van Cott, followed by Mr. Gelston of the Eagles, Mr. Dahin of the Putnams, Mr. Thorn of the Empires, and ... and...

By the time we sat down to eat, we *were* old men.

After dinner, in honor of the national game of base ball, I sang (if that be the most appropriate word) a song, "Ball Days" I had written about the game, with the assembled joining me for the chorus which I taught them. Everyone had a great time with that.

We had great fun singing it, although listening to Charlie DeBost struggling to find anything even close to a melody might be stretching the word "singing." What he was singing I do not know, but the rest of us sang it to the tune of "Uncle Sam's Farm."

Regardless, the song became something we sang at many a dinner, always with the words changed appropriately to suit the circumstances. Every year I was expected to come up with new verses, but I was happy to oblige.

It always started like this:

> Come, base ball players all and listen to the song
> About our manly Yankee game, and pardon what is wrong;
> If the verses do not suit you, I hope the chorus will,
> So join with us, one and all, and sing it with a will.
>
> Then shout, shout for joy, and let the welkin ring,
> In praises of our noble game, for health 'tis sure to bring;
> Come, my brave Yankee boys, there's room enough for all,
> So join in Uncle Samuel's sport — the pastime of base ball.

Then it went into verses appropriate to the circumstances.

> First a welcome to our guests, the brave Excelsior boys;
> They play a strong and striking game, and make a lively noise;
> They buck at every club, without breaking any bones
> Assisted by their president, the witty Doctor Jones.
>
> They well deserve their motto, and may they ever keep
> Their men from slumbering till their score "foots up a heap";
> And their names will resound through village and through town,
> Especially by older clubs who've been by them down brown.
>
> They have Leggett for a catcher, and who is always there,
> A gentleman in every sense, whose play is always square;
> Then Russell, Reynolds, Dayton, and also Johnny Holder,
> And the infantile "phenomenon," who'll play when he gets older.
>
> The Nestors and the parents of this our noble game,
> May repose on laurels gathered and on records of their fame;
> But all honor and all glory to their ever-fostering hand,
> That is multiplying ball clubs in towns throughout the land.
>
> Then treat the fathers kindly, and please respect their age,
> Their last appearance is not announced, as yet, on any stage;
> Some vigor yet remains, as you very well must know —
> It shines out like a star in our agile Charles DeBost.
>
> Now we'll sing to the Gothams who hold a foremost rank;
> They have taken many prizes, and they seldom draw a blank;
> Their players are hard to beat, with Van Cott in the race,
> And Wadsworth is bound to die on the very first base.

There's a club that's called the Eagle, and it soars very high;
It clipped the parent's wing, and caught them on the fly
Little Gelston plays behind, and Bixby pitches well,
And Hercules he bats the ball — oh! dreadfully to tell!

And here we have the Putnams — they bear a gallant name;
They are jovial, good fellows, as everyone will claim —
For Dakin is a trump, as the Brooklyn boys well know,
And with Masten for a catcher, they have a right to crow.

See, the conquering hero comes from the broad Atlantic's ocean,
And the Nestors' hearts do swell with grateful, glad emotion;
They've so many star players, you can hardly name the lions,
I think you'll all agree with me as to the O'Briens.

But we'll cross to the westward, where Empire takes its way,
At our home, the Elysian Fields, this club enjoys its play;
They've Benson, Hoyt, and Miller, Leavy, Thorne, and Fay,
And are noted for their even play on every practice day.

There's the aspiring Eckford boys, justly considered some;
When they send a challenge, that club looks very Grum;
Their Pidgeon's ne'er caught napping, and they never are cast down,
With such splendid fielders as Manolt and Eddy Brown.

There's a club in Morrisania, that's a very strong bulwark;
It forms a solid "Union" 'twixt Brooklyn and New York —
They've Gifford for their pitcher, and Booth plays well behind,
And Pinckney, on the second base, is hard to beat you'll find.

The young clubs, one and all, with a welcome we will greet,
On the field or festive hall, whenever we may meet;
And their praises we will sing at some future time;
But now we'll pledge their health in a glass of rosy wine.

Your pardon now I crave — this yarn is spun too long —
The Knickerbockers' "fiend," you know, he always goes it strong;
On America's game of base ball he will shout his loud acclaim,
And his "tiger" shall be telegraphed to Britain's broad domain.

JAMES WHYTE DAVIS   Around 11 o'clock we broke up and with Dodsworth's Band leading the way, we marched escorting the Excelsior Club to the Ferry where, on parting, repeated cheers were given on both sides.

This was the base ball culture as it was supposed to be but, as we were to discover, was not long for this world.

## 79

# *Beginning of the End*

JAMES WHYTE DAVIS   These were the years that really marked the beginning of the end of "The Gentlemen's Game," as we created it, knew it, played it, loved it. Gambling and greed, those evil monsters forever locked in a dance to the death, were every year, every month gaining the upper hand. Yes, the game was thriving, but it was thriving on avarice.

I suppose it could be argued that gambling is what drove the game to attract the highly skilled players and immense crowds. But at what cost? I suggest no matter how it is calculated, the cost was very much too high.

Corruption follows in the footsteps of money and money follows in the footsteps of base ball. Because of what happened on the field, money was changing hands. Miss a fly ball that should have been caught and someone somewhere hands over ten dollars. So clubs were looking for those who could catch the ball every time (unless ordered to do otherwise), and it didn't matter who the players were, where they came from, what characteristics they displayed, what values they espoused.

Base ball had become lucrative.

Rowdy crowds with pecuniary interests were increasingly in evidence, thus making the experience of visiting ball grounds uncomfortable, if not dangerous, for respectable citizens. Umpires were subjected to verbal abuse. Ruffians, gangs, and pickpockets were everywhere.

On the field itself, taunts were hurled and tactics developed to win games at all costs, including the cost of fair play.

HORATIO STERNE   Gambling and corruption in base ball you say? The spirit of the times, my friend, the spirit of the times. You couldn't pick up a paper without reading of allegations of corruption—corruption in Mayor Wood's office, among the city aldermen, in the post office, with the police. There were stories of the bribery of city officials for construction contracts, including those at the Brooklyn Navy Yard, stories of bribing members of the Croton Water Board. Even church bishops were accused. There was the "Railroad Swindle," the "DeGroot Swindle," the "Fort Snelling Swindle," the "School Board Scandal," the "Harbor Masters Corruption Trial." The Brooklyn Ferrys were said to be run by a corrupt board. Contracts for the city's new steam fire engines were apparently awarded to friends of the city administration. There were charges of corruption leveled at social clubs, political clubs, fraternal clubs.

Not even the dead were exempt. It seems the Common Council was charged with corruption when it entered into a $9000 contract for the removal of human remains at Potter's Fields.

I could go on at great length. Base ball our national sport? I think not. Corruption was our national sport and we played it well and often.

DOC ADAMS    I went with Walter Avery over to Cooper Union to listen to Abraham Lincoln deliver a depressing speech on slavery.

"I'm worried," he said.

"I know. Me, too."

"I read the other day that Mayor Wood made a proposal that Manhattan, Brooklyn, and Staten Island secede from the state and form a new one called Tri-Insula."

"Is that supposed to keep us out of any of the unpleasantries?"

"I suppose."

"The Knickerbockers of Tri-Insula."

Everyone else thought he was nuts. Still the concerns about slavery hovered. We talked about them some at dinners or meetings, but never at practices or games. Those were for other purposes.

Spending a lot of time playing base ball was fine and good, but troubling winds were wafting in the air. Some states in the South were openly talking of withdrawing from the Union.

Henry Ward Beecher had been giving a series of lectures on "How to Save the Union," and so one night I talked Jamie into going to hear him.

"We need to pay attention to these things," I said.

"Why, do you think Beecher might make a useful pitcher?"

"He might save the Union."

"Unless and until they get some good clubs down there I'm not so sure it matters."

He did care, of course, but it was also part of his personality to disavow such serious sentiments. It wasn't all base ball, all the time, although it was close.

Before the night was over, the police had to be called to quell the ugly disturbances that continually interrupted the speeches.

General Pilsbury got up and pleaded with the audience to remain seated and calm but his appeal was to no effect. The chaos only increased as the band struck up "Hail Columbia."

Over the shouting and the music Jamie leaned towards me and said, "And I thought the Atlantics crowd was rowdy!"

It was, I'm afraid, a sign of the times.

In November, Lincoln, who had declared, "Government cannot endure permanently half slave, half free," was elected president although he only received 40 percent of the popular vote. A month later, South Carolina seceded from the Union.

I'd like to be able to say that all of us were true blue Americans who defended liberty and freedom and understood slavery as the evil it was, but I can't.

I remember one particular conversation with Fraley.

"This slavery thing is going to tear us apart, you know," I said as we were walking along a crowded street.

"I don't know, maybe."

"I just don't understand why everyone can't see how pernicious slavery is. How can any right-minded, sane-thinking individual defend it? I tell you, Fraley, it's beyond my ken."

"I understand how you feel, but you have to understand that the cotton trade brings some $200 million a year to this city. That makes cotton a huge financial issue here."

"That doesn't make slavery right."

"It makes it important enough that many of this city's merchants, worried about their cotton investments, are siding with the South."

I'm not sure where everyone in the club stood on slavery, but I'm reasonably sure that I'm safe in saying that as a club of educated gentlemen we were predominately on the right moral side of the issue. I wouldn't have belonged to a club that was otherwise.

That being said, please don't think me callous when I say that I knew if war were to come, and some were opining it would, I could envision so many of our fine young ball players toting muskets rather than bats. The very thought sickened me.

JAMES WHYTE DAVIS   So one gorgeous night in July we're riding the ferry back from the Elysian Fields, and I happen to look up just in time to see a hazy ball of fire high in the sky. As it advanced, it seemed to resemble a rocket, but it was larger and more imposing. Once overhead, it appeared as two bodies, the larger a short distance in advance of the smaller. Both were surrounded by lustrous halos. Behind them were a number of balls of fire as if strung on an invisible cord. It was a magnificent spectacle that lasted only a few moments before fading.

I was sitting with Doc and DeBost and we were all awe struck by the meteor's unannounced appearance.

"Do you suppose that's like us?" I said.

"Why, are you on fire or something?" asked Charlie.

"A bright, burning star that shows off for a brief period of time and then burns itself out and is of no use any more."

"Have another beer, Jamie."

Still, the thought persisted.

---

## 72

# *Going National*

ASHLEY HYDE    Despite the Elysian Fields and all those romantic drawings of base ball games being played in bucolic settings, the fact remains that base ball was, is, and probably always will be a city game, and among the big cities, New York and Brooklyn dominated.

JAMES WHYTE DAVIS    I went with Doc one day up to Boston where we had been invited to meet with some men to help them organize their new club. The amazing thing is that with the new railroad we made the trip from New York to Boston in seven hours and seven minutes—and that included ferrying the trains over the Thames and Connecticut rivers.

What was evident was that with such faster forms of transportation, base ball clubs were going to be able to travel more easily to play clubs in other cities.

DOC ADAMS    If there ever was a year in which the peacock of base ball showed off its colors, it was 1860. I don't know whether the looming war induced men to invest more time in pleasurable activities, but I do know that as fast as the game had been spreading, it was now spreading even faster.

Okay, here's my medical training explanation: It was pure ontogeny, the process of an organism growing organically; an unfolding of events involved in an organism changing gradually from a simple to a more complex level.

According to what I read, there were teams regularly playing in the public square of Cleveland, and in Chicago, Detroit, Washington, D.C., and even as far away as the Minnesota Territory.

Anyway, as I saw it there were a number of factors accounting for this proliferation. One, certainly, was the Excelsior tour. They took the baton from us and brought high-level base ball to the hinterlands.

JOSEPH JONES    We decided to embark on a tour of upstate New York and to play the country clubs there. By this time, we were generally considered the top club. Maybe the Atlantics could give us a tussle for that title, but certainly no one else. We were, after all, the Excelsiors and we knew there would be great interest in engaging us.

When word got out that we were available to engage in friendly competitions, we received scores of invitations. We eventually accepted six.

We agreed that in order to put our best foot forward everyone on the tour would refrain from using intoxicating beverages, and for the most part we did. We also agreed that each member of the club would pay his own expenses.

Some thought was given to sending our second or even third nines so as not to overwhelm the opposition, but in the end we decided that in order to show off base ball at its best, we would send our best. Now as it turned out, not everyone on the first nine could arrange his schedule to allow him to be away for two weeks. Nevertheless, seven of our first nine made the trip, including Jim Creighton who by then was recognized by many as the finest player in the game, and Asa Brainard who wasn't far behind.

"The Excelsiors Are Coming" proclaimed many a newspaper. Everywhere we went we were greeted by large contingents of excited spectators and civic dignitaries. The idea was to test the mettle of the local nines against the best in the world. Perhaps some of the locals were disappointed with the results, but we had determined in advance that we would not "lay down" to these clubs.

We started up in Albany where we beat the Champion Club of that city 24–9, then over to Troy where we beat the Victory Club 13–7. When we got to Buffalo to face the Niagara Club, we found a community of enthusiasts who were not only excited by our visit, but who entertained the belief that they would actually beat us. Apparently no club in the area was their equal and the city was justifiably proud of their "champions."

Their grounds were decked out with pennants and flags, the biggest flying from a new flag pole they had put up for the occasion. Spanking new stands had been erected on each side of the field with seats available to the city's finest ladies and gentlemen. The place was jammed with people not only around the grounds but also on the rooftops of nearby buildings. Such was the allure of the Excelsiors.

As the game time approached, the mayor introduced me to the leading lights of the city and said to me, "Well Dr. Jones, we understood you had your way with the clubs in Albany and Buffalo, but I think you'll find we're a tiger of another stripe."

"If that be the case," I said, "then we'll welcome the opportunity to learn the finer points of the game from you."

"It's not just you big city boys who know how to play the game."

"I don't doubt that."

"May I offer you a segar, Dr. Jones? Call it an early victory segar."

"Thank you," I said pulling my own segar from my coat pocket. "May I offer you one of ours."

With Jim Creighton leading the way with superb pitching we won the game 50–19.

I think it's safe to say, that the good folks of Buffalo had never seen ball playing like that. Not wanting to rub it in, I told the Mayor we were very lucky to have won by that score.

"I'm afraid we didn't play with our usual skill and coolness," he said.

"That happens sometime."

I think probably their cock-sureness added to our fervor in shellacking them by one of the largest score we had ever made.

We went on to beat the two Rochester clubs, both by respectable scores, although nothing like how we beat the Niagaras. At our last stop in Newburgh where we were to play the Hudson River Club, we were met by a score of players who had made the train trip up from New York and then accompanied us back home. That game we won 59–14.

JAMES WHYTE DAVIS    It wasn't a base ball game, it was a slaughter. Where's the pleasure in that?

One thing I will say for them, though. True to their word, there was no wine or liquor to be found on the grounds.

JOSEPH JONES    Later that summer we made another trip, this time south, where we played matches in Philadelphia and Baltimore. Of course, we won there, too. We had become the great ambassadors of base ball.

We took the night train down to Baltimore, arriving shortly before dawn. Our hosts, the Baltimore Excelsiors, provided carriages to show us the various interesting historical sights of that fair city.

They did everything they possibly could for us. All any of us had to do was say something like, "Gee, while we're here, wouldn't it be nice to..." and a carriage would be arranged for that very purpose. And we couldn't spend a penny of our own money either. Everything, and I do mean everything, was made available to us. About an hour before game time, a city car decked out in bunting and flags, and drawn by four beautiful horses, arrived to take us to the ground.

Royalty simply could not have been treated any better.

After the game, which we won 51–6, we were feted by our hosts in a most magnanimous fashion.

"I would like to offer a toast," said Dr. Hawks, their president, "to the champion club of the United States."

"Thank you for your sentiments," I said, "but I think that will have to wait until after our match with the Atlantics. I would instead offer a toast to our magnificent hosts, the Excelsior Club of Baltimore."

HENRY CHADWICK    Lopsided results or not, the fervor that was unleashed by the Excelsior tours cannot be underestimated. It's human nature to admire greatness, and to those who saw them play in the hinterlands, that's what they represented. The neophytes dreamed of one day representing their cities the way these men represented Brooklyn.

Where once the Knickerbockers represented the acme of the game now the Excelsiors/Atlantics did.

Here's the important thing, though: the fact that the Excelsiors ranked second to none in social standing did much to establish base ball on a permanent and reputable footing.

JAMES WHYTE DAVIS    Other clubs caught the touring fever from the Excelsiors. First the Enterprise Club went off and then others. We, however, stayed on our grounds playing our twice-a-week intra club games. In fact, we only played one match that year with another club, and that was a match with the aforementioned Excelsiors which we lost 32–9.

Our days of playing big games with other clubs were coming to an end. Unless we were willing to open our membership to players based solely on their ball skills (which we weren't), we could no longer be competitive with those clubs that did. No matter. We were happy doing what we were doing.

---

## 73

# *Sunday Play*

HIRAM BREWSTER    I was just 16 when I went with a few of my Jersey City school chums to watch a game between the Knickerbockers and Eagles.

We had so much fun that we decided to try to play the game ourselves. At first we weren't sure where we were going to find a ball and a bat, but Alfie came up with a ball someplace. We made a bat out of a rake handle and headed over to an open field near our school where we proceeded to do our best to copy the actions of the Eagles and Knicks. We had played a version of it in school, so it wasn't all new to us. Well, we played for hours on our makeshift field and agreed we'd do it again when we got the chance.

The chance came two days later. We weren't at it for more than a few minutes when a Jersey City policeman came strolling across the field twirling his nightstick and grinning like he had just caught a cat burglar in the act.

"Hello, boys," he said. "Having a good time?"

"Yes, sir, we sure are," I said.

"Do you know what today is?"

"The last day of the month, I believe."

"And what day of the week might that be?"

"Day of the week, officer?"

"As in Monday, Tuesday. Perhaps you've heard of them."

"Why I do believe today is Saturday."

"And the rest of you boys, do you believe it's Saturday too?"

They all shook their heads sheepishly, knowing very well, as I did, that it was Sunday.

"Well now, we've got a little problem here with the calendar, because according to this morning's paper, which I believe is often accurate, today is Sunday. Sunday, the Sabbath day."

"Is it really? I guess we must have looked at yesterday's paper by mistake, Officer, because we all thought it was Saturday, didn't we, boys?"

"We surely did, officer," said Alfie. "We surely thought it was Saturday and we surely appreciate your setting us straight."

Alfie, whose father was a teacher, was sure about a lot of things, but how to pull the wool over a policeman's eyes wasn't one of them.

"I suppose, too," said the officer, "that none of you had any idea it was illegal to play base ball on Sunday."

"Is it?" I said. "Imagine that."

"I'm trying to," said the officer.

"I'm surprised no one ever told us that before."

"I've got another surprise for you. You're all going to spend a little time in the City Prison."

Needless to say we all knew what we were up to, but never for one moment did we think it would have come to this. We were young boys, albeit smart alecks, but no policeman was going to go so far as to put young boys in a prison with drunks, knucks, and burglars.

"Now be good lads, and just follow me, and don't make no trouble."

We looked at each other with faces of stony panic.

"We got nice bunks for you all. Of course, you'll have to share with the vagrants we've already got in there, but that shouldn't be a problem because none of you boys are too big to go two to a bed."

"Officer," I said in my meekest voice, "if we promise not to do it again, do you suppose you could overlook it this time?"

"Overlook a serious crime? Well, I don't know."

"Because we've learned our lesson."

"We surely have," chimed in Alfie.

He stroked his chin for a moment like a bad actor in a melodrama of no account. "Well, I tell you what. Let me see that bat."

Alfie handed it to him like an altar boy handing the cup to the priest. "It's not a real one," he said. "We made it ourselves."

"Let's take a look and see how it works. You pitch to me, and the rest of you go out in the long field."

With smiles that lit up the gray afternoon, we took our places while he proceeded to hit a ball about as far as a man can.

As it turned out, we were spared a prison term but four others who were caught in our city later in the summer weren't. Whether they had to share bunks with big men I don't know. I do know it was the last time I played Sunday ball. As for the policeman, he was a member of the Liberty Base Ball Club of New Brunswick which is probably the only reason he let us go. Us players stick together.

---

## 74

# Chadwick's Guides

DOC ADAMS    The Excelsior tour had a huge impact on the spread of the game, but it wasn't the only thing that did.

The game was now receiving greater coverage in the press, most notably from Henry Chadwick, reporter extraordinaire. He was regularly covering base ball for the *Clipper* but also contributed to several other New York and Brooklyn papers.

In 1860 he began writing what would become an annual book — *Beadle's Dime Base Ball Player*, or, as they were to become more popularly known, *Beadle's Guides*. In them, one could find numbers, numbers, and more numbers. He must have had a lot of time on his hands, because these complicated statistics were worked out in great detail.

DOC ADAMS    In these *Guides* Chadwick offered all sorts of advice on how to form your very own base ball club, including sample constitutions, by-laws, rules for playing, and pages and pages of instructions including "how-to" sections on pitching, batting, catching, and position playing. The publisher claimed that 50,000 copies were sold.

For one thin dime, shiny or otherwise, you could buy a book with everything (and more) that you would need to start your own base ball club, including Father Chadwick's moral imperatives for the game.

Want to play base ball? Pick up a copy of *Beadle's Guides*, follow the instructions, and you too might one day play for the Excelsiors.

HENRY CHADWICK    I have to admit the *Beadle's Guides* were extremely successful, and probably by extension, influential. How many clubs were organized because of the *Guides* I don't know but I do know that any men considering such an action were well served if they followed the prescriptions and proscriptions I recommended.

Two statements I thought particularly noteworthy: 1.) It is desirable to secure the services of one or two men in a club who will take as much interest in its welfare as if it was a pet stock company, yielding them large pecuniary returns. Without such supporters, no club will flourish. 2.) Don't elect bad-tempered men in your club, no matter how noted as players they may be, for they will eventually do more injury to a club than benefit.

WILLIAM TUCKER    Chadwick undoubtedly did much to popularize the game, and his insistence on moral probity was important, but I found his constant moralizing something of a bore. If I wanted a sermon, I'd go to church.

---

# 75

# *Out-of-Control Cranks*

JAMES WHYTE DAVIS    Those who can't or won't, live their lives through the accomplishments of those who can and do. It's sad really.

FRALEY NIEBUHR    It was getting to the point where some cranks were out of control, shouting at batsmen such things as "shanks," "Shanghai," and worse. I saw games where there were so many cranks spilling out onto the field that fielders had to weave their way through a forest of legs to retrieve balls and where there were so many men crowded around third base that I couldn't even find the runner. Gangs of young ill-bred urchins were particularly obnoxious in both their behavior and their language.

This was partly the reason we were playing more games amongst ourselves and very few games against other clubs. It just wasn't worth the aggravation.

DUNCAN CURRY    One day, in a game involving the New York Mutuals, a huge crowd of some 7,000 spectators and hundreds of vehicles surrounded the field. In the fifth inning a disturbance involving a pickpocket broke out and quickly turned into a full-scale riot that overflowed onto the field. Since there were no police, the crowd had to be driven back by bat-wielding players. One player was so badly sucker punched that when they finally managed to gain control and re-start the game, he had to be replaced.

I was glad I was no longer playing regularly. In my wildest imagination I could never conceive of a time when bat-wielding Knicks would have had to beat off fans at the Elysian Fields.

JAMES WHYTE DAVIS Upwards of 18,000 spectators crammed into the Putnam Ground in Brooklyn to watch a match between the Excelsiors and Atlantics. Unfortunately I was among the thugs, gamblers, thieves, and plug-uglies who decided to spend their afternoon watching a game. The actions of a few in the crowd was shameful but perhaps not unexpected for statements had been made in the days leading up to the contest that the Excelsiors would not be allowed to win in a close contest. I for one could not believe that the Atlantics could be involved in any such plot, but I do believe that regardless, stricter enforcement of order on their own ground would undoubtedly have led to greater quiet and more agreeable results when their hangers-on followed them to other grounds.

In the Atlantic fifth inning, McMahon, after overrunning the third base, was put out much to the dismay of the Atlantic supporters who thought the result was an injustice. During the next inning, the rowdy element, which had been excited by the fancied injustice to McMahon, now became unbearable. Disgraceful shouts from all over the field arose for a new umpire to replace Thorn of the Empires. Leggett, the Excelsior captain, was supported by the Atlantic Nine in his endeavor to restore order and together they managed to secure a temporary lull, but it did not last long. Despite his telling the crowd that he would withdraw his side if the tumult was renewed, the shouts began again this time with increased vigor.

With the crowd in an uproar, Leggett handed the ball to Matty O'Brien, the Atlantics' captain.

"Here, Matty," he said. "You keep it."

"Will you call it a draw?" said O'Brien.

"As you please."

With that and true to his word, the Excelsiors immediately left the field followed by a crowd of roughs alternately lambasting the Excelsiors and cheering the Atlantics.

The game was declared drawn with the tacit understanding that if it was ever to be played out, it would take place in the privacy of some enclosed ground.

I was pleased to see that action of the Excelsiors and applauded them accordingly. Things like this should never happen, but I put the blame squarely on the very idea that 18,000 spectators should be at any match.

The next day the *Clipper* opined that it was "the foreign element" that was responsible. By that they meant the Irish-Americans. I don't know if that was right or not, but it was not out of the question. The Atlantics was a team composed mostly of Irish-Catholic workingmen.

There was no doubt — absolutely none — that the actions of the spectators that day were due in large measure to strong feelings of partisanship born of gambling.

Look, there were plenty of opportunities to gamble in the city without involving base ball, not the least of which were dozens of new luxury casinos, apparently equal to Europe's finest. At these establishments one could dine in splendor and then repair to the glass-domed, velvet-carpeted, rosewood-furnished gaming rooms for high stakes faro and roulette. It was said that one night August Belmont lost $60,000 in one of these. Better there than at a ball ground. As far as I know, roulette wheels can't be bribed.

ASHLEY HYDE    In some respects, the game was surely but inextricably slipping away from the Knickerbockers. The spectators were no longer just convivial family and friends, but boisterous partisans. The ugly twin-headed hydra of commercialism and professionalism was growing by the day.

# 76

# *The Spectre of Professionalism*

JAMES WHYTE DAVIS    We must have been running out of good club names because we ended up with new clubs like the Wild Wave, Good Intent, Alert, Invisible, Vigilant, Starlight, Eclipse, Reindeer, and many score others. I have no idea how many clubs there were but the number was astounding. I even heard of teams playing regularly in the backyard of the White House. Out in San Francisco, a club called the Eagles was started by Will and Jim Shephard, two former Knickerbocker members.

Even colleges were taking up the sport. I read that Amherst defeated Williams 73–32 after which the students rang the chapel bell, set off fireworks, and lit a huge bonfire. The report went on to say Amherst also defeated Williams at chess. Bright boys, those Amherst lads.

On any given summer's day there had to be hundreds of thousands of men and women watching games. Seldom did a newspaper report fail to comment on the size of the audience with words like "huge," "immense," or "vast."

When 10,000 spectators became rowdy, how could players stop them?

Doc Adams   Our Association wasn't always the most effective organization at reinforcing rules and policies. Still it was better than not having one.

At our annual convention of '59 there was talk — just talk mind you — that some clubs were looking to pay some men as an enticement to play for their club. Francis Pidgeon, president of the Eckfords, stood up and loudly proclaimed that he and his club firmly opposed any form of compensation for players. He insisted the game was for pleasure, not profit.

I assured everyone who would listen that the Knickerbockers were in full agreement with Mr. Pidgeon.

Sam Kissam   What was happening all over was that many clubs — not us — were admitting non-playing members as financial supporters, club officers, delegates, and business managers of all sorts. As long as there was money to be made, and there definitely was, there would be men interested in promoting the game for gain. There was the management and there were the players and I couldn't help thinking their interests just weren't the same.

The Knickerbockers, though, were always a club of, for, and by the players.

Doc Adams   When a group of crack professional English cricketers visited, they attracted some spectators who opined that were the cricketers to play base ball their skills would easily translate into victories over real base ball players. So one evening a number of us got together at the Astor House to consider a challenge. As I recall, we represented the Knickerbocker, Eagle, Empire, Excelsior, Putnam, St. Nicholas, and maybe a few other clubs.

At the time the cricketers were playing upstate so we agreed that Dr. Jones of the Excelsiors would go up to Rochester and challenge them. I would have gone myself, but as he volunteered, I let it go at that. The idea was that we would select a team made up of top players from both New York and Brooklyn.

"They're not called professionals for nothing," I said.

"Then we'll offer them a pot of gold," said Jones.

"And whose pot is that going to be."

"How much do you think it will take?"

"Hard to say."

"What would you think of $5,000?"

"For that much I think those mercenaries would play naked if we asked them."

"That's an unsavory thought."

"But we'd never get the clubs to come up with that much. We have trouble enough just getting some our members to pay their dues on time."

"I think I could arrange for it," Dr. Jones said with nary a smile. "Why don't we see if they'll give it a go?"

I never asked, and he never offered, but I suspect I know where he thought he could raise that amount of cash. I suppose I didn't want to know.

Anyway, we had little doubt that those touring soldiers of fortune would accept our challenge and so we began considering the constitution of the side we would put up — Price, Pearce, Creighton, Wright, DeBost, Leggett, et al. The possibilities were as endless as was the enjoyment in the consideration. The "what-ifs" that base ball promotes is one of its joys.

While we waited for Jones to return, we looked into possible playing grounds, knowing that we would need to accommodate a large crowd.

I met Dr. Jones at the station on his return. "They turned me down flat," he said.

"Why?"

"I don't know why. I can only tell you what they said."

"And that was?"

"It wasn't enough money."

"Five thousand dollars wasn't enough money?"

"That's what they said."

"That's hard to believe."

"Isn't it, though?"

The distinction between professionals and amateurs was just beginning to be an issue, and it wouldn't go away for a long, long, time.

# 77

# *To Be Competitive*

JAMES WHYTE DAVIS    In June 1860 we held a club meeting to deal with a number of pressing issues including the designating of our first and second nines. After nominations and due consideration, I was elected to the first nine along with Doc, DeBost, Wright, Morrow, Welling, Keeler, Wood, and Walker.

WALTER AVERY    I'll admit it. I was put off by not being selected for the first nine. In my mind I was as good as several of those who were elected. Then, when I wasn't selected for the second nine either, well, that really irked me. And I was the club's vice-president! Finally after the members choose three players from the second nine to serve as alternates for the first nine, they got around to naming three alternates to the second nine. Huzzah, I was at least an alternate to something.

Well it was better than nothing. Being on the second nine beat being on the no nine.

CHARLES DEBOST    I told Jamie that with my work schedule, commitments at home, and a slightly sore back I would be unable to play in matches with any other clubs for the foreseeable future.

"Sorry, Jamie, but I really don't have any choice at this point."

"When do you think..."

"I don't know."

"But surely you can..."

"I don't know."

"Maybe just one or two..."

We didn't call him the Fiend for nothing.

HARRY WRIGHT    I had to tell Jamie that I was too much engaged with cricket to be able to make any calculation about playing in a match.

JAMES WHYTE DAVIS    What choice did I have but to call the membership back to a special meeting? Let's face it, DeBost and Wright were our two best players. Invitations from the Excelsior, Star, Charter Oaks, Independent, Empire and Lexington Clubs were put on hold. So too was an invitation to play a third nine match with the Excelsiors. We didn't even have a third nine!

Our Committee on Matches arranged for games between the 22s. These were the 22 members not on the first and second nines. They also organized games between our two designated nines and between the married members and single members. When we would again play against other clubs was uncertain, but we agreed that McLaughlin and Stephens would be substituted in the first nine for DeBost and Wright. I volunteered to withdraw from the side whenever Wright could play. Avery and Rogers were promoted to the second nine.

GEORGE GRUM    Simple. The Knicks were turning down games because they didn't think they could win.

SAM KISSAM    It wasn't so much a matter of winning, but of being competitive. With DeBost and Wright we could be; without them we didn't think we were. Games where one team is simply overmatched doesn't make for much of a contest.

CHARLES DEBOST    To those who say we weren't a competitive lot, all I can say is balderdash. We wrapped our losses in the rhetoric of chivalry, but the losses bothered us as much as anyone.

GEORGE GRUM    Look, competition has always—and I do mean always—been a part of base ball. Oh, I know, it was not always considered appropriate to acknowledge that in public. Some club members argued that one should politely show contempt for anyone who put competition above character, but that was just so much malarkey. Show a vulgar approval of winning and losing and some looked down their hypocritical noses at you. Winning and losing. That what the game was about, then and always. The rest is pure lip service, unctuous pretentiousness.

JAMES WHYTE DAVIS    Although I have no concrete proof of this, a story was floating around that the Excelsiors actually paid Creighton to play with them. This was, of course, absolutely against the rules of any Association member club. The claim was that although his father was a clerk at city hall, the family was in some financial difficulty, so Creighton needed to work in order to help support them. He was such a wonderful player that his club agreed to compensate him for time lost when he played games or when he was on that tour. I have no firsthand knowledge of this but the rumor was repeated so often, I have to believe there was at least some truth to the story.

I asked Dr. Jones about this and I believe him to be an honorable man. His response was, "Jamie, the Club is not paying Creighton or anyone else."

What very well may have happened was that the Club was not paying him, but perhaps a wealthy club patron was. I also heard that some players had their club dues paid this way or received special gifts from supporters.

To play to win, or to play to play: that was the question.

SAM KISSAM    There was no doubt Jim Creighton was the game's greatest player. As a pitcher, he not only delivered the ball with great speed, but also threw balls within a few inches of the ground that rose up to the batsman's hip, making it almost impossible to hit well.

Now it was rather widely known among base ball men that the Excelsiors, in direct violation of Association rules, compensated. Were other players being compensated at the time? I can't say for sure, but I'm willing to bet they were.

---

# 78

# *On Running a Club*

FRALEY NIEBUHR    I suppose it was much the same on other clubs, but we sure did have a lot of meetings, so being an officer of the club meant you had to make a huge investment in time. There were practices or games twice a week, a monthly Board meeting, an annual Club meeting, and special meetings as needed, and it seems as if we needed a lot.

Most of the business was routine — voting on membership proposals, approving bills to be paid, those sorts of things.

The Club was very much a democracy. We voted on just about everything.

Moved: That President Davis be appointed a committee of one to confer with the Eagle and Empire clubs in reference to getting suitable benches to be used on the grounds on play days.

Moved: That an invitation be extended to the Excelsior Club to play a friendly game and suggest that it be played on the fly.

Moved: That the secretary be empowered to have the tops of the lockers grained at an expense not to exceed $8.

Moved: That the secretary be instructed to notify those members selected for the first and second nines of their positions on the teams.

Moved: That the Board considers as satisfactory the excuses received from Mr. Taylor and Mr. Kirby for non-attendance on play days.

Moved: That we decline the invitation from the Hoboken Club to play a second nine game on consequence of severe indisposition of Mr. Stansbury.

Moved: To go into ballot to fill the vacancy created by Mr. Stanbsbury's unavailability.

Moved: That Mr. Lasak be empowered to procure a suitable carpet for the use of the members on play days.

Moved: To notify the members to attend a meeting of the Board on Thursday evening next.

Moved: To accept the resignation of Mr. Leggett.

Moved: To go into ballot for a director to fill the vacancy caused by the resignation of Mr. Stansbury.

Moved: To appoint a committee of two to select a new cap for the club and to report on same as early as practicable.

Moved: To pay the bill presented by Mr. Brown for the collation furnished at the game with the Excelsior.

Moved: To accept the report of the Committee on Caps in favor of the blue and white cap furnished by Mr. Stevens.

Moved: To appoint a committee of two to select a new belt for the use of the club.

Moved: To accept the report of President Davis serving as the Committee on Benches stating that he had conferred with the officers of the other clubs who were opposed to furnishing benches, but that Mr. Perry had volunteered to provide benches for spectators.

Moved: To notify the first nine that a game with the Excelsiors would be played on the afternoon of Thursday the 30th to commence at 3 o'clock.

Moved: To accept the invitation from the Excelsior Club to make up a muffin game and to empower the president to appoint a captain to select the muffin nine and have full charge of same.

Moved: Upon request of Mr. Wenman to be removed from the second nine, to appoint Mr. Wood in his place.

Moved: To appoint President Davis a committee of one to procure a suitable trunk for the use of the club principally to carry the clothes, bats, etc., when matches were played on grounds distant from our own.

Moved: To accept the report of President Davis serving as the Trunk Committee to purchase a trunk for $2.

Moved: To approve the proposal of Mr. Manning for membership.

All of this from just a couple of meetings! And remember, on top of this, we met twice a week for play!

I always enjoyed my association with the Knicks. I liked the men and I liked the game, but sometimes it was difficult to keep up with the demands it made. I had a family and I had a company to look after. I also belonged to other organizations. I was a member of the Brooklyn and Civic clubs. I was a director of the Prospect Park and Coney Island Railroad Company as well as the Gebhard Fire Insurance Company.

I feel I did my share and more for many years, but it was nothing compared to what Jamie and Doc did. Doc represented us so often at conventions and in meetings with other clubs, and Jamie must have acted as a committee member on a thousand committees. Need something done in a hurry? Ask Jamie. Need to have something fixed in the club house? Ask Jamie. Need a good fielder to fill out a side? Ask Jamie. He was indefatigable in the cause of the club, and he was loyal to it to a fault.

Of course, this all came at a price. He needed to be appreciated. He needed people to acknowledge his contributions, and as is always the case with such men, he was quick to irritation if you disagreed with him. It was as if he was saying, "I put in the time to do it, so either do it yourself or shut up about it."

I once asked him why he worked so hard for the club.

He shrugged. "Why does anyone do anything by choice? Because there's something in it for him."

"And what is that for you?"

He grinned but never answered.

JAMES WHYTE DAVIS   There were times when I grew frustrated. Too damn many members didn't want to do anything other than play in games, and some of them did little of that. I got almighty tired of the shirkers.

I got tired, too, of those who were selected for the first or second nines and then couldn't make it to the matches. I can't tell you how many times we had to vote on a resignation of someone from the second nine and vote on a replacement and then maybe reverse it a month later. It seems to me if someone makes a commitment to something like a nine, then dammit all, he ought to honor that commitment.

FRALEY NIEBUHR   I knew a photographer who asked me if we might like to have a club picture taken. In those days it was not possible to take an action picture because, as he explained, the players and the ball would be moving too fast, but a still, posed picture would work.

I put the proposition to the members. We had a first nine game coming up with the Excelsiors, so I put a motion on the floor that before the game we pose for a photograph with both teams. When our treasurer questioned the expense involved, I added, "at a cost not to exceed $10."

A fine picture it turned out to be. I wish we had more testaments such as that as a record of our club, and of base ball in general for that matter. Some of our most important members were in that picture — Davis, Adams, DeBost, Sam Kissam.

Looking back on it, wouldn't it have been fine if we had a picture of the club members in the first year with Cartwright, Wheaton, Curry, Dupignac, and all the others?

WALTER AVERY   Managing the finances of the club was always a bit tricky as we never had much, if any reserve, so we were constantly operating on the thin edge of solvency. At one monthly meeting, David Keeler, our treasurer offered a report showing a deficit for the year. He also cited several members for non-payment of dues — me among them.

"Mr. Keeler," I said, "I assure you I never received notice that I was arrears in dues."

"I'm sure I notified everyone."

"You did not notify me."

"Perhaps then I missed your name on the list."

"Indeed you did."

Mr. Keeler looked a little sheepish.

Mr. Wenman, our secretary that year, rose and moved that a fine be issued to Mr. Keeler for neglect of duty. The motion was passed in a spirit somewhere between a rebuke and a joke.

"Check our books, now," said Mr. Davis, "and tell us if we still have a deficit."

"It seems to be smaller than it was a few minutes ago."

"At least we're heading in the right direction. Now who else can we fine?"

"I propose, rather," said Mr. Lasak," that we levy a fee of $3 per man on the members for the purposes of meeting the current annual expenses and that the treasurer notify those members in arrears that unless they settle their accounts before the 12th they would be reported to the Board for action. Would that handle the deficit, Mr. Keeler?"

"Assuming everyone pays up, it would."

"Make sure you send the notice."

"I'm making a note."

After the motion carried, President Davis vacated the chair and asked me as vice-president to take over.

"I am compelled to make charges against Mr. Welling," he said. "The charges are that he used abusive language in reference to the Board of Directors."

"What action are you asking us to take?" I asked.

"I am asking to have the matter investigated."

Since Mr. Welling was not present, I asked Mr. Davis if he had notified him to appear at the meeting."

"I personally sent him a note to that effect. I put it in the post myself."

Mr. Keeler then stood up and said: "Inasmuch as Mr. Welling has not seen fit to pay any attention to the notice, I move that he be expelled from the club."

"Perhaps Mr. Welling never received the note, said Mr. Wenman, "as it was sent through the post office. So I would amend Mr. Keeler's motion, that Mr. Welling be notified that unless he appears before the Board on the evening of the 9th, he will be expelled."

The motion including the amendment carried.

At the next meeting, I was again sitting in the Chair for the purpose of taking up Mr. Welling's case. This time he was present and was informed of the charges preferred against him by Mr. Davis.

"I'll admit to having made use of the language," he said, "but I assure you I had no intention of reflecting on the Board either individually or collectively and I am most willing to make any apology necessary."

On motion the apology was considered satisfactory and the case dismissed.

I don't know whether or not this satisfied Jamie, but he didn't say anything. He could be a real stubborn son-of-a-gun when he wanted to, and he frequently wanted to.

SAM KISSAM    One thing about our club that drove me crazy was that I don't think a year went by that we weren't assessed additional dues to meet the demands of the club. I don't understand why we didn't just raise the darn dues in the first place.

DOC ADAMS    Once when I proposed that we amend some of our rules so as to conform to the rules of the National Association, Mr. Stanbury moved that we withdraw from the Association. The motion was laid on the table and not then acted upon but it did indicate a current of disaffection with "surrendering to the masses."

Although I tried to be as persuasive as I could, what these members didn't understand is that the Association was the future of the game whether we liked it or not and that if we wanted to have any influence on that future we had to remain as a member.

# 79

# *Other Clubs to the Forefront*

JAMES WHYTE DAVIS    In '59 I was again elected Knickerbocker president and was glad to have Walter Avery back as vice president. We only played four intra-club games that year and a couple of muffin matches. In every one we played the fly rule and although we lost three of the four club games, we were insistent that if we were to accept a challenge from any club it would have to be with that rule. Most of the other clubs were reluctant, but in each of our matches we used umpires who we felt would be influential in convincing their members.

JOE LEGGETT    The first Great Base Ball Match may have been won by New York, but the Brooklyn clubs were proving to be the strongest. The Atlantics were 11–1 for the '60 season; the Eckfords, 11–3; the Star, 8–1; and my Excelsiors 12–3. In fact, all year, only two of the losses for these clubs were against New York clubs.

We also played a game of base ball against the St. George Cricket Club. They were an almighty arrogant bunch, so it was with great pleasure that we soundly trounced them 25–0. Afterwards it was reported that this was the first time a club shut out another team. Bowled for a duck they might say.

We thought it was still appropriate to play against the Knickerbockers out of respect for their seniority if not their playing skills. We won both games against them that year, the first game 26–22, the second 20–5.

I had a particularly good season, ending up tied with John Gram of the Eckfords for the most runs scored at 49.

ASHLEY HYDE    Another year and scores of new clubs sprang up — Amity, Esculapian, Exercise, Good Intent, Hiawatha, Ivanhoe, Katydid, Oriental and Osceola. There was also a spate of clubs flying the patriotic flag — Liberty, Columbia, E Pluribus Unum, Eagle, Excelsior.

One afternoon with a day off and nothing pressing, I went over to Bedford to watch a match between the Atlantic and Harlem clubs. When I got there, however, I was informed that the game had been postponed because of wet grounds. So I decided to take a walk around Bedford, a pretty village that would become part of Brooklyn. I hadn't gone very far when I came upon a crowd watching a base ball game played by the Unknown and Monitor clubs. What was remarkable about this is that the players on both clubs were of African descent and all in the large crowd were as black as the ace of spades.

Yes, the game was spreading.

JERRY FRUIN    Well, I don't question that the mighty Excelsior Club was the strongest club around, but when they accepted the invitation of our new club, the Charter Oaks, they thought so little of our chances that they didn't bother to send their first nine. So we ended up scoring two runs in the bottom of the ninth inning to win the game.

This apparently irritated them so much that for the return match they did send their first nine who managed to "squeeze out" a 62–13 win.

Later that year we invited the Knicks to our new home grounds in Brooklyn, but they declined. You think they were afraid of us?

DOC ADAMS    Another reason base ball was spreading like wildfire was that it had the imprimatur of New York on it. For better or worse, New York was the commercial and cultural hub of the country. A game that came from New York and was for a long time referred to as "New York Game" suggested a connection with our city that to many was appealing and that perhaps suggested a certain legitimacy.

It was around this time, too, that the Massachusetts game was replaced by the New York game, and down in Philadelphia even such stalwarts of their game as the Olympic Town Ball Club came over to our rules.

Base ball as envisioned by Knickerbockers and adopted by virtually everyone else had taken on all challengers and came out the unquestioned victor. We all knew now it was here to stay. The only question was, to what influences would it succumb?

JOE LEGGETT    By the end of the '50s, amateur base ball was in its glory. In some ways it might have been considered the beginning of true base ball, and everything that came before, a series of trial trips.

---

# 80

## *Of Bounders and Flys*

HENRY CHADWICK    It seemed to me that the Association delegates were defeating the fly rule proposal despite the fact that most players supported it. Here's the irony: The Knickerbockers, the most fraternal of all the clubs were on the side of those favoring the competitive nature of the fly game, while at the same time, they were being criticized for "holding back the progress of the game."

JUDGE VAN COTT   I had always opposed it on the grounds that it made it more difficult for youngsters to learn and play the game, but out of courtesy to Adams and Davis, who seemed so earnestly to believe it would be a desirable improvement, I agreed to support the proposal.

DOC ADAMS   I was hopeful that with Van Cott's reversal, the fly rule would be passed at the next Association meeting.

In March of '60 we had the meeting at the Cooper Institute. Van Cott again presided. The first order of business was a report from the Committee on Nominations, read by Mott, who once played with us but who was then with the Eagles. When all was done we had admitted something like 20 new member clubs.

As soon as that was completed, Van Cott asked if there were any representatives of clubs present who had not been considered. Up popped a man on crutches whom none of us had seen before.

"Yes, your honor," he said, drawing a big laugh.

Van Cott, assuming the judicial role said, "You may approach the bench with your application."

"I represent the Bunker Hill Club, your honor."

As it turned out, the old soldier didn't have the proper documentation for membership so the Bunker Hill vets were put off for the time being.

When it was time to elect officers for the coming year, Dr. Jones was elected president.

Then it was my turn to take the floor as chairman of the Committee on Rules and Regulations. Yet again I reported that the committee was unanimous in their proposal to adopt the fly game. Because I figured that the members were tired of me haranguing on about it, I asked Tom Dakin to take up the cudgel, which he did with great conviction.

We lost the battle again, this time, 37–55, but slowly we were gaining on the opposition and I vowed to continue to press the question whether the stuck-in-the-muds liked it or not. Surely the day would come when we all played the fly game all the time. It simply had to be.

SAM KISSAM   I have no doubt whatsoever that had the clubs sent the best players to the convention instead of the best talkers, we would have been better off. Many of them weren't first or even second nine players. For all I know, some of them didn't even play the game any longer. Ignoring the appeal of the fly game was just stupid.

JAMES WHYTE DAVIS   I don't know what else we had to do to get the blockheads to accept the fly game. Maybe if we played games where we tried to catch the balls in our mouth, the fly game would have looked easier in comparison.

CHARLES DEBOST   One part of the game that I got pretty stubborn about was fielders running into each other trying to catch fly balls. Even a player as good as Harry Wright sometimes did it. Since we were playing the fly rule I took to telegraphing the direction fielders should take in chasing a fly ball when it appeared two or more might arrive at the same point at the same time.

In one game a fly was lifted to the infield and I could see Jamie and Harry both heading toward it, so I signaled Jamie to go to his left so as to leave it for Harry. Hell, I even shouted to that effect. But Jamie was either blind, deaf, or stubborn (I think I know the answer) and ran right into Harry, dislodging both the ball and the little finger on Harry's hand.

"For Christsake, Jamie, didn't you see me?"

"I saw you."

"Didn't you hear me?"

"I heard you."

Then what the hell happened?"

"I didn't believe you."

I suppose the bound rule would have prevented these sorts of things, but then again, so would have paying attention.


ASHLEY HYDE   I loved watching games at the Elysian Fields. The ferry ride across the busy river was in itself an enjoyable experience with views of the bustling New York marine activity on one side and the verdant bluffs on the other.

Once the ferry landed I would make the short climb up to the fields above where I would find a place along the sidelines. A few visitors who lived nearby would sit in parked carriages, but the rest of us would stand. I was, at the time, seeing Elizabeth, a young lady of considerable charm and wit.

The field was all grass except for a few worn spots near the bases and around the pitcher's line. Leafy green trees almost completely encircled the field such that any ball hit foul had a good chance to bounce off branches. If the word "Elysian" is taken to mean "inspired by the gods," then this marvelous place was certainly that.

I remember one particularly interesting game that year that I saw with Elizabeth. The Knicks were playing the Excelsiors and what was particularly noteworthy about the game was that they were using the fly rule.

The Excelsiors were already batting as we came over the rise to see the field in all its summer glory. Along the third base line the Excelsior players were lounging in the August sun while waiting for their turn at bat. They were a good looking group of lads in their immaculate white uniforms, and sporting neatly trimmed beards and moustaches.

Sitting at a table mid-way along the third base line, were the two umpires—Young from the Excelsiors, Wood from the Knicks. They looked like opposing attorneys at court. Along the first base line stood Mr. Hawkhurst of the Atlantics in top hat and frock coat leaning insouciantly on his silver-topped cane.

He was the referee who would rule on the arguments of the opposing barristers.

We found a place in the tent, spread a blanket on the ground and put out the picnic lunch Elizabeth had prepared. Elizabeth, who had been to many games with me, greeted a few of the ladies and then took out the needlework. I enquired about the score and was told there was none yet.

When Leggett came to bat, Elizabeth said, "He's a very scientific hitter, isn't he?"

I smiled at Elizabeth's knowledge of the game. "He certainly is," I said.

"He'll hit a home run this time," she said.

"Now, what makes you think that?"

"It's just what I think. Call it intuition."

"Well that's not very scientific."

"I said he was, not me."

"Oh, I see."

Unlike many scientific batsmen who gripped the bat part way up so as to be able to poke the ball between the fielders, Leggett gripped the bat down near the end and often took a mighty swing.

"He hits too many high fly balls," I said.

"Playing the fly rule, that will be less of a problem," she said.

This brought a little laughter from a few spectators. How many women would know such things? Elizabeth was special.

"You like the big strong types then, do you?"

"I like good players."

"Well I don't think he will hit a home run at all. I think he'll hit a fly ball that will go for naught."

She turned back to her needlework. "We'll see," she said.

On the third pitch, Leggett swung his big bat as hard as he could, sending the ball deep into the field over the head of Davis who turned his back to the infield and raced after it. At full speed he reached out his left hand caught the ball, his momentum carrying him nearly to the trees. It was the most beautiful of base ball plays—fast, graceful, daring.

The spectators responded with well-deserved applause. As if it needed it, that one play itself was justification for using the fly rule

"I told you he'd make a fly out," said Elizabeth without smiling.

"You're always right, dear. I shouldn't have doubted."

JAMES WHYTE DAVIS  Here's a little ditty in celebration of the fly rule:

> How dear to the heart is the green-covered ball field,
> Where good rival captains their men rightly place,
> The pitcher, the catcher, the right field and left,

The good men, the true men, who guard well each base!
The shortstop so lively, the center field handy
The ball and the striker who aims to send high!
But dearer than all to the hearts of good fielders,
Is the leathern clad base ball we catch on the fly —
The jolly old base ball, the well-covered base ball,
The leathern clad base ball we catch on the fly.

---

# 81

# *Banning Entertainments*

JAMES WHYTE DAVIS    To those who were claiming that the Knickerbockers were an old-fashioned, conservative organization, holding back the inevitable progress of the sport, all I can say in response is look at the progression in the rules proposed by our club through Doc. The fact is, we were at the head of the pack pushing to make the game ever more difficult and thus challenging. And that's the way we played it!

Now get this. According to the Association, a "sad but necessary" rule was added. They, in their infinite lunacy, decreed that post-game dinners hosted by the home clubs would be banned. Why? Because they claimed that these expressions of fellowship and good feelings had degenerated into a further spread of club rivalry and rowdy behavior.

I remember the look on Charlie DeBost's face when I relayed this exciting piece of information to him.

"Well, Jamie," he said, "they can shove their rules..."

I can't repeat the rest, but suffice it to say, our dinners were always lively, but never rowdy and we weren't about to change anything because some Association bigwigs thought they could legislate not only the game but our behavior as well. Our behavior didn't need any legislation.

"Come on, Jamie," said Charlie, "let's go have a drink and be rowdy."

"What if someone from the Association sees us?"

"I'll buy them a drink, too."

Ever since bases were posts, the after-game festivities were as important to the game as bats and balls. Unlike cricket players, who indulged in the middle of the match, we waited until the game was finished. You just can't play a good game on a full stomach. But when the day's play is done, well, that's a different story.

A well-laid banquet table was as important as a well-played game. We gathered after most games, we held special banquets after matches with other clubs, we had season-ending balls when we invited wives and friends.

I understand that for some clubs these events were becoming as hotly contested as the games themselves. Contested in the sense that clubs tried to outdo each other in putting on better and more elaborate events. But ours were characterized by propriety and dignity. Oh, occasionally someone might arrive a little upset over something that happened in a game or have a little too much to drink, but these were relatively minor and few. We were gentlemen, not saints.

CHARLES DEBOST   According to one story I read in the *Clipper*, after having downed a keg of lager, the players on one club were unable to recall the score of a game they had played only hours earlier. Reports like this didn't help with those Victorians who wanted to believe the game of base ball was a one-way street leading directly to hell.

Now we could put away the lager, no doubt about that, but I don't remember ever forgetting a day's game. Now that I think of it, maybe that was the point.

SAM KISSAM   You simply can't legislate against having fun. What would be the fun in that? We remained very active on the social front, particularly during the winter months. We'd organize dinners, various outings, skating parties, promenades, and such. And always there was the annual ball. We had a committee to organize it and included some of the wives to help with the details. As you can imagine, these were highly festive occasions with a rented ball room decked out in bunting, flowers, and sometimes the colors of other clubs.

We hired a band, and, very Paris-like, swept our ladies across the floor with as much panache as we could muster. Jamie was particularly light on his feet and often presided on the dance floor to the applause of all.

Some of the clubs became so elaborate with their annual balls that the newspapers covered them as if they were important matches.

Call us social/athletic clubs if you will, but we never dreamed of one without the other.

# 82

# *A New Park*

DOC ADAMS   At one of our Association meetings, the discussion turned to a topic about which we had been hearing much lately — the creation of a large new park to be called Central Park. Francis Pidgeon of the Eckfords was particularly excited about the possibilities.

FRANCIS PIDGEON    The city was becoming so crowded that people were clamoring for more open spaces. During summer afternoons, even the cemeteries were filling up with those looking to escape the noise and bustle of the city. Then William Cullen Bryant, editor of the *Evening Post*, and the architect Andrew Jackson Downing began campaigning for a green space in the city equivalent to the Bois de Boulogne in Paris, or Hyde Park in London. Eventually the New York Legislature designated 700 acres stretching all the way from 59th Street to 106th Street for a park at a cost of 5 million dollars for the land alone.

The state then appointed a Central Park Commission to oversee its development and to select a winning design. The writer, Frederick Law Olmstead, and English architect, Calvert Vaux, won the competition with their "Greensward Plan."

Everyone with a vested interest in the park came forward with proposals for setting aside specific areas for specific activities. This is where we came in. I proposed to the Association that we appoint a committee to work on our behalf to secure a portion of the park to be set aside for several base ball fields. I was hoping that the new Central Park would become the home of base ball for the entire New York area. What more beautiful use of that space could anyone imagine?

DOC ADAMS    The potential was exciting. The idea of a permanent home for the game and a place to stage all the big matches was extremely appealing and great enthusiasm for the project was voiced.

The Commissioners claimed it would accommodate more athletic interests than any other park in the world. The question was, would the base ball space be for occasional or permanent club use?

FRANCIS PIDGEON    The creation of Central Park got under way but in the process established communities like Seneca Village were razed, churches removed, and according to the papers, 1,600 people dislocated.

Many of the city's poorest claimed they wouldn't be able to afford the fare to get to the park when it was completed. This was brought up as an argument against putting in permanent base ball fields for championship matches.

Nevertheless, some of the oldest and most respected clubs in the city — the Knickerbockers, Eagles, and Empires — all urged the Central Park Board to include more ball grounds.

FREDERICK LAW OLMSTED    It was obviously impossible to accommodate more than fifty ball clubs with fifty members each. The space was not sufficient to acquiesce to all the club requests and at the same time preserve an appearance that would be satisfactory to those who would frequent the park for the enjoyment of the refined and attractive features of its natural beauty. Whatever might injure or deface this picture would make it less attractive to the general mass of visitors. Therefore, for the general good, we had to reject the applications of all base ball clubs.

DOC ADAMS   Shortly after it was completed, some of us went up to the new Central Park and rode on the carousel they had just put in. We enjoyed it as much as the children. It might have been nice to have had permanent ball fields but I understood Olmstead's position. Besides, the Elysian Fields continued to serve our needs very well.

---

## 83

# *Rule Changes*

DOC ADAMS   The Rules Committee continued to adjust, reconfirm, and change rules, most of which had something to do with cheating, ill behavior, or violations of one sort or another. I suppose, looking back on it, there was a clear indication that not all was well with the game.

Although I don't think any of us actually believed that putting in a rule about betting would stop that odious act, it was a place from which to begin. So we wrote in a statement saying that no one engaged in a match as umpire, scorer, or player shall be, either directly or indirectly, interested in any bet on the game. There it was as an unequivocal position of the Association—for all the good it was likely to do.

We also added a prohibition against any club using players who were in arrears to any other club, or who received compensation for his services as a player. This was an important rule, although at the time we didn't realize just how important it would become.

Some other rules we added or adjusted included:

Clubs could adopt their own rules on balls knocked beyond or outside of bounds of the field, as the circumstances of the ground demands, as long as they are made known to every player and umpire, prior to beginning the game.

No person could approach the umpire in any manner that interrupted or interfered with the progress of the game.

No person could act as umpire or scorer unless he was a member of a club governed by our rules.

If either club failed to produce their players within fifteen minutes of a game's designated starting time, they had to admit defeat.

All nine players on a side had to be regular members of the club they represent, and of no other club, for thirty days prior to the match, and no change or substitution could be made after the game begins, unless for reason of illness or injury.

Any player who intentionally prevents an adversary from catching or fielding the ball would be declared out and if a player was prevented from making a base by the intentional obstruction of an adversary, he would be entitled to that base.

Any player running three feet out of the line between the bases for the purpose of avoiding the ball in the hands of an adversary, would be declared out.

We specified that the bases must be so constructed as to be distinctly seen by the umpire, and must cover a space equal to one square foot of surface. The first, second, and third bases had to be canvas bags, painted white, and filled with sand or sawdust; and the home base and the pitcher's point each marked by a flat circular white iron plate.

We also clarified the pitching delivery to state that the pitcher was not to let his pitching arm touch his side, or be "jerked," in the act of delivery. There was a very good reason for this inclusion — Jim Creighton.

JAMES WHYTE DAVIS    James Creighton had become simply the most highly regarded player both for his batting and for his pitching. In fact he was such a star that spectators came to games just to see him play and it wouldn't have mattered for whom he was playing.

He was a natural and it quickly became obvious that he was better than any of the Brooklyn lads with whom he was playing. He helped organize a club, the name of which indicates what they thought of themselves — the Young America Base Ball Club. The club folded before the Young Americans could become old Americans, but he immediately helped start the Niagara Club.

One day while playing in the field, his club fell a number of runs behind so they switched Jimmy to pitcher. What he did then had never been seen before.

Believe me, I know whereof I speak when I say that his delivery was near on unhittable.

HENRY CHADWICK    Now the question was, of course, was Creighton's pitch a jerk, or a fair square pitch? I believed it was the latter. He was both a wonderful player, the likes of which I had never seen, and a wonderful young man demonstrating the best values of the game.

WALTER AVERY    As far as I was concerned it was simply an illegal pitch and a lot of players agreed with me. The rules said the ball must be pitched, not jerked. I rest my case.

DOC ADAMS   The Rules Committee was constantly wrestling with attempts to define exactly what the pitcher could and could not do. First we established a rule stating that both of the pitcher's feet had to be on the ground when the ball was released. Later we modified that to allow a step before the release.

The fact is, that no matter how we tweaked the rules, umpires found it difficult to enforce them. This was particularly so when it came to the straight-armed requirement. The pitcher's arms were moving so fast, it was really hard to tell.

What all of this amounted to was simply this: The game was shifting in favor of the pitcher and Creighton was at the forefront of that change. He was so good and so popular that teams were even named after him.

CHARLES DEBOST   There were two types of balls that the pitchers threw: the fast ball and the slow ball. Of the two, it was that damn slow ball that nearly drove me to the nut house. Harry Wright could throw it real good, and so could "Old Slow Ball" Alphonse Martin of the Eckfords. I watched him throw the ball with a delivery so damn drawn out and twisty that batters got exasperated and swung much too hard. As far as I was concerned, pitchers like Martin need to be confined to the nether regions of hell for all eternity.

"Patience, Charlie," Jamie used to say all the time. Then he'd come up against a slow, tricky thrower, swing too hard and come back swearing a blue streak.

"What was that you said, Jamie?"

"I said, that old honey-fuggling ... oh, never mind. Just wait till you try it."

Some pitchers, too, now lifted the back foot before delivering the ball, which was illegal, but if a pitcher did it quickly enough he could usually get away with it. All pitchers had a black heart. They were born hornswogglers and remained so all their tricky lives.

# Part Nine: Playing Through the War 1861–1865

## 84

## *Things Unravel*

DOC ADAMS  Until it actually happened, never in my wildest dreams did I think it would come to this. We were at war. In April of '61 President Lincoln issued a proclamation calling for 75,000 militiamen. Command of the Union Army was offered to Robert E. Lee, the son of a Revolutionary War hero with 25 years of distinguished service in the United States Army and former Superintendent of West Point. He declined.

To show its support for the Union, thousands of people assembled in Union Square and the city was decked out in red, white, and blue bunting. By July, the 1st New York Cavalry Regiment had been organized and sent off to defend Washington and Alexandria. A call went out by our governor for another 25,000 volunteers to enlist for a three-year term.

FRALEY NIEBUHR  The patriotic press was constantly pointing out the similarities between sports like base ball and war—the need for team play, courage, good judgment, sobriety, even tempers, developed muscles, courtesy of manner, and gentlemanly language. All of these represented the qualities of a good soldier, went the argument. "Better to join in boys," wrote the *Clipper*, "than be loafing the streets or hanging around bar rooms."

Many a good player in the city joined up, but not so many as to stop games from continuing, for in reality there was considerable criticism of Lincoln's policies and so lots of men, including ball players, were not eager to put their lives on the line for the Union cause. Since the military was made up mostly of volunteers and it was fairly easy to avoid the conscription laws, plenty of first-rate players remained in the city and continued to play.

Our club activities, largely suspended during the early days of the war, were eventually reinstated. Of course it would be absurd to say that the status was quo.

Mostly during our games we avoided talking about the war or the involved politics surrounding it. At other times, though, there was talk of little else. While most of us saw the war as a necessary evil, many others urged conciliation with the Confederacy. Simply put, the New York economy depended heavily on southern cotton. As our economy floundered and casualties mounted, opposition to the war escalated.

One in every four residents here was an Irish-born immigrant, most working as unskilled laborers on the docks, as coal heavers and street pavers, or in other similar positions. As such they were in competition with many of the Negroes who had worked in the city as either slaves or free men since before the Revolutionary War. So, since many white workers viewed the war as leading to increasing unemployment in the working class neighborhoods, racial tensions mounted.

Although perhaps somewhat of a simplification, I think it fair to say that on the whole, the white working class did not support the war effort and abolition, while the middle and upper classes did.

As one might expect, the Knickerbocker membership mostly supported abolition, and those who didn't largely kept quiet about it. Doc was always the most vocal supporter.

HENRY CHADWICK   I suppose it sounds callous to say this, but if nothing else, the war was an ideal breeding ground for the spread of the game. Soldiers from the North took the game with them and played on fields all over the country. According to the many stories which were passed on to our papers, officers and enlisted men alike used the game to help them forget about the horrors of war. Players were chosen to play on the sides not because of their social status but because of their playing skills and once again the democratization of the game was on display. Since it was by then considered our national game, it was intrinsically linked in the minds of many with patriotism.

Many young men from our city were fighting in the Union Army, and it was they who were largely responsible for teaching the game.

We received one story of a game between the Washington Nationals Base Ball Club and soldiers from the 71st New York Regiment played in the "President's Backyard." The Nationals won that game 41–13 and the rematch 28–13. Apparently the difference in the scores was a result of the death of many of the regiment's best players at Bull Run during the time between the two matches. Another story which reached us claimed that a Christmas day match in 1862 featuring the 165th New York Volunteer Regiment known as the Duryea Zouaves at Hilton Head, South Carolina, with 40,000 troops watching.

Some of the young players from New York went off to war toting their ball playing equipment, but when the right equipment wasn't otherwise available, they would improvise. A fence post or a barrel stave might make a passable bat; a yarn-wrapped pine cone, a ball.

DOC ADAMS   As the war dragged on, the Union faced a military manpower shortage, so Congress passed a conscription act to draft men between the ages of 18 and 35. The reality was, however, that not many men were actually drafted.

For one, many officers and volunteers resented those drafted against their will, and for another, even if drafted, it was possible to buy one's way out. This was a process known as "commutation" whereby a drafted man could put up $300 or a substitute in order to procure exemption from service. This led to the derisive term, "300-dollar man." As many would say, it was the rich man's war but the poor man's fight.

As a result of the draft, some 750,000 men Union-wide were selected for conscription, although, according to official reports, only about 45,000 actually entered the service.

Many clubs simply disbanded during this time, although most of those that did were junior clubs. Most of the senior clubs, despite losing members to the war effort, managed to survive although often with limited schedules. The Atlantics, for example, didn't play a game in the first year of the war until sometime in August and we didn't play at all that year, nor did the Excelsiors. Part of their problem was that their outstanding player, Joe Leggett, left with the Thirteenth Regiment. About 90 other club members also enlisted.

Early in the war, a number of the top players who were of good social standing were commissioned as officers even though they had no military background. It appears that social position was equated with leadership ability, a correlation you could not prove by me. Then, too, a couple of players who went off to war were captured by the Confederates and then released to come home under an agreement that allowed officers to be released on condition that they promise not to return to battle.

One of our club members who joined was Otto Parisen. A patriot always, he was commissioned as a captain in Company C of the 9th Infantry Regiment, New York Volunteers, and was involved in perhaps the most momentous battle of the war — Antietam — and survived.

After he returned to New York with an honorable discharge, he came over to Hoboken to watch a game and was given a hero's welcome by the members. Of course, as was the right of every returning soldier, he regaled us with stories of the great battle.

"Well, on the eve of the battle I found myself with Hooker's Corps along with brigadier generals George Meade and Abner Doubleday when we faced off with Lee's forces along a low ridge behind Antietam Creek. See, we had some inside information — a copy of Lee's detailed battle plans wrapped around three cigars that a couple of our boys had discovered. Now if only McClelland would move fast enough we could..."

He went on for some time and we listened with all the diligence due the returned hero. He was either very lucky, or very smart, or both, for the papers reported that it was the bloodiest single-day battle in American history.

We all congratulated him and welcomed him back to the Club.

"Thank you, Gentlemen," he said, "but I think I'll join up again."

"You're not serious," I said.

"Once the smell of gunpowder gets in the nostrils..."

The odd thing is, Otto had a lovely wife waiting at home. But he did go back. I guess it ran in the family because he served with his brother and a cousin. Otto came through unscathed. His cousin was killed.

Not all the players who volunteered were as lucky as Otto. Holt of the Eckfords was killed when accidentally shot by another Union soldier.

Although none of their first nine joined up, scores of Excelsiors volunteered, including Pearsall, who joined the Confederate army as a surgeon. The Excelsiors immediately expelled him.

OTTO PARISEN    When I left home I assumed my ball playing would have to be put on the table for the duration. Was I ever wrong about that! Many volunteers, it seemed, toted bats as carefully as they did their rifles, and we played many a game both to relieve the boredom that attended most of our time and the fear that accompanied our every day. My initial thought was that the high-ranking officers would frown at games or even prohibit them in the name of military discipline, but in fact they frequently not only encouraged them, but sometimes even played along. One thing I did learn, however, is that rank didn't necessarily equate with skill.

I remember one particularly impassioned game being played between the officers of the 140th New York Volunteers and those of the 13th New York Volunteers. I tell you, there were so many soldiers watching the game that you might have thought you were back at the Elysian Fields. The game was played with such school-boy ardor that for the duration we all forgot about our dire situation. How much the sprained ankles and sore backs that resulted may have effected subsequent military actions I don't know, but I suspect that once shells started exploding, minor infirmities quickly disappeared.

I played in scores of games, some of which were interrupted by a call to arms. War can be rather bothersome at times. It's quite astonishing really how a man can put the threat of danger out of mind even if the report of musketry echoes off the nearby hillside.

I remember one player, a man by the name of Ezell, who threw the ball harder than any man I had ever seen play. In fact he threw so hard that some of the men refused to play with him. I wonder what became of him, for certainly he could have been successful with any base ball club in the land. I wonder what happened to a lot of the boys I played with, but I guess I know the answer.

One story that made the rounds of the camps was that the president and his son, Tad, used to watch Union soldiers play games behind the White House. The story claimed that the president himself played the game back in Springfield and that when informed that the Committee of the Chicago Convention was waiting for him, Lincoln responded: "Tell the gentlemen that I am glad to know of their coming; but they'll have to wait a few minutes till I make another base hit."

Whether there was any truth to the story I don't know, but I do know it was repeated frequently.

I also heard that games were played in both Union and Confederate prison camps and that many Confederate prisoners learned the game from their northern guards and then when they returned home, taught it to others.

GEORGE PUTNAM    I was a Union soldier playing a spirited game of base ball when suddenly shots rang out. We managed to repel the attackers but our center fielder was hit and captured and so we had not only lost our best long fielder, but also the only base ball in Alexandria.

DOC ADAMS    In March of '64 I witnessed a quite remarkable display. A thousand black men in uniform marched through busy city streets, all the while receiving a grand ovation and the showering of bouquets from the hands of many of the city's most respectable ladies and gentlemen.

Only a year earlier, the draft riots saw the lynching of several Negroes.

We had come a long way in one year. There was still no question of any kind of social integration between the Whites and the Negroes, but we were moving in the right direction.

Play base ball with them? The issue wasn't even being discussed.

There were, however, a number of all–Negro teams playing in the city. One team, the Unions, comprised of former slaves, had played several games here a few years earlier.

JAMES WHYTE DAVIS    As the war dragged on, enthusiasm for base ball gradually returned. Before the war was over, many matches were again attracting large crowds. Occasionally, these matches were connected to a gimmick as in a match between the Atlantics and the Eckfords where the proceeds were advertised as going to the Brooklyn Sanitary Commission for sick and wounded soldiers. That took the guilt away from going to a game while so many men were off and dying.

A lot of the clubs had to rely on younger players and sometimes struggled to muster enough to make a good match. This affected us too. In one match against the Excelsiors we had to "borrow" two of their members to complete our side.

DOC ADAMS    The Association struggled some to survive during the war years. Attendance at the annual conventions declined as some clubs disbanded and others sent no delegates. Nevertheless, we continued to address issues related to the sport. We considered a resolution to distribute our surplus funds to army volunteers, but the resolution was eventually tabled because, according to some, the Association couldn't afford it, and to others it was too difficult to decide who should get the money, the soldiers or the families of those who had lost loved ones in the war. Another suggestion was that we hold a grand ball specifically to raise money for the war effort, but this too went nowhere.

I'm ashamed to say that although many players enlisted and some died for the Union cause, the fact remains that our base ball fraternity as a whole did little to aid the families who suffered losses. This remains a black mark against all of us. We could have and should have done more. That we didn't just shows how petty and argumentative we could be.

Is it any wonder that we had such difficulty on agreeing to play the fly game?

---

# 85

# *Membership Matters*

DOC ADAMS      I was still playing with the club, but not as often as I once did. It wasn't just the war, though. There was another important reason: I got married.

SAM KISSAM      We had given up the thought of Doc ever getting hitched. We were so used to thinking of him as single — well, maybe married to his practice and the club, but otherwise single. He was pushing 50 when he announced he would be marrying Cornelia Cook, a bright young lady who shared many of his interests. Base ball, however, did not particularly seem to be one of them. Nevertheless, she was very much a lady and was always polite if not overly enthusiastic around us.

Before the wedding, Doc took a lot of kidding, particularly from DeBost who had been married seemingly forever.

"Hey, Doc, aren't you getting a little old for this sort of thing?"

"Don't you know people improve with age?"

"I hadn't noticed."

"Experience."

"If you need lessons, let me know."

"I'll be sure to do that."

"Because at your age ... I mean you do know how it's done, don't you?"

"What's that?"

"Your marriage obligations."

"I read the instructions in a book."

"What book, 'How Old Men Do It?' Did it have good pictures?"

JAMES WHYTE DAVIS   Of course we feted Doc at a club dinner.

"I hope you're getting married early in the day, Doc," I said. "That way if it doesn't work out, you haven't wasted the whole day and you can still join us for a game in the afternoon."

"Doc, let me give you some advice about marriage," DeBost told him. "It's something like when we all go to a restaurant together and you order something you think you want, then you look around and see what someone else has ordered and you think maybe that would have been better."

"Not me," said Doc. "I'm very happy with what I've chosen."

"Yeah, now. Let's talk about it next year."

Doc took it all in the spirit in which it was intended, but I could sense that perhaps the days of Doc's participation with the club might be winding down. His age, his marriage, and frankly, some health issues were all telltale signs.

DOC ADAMS   I can honestly say my marriage was the crowning achievement of my life. Cornelia and I were looking forward to raising a family. I knew my days with the Club were limited.

CHARLES DEBOST   We may have been losing Doc, but the base ball fraternity absolutely lost as fine a young man as you could ever want to know.

When Jimmy Creighton joined the Excelsiors in '60 he turned what was already a good club into arguably the best. That year, with him pitching most of the games, they won 18 of their 21 games. And here's the interesting part: he allowed the opponents less than eight runs a game. That was unheard of in those days. The next year, although the Excelsiors abstained from playing club matches because of the war, he did pitch an all–Brooklyn side to an 18–6 win over our New York boys. Also, for the record, I add that Mr. Cohen was the catcher for the New York side while Mr. DeBost watched from the stands.

Yes, sir, he was good all right; however, irony being what it is, his reputation skyrocketed because he left us at such an early age.

The story that was published in every paper that cared about base ball, and probably a few that didn't, is that while batting in a match against the Union Club on October 14, 1862, he swung so hard that he ruptured his spleen and died a few days later.

I heard, though, from his teammate Joe Leggett, that actually he had been injured some days earlier in a cricket match while bowling for the St. George Club.

Jimmy was only 21. I went to the services for him when was buried out in Greenwood Cemetery with Joe Leggett serving as one of his pallbearers.

One paper on reporting his death wrote that it should be taken as a warning to others. "Exercise is a good thing," they wrote, "but like other good things, one may take too much of it." I never heard anything so stupid in my life. How many of us have swung hard at pitches and not died in the effort?

It has since frequently been claimed that he was the first great star of American base ball. The only pitcher who never had an equal, they said, but I can't help wondering how much his reputation is because of the circumstances and timing of his death.

FRALEY NIEBUHR   Wonder of wonders! They established a telegraph link between New York and San Francisco and naturally it made me think of my old friend Alick.

"I wonder what the old boy is up to," I mused one evening as we gathered after a game.

"Alick?" said Tuck. "He's probably telling the city fathers out there how to run their city."

"Hell, he probably is a city father."

We talked about trying to contact him, but never actually did. Anyway, I wonder what he would have thought about the game then? Much of it was exactly as he knew when he left; but much had changed, too.

JAMES WHYTE DAVIS   By the end of the war, base ball was struggling with a number of critical issues: commercialism, threats of professionalism, maintaining control at championship matches, and the inevitable pains associated with growth. Some suggested the game was getting out of control.

---

# 86

## Maintaining Control

FRALEY NIEBUHR   I wouldn't necessarily agree with some who thought the game was spiraling out of control, but I would agree that there were issues that needed to be attended to.

CHARLES DEBOST   I went with Jamie to a match of some import between the Brooklyn Atlantics and the New York Mutuals. Despite the oppressively hot weather about 5,000 spectators turned out, but a committee of the members did a good job in keeping order. I might add that, by my estimate, there were more than a hundred ladies present. The field was bounded on either side by a row of spectators some two or three deep behind which were dozens of carriages and behind them tents decked out with flags and surrounded by thirsty applicants for the popular lager.

Both clubs were fielding their very best nines so anticipation of a first rate match was in the offing. "Anticipation" I say for the display of fielding from two of the best clubs around was in a word, "atrocious." By the close of the eighth inning, the score stood at 26 to 18 in favor of the Atlantics. Even the most sanguine of the Mutuals appeared to have given up the game and those who had a heavy wager pending either felt good humored or angered and annoyed according to their bets.

"Our muffins could put on a better display of fielding," said Jamie.

"And frequently do," I added. "Do you want to call it a day?"

"Let's see it through."

"Why, are you a glutton for punishment?"

"Apparently."

The Mutuals then put on the best batting of the match and pulled to within two runs of the Atlantics.

"Will wonders never cease," said Jamie.

At this point, considerable chaffing broke out among the players. All pretense to gentlemanly behavior evaporated. The Atlantics continually baited the Mutuals with angry comments which agitated spectators, some of whom began joining in by adding their own obscenities to the din. Suffice it to say, it was an ugly, disreputable scene.

"Damn," said Jamie, "makes me sound like a saint."

"Well that's something I've never heard you called before."

Insults were being hurled across the field with abandon. Then to make a bad situation even worse, a ball was hit toward Start at the first base, but he appeared to make no effort to catch it. Start said it was too dark and that he just couldn't see the ball. Apparently this was all the Atlantic players needed to appeal to the umpire to stop play on the grounds that there was not enough light left in the day. Granted, it was nearly seven and clouds were rolling in, but this shameful display of poor sportsmanship was beyond my ken. When the umpire, who did his duty correctly and manfully throughout, stated the game would continue, the Atlantics then appealed to him to call the game because of the terribly excited crowd and the "threatening aspect" it presented to the umpire.

I looked over at Jamie who was now silently seething.

The umpire, to his credit, sent the sides back out to finish the game and cleared the field of the spectators who had descended upon it. Beard took his stand at the bat, struck three times at the ball without touching it, the third time, running for his first base when Pearce missed the ball and made no effort to retrieve it. Beard made it all the way around to score. Wansley then followed suit by striking three times at the ball, and again no effort being made by the catcher, he made it half-way between the second and third bases before Smith ended the game by touching him with the ball and received three cheers from the Mutuals for his credible actions. The umpire then signed his name on the score book giving the game to the Mutuals.

As we were leaving the grounds, Jamie turned to me and said, "Is this what we started? Tell me it isn't so."

JAMES WHYTE DAVIS    That game put a lot of pressure on the umpire and despite insinuations to the contrary, I only argued with the umpires when I was right.

The situation was made all the more difficult by the fact that the umpires were all players themselves so, of course, they often knew the other players on the field, yet for the sake of fairness they were to pretend they didn't. Once they assumed the mantle of umpire, they became the most equal among equals. It was such an artificial situation that no wonder there were problems.

CHARLES DEBOST    I saw a game once where the Mutual's Eddie Brown stole the third base. Although the play was very close, he jumped up and offered to take on any of the Eureka players who cared to fight him. As those taking him up on his offer rushed to the base, he ran home with the winning run. Is this fair trickery or cheating? Either way, it stunk to heaven.

Here's another piece of chicanery that was often resorted to by catchers like Cohen. We played a rule that said a runner could not advance on a foul ball until the ball had been returned to the pitcher. So what he would sometimes do if a batter hit a high foul over his head was to return the ball to his pitcher (usually McKeever) who on purpose let it slip though his hands. What a clumsy fellow he was. Anyway, sometimes a runner would not see it get away from McKeever, who would then blithely move to the base from which the runner left and stand there like an idiot but, nevertheless, the runner was out.

Most of us catchers didn't play that way, but such hanky-panky was widely applauded in some quarters.

# 87

# *Creeping Commercialism*

JAMES WHYTE DAVIS    Here's a perfect example of the creeping commercialism in the game. Or to put it another way, how to pay players to play base ball.

The "friends" of Dickey Pearce got up the idea of staging a benefit match for him, the friends being, I'm sure, the club. What could possibly be the purpose of a benefit game for someone other than to indirectly pay him for his services? It wasn't as if he was destitute or ill. He was, in fact, healthy, employed, and a damn good player. The game was to be played at the St. George Cricket Ground with an admission charge of ten cents per head.

The day in November chosen for the game was clear but cold enough that several of the players who agreed to play did not show up and several clubs failed even to send representatives. Eventually, they managed to round up enough warm bodies to play.

The papers the next day reported that between two and three thousand people were there to watch Little Dickey and his friends

Let's take the middle ground for the sake of computation. If there were 2,500 spectators and each paid ten cents then that would have meant a gate of $250. Not a bad day's work for playing a game, and this at a time when you could buy a paper for one penny.

That wasn't the only way of making money on the game, however. Gambling was as much a part of the game as peanuts. Hell, sitting in the stands you could hear veteran punters shouting out the changing odds for any and all to hear. You could lay down a bet in the stands just as easily as you could stand and cheer, and many a man did.

Then one September afternoon, the Mutuals played a game against the Eckfords. According to those who decide such things, the Mutuals were heavily favored to win the match. They ended up losing the game 23–11, but that's hardly the story.

Now I wasn't present, but according to some of the 4,000 who were, they could smell a rat, the stench of which might have been detected all the way out to Coney Island. To call the fielding of the Mutuals "loose" would be like calling George Washington a patriot. They looked more like clowns at the circus or drunks at the Five Points than ball players. Bill Wansley, their very capable veteran catcher, accounted for 10 miscues all by himself. I'm not sure he had 10 all the rest of the season. Apparently there were more wild throws and passed balls than there were pickpockets in the stands and there were always plenty from that fraternity.

So with the stench still burning in their nostrils, the officers of the Mutuals, to their credit, formed a committee to look into the game and possible charges of "selling," or as we called it then, "heaving" the game, or "hippodroming." After an extensive investigation that couldn't have taken more than ten minutes, they concluded that, indeed, the game had been heaved. In their report they stated that Wansley was the ringleader, ably assisted by the bungled playing of Ed Duffy at the third base and Tommy Devyr stumbling around at short stop. With all due respect to the august committee, a group of the deaf, dumb, and blind apparently would have reached the same conclusion.

The Mutual Club, acting in the best interests of the game and their organization, expelled all three cheaters with the full understanding that at the next convention, they would be barred from playing for any other club.

THOMAS DEVYR    Obviously I can offer no apology for the injury done my club or the disgrace brought on myself by my connection with this affair, but in order that I may put myself in the true light (which, God knows, is bad enough) I can explain what happened. Between eleven and twelve o'clock on the morning of the match, I was going toward the ferry when I met Wansley, Duffy, and another man in a wagon. Bill pulled up and asked me where I was going.

"I'm heading over to the ground in about an hour," I said.

He said, "Do you want to make three hundred dollars?"

"Who wouldn't?"

"You can make it easy."

"How is that?"

"We are going to heave this game, and will give you three hundred dollars if you stand in with us; you need not do any of the work, I'll do all that myself and get all the blame. Let them blame, I can stand it. We can lose this game without doing the club any harm. I know you ain't got a cent, neither has Duffy."

"True enough."

"You can make this money without any one being a bit the wiser of it."

"Bill, if you don't want me to help you why would you let me into it?"

"I want to give you a chance to make some money and make the men with the money sure that it can be done."

Well, to make a long story short, I agreed. We went over to a house in the city, received a hundred dollars, of which I got thirty. That was all I did receive since or before. This is the whole substance of it.

I simply say this to explain how my connection with this unhappy affair was brought about. For what! For thirty dollars, which I could do nothing with but lose playing faro. I had 30 hundred worth of disgrace, all to myself and never to lose.

I am sorry I had anything to do with it but my sorrow, like my confession, comes too late to help.

DOC ADAMS    I guess *mea culpas* work, because the Association wilted under pressure from the Mutuals and two years later he was again playing short stop for them and it wasn't long before Ed Duffy was once more patrolling the infield, and incredible as it sounds, Bill Wansley was also reinstated. The shame belongs to the Association. Apparently perfidy has an expiration date.

JAMES WHYTE DAVIS    It had come to this: The reputation of many clubs was less determined by its decorum than by its winning percentage.

How do you win? By attracting the best players. How do you attract the best players? Make it worth their while. How do you make it worth their while? Pay them, of course. Oh, but that's illegal you say? Okay, so do it sub rosa and then deny it so loudly and often that no one will want to question it.

Look, we all heard the stories, the rumors, the innuendoes. We knew. Some clubs began secretly paying players under the table.

Three clubs in our area were heads and shoulders above all others in their ability to win games—the Eckfords, the Mutuals, and the Atlantics—and it was these clubs who were the most active in compensating players. Mostly what they did was to find someone who could hire a player to work for him in some capacity or other where the player had to do minimal, if any, actual work.

"What's that you say, son? You need the afternoon off to play ball? Why, sure, take off the whole week if you need to get ready for the game. Don't worry about the U.S. Treasury, we'll just print up a few more dollars to make up the difference."

It was all a sham—the salaries, the lies, the game. Ball playing was edging toward becoming a regular business, an occupation just like a bank clerk or a customs officer.

What if you were being paid to play for one club and another club wanted your services enough to offer you more money to play for them? Why, jump to that club, of course. And if another club offered even more? Jump again. And again. This act of betrayal became known as "revolving." According to a newspaper report, one such double-dealing traitor actually played with six different clubs in a three-season span. Although the paper didn't say it, I assume he then retired to live on his yacht.

Let it be said, the Knickerbocker Base Ball Club did not pay its players, the players through their dues, paid to play.

SAM KISSAM    One enterprising gentleman by the name of William Cammeyer came up with a rather clever way to make money on the game. He found a barren lot on the corner of Lee Avenue and Rutledge Street over in the Williamsburgh area. So, apparently after being struck by a bolt of inspiration, he smoothed it over nicely and erected a fence around it. Voila, he now had an enclosed level plot of land just the right size for a ball field, stands for about 1,500 people, a clubhouse, and a saloon—all the requisites to make a pile of money, which he did by attracting teams to play there and then charging for spectators to walk through the gate in his fence. And because he was such a patriot, he named his enclosed field the Union Grounds, flew the American flag, and hired a band to play "The Star Spangled Banner" before games.

In winter, he flooded it and charged to ice skate there. I guess he needed the money because, although he owned a shoe company, he had thirteen children. Presumably they could skate and watch games for free; everyone else paid ten cents.

This was in 1862. Within two years, a second enclosed ballpark in Brooklyn, the Capitoline Grounds, opened, and soon after that, others followed.

A new term entered the everyday vocabulary of those interested in base ball — "gate money." Who got how much of it became a matter of great interest and a great influence. With money to be made by ball ground operators, some of which was passed on to the clubs as an inducement to play on their grounds, is it any wonder that ball players wanted their share?

When players began demanding a share of the gate receipts, Cammayer initially refused on the grounds that it was he who stood to lose money if a game didn't draw big enough crowds, but eventually he capitulated and gate money-sharing became a huge issue.

JAMES WHYTE DAVIS   Money-grabbing operators of ball grounds were not above conspiring with one or maybe even both clubs to fix the outcome of games so as to increase attendance at subsequent games between the clubs.

HENRY CHADWICK   I, for one, always believed that as soon as players and grounds owners began sharing the gate money, the tendency to develop evil habits quickly followed. So for this reason, if no other, I thought it was a lesser of two evils to go ahead and pay the players straight salaries.

JAMES WHYTE DAVIS   Ah, to pay or not to pay, that was the question. Meanwhile anyone who wanted to watch a good base ball match could do so for the cost of a lovely ferry ride to the Elysian Fields. Since we had no gate, there was no gate money to haggle over, and since there was no haggling, we could play just for the hell of it. The Just-for-the-Hell-of-it Knickerbocker Base Ball Club for gentlemen played on untainted and untempted. Well, almost.

CHARLES DEBOST   If anybody was pushing the game towards more commercialism, it was the Wright brothers, particularly Harry, who had once been a member of our lowly club of unpaid gentlemen. One year during the war, I know for a fact he was paid $1,200 to play cricket for the Unions of Cincinnati while also playing cricket that year for the St. George and Philadelphia clubs, and base ball for the Gothams, Morrisania's Unions and Washington Nationals. I don't know how much, if anything, he made, but the rumor was he was thinking of buying the Astor House.

JAMES WHYTE DAVIS   Let me be as clear about this as I possibly can. We didn't play for goddamned gate receipts. We played for fun and anybody who said or implied otherwise was full of crap.

GEORGE GRUM  It's pretty simple, really. The Knicks played for fun because they couldn't play for anything else.

---

## 88

# *How They Played*

DOC ADAMS  Occasionally I was called on to help a new or a junior club set up their field for play. Although we could manage on a smaller field, what we generally looked for was a ground about 600 by 400 feet.

So to lay out the field, first we located the home base where we wanted it relative to the space available. Then we took a length of cord that I had previously measured at 27 feet, four inches, and stretched it out to fix the point of the second base at the end of the cord. Taking a second pre-measured cord of 80 feet, we then fastened one end to the home base and the other at the second base. Then we took the center of the cord and extended it first to the right side to fix the point of the first base and then to the left to fix the third base. This created a square of 90 feet. On a line from the home base to the second base, we marked the pitcher's point at 45 feet.

To fix the location of the bases permanently, we took a small block of wood and embedded it in the ground level with the surface held in place by screwed-in staples. Initially, most of the clubs made their own bases out of double-thick canvas, stuffed with sawdust. A few clubs filled their bases with sand, but these proved heavy to carry around between games so just about everyone sooner or later switched to sawdust, or in some cases, hair. The best bases were about 14 by 17 inches but anything at least a foot square satisfied the rules. Around the bases we ran heavy harness leather straps about an inch and a half wide which were then used to hold the bases in position.

The pitcher's point and the home base we marked with iron quoits at least nine inches in diameter that were held in place by iron spikes that protruded from the underside. These we could get made up especially for us by various smiths in the city. The pitcher's line we marked by a couple of pieces of hard wood at each end protruding just enough that the umpire could see them.

That was all there was to it, really.

CHARLES DEBOST  I suppose it would be fair to say that there were as many different ways of swinging a bat as there were swingers. Some gripped the bat with the left hand and then slid the right hand from the fat end down towards the handle. Some of the more "scientific" hitters grasped the bat near its middle, and others, like me, held the bat with both hands well down on the handle. This gave me the best ability to drive the ball. Lots of other hitters kept their hands slightly divided so as to have better bat control.

In the field we slowly but surely adopted the policy of assigning each man to the position he was best capable of playing and having him play there every game.

Some opined that the second baseman was the most important player and thus the best fielders were often stationed there, and that right field was the least important since the fewest balls were hit in that direction.

We catchers were the ones best able to keep our eyes on the entire field which is why catchers were often the captains—and naturally, I would argue, the most important.

DOC ADAMS    I was beginning to despair that the fly rule would ever win the day. At the convention in 1863, after more impassioned discussion, the negatives, led primarily by the muffin fraternity, defeated the proposal, but the vote was closer than it had been. We were gaining.

Then in December of the next year at the eighth annual convention the question was again put to the membership. This time several clubs, including the Resolute, Mutual, and Enterprise, that had previously voted against the fly game came out in support of it. By a vote of 33 to19, the fly rule was adopted!

Finally! A boy's game was forever changed into a man's game. A foul ball could still be caught on the bound, and although that also needed to be changed (and eventually it was), it was a lesser issue.

That representatives from such established clubs as the Active, Atlantic, and Eagle voted against it seems incredible but the record speaks for itself.

A year earlier, in an effort to stop the stalling tactics, the Convention had voted to allow the umpire to call balls on the pitcher. Now, with the fly rule in effect, the game was cast almost in the form it would take long into the future. The only important major rules that would change in the years to come were those relating to the fair-foul hit and overhand pitching.

We had come a long way in a relatively short period. Now if only the commercialization of the game and the gambling interests didn't kill it...

JAMES WHYTE DAVIS    The adoption of the fly rule was another example of the influence of the Knickerbockers on the development of the game at the very time some were complaining that we had become irrelevant. Far from it, we were essential. What do you suppose base ball would look like today were it not for our efforts?

HENRY CHADWICK    The rule change that allowed the umpire to call balls as well as strikes was a correct one, but the problem was, it brought about more arguing with umpires. The unceasing cries of "how's that" from players asking for judgments had developed into a real pain in the neck. Only the captain should be able to make an appeal on a point of play which is the duty of the umpire to decide without any appeal whatever. Balls and strikes are perfect examples.

The issue of what was and what wasn't a strike took some time before it settled into a consistent policy. Here's the way it worked: The umpire asked each batsman where he wanted the ball, and the batsman responded by saying "knee high," or "waist high," or by naming the character of the ball he wanted, and the pitcher was required to deliver the ball accordingly. What was happening though, was that with men on bases some batters would try to change their request from the previously asked for high balls to low balls under the assumption that low balls might be more easily missed by the catcher. Although some umpires were induced into accepting this, it was strictly against the rules.

There were also some problems in standardizing exactly how close a delivery had to be to that which was requested for it to be called a strike. Some umpires were very strict in adhering to the request, others more lenient. Naturally, what this led to was even more criticism of the umpire. Sometimes the umpire would consult with the two clubs as to how they wanted this to be enforced, but as one might expect, the clubs didn't always agree, which then led to even more bickering and criticism.

But nowhere was there more confusion than in the calling of "balls." Some umpires decided that a "ball" was only to be called if the delivery was over the head of the batsman or on the ground before it reached the home plate. No two umpires seemed to agree. Some even just stopped calling them altogether. A few called balls, but never strikes.

Here was another issue. What was an umpire to do if say a batsman asked for a knee high pitch, but then swung at a pitch around his shoulders although the umpire had already called "ball" while the pitch was in flight? I saw this happen on more than one occasion.

The rules requiring the calling of balls and strikes were valuable. Before the rules, as many as 70 pitches might have been delivered to a given batsman. I know one game in which almost 700 pitches were thrown in three innings.

What was happening is that over time, the rules that were implemented to restore equilibrium to the pitcher/batsman battle were in reality giving new power and importance to the umpire.

Whether this was good or bad we were going to have to figure out. Either way, it was important that we began to standardize the calling of balls and strikes.

DOC ADAMS  A rule was put in place saying that the pitcher could no longer get a running start, nor could he have a foot outside the pitcher's box. The pitching distance of 45 feet was measured from the front line of the pitcher's box to the home base.

This was another example of attempting to address the balance between the pitcher's and hitter's game, a delicate, but pivotal issue with which all us rulemakers tinkered for many years. Some 20 years after I had left the game, they moved the pitcher's distance to 50 feet and then a few years after that, to 65 feet, six inches. Who knows, maybe someday it will be 100 feet. The important thing is to maintain an equilibrium that matches offense and defense in a reasonable way.

Another rule that they put in was that runners actually had to touch their base. Now this may sound strange, but in the old days when the bases were posts, or rocks, or other such hard objects, we always played such that a runner had only to be near the base to be safe.

The Knickerbockers created good rules, but we were always adjusting them in an effort to make the game better and I don't know that will ever stop. The basic rules of the game, though, are still the ones we created.

# 89

# *Other Clubs' Matches*

CHARLES DEBOST   Chadwick decided it was time to revive the competition between the Brooklyn and New York clubs and so he offered to put up a silver ball as a trophy to go to the winning side. Actually it was to go to the club whose players made the most runs in the contest. So a nine was chosen to represent New York.

This time, however, the side was made up of four players from the Mutuals, three from the Gothams, one from the Eagles, and one from the Jeffersons. Cohen of the Mutuals was the catcher. Just for the sake of accuracy, of course, I add that he scored no runs.

The Brooklyns won the match 18–6. Pearce received the ball on behalf of the Brooklyn nine and the Atlantics since their players made the most runs.

According to published reports, delegations from all over except those from "Secesshin" states were present. The Knickerbockers were nowhere to be found. A sign of the times, I suppose, but I don't know that we had any interest in participating anyway.

JAMES WHYTE DAVIS   It's true that the Association never established formal rules for determining a national champion, but the press certainly did. The accepted principle was that once a club was considered the champion, it could only lose that title if it were beaten twice in a three game series with a challenger.

Now what this accomplished in fact was that many of the better players were scooped up by a handful of clubs, thereby reducing the number of viable challengers.

Shortly after we had played the Excelsiors, one paper wrote that they had played but three first nine games all season "for certainly no one with brains would call the Knickerbocker games first nine matches."

The *Brooklyn Eagle* wrote: "Look at the Knickerbockers of New York, how it has declined in position as a playing club, and all because it refused to revive itself with young blood."

Decline in position? We never aspired to any position, and as for young blood we had plenty of new members.

Another time the *Eagle* reported that in a match against the Excelsiors, we "did the muffing business up in first rate style."

I can remember one particular game we played in '65 against the Excelsiors. I pitched, and Sam Kissam played third base. Other than that, our side was composed of club members none of whom probably even knew who Alick Cartwright, Duncan Curry, or Will Wheaton were. I'm not sure a couple of them could even grow beards yet. What I remember about that game is that there was not one single ball missed by either side and that included more than 15 fly catches, two of which this old man made himself. Muffin? Like hell we were!

HENRY CHADWICK   The Atlantic Club of Brooklyn had developed into the most powerful base ball club anyone had ever seen. By 1864 they had succeeded the Eckfords as the dominant club by playing a season of 21 games without a loss.

The idea of selecting a championship club each year was now on everybody's mind.

DICKEY PEARCE   We — the Atlantics — were unquestionably the best team in the game during a good part of the '60s. During one span of almost four years, we didn't lose a single game. Other clubs would come to the fore for a season or two to challenge us only to fade away when they understood how overwhelming that task would be. By our play on the field, we earned the title as "champions" of base ball.

WILLIAM TUCKER   The Atlantics and the Eckfords were considered the "best" clubs. Nevertheless, I challenge that designation. We were still playing the game the way many of us considered the "proper" way, the way the game was conceived with our values in the right places. I will argue that we were still the "best" club when taking into consideration all aspects of base ball including character, sportsmanship, fair play, camaraderie, decency, and skill. I include skill as only one quality among others.

DOC ADAMS    The quest to be the best may not have been in the best interests of the game, but it sure didn't hurt attendance. I remember reading the paper one September day in '62 when a story claimed that there were 15,000 casualties at a recent battle down in Antietam, Maryland, while another story said that 15,000 people turned out to watch the Eckfords play the Atlantics, in Brooklyn. Something was sadly wrong with our world.

JAMES WHYTE DAVIS    Championship fever was running rampant, but count me not among its victims. I didn't give a damn which was the strongest club, I only cared which was the best and those aren't the same things—not by a long shot.

# 90

# *Down to a Few*

DOC ADAMS    When P. T. Barnum's midget star, Tom Thumb, married Lavonia Warren in a public ceremony, thousands of people showed up at Grace Episcopal Church to greet them. Afterwards they were received by President Lincoln at the White House.

I couldn't help thinking about what made people so fascinated by such side-show attractions during a time of such a national crisis. I suppose it was the same instinct as lured people to base ball games—to spend a few hours investing in the lives and activities of others so as not to have to consider the state of their own.

I read once where somebody said that the Puritans hated bear-baiting, not because it gave pain to the bear, but because it gave pleasure to the spectators. I suppose base ball is similar in that the game isn't really played by the player alone; the spectator brings the game into contact with his world by investing his emotions and thus in some way contributing to the game itself. By providing drama, the game has the ability to inspire vicarious feelings of victory or power in the viewer. This seems to me to be particularly so when they themselves are deficient in those values.

Certainly social bonds form among spectators as they come together to celebrate the victories and lament the losses of the teams and players with whom they identify. But I suppose there are negatives, too, such as when the involvement leads to excessive gambling or when the spectator becomes so involved with watching the game that he ignores his responsibilities to his family and job. I have seen too many examples of both.

Thoreau used the term "spectatordom" to refer to spectators collectively, so I think it fair to say that spectatordom was taking over base ball in that more people were watching it than playing it although there was no shortage of the latter.

Nevertheless, everything in its time, and the time had come in my life to move from active player to spectator.

JAMES WHYTE DAVIS   Not all wives are as amenable as others to having their husbands off playing a game a couple of times a week. I suppose Doc's resignation from the club was inevitable and although he always said Cornelia had nothing to do with it, I imagine it was a factor.

DOC ADAMS   It was 1862. The war was still forging on. I was all of 48 but had a few health issues, and a strong desire to spend more time with my wife and family led to my decision to end my association with the Knickerbocker Base Ball Club.

Life comes in tidy bundles of time — stages if you will — and you can't hold them back. They are immutable. There was a time for me to belong to the KBBC and there was a time to move on. Moving-on time had come.

I had been a member of the club for all but the first month. I served as vice president for a couple of years, and president I think for six. I was a club director for at least five.

Looking back on it, I think I had made some contributions to the club and to the game of base ball.

JAMES WHYTE DAVIS   I can't say it was really a surprise when Doc said he was leaving, and I can't say that given his situation, I blamed him, but I sure as hell tried to talk him out of it.

"It's not going to be the same," I said.

"Nothing ever is. All things must change to something new, to something strange.

"We don't need strange."

"Anyhow, that's how Longfellow put it."

"But he can't play short stop."

"How do you know?"

"Just a guess. It's a critical time for us."

"It's always a critical time."

"Well this time it's criticaler."

"Why is that?"

"We've got to keep things the way they ... should be. There are so many wrong influences pulling at the game — rowdyism, gambling, professionalism...

"Jamie, like everything else in this world, the game will change. You can't stop that."

"The hell you say. And you, what are you going to do now, go off and watch sunsets?"

"Well, we want to raise a family. I think maybe one of these days we'll move back to New England someplace."

"Are you insane? There are wild animals up there. You can't live in the country. It's ... uncivilized."

"We'll take our guns."

And so reluctantly, in April of '62, I sent Doc a letter. The last line was just in case.

> D.L. Adams, Esq.
>
> I beg to acknowledge receipt of your note of 26 last tending your resignation as a member of the old Knickerbocker B.B. Club, and that it was reluctantly accepted with great regret and you were unanimously elected an Honorary Member.
>
> Permit me to add my personal regret of the necessity that induced such a course and tendering you my best wishes for your health and prosperity. I indulge the hope that the "spirit" you express of being with us always may be accompanied by the body on the old Play Grounds.
>
> > Yours very truly,
> > James Whyte Davis
> > Secretary
>
> Playing commences on the 21st.

WILLIAM TUCKER    In March when Doc came to his last meeting, we instantly and unanimously elected him to honorary membership and presented him with a special resolution.

The resolution which I helped compose read:

> Resolved, that by the resignation of Dr. D.L. Adams, the Knickerbocker Base Ball Club has lost one of its most honored members; one who for a period of 16 years in the performance of every duty whether at the bat or in the field, as our presiding officer, our representative in the National Association of Ball Players, or in the daily walks of life, has ever been faithful and uniformly proved himself the courteous big-minded gentleman, and the zealous advocate of our noble game.
>
> Resolved, that to him as much if not more than any other individual member are the Knickerbockers indebted for the high rank their club has maintained since its organization, and we claim for him the honored title of "Nestor of Ball Players."
>
> Resolved, that with unfeigned regret we yield to the imperative necessity that compels his withdrawal from the roll of our active members, and beg to assure him, that in leaving us he carries with him our heartfelt

wishes for his welfare, happiness and prosperity, and we cherish the hope often to be the recipients of the benefit of his good counsel and long experience.

DOC ADAMS  Nestor — a wise old counselor to the Greeks at Troy. I don't know about the "wise" part, but I guess by the standards of base ball, they got the "old" part right anyway.

FRALEY NIEBUHR  It would be difficult to overestimate the contributions made by Doc. Whether in office or not, he was our leader, the man we looked to for guidance and representation when critical issues needed to be addressed. He was at once perceptive and analytic, seeing information as the lifeblood of the club, and he was able to synthesize that information to make truly informed decisions. Actually, he could be annoyingly analytic at times, but I suppose every organization needs someone like that. Since he always seemed to be concerned with why things are the way they are, he wasn't always the easiest to connect with emotionally. He seemed to think that being as self-sufficient as he are, he didn't need things from others. Nevertheless, I think everybody looked up to him and respected the leadership he provided. Maybe we wouldn't even have survived as a club in those early years had it not been for his steadying influence.

HENRY CHADWICK  I'm not sure Doc Adams ever really got the recognition he deserved for his contributions, but the regard in which he was held by the Knickerbocker members and the wider base ball fraternity is undeniable. He was always articulate, bright, and exceptionally level headed. When Doc spoke, people listened.

He was particularly influential in arranging the new codes of playing rules which were adopted in 1854 and 1857.

Base ball owed Dr. Adams a great debt.

JAMES WHYTE DAVIS  It wouldn't be the same without him but I knew that if we had done our job properly, the structure of the club was such that no one man was critical for its survival. As important as he was, it wasn't the Doc Adams Base Ball Club. We had new blood coming in all the time and younger men like William Bensel were assuming the leadership. Bensel, who had been a captain in the Union Army and who was used to leading men, became, for a number of years, our new president.

But Doc wasn't the only old timer to leave the club during these years. Charlie DeBost and Fraley Niebuhr also left.

CHARLES DEBOST  I was 35 when I resigned from the club in 1863. I was busy at work; I had a big family with more to come, and my once lithe body was becoming less so with each passing year. Oh, I could have played at a good level for several more years, but I don't regret my decision.

JAMES WHYTE DAVIS    I wasn't surprised when Charlie quit either. Actually I was surprised he lasted as long as he did. He easily could have jumped ship and joined any of the best clubs in New York or Brooklyn and I don't doubt that he was frequently asked to do just that. It wouldn't have taken much imagination to picture him playing with Dickey Pearce and Joe Start with the Atlantics, or with Al Reach on the Eckfords, or with any of the other top clubs for that matter.

I don't want to speak for Charlie, but I think he stayed with us because he relished the things for which we stood and because he valued having a good time with good friends more than winning.

Behind his big full beard was a man who could be as funny as anyone I ever played with but he could also at times display self-deprecating insecurities. Yet he was always upbeat, always charming. Charlie was one of those people who maybe made the world out to be a better place than it really was. He had a zest for life and adventure that was infectious. I would miss him. We all would.

Fraley had been one of the original Knicks and had played more or less continuously with the club since then. Never one to get very involved with club politics or leadership positions, he nevertheless was a loyal member, and in his younger days, a pretty good player.

FRALEY NIEBUHR    It's funny how some things stuck in the memory all these years. I can't even begin to guess how many games I played with the club. The memories of most of the games have all melded together, but that first game, in October of '45 with Cartwright, Tucker, Birney, Curry, Dupignac, well, that stands out all by itself.

I still enjoyed playing but my duties at the Customs House had increased, and I had taken on new responsibilities as an officer in the Prospect Park and Coney Island Railroad Company. I was finding myself with less and less time for base ball. Then too, Mother, who was born in Scotland, died suddenly and I had to take care of Father.

I guess that's the way things go in life. All of a sudden one day you wake up and you find yourself with so many responsibilities that you have no more time for games.

For a while I stayed in touch with the club, but as new members came in and the ones I knew left ... well, eventually I lost contact altogether.

The game had changed so much. By the time I left, the Knickerbockers were an afterthought if thought of at all by those who knew and followed the game. And that was okay with me. Nobody could ever take away the memories.

JAMES WHYTE DAVIS    We made both Fraley and Charlie honorary members and they deserved it. Now, me, and Tuck, and Sam were about the only old-timers left.

# PART TEN: COMMERCIALISM 1866–1870

## 91

# *Base Ball Mania*

JAMES WHYTE DAVIS    It was time for base ball mania, much of which came as a result of the return home of so many soldiers, ready for healthy diversion.

If you could believe the reports in the papers, as the war ended, there were as many as 1000 active clubs playing base ball and according the *Clipper*, "nearly every trade and occupation had its votaries in the game of base ball." Two years later there were said to be 2,000 organized clubs with maybe 100,000 players. The Association boasted it had over 300 members and that over 200,000 spectators had watched the important matches. I don't even want to speculate about what they meant by "important."

The *Times* claimed that 40,000 people turned out to watch the Brooklyn Atlantics play the Philadelphia Athletics. They were hanging out of windows, jammed onto rooftops, perched on tree branches, and apparently overflowed onto the playing field causing the game to be canceled. What does that say about a game that's become too popular to be played?

It was said that Philadelphia had five times as many clubs as New York and that Buffalo had as many as 80 clubs playing regularly. The fact is, there were clubs everywhere — Kansas, Iowa, Missouri, Wisconsin, Illinois, Michigan, Indiana, Ohio, Minnesota, Missouri, Tennessee, Kentucky, all over New England, even out west in Oregon and California. Since Alick was out in Hawaii they probably had clubs there, too.

Most of the papers gave base ball increasing attention. Some, new ones like *The Ball Players' Chronicle* and *The Bat and Ball,* were devoted completely to the game.

Our Association meetings, once a gathering of players all of whom I knew, had now grown into a conflagration of clubs drawn from God knows where.

THOMAS TIMBERLAKE    Our club was probably typical of the era. I was living in Louisville, Kentucky, when a number of us who had been playing the game for a few years got together and decided to create a formal club. To that end, we incorporated a legal act that allowed investors to pool resources so they could purchase playing grounds and to build facilities appropriate for first-class games.

We sold shares and then selected a board to run the corporation.

The board was authorized to acquire real estate in an amount not to exceed twenty thousand dollars. It could borrow money in any amount it deemed necessary just so long as it did not exceed the capital stock of the company, and it could mortgage the property and all appurtenances belonging to the corporation, provided it did not authorize the creation of drinking saloons or other establishments calculated to promote dissipation.

JAMES WHYTE DAVIS    Actually, we had incorporated also, and so, according to the State of New York, we were "a body corporate and politic," and as such we could "sue or be sued, plead or be impleaded, defend and be defended, in all courts and places whatsoever." We were then legally able to purchase or lease real estate up to the amount of $25,000.

According to the state, "The object and purposes of this incorporation shall be the providing and attainment of healthful recreation and amusement for the members of the club hereby incorporated, by and through the means of the game generally known as 'base ball.'"

So I guess now we were legally allowed to engage in healthful recreation. I can only assume that before that what we were doing before then was either unhealthful or illegal — maybe both.

WILLIAM TUCKER    If big means better, then the game was getting better. If big means less controlled, then the game was that, too. It seems like things were always better in the old days, but that's probably less true than we like to think.

ASHLEY HYDE    For better or worse, by the end of the decade, the game would come to be dominated by a small group of paid players, a commercialized, spectator sport stretching from shore to shore.

---

# 92

# *Paid to Play*

JAMES WHYTE DAVIS    Pay for play had been sneaking into the game for some time. How many clerks and insurance salesman were in reality being paid to play base ball, I can't say, but the numbers were not small. Hypocrisy reigned.

FRANK PIDGEON    I wrote the Association bill against professionalism arguing that base ball should be played for pleasure not profit. This was not a position of "snobbish inclinations" as some claimed, but rather it sprang from the convictions that professionalism would only give the wealthier clubs an undue advantage on the field, whereas skill, courage, and endurance should decide the victors. I hated the idea that players could be bought and sold like sacks of wheat.

ALBERT SPALDING   When still in my teens I showed some skill on the ball field, so I was offered a job for $40 a month as a grocer in Chicago with the understanding that I would earn my way by playing ball, not by polishing apples. I was to play for the Chicago Excelsiors. At first I was rather put off by the idea. Taking money for play was something that ran counter to my upbringing. Men were paid to work, not to play. Besides, I knew, as did everyone else, that it was strictly against the rules.

The man who was making the arrangements told me that what I would be doing would be a benefit to the good people of Chicago. They would take pride in their team, in their city.

Still, I balked.

"Look, son," he said, "don't actors get paid for what they do?"

"I suppose they do."

"Don't singers and musicians get paid to entertain the public?"

"I imagine."

"Then what's the difference?"

"I never thought of it that way."

"Ball players are entertainers, only they're more important than singers because they carry the hopes and dreams of the city in ways that singers never can. Consider it a civic responsibility if you want."

Well I was persuaded, and I did play, and yes, I took the money. I'm sure I wasn't the only one.

HARRY WRIGHT   In '68 I was offered $1,200 to play for the Cincinnati Base Ball Club and to serve as the side's captain. Since this was the same amount that I was getting paid for playing cricket with the Union Club, and by that time I preferred base ball anyway, I accepted the offer and set out back east to search for the most talented ball players I could lure out to Cincinnati. We were considered an amateur side but one that paid a number of its best players.

JAMES WHYTE DAVIS   What Harry was up to was his business. He had been a good member of our club once but now he was taking base ball in another direction entirely.

In 1867 Harry's brother, George, left the Gothams to play for the Washington Nationals. Why did he leave New York to go down there to join a base ball club when we had many perfectly good ones here? There's only one possible answer: they paid him. In point of fact, I was told that on the Nationals' roster his occupation was listed as a clerk in some government office along with a number of other players on the club. The address of the government office was 238 Pennsylvania Avenue. Go ahead, look it up on a map. It's a public park!

Probably the worst offender of the ideal of amateurism was old Boss Tweed himself. In addition to his other scandalous activities on behalf of corruption in New York City politics, he was for many years president of the Mutuals. Most of their players were paid to be "city employees." Never before or since has the city had so many excellent street cleaners. According to one paper, Tweedism in base ball cost the city $30,000 annually.

GEORGE WRIGHT   What young man if gifted enough to play a game and be paid for it wouldn't do so eagerly? To earn one's living playing ... well, that was not something any right-minded young man could refuse.

SAM KISSAM   I have to say that it was looking as if the time would come when every player on a first-class nine would be paid.

CHARLES "POP" SNYDER Why did the Association prohibit paying players? Simply because the old men of the game longed for a return to old Puritan values. What it meant in reality, however, was that the inevitable payment to players had to be made secretly. That is, it supported cheating.

HENRY CHADWICK   To my way of thinking, the whole debate about professionalism in base ball was a waste of time because players were being paid, and I could see no reason why a man should not be able to honestly devote his time and talents to a base ball club as a paid employee. Teachers of sport were paid. Why not the practitioners?

JAMES WHYTE DAVIS   Amateurism is, was, and always will be the purest expression of the game. The professionals can whine all they want about being "misunderstood," the fact is that playing the game (any game) for the pure joy of playing is always different than playing because someone bribes you with money.

Nevertheless, when players began to be paid to play the game, our old fraternity of players was in effect split in two.

---

# 93

## *To Distinguish Between Amateur and Professional*

JAMES WHYTE DAVIS   The word "amateurism" is sometimes used in a disparaging sense suggesting the amateur is a "dabbler" or somehow superficial, but permit me to point out that the word comes from the old French meaning "lover of." So an amateur is someone who engages in an activity out of love. It elevates things done without self-interest above those done for pay.

I saw all sorts of people become angry or even sick if "their team" lost an important game. "We," they say, lost the game. But it is not "we," it is not "their team." It is men paid (sometimes very well paid) to play.

I feel sorry for those whose happiness depends upon the toil of others.

HENRY CHADWICK    It was well known that nearly all the leading clubs—certainly all the aspiring applicants for the championship—began employing professional players. The rules prohibiting the custom were mere dead letters and it was almost impossible to frame a law on the subject that could not be evaded. So in 1869 the Association introduced a new rule: "All players who play base ball for money, or who shall at any time receive compensation for their services as players, shall be considered professional players; and all others shall be regarded as amateur players."

Clubs could then openly advertise for professional players, and the players could openly solicit employment. All clubs who had a majority of their nine composed of professionals were to be considered professional clubs.

I believed that the result of the change would at once give the amateur players a new interest in the game. With the new rule, it no longer mattered how well the amateurs fared against clubs employing professionals because their status would only be affected by the results against other amateur clubs. Conversely, the professional clubs would be playing more with their own class than previously, and the gambling, betting rings, and all the objectionable surroundings would then be confined to the big contests between the professional nines.

JAMES WHYTE DAVIS    The new Association rule said that amateur clubs could employ a professional for the purposes of taking care of the grounds and teaching new members, but he could not play in a match without the consent of the opposing club, unless they too, employed a professional on their nine.

With the division into amateurs and professionals came the desire of some amateur clubs to rise to the top of the amateur ranks—the Alphas, the Stars, the Athletics, to name a few. We, on the other hand, chose to stay apart from such intentions—may I say "stay above" such intentions? The Excelsiors likewise made this commitment. When our intentions were made known, one paper wrote, "Though this is a sensible idea in a way, it does not suit the notions of the general class of the fraternity, and the consequence is that clubs who favor that line of policy are classed as 'old fogeyish.'"

So let me, the oldest of the old fogies, be the first to say, that's the damn way we wanted it, and who the hell asked the press for their opinions anyway?

## 94

# All-Professional Clubs

JAMES WHYTE DAVIS   One city that had a particularly active base ball scene and would prove to be exceptionally influential in the years to come was Cincinnati, or as we sometimes referred to it, "Porkopolis." The Cincinnati Base Ball Club was organized right at the end of the war with our Harry Wright as their star player. The club was supported by hundreds of prominent and well off Cincinnatians, who while they didn't actually play the game themselves, wanted to support a top notch club to represent their fair city.

Exactly how influential (or should I say "devastating?") this organization was, would shortly become clear.

HARRY WRIGHT   In 1869 we were able to put together a group of Ohio investors headed up by Aaron Champion, who saw the potential to make the Cincinnati club into a fully professional organization. And, oh yes, to turn a profit. I convinced the investors that many in the public who gladly paid seventy-five cents to a dollar to go to the theatre would do the same to watch base ball. Not only that, I told them, but there were far more people who would pay for ball as wanted to go to the theatre.

It was all about the profit potential. I honestly believed what I told them. The only thing I wasn't sure about was whether the public would continue to pay after the novelty wore off, but I was assuming they would if the product we put on the field was of a consistently high caliber.

After discussing the matter with Mr. Champion, the investors agreed to a figure of $9,300 for player salaries—surely enough to attract skilled players. My brother George agreed to join us for $1,400. Asa Brainard, who had been a Knickerbocker while still working as an insurance salesman, was a first-rate pitcher who delivered the ball about as fast as anyone, and with a wicked twist to boot, signed on for $1,100. Most of the others received $800.

Mr. Champion was pleased.

"Just so long as you win," he said.

"We'll certainly try," I told him.

"Try? We're not paying you to try. We're paying you to win. We're paying you to make Cincinnati proud."

"And you to make money."

He couldn't help but to smile. "That, too."

To mark our inauguration as a fully professional team, I arranged to have new uniforms designed. We needed a new look to distinguish us from the amateurs, so we came out wearing knickers with long bright red stockings. And so we came to be known as the "Red Stockings."

Next up was to arrange a schedule against clubs that could guarantee a good gate.

We were ready to show the base ball world just what a professional side could do.

"I would rather be president of the Cincinnati Base Ball Club than president of the United States," Champion said.

JAMES WHYTE DAVIS   Exactly what they were out to prove I don't know. Paying some of the best players in the land to beat up local amateur clubs isn't exactly high on my list of the principles of good sportsmanship.

HARRY WRIGHT   In order to make ends meet, we had to play a lot of games. We started in the Ohio area, toured in the East where we played the Association's strongest clubs, and even traveled by steamboat and by train on the new Union Pacific–Central Pacific transcontinental link all the way out to San Francisco.

Spectators turned out everywhere to see us play well, and play well we did. We easily won all our early games, including matches with the mighty Atlantics and Eckfords. Our closest call came in a game against the Union Club, from, of all places, Lansingburgh, New York. With the score tied at 17, they walked off the field to protest the decision of the umpire so we were declared the winner by forfeit.

By season's end our record stood at 57–0.

"That good enough?" I asked Mr. Champion.

"Well, we turned a profit of $1.25."

"For the whole year?"

"I was hoping for at least $2.00."

"We'll try to do better next year."

HENRY CHADWICK   The Red Stockings were certainly not the first club to pay players, but it was the first club that engaged all its players by offering season-long contracts and the first to offer stock to investors in the name of profits.

What Harry and the other professional ball players did was to demonstrate to any who cared to watch just how well and how beautifully the game of base ball could be played.

WILLIAM TUCKER   Harry was a very decent soul. Men just naturally liked and trusted him, and I believe it was for this reason alone that the Red Stockings succeeded to the degree that they did. He was also one heck of a fine ball player, and that didn't hurt the cause either.

Harry needs to be given credit for what he did for the reputation of the professional sportsman.

HARRY WRIGHT   In the minds of many, professional athletes were seen as being on the same level as drunks and gamblers, so I did everything in my power to see that neither of these two things were connected in any way with the Red Stockings. As the captain of the ship it was my responsibility both to demonstrate and demand the highest standards of behavior. Anything less and the venture would surely fall apart.

JAMES WHYTE DAVIS   "It's a game, Harry," I said to him once as we were coming from Augustin Daly's melodrama *Under the Gaslight*. "It's not a profession."
   "You mean like acting."
   "That's different."
   "Is it?"
   The thought that we could be considered in the same category as dancing girls was frankly abhorrent.
   "If we can have professional cricket players, why not base ball?"
   "Cricket, is that a sport?"
   I'll say this about Harry, though. He was a regular base-ball-thinking-machine. He approached his game like a scientist might a complicated experiment. He was always looking for ways to make it work better, always thinking about it, always tinkering with it.
   He played his first game with us in '58. Harry never got involved much with the running of the club, as he would later with other clubs, but precisely because he studied it so carefully, he became an excellent teacher of the game.
   I would have to say that Harry Wright was the most skilled player to ever have joined, and then abandoned, the Knickerbockers. But that was hardly the point was it? He changed the game forever. Of course, had he not done so, somebody else certainly would have.

HARRY WRIGHT   I was three when my family moved from Sheffield, England, to New York. Father was a wood turner by trade, but a cricket player by instinct, so I learned the game as soon as I was old enough to hold a bat. Because we had a large family, I was forced to drop out of school when I was 14 to work in the jewelry business with Tiffany's.
   In those days cricket was my passion, my only real passion. We lived in a house looking out on the St. George Cricket grounds where Father worked. I guess some of the older members saw me play enough that they asked me to join them when I was only fifteen.
   Father was by then the best bowler and a club professional, so in 1857, they offered me $12 a week to serve as assistant professional of the club. That was better pay and a whale of a lot better than working for Tiffany. I jumped at the chance.
   That was also when the club moved over to the Elysian Fields. It was there,

while practicing cricket with my brother, that we looked over at the Knickerbockers playing base ball. For some days we watched from a distance trying to figure out the rules of the game simply by observing it. One day, when they were short of players, one of them asked us to join them. It was love at first swing.

I still loved cricket, but I could see that base ball was the game that the Americans were taking to, and a fine game it was.

DOC ADAMS HARRY   was never showy, never acted as if he were better than the rest of us, even if he was.

.  I saw in him a fine young man and a fine young player. That he would eventually change the game forever, well that I never would have guessed.

HARRY WRIGHT   To put it simply, Father was not happy.

"It's a passing fancy, Harry," he said. "In a few years it will be gone. Cricket has a history. It will always be with us."

"I won't give up cricket," I promised him. "I'm just adding base ball."

"You can make a living playing cricket, and a good one. Can you say that about base ball?"

"Maybe someday."

Nevertheless, in deference to my father, I continued working for St. George's by playing, coaching, and arranging matches while playing base ball with the Knicks at every opportunity I could find.

JAMES WHYTE DAVIS   When we all but dropped out of playing formal competitions with other clubs, it meant that a few of our members left us to join clubs that were more active in that area. Harry Wright was among them. He left us in 1863 to join the Gothams. Now the Gothams weren't all that much different from us but they were still playing games against other clubs, and I guess Harry wanted that. Then, of course, came the Red Stockings.

CAL MCVEY   Every person who ever watched a game of professional base ball owes Harry a debt of gratitude; every investor and business man who ever made a dollar in the game owes him a word of thanks; every one of us who made base ball our livelihood owes to Harry ... everything.

JAMES WHYTE DAVIS   Let's see if I can put the Red Stockings' season of '69 into perspective. They won every game they played — 57 in all. (The Olympics, incidentally, lost every game they played.) They scored 2,400 runs, meaning that they averaged about 42 per game. In a new statistic that writers were then beginning to use, they had a batting average of about .500. George Wright scored 339 runs, made 304 hits totaling 614 bases, hit 47 home runs and batted .629. The team won games by as much as 103–8.

Now I ask. Was this in the best interests of base ball? Is this how the game should be played?

HARRY ELLARD    The Red Stockings were the sensations of the game. Even though there wasn't much profit, Champion and Wright made their point.

Some years later, I published a poem about that incredible season of '69.

> When I was young and played base ball
> With the Reds of Sixty-Nine,
> We knew how to play the game,
> We were all right in line.
>
> And when our bats would fan the air,
> You bet we'd make a hit;
> The ball would fly two hundred yards
> Before it ever lit.
>
> Well, well my boy, those days are gone;
> No club will ever shine
> Like the one which never knew defeat,
> The Reds of Sixty-Nine.

JAMES WHYTE DAVIS    Following the Reds' season of base ball bullying, the "enclosure movement" ran rampant. Clubs all over began erecting fences around their fields so as to be able to charge gate fees.

"You mean we can make money playing games here?" said the managers.

"Money, money, money," said the players.

"So if we play more games we'll make more money?"

"Play more, make more."

"And if we tour around the country...?"

"Even more."

"And if we have the best players?"

"More yet."

So build the fences high, charge all you can, pay the best players you can find ... and ... and ... and...

WILLIAM TUCKER    The fraternal nature of the game that had attracted us to it in the first place was fading away. Friendly games played among members were shunted to the "who cares?" back field. That being said though, I don't want to fall into the "life was better when I was young" mode. Let's leave it as "life was different when I was young."

A professional club was now a small business, and the membership, hired hands imported to represent it in matches. No doubt the good people of Cincinnati were proud of their team, but was it really "their" club? The players were hired professionals, almost all of whom came from someplace else.

So be it.

ALBERT SPALDING    Professional ball raised the level of playing to new heights and attracted ever more spectators in ways the old fraternal organizations never could.

Of course there were problems, too. Some players, revolvers, lured by ever greater salaries, moved from club to club without so much as a by your leave. When spectators of a town supported their club, they had a right to expect loyalty from the players but this didn't always follow.

JAMES WHYTE DAVIS   After the great "success" of the Red Stockings, Chicago felt jealous. So they advertised for top players, raised the money, outfitted themselves in knickers like the Cincinnati players, but to show just how different they were, they wore white. Naturally they became the White Stockings. Most original. That just opened the door a little wider for other clubs, and in they streamed. I don't know how many different colored stockings there could possibly be, but I'm sure investors were looking into it.

JAMES WHYTE DAVIS   Asa Brainard, who had been a member of our club for a short time some years earlier, joined the Red Stockings as their premier pitcher and in so doing, deserted his wife, leaving her destitute and struggling to raise their infant son. Apparently making money playing base ball was more important to him than supporting his family.

---

## 95

# *A Question of Race*

JAMES WHYTE DAVIS   Let me make one thing very clear. Colored base ball was around and I had no objection to coloreds getting together to form their own clubs and playing games amongst themselves. I'd been told, and had no reason to believe otherwise, that some of them were excellent players indeed and that some of their games had been first rate. The Pythians of Philadelphia, for example, were known to be a very adept club. The Brooklyn Uniques and the Philadelphia Excelsiors were also colored clubs that people said played good ball.

The Excelsiors and the Uniques played a game in Brooklyn for the "colored championship of the United States" in '67. I understand the game was reasonably well played but the gaudy fife and drum corps that led the nines to and from the grounds did not add much to the seriousness of the situation. Such corps may be fine for some occasions, but certainly they are not appropriate for base ball.

HENRY CHADWICK   In point of fact, Octavius Catto's colored Pythian Club, founded in 1866, played many splendid games against other colored teams. The year after their founding they won eight of the nine games they played. In later years they played many matches against white clubs.

JAMES WHYTE DAVIS   In 1867 I was acting chairman of the National Association's Nominating Committee at a time when a difficult issue was before us. The Pythians, through Octavius Catto, had applied for membership in the Association. It was up to our committee — me, William Bell, and William Sinn — to make a recommendation to the Association. It was indeed a prickly situation that I had discussed some with Walter Avery, the other Knick delegate to the convention.

"You don't have a choice," he said.

I think that was the prevailing attitude. If we let the Pythians in, we would have lost so many members, the Association would have collapsed. And then what? Another organization would have started and they would be right back at the same place. Look, we were a base ball organization, not a political one. The question of colored and white working or playing together was a political issue to be sure and there were places for debates on that, but this was not one of them.

Our three-man committee was in agreement.

"If we let them in we'll have all sorts of hell," said Bell.

"I agree," said Sinn. "Personally I wouldn't mind, of course, but I know others would. I can guarantee you some of our members wouldn't play against them."

"And do what? Quit?" I said.

"Probably. And more. We'd have chaos."

"Leave the politics to the politicians," said Bell. "Besides it's in the best interests of the colored clubs. They don't really want to join our organization anyway. Why would they? They know damn well the problems they'd have. It's just a few instigators like Catto who bring all this on. They're not interested in base ball, they're interested in agitating. What's the matter, the Emancipation Proclamation isn't enough for them?"

We all agreed that to admit colored clubs would inevitably have led to a division of feelings, whereas by excluding them, no injury could result to anyone. It was in the best interests of both our clubs and the colored clubs to keep the groups separate.

When the time came for our committee's report at the December convention, everyone knew what was coming, but rather than engage in a long and potentially divisive political debate, by a majority vote we agreed to close the discussion and move to my report.

I began by recommending that we admit 28 new clubs whose applications we deemed to be correct and eight others whose applications contained some irregularities. Then I said it was the unanimous recommendation of our committee that we deny the admission of any club which may be composed of one or more colored persons.

The report was accepted by the convention. By excluding the colored clubs we assured that no injury would come to any club, white or colored.

Doc Adams   Had I been at that convention, I would have argued against the report of Jamie's committee and told him so. That being said, it's important to understand that the committee was merely reflecting the prevailing feelings of the times. I know Jamie came under fire later for being a racist, but in my long association with him I can't remember him saying anything other than reflecting the political situation of the day. The Negro issue was still a hot topic whenever and wherever it came up. The action of the Association simply reflected where we were as a nation.

Octavius Catto   I was the founder and captain of the Phythian Base Ball Club. I could play short stop, but not against white players. I could hit the ball with some skill, but not against white players. I could throw a ball straight and true, but not against white players.

Base ball was considered a gentleman's game and the gentlemen didn't play against Negroes.

I, a college graduate and class valedictorian, was not up to the standards of the white gentleman, said the National Association of Base Ball Players. I was neither surprised nor quieted by their actions. I would continue to fight for the rights to be judged as a player by my abilities on the field and not on the color of my skin.

Ashley Hyde   Base ball may have been the national pastime — and I don't claim that it wasn't — and as the national pastime it reflected American society, including its racial attitudes. Despite the events of the recent years, blacks were not to become a part of organized base ball for a long, long time.

---

## 96

# *Leaving the Association*

James Whyte Davis   I was simply sick and tired of the politicking that was running rampant through the Association.

Then, as the decade was drawing to a close, owing to the contentious issues surrounding the issues of professionalism, I suggested to the members that we withdraw our membership in the Association altogether.

"But we're the Knickerbockers," came the cry from some members.

"Exactly the point. We don't need the Association."

"Maybe the Association needs us."

"Maybe, but out responsibility is to the club, not the Association. Let's not kid ourselves, the professionals are in charge and that's not about to change. What do we need the Association for? Tell me. We can manage our club just fine without them, can't we? We can continue to play our games just fine without them, can't we? Unless someone can tell me otherwise, I can't see why we as gentlemen amateurs should associate ourselves with hired hands. Let the pay-for-play-crowd forge their own damn path to wherever the hell they're going. Let's remain above it all."

There were some objections. Not a lot. When the vote was taken we easily won the day, and I sent a letter to the Association informing them of our actions—another move I never regretted.

HARRY WRIGHT   The Association, I think rightly, voted in '68 to recognize the two classes of players—amateurs and professionals. However, the next year, in response to pressure from some in the unhappy membership camp, the Association reversed its stand.

Then the following year, two-thirds of the membership voted down a resolution stating that professionalism was "reprehensible and injurious to the best interests of the game." Well, it was no surprise that some amateur clubs headed by the stalwart Knickerbockers withdrew from the Association.

I think all of us who had any sense of what was happening not only within the world of base ball but also in the wider context of American society understood that professionalism would be the way of the future. Those reactionaries like Jamie Davis and his brethren seemed to me to be very out of touch with the way the world was operating. Still, they had a right to their opinions and ways, and I bore them no ill will, although I'm not sure the reciprocal was true. There will always be a place for the dilettante and amateur in the world of sport, just as there will always be a place for the professional in any sport that people are willing to pay to watch.

GEORGE GRUM   Despite the reality of the situation, the Knickerbockers continued to wear the genteel but shabby cloak of amateurism. Surely they could see the writing on the wall. Or could they? Still, they doggedly professed adherence to social exclusivity and were never competitive with the top clubs again.

HENRY CHADWICK   The Knickerbockers' defection from the Association was, without doubt, a serious blow to that organization in particular, and amateur ball in general. I only hoped this was the initial move towards the organization of a strictly amateur association.

JAMES WHYTE DAVIS   I was right that we didn't need the Association. We continued to hold our practices as we had in the past and occasionally played matches against other amateur clubs.

## 97

# *On Their Own*

WILLIAM TUCKER   I had thought about resigning for some time. Finally I did. I enjoyed my years with the club, but I was playing less and less and decided it would be best if I stopped altogether.

JAMES WHYTE DAVIS   I was sorry to see Tuck go. He was one of the original Knicks who was in on the writing of the rules. A good humored chap. He would be missed — again. I say "again" because he had missed a few years of playing while he was out chasing the gold.

We had a nice dinner for him and made him an honorary member.

WILLIAM TUCKER   At the going away dinner they made it sound as if I was going off to die.

"This ain't a funeral," I said. "I'll still be around. I'll always be a Knick."

"That's what we're afraid of," said Jamie Davis.

And that's what I missed most — the camaraderie of the men.

JAMES WHYTE DAVIS   One day I read in the *Clipper* that it would present a gold ball of regulation weight and size to the club proclaimed Champions for the season of '68 and that it would give gold medals to the nine best players.

We played all of six match games that season — three against the Excelsiors, two against the Eagles, and one against the Uniques of Staten Island. I pitched in four of them and we won three.

"Think we'll win the gold ball?" asked Sam.

"Since the Atlantics won 44 more games than we did, I somehow doubt it."

"Maybe you'll win a gold medal."

"Well, I did score nine runs for the season."

"That should do it."

"After all, it was only 226 runs fewer than Joe Start scored."

"Close enough for my vote."

Had they counted how much enjoyment each player got from playing the game, I might have won ... something.

The fact is, we were receiving fewer match invitations every year, but that hardly mattered.

"Maybe we should challenge the Atlantics," Sam said after we beat the Uniques 40–34.

"They'd probably be afraid of us."

"As they should be."

SAM KISSAM    We base ball players were not averse to extraordinary displays that might have been staged by P.T. Barnum.

During the "velociped fever" some years ago, a game was played in Brooklyn with the fielders perched on bicycles and the base runners traveling around the bases similarly mounted. A burlesque game was once played in which the 18 participants were costumed in masquerade suits and were conveyed in wheelbarrows from base to base. Then there was the "Donkey" game in which the nine having the least number of runs at the end of the game were considered the victors. The players on each side were matched against each other, and each run made by a player was credited to his opponent on the opposite side.

Once, in a Philadelphia game between amateur clubs, a herd of cattle that was being driven through the adjacent street made a raid on the ball players and tossed five of them into the air. No one was hurt, but all were mightily scared.

JAMES WHYTE DAVIS    One of the other stalwart amateur clubs was the Staten Island Base Ball and Cricket Club. We played a number of matches with them over on the Camp Washington Grounds in New Brighton. Their captain apologized profusely for their lack of conditioning and playing skills, then they went out and beat us 40–16.

We also continued to play cricket occasionally. I recall one such match against the Manhattan Cricket Club. Thank goodness Chadwick was one of our two bowlers and he took six wickets himself. We ended the match winning 77–50. I loved to beat the cricketers at their own game.

It had become traditional for the veteran Knicks to meet the veteran Excelsiors twice a year. It was an opportunity for us to renew the sport of our younger days. I remember particularly one such occasion in September of '68. We played a game of seven innings running up 51 runs in a nice win.

A few days later, when the *Eagle* reported on the game, it referred to "J.W. Davis, Esq., ye wily and tricky pitcher of the Knicks." I rather liked that.

DOC ADAMS    When the deadly scourge revisited New York, killing as many as 10,000, there was concern that crowds like those at base ball matches would be more susceptible to the ravages of the disease. The last time cholera had ripped through the city in 1849, there was little medical information as to its causes, much less the treatment. This time, however, armed with new research on how cholera traveled, the city was much better prepared to meet the threat.

I received a letter from one of the new members of the Knicks asking my advice. I assured him base ball posed no threat — bad sewage treatment did, which is why so much damage occurred in the overcrowded lower class areas of the city.

Although no longer a member, I continued my interests in the club's activities, and in general what was going on in the game. It was with some interest that I noticed several mentions in the papers of players, mostly catchers and first basemen, using leather gloves on their catching hands. As hard as I tried, I just couldn't picture Charlie DeBost with a leather glove. His hands were leathery enough. Now I know some cricket players wore gloves, but the idea of a base ball player using them seemed to go quite against the idea of manliness that the game had sought to promote. To that end, a few players actually resorted to using flesh-colored gloves so as not to draw attention to them.

I also noted with considerable interest that the manufacturing of bats and balls had become a big, and I can only presume, profitable business. I read someplace that the demand for balls had reached half a million per year. I know they were using colored balls, too. In fact one company brought out a ball that they called the "Dead Red Ball," which they claimed did away with the dazzling whiteness which blinded batsmen and fielders on a sunny day. Funny, I don't recall ever being blinded by a ball. Hit by a ball, yes; blinded, no.

A note in the papers said that new balls had been adopted for all match games. The balls were apparently stamped with the maker's name on them along with figures indicating the exact size and weight of the ball, and to top it off, the word "guarantee" was added. The makers guaranteed to forfeit any ball with their stamp on it — provided it is not a forgery — if it was found over weight or size.

I had to laugh. In the old days when I made the balls, they were exactly the right weight if they felt right. I guarantee that.

Naturally, too, since I had been so involved in the formulation and revision of the rules, I still followed with interest the changes they were making. One thing they did was to prohibit the batter from stepping forward or backward when striking at the ball. He had to stand on a line drawn through the center of the home base that ran three feet out from the base on each side and which was parallel to the pitcher's line. I thought this a good addition and another example of the intention to balance the game between pitcher and batsmen.

## 98

# *Dirty Dealings*

JAMES WHYTE DAVIS    In many people's minds, base ball was in the same class as gambling halls, brothels, and saloons—a dirty business to be sure. Base ball and the underworld were seen to be in bed together. Maybe this shouldn't have been surprising during the Grant administration, which itself was rife with scandal and moral turpitude.

The city was home to any number of gambling halls, lavishly decorated dives with thick carpets, soft chairs, and marble tables where for a pittance one could buy a brandy and segar so as to lose one's money in faux style. I read someplace that in our city alone as many as 30,000 people earned their living off the gambling industry.

Because gambling had become so much a part of base ball, spectators were wont to think that any game which their team lost when highly favored was because the "fix was on." In most cases it wasn't, but so long as the suspicions surfaced, the game remained tainted. And because they so often played three-game championship series, the temptation to purposely split the first two games so as to force a third game with a big gate was always in the air. Suspicion, justified or not, was everywhere. It's but a short step from gambling to fix. A sure thing is a whole lot better than a chance.

The Haymakers from upstate in Troy were widely thought to be the dirtiest team on the planet. Controlled by the notorious gambler, John Morrissey, they apparently took hippodroming to a new level by arranging a series of close games so as to attract larger gates for future games.

Then there was the time James Devlin and a couple of his club mates were turned out by their clubs and banned from professional base ball for life. By all accounts Devlin was a fine pitcher who at 28 stood to make a good living from the game for years to come. He apparently confessed to receiving bribes for selling games and then swindling his co-conspirators out of their share of the money. Why would he throw it all away like that? It's beyond me.

The problem in base ball was simply that the Association was powerless to deal with the problems. Its rules against betting were simply scoffed at by those who chose to do so. Even when a case did make it to the Judiciary Committee, the committee was impotent to enforce punishments. Half the time when a player was summoned, the player simply "forgot" to make an appearance. Case over. Other times they just didn't or couldn't follow through, or like in the Devyr case, the clubs simply nullified their decisions.

It was an ugly situation. Would spectators continue to follow and support a game that they knew or thought they knew to be fixed?

HENRY CHADWICK    Without question the greatest single evil in the great game of base ball is pool selling. If ever the game ceases to exist, the proper inscription to place upon its tombstone will be "Died of Pool Selling."

Before the pool selling it was anybody's guess how much had been bet on a game. However, with the advent of pool selling, the amount bet could be easily determined, and so the temptation was there to enter into some arrangement to "sell" or "throw" a game.

With pool selling it was not unusual to see as much as ten to twenty thousand dollars being put down on a single game. With this knowledge there were those who had an interest in seeing that the game ended as it "should."

JAMES WHYTE DAVIS    The State of New York eventually prohibited pool selling on base ball games, but the very fact that they had to said it all.

SAM KISSAM    I read where in California gamblers would shoot off six shooters just as a player was about to catch a ball that would spoil their bet. I don't know if that's true or not, but it sure made for a colorful image.

HARRY WRIGHT    I don't deny that gamblers and gambling had become part of the game, but the influence of both was greatly exaggerated — and I emphasize "greatly." By far most games were strictly on the up and up. I don't think I ever played in one that wasn't, and I played in an awful lot of games during my career.

Anyway, you can't stop a gambler who wants to put down a bet on anything. Five to one it rains this afternoon. Three gets you four I can down a mug of lager before you can.

The reality is the cheats and scandals make more news and sell more papers than the honest and fair. Newspapers were jumping to conclusions for their own ends. By far, by far, by far, most players were honest decent men who played the game fairly and squarely.

HENRY CHADWICK    There was no place in our game, either professional or amateur, for men who lacked character. It was that simple, it was that clear, but it wasn't that true.

# 99

# *Gate Money Principles*

JAMES WHYTE DAVIS   After considerable discussion, the Association gave tacit consent for amateur clubs to receive gate money when on tours or under circumstances involving the question of their having a ground to play on or not. Although players were not to be paid, this was a compromise to which I could not subscribe.

According to reputable sources, by 1868 the leading clubs in the New York area took in about $100,000 in gate money. Players in Brooklyn were particularly eager and able to take advantage of this. After Cammayer and his ilk took their cut, the top Brooklyn clubs made up to $900 each. If this doesn't sound like much consider that at that time $500 a year was a hell of a good salary for most clerks.

What it had come down to was this: Amateur games were being played for gate receipts.

"It doesn't make us professionals," went the argument. "We're not paying salaries. It just allows us to cover our expenses."

The "enclosure movement," as it was euphemistically called, was nothing more than insincerity wrapped in hypocrisy and presented with unctuous apologies.

We — the Knickerbockers — were one of the last bastions of the code of pure amateurism, but we had a lot of new members, men who didn't know the game as us old-timers did. Younger lads like Peck, Stanwood, and Lyon didn't see anything wrong playing games for gate receipts.

"It's not as if we're going to be paid personally," said Peck. "The money will go to the club for legitimate expenses. I don't see anything wrong with that."

"I do," I said. "I see something definitely wrong with that. I see a corruption of the very spirit that is base ball."

"Nothing is forever. The game changes. You've got to expect that."

"If we don't stand for right, who will?"

"Just about everybody else is playing for gate receipts."

"Which is why we shouldn't."

"Except there's a reason they do it. It keeps their club afloat."

"We've been floating for a long time without it, and we'll continue that way."

"I don't see how it changes our position as upholders of the amateur position. We're not talking about turning professional, but if people are willing to pay to see us play, I can't see any reason why we shouldn't use that to benefit our club, that's all."

And so the argument went at meeting after meeting. At one, the secretary read an invitation from the Yale Base Ball Club offering to play us for a guarantee of $50 and one third of the gate for anything over that.

"Out of the question," I said.

"We sure could use the money," said Stanwood.

"Has anyone seen our account books?" said Peck.

"Even an amateur college nine wants to play for gate money. I don't see what's wrong with that," added Stanwood.

"As long as I'm a member of this club," I said, "we're not going to play games for money. I don't care if it comes from the gate, from investors, or from Santa Claus, and if you do decide to accept money, you will find yourself with an opening in the membership rolls, for I will no longer continue my membership in this club. The day the Knickerbocker Base Ball Club of New York accepts money for playing the game it created is the day I quit, for it will be a slap in the face of Adams, Cartwright, Curry, Wheaton, Dupignac, Tucker, Ransom, Lee, and the others who worked hard to make this club what it is today, a club of gentlemen playing the game according to a code of sportsmanship and amateurism that honors the game, the members, and the founders."

I won the day but I could see what was coming. We wrote to the Yale Club, thanked them for their invitation, but informed them that we would adhere to our amateur code and so decline the invitation. They wrote back saying they would still like to play us and of course they would not charge gate money if we objected.

"I propose a compromise," Peck said at a subsequent meeting. "Given the objections of some of our members to playing for gate money, and given that almost every other club that we could play against is charging gate money, I propose that we accept invitations for games with these clubs where appropriate but decline to partake in the receipts. I trust this will meet with the approval of all our membership."

By "our membership," he meant me, and perhaps a few others. I suppose Peck's proposal adhered to the letter of the law in maintaining our amateur status, but it was a step, albeit a small one, in the wrong direction. I knew once we started going down that road, there would be no turning back. There never is in these sorts of things.

"It's a reasonable compromise," said Collingwood. "After all we can't dictate what other clubs do, only what we do."

"It makes sense to me," said Stanwood. "I think we should put it to a vote. It's a good compromise."

I didn't say anything. I didn't have to. Everyone in the room knew where I stood. Hell, every player in the city knew where I stood.

When the compromisers carried the vote, I simply went home and wrote a letter to the club.

> Gentlemen of the Knickerbocker Base Ball Club:
>
> Given that the club has desecrated its time-honored principle of playing base ball for health and recreation merely, it is incumbent on me to quit the dear old club. I can no longer be a part of a club that has leant its good name to the odious practice of charging admission to games.
>
> Yours sincerely,
>
> James Whyte Davis

SAM KISSAM    Jamie's resignation was, to put it mildly, a huge blow. It didn't seem possible to run the club without him. That's not true, of course, but that's the way it appeared at the time. He had been such an integral part of it for 20 years that it almost seemed as if the Knickerbocker Base Ball Club was James Whyte Davis.

JAMES WHYTE DAVIS    Somebody had to stand up for the sanctity of pure amateurism.

With my resignation, they were spared the rambling discourses of this old relic. I didn't doubt that many were glad to see me go.

SAM KISSAM    But we weren't — not all of us anyway.

"Jamie, don't be rash," I said to him. "You're not a foolhardy man, and this..."

"It's not rash. I've thought about it quite a bit."

"You didn't think about it at all. You got angry and acted impulsively. I know you."

"You're damn right I'm angry, and you should be, too. All this business with gate money is wrong and you know it."

"Maybe, but it's here, Jamie, and it's not going away."

"No, but I am."

"And what good does that do? If you're away from the game, then there's no way you can influence it as you ... we ... wish."

"It does me good."

"Like hell it does. Deny yourself something you love because you're mad at it? Jamie, you, not the game, come out the loser in this. Look, we all get angry at things from time to time. That's life, but if we run every time anger comes to us, well we wouldn't have much left in our lives."

Despite his protestations, I think Jamie wanted someone like me to try to talk him out of this act of self pity. The name, "Poor Old Davis," was not pinned on him without cause.

"Get off your high moral horse. 'Oh, woe is me. They want me to play the game the way others want, not the way I want.' You know what, Jamie? That's just stupid."

"You're saying I'm stupid?"

"No, let me re-phrase that. Maybe muttonheaded. I dare say that's a little more gentlemanly."

"Maybe dunderheaded."

"No 'maybe' about it. You're that and more."

"Some friend you are."

"It's because I am your friend that I can say such things. No, it's because I am your friend that I do say these things. Stop feeling sorry for yourself."

"Is that what I'm doing?"

"The club needs you."

"I'm not sure."

"The game needs you."

"It has no interest in hearing what I have to say."

"Poor old Davis."

In time he relented and came back into the fold. His impetuous act of resignation was really just that—a moment of pique, which upon reflection and the gentle urging of a friend, he came to rescind.

With so many new members coming into the club it was important to have some of the older, and in some ways base ball wiser, members there to help guide the ship. Certainly no one fit that bill better than Jamie.

Would the club have survived had his resignation become permanent? Probably, but we were clearly better off with him leading the way, and make no mistake about it, he was by then our unquestioned leader.

---

# 100

## *Difficult Times for Davis*

SAM KISSAM   Many of us knew about the difficulties Jamie was facing. His wife, Maria, was seriously ill and the toll it was taking on him and his boys was apparent. He didn't talk much about it, but the stress showed. Still, he forged on with his club activities. I suppose in a way it was therapeutic, an escape from having to think about the inevitable.

When Maria passed, everyone in the club was there to offer whatever support we could. Such is the nature and strength of the fraternal friendships club membership offered.

So with two young sons still at home, Jamie became a widower at a relatively early age.

I have seen men who experienced the death of their spouses respond by entering into a stage of social isolation; I have seen some become extremely angry or frustrated; I have seen some become utterly helpless, or express such feelings of hurt that they were unable to function effectively.

Then his brother, Sam, died at 25.

Yet, or perhaps because of his losses, Jamie became even more involved with the club than he had ever been. At least it seemed that way to me.

WILLIAM TUCKER    Jamie was deeply wounded by the death of Maria. There was no doubt about that. The club came to his aid as best we could. At the very least, we supplied a diversion from the heartache I know he felt but didn't always express.

I told Jamie I was there if he wanted to talk about it. If nothing else, I'm a very good listener, I told him.

"I know you are Tuck," he said, "and I appreciate that, but I just have to get on with ... everything."

We didn't broach the subject unless he did first. Mostly he just threw himself back into his work and play.

A base ball club can serve many functions.

---

# 101

# *Collapse of the Association*

HENRY CHADWICK    Of the some thousand organized clubs, not fifty could be ranked in any way as professional clubs. And yet it was the ambition of this small minority to rule the whole thousand.

It is true the apathy shown by the amateurs afforded the professionals the opportunity to take the reins in their own hands, but that did not absolve the professional leaders from the charges of blundering management.

JAMES WHYTE DAVIS    By 1870, the Association was rapidly sinking under the sheer weight of its many problems, most of which had to do with professionalism and its unwieldy size. Look, it had grown into a national octopus with hundreds of members spread to hell and back with some state associations maintaining control over their members. The professional clubs were in total control and the amateurs were pushed aside as so much detritus.

It was clear that either all the other amateur clubs had to withdraw from the Association as we did or the professional clubs had to be expelled. The interests were just too damn different for the two groups to live together under the same tent.

Of course, I wasn't at the convention, but I heard all about it from Harry McLean, a long-time player in the Washington area whom I came to know a little through business connections.

HARRY MCLEAN   From the very outset it was clear this was going to be a contest for control between the amateur clubs and the professional clubs. It was equally clear the professionals had the upper hand.

In the opening proceedings, the animus of the controlling clique became quite obvious, first by an unsubstantiated charge about rules abuses and then by questioning the right of Mr. Chadwick to occupy the position of chairman of the Committee on Rules. Both these efforts failed. Then animosity was directed against the treasurer of the Association whose own misfortunes in business had prevented him from fulfilling his financial obligations.

The fact is, that before an hour had gone by, those of us representing the interests of the amateurs had become thoroughly disgusted by the whole business.

The wildest discussion followed a resolution introduced by Mr. Cantwell of Albany.

"I propose the following resolution," said Mr. Cantwell with all the authority of a Lincolnesque pronouncement, "that this Association regard the custom of publicly hiring men to play the game of base ball as reprehensible and injurious to the best interests of the game."

There it was, out in the open and on the table for debate—and quite a debate it became. You would have thought we were debating the abolition of slavery so heated were some of the comments. Acrimony darted about the room as if it were a chicken barely evading a fox.

One delegate I didn't know assailed Harry and George Wright for their deleterious effect on the game, whereupon Mr. Ford quickly and staunchly defended them.

When the motion finally came up for vote, but nine of us voted for the resolution. There were seventeen votes against the resolution.

There it was, once and for all.

Other actions on rules and such things were taken up by the Convention, but that vote killing the Cantwell resolution also killed the Association.

JAMES WHYTE DAVIS   After that contentious meeting, the National Association gave up the ghost. It adjourned *sine die*—that is without setting a date for its next meeting. The Association, which had once served a purpose, disappeared without tears in this quarter. The move toward professionalism tore it apart just as I believed it would do to the game itself.

ALBERT SPALDING    The death of the National Association of Base Ball Players was expected, natural, and painless. The organization had outlived its usefulness; it had fallen into evil ways; it had been in very bad company.

HENRY CHADWICK    The fact is we did have amateurs and we did have professionals and we needed to be honest and accept that. There were problems in the game to be sure, but the root of these problems stemmed from the gambling interests, not because players were being paid to play. Wherever there is money to be made, men will make it. That's part of the fabric of our country; it's essential for a thriving democracy. It was essential for us to recognize the facts of our situation and recognize the professional base ball player for what he was.

The Association had fallen prey to the same evils bedeviling the city — greed, corruption, deceit. Disgraceful maneuvering by an unscrupulous clique of men hailing from the professional clubs pushed the amateurs to the dusty corners of their organization. Among the shenanigans of the clique was the scandalous act of welcoming back Wansely, Duffy, and Devyr, the three Mutual players who had been banned for throwing games a few years earlier.

I know James Davis among others was irate at this, and I know he began talking to others, fomenting disgust at the takeover by the professional scalawags.

# PART ELEVEN: AMATEURS AND PROFESSIONALS 1871–1875

## 102

# Red Stockings Reversal

SAM KISSAM   "Did you hear about the Red Stockings?" I asked Jamie as we were walking out to the ball grounds.

"What, that they beat up on some poor team 100–0?"

"No, that they've decided to return to the ranks of us poor amateurs."

"Why, were they being paid in counterfeit money or something?"

"Or something."

JAMES WHYTE DAVIS   I shouldn't have been surprised. It was as inevitable as Alick chasing gold. If Harry Wright couldn't keep them afloat, nobody could, for he was as clever with the books as he was with the ball.

While the hired hands were racing about the country engaging in games for lucre, the real members of the club were sitting at home with the understanding that they would have to dig into their own pockets to make up any losses.

The team of professionals known as the Red Stockings was a fraud; the players were hired assistants. The real club members were nothing more than spectators with everything to lose and nothing to gain.

HARRY WRIGHT   The reaction with which some people greeted our return to amateur status was hypocritical, mean-spirited, and downright wrong. We had been the standard bearer for greatness in the game and brought honor to our city and our club. We were universally applauded for our accomplishments and admired for our sportsmanship.

To suggest that only an amateur could play the game with honor and dignity is pure unadulterated humbug.

ASHLEY HYDE   For some time after the Red Stockings announced they were returning to the amateur ranks, the sporting press fueled the professional vs. amateur debate.

WALTER AVERY   Professional base ball was no different than any other business in that it needed to be run on the up and up if people were to respect it.

But in base ball's case it was rife with squabbles and unsavory practices and consequently lost favor with many, not because it was a business, but because it was a business badly run.

A good example was the specious reporting of gate receipts.

# 103

# *All-Amateur Association*

JOSEPH BAINBRIDGE JONES    I was president of the Excelsiors when the flap broke out over the Red Stockings' abdication of its professionalism.

The professionals formed their own National Association of Professional Base Ball Players, and so it was time for all of us who championed the amateur cause to come to the fore and take a public stand. I called on representatives of the city's oldest and most respected clubs to gather with the purpose of organizing a national association of strictly amateur base ball players.

Among those invited were the Knickerbockers. Now I know they had dropped out of the Association and even though they weren't playing many games by then, they were still the yardstick against which other amateur clubs were measured.

I had several long conversations with Jamie Davis about this and he concurred that by organizing, we could reclaim the game from the evils attendant upon it by the professionals.

GEORGE GRUM    By calling together the old clubs, the doctor was trying to revive a game that never existed, not even in the "good old days." And as for the Knickerbockers, they had become more of an ideal than a reality. The game quite simply had passed them by.

HENRY CHADWICK    I suppose it was my prodding that got the amateurs started re-organizing. To that end, a convention was held under the joint call of the Knickerbocker and Excelsior clubs.

DOC ADAMS    In March I received an invitation letter from Dr. Jones inviting me to a convention of amateur base ball clubs to be held in the rooms of the Excelsior Club.

The invitation read in part, "The committee hopes to see such veterans as Messers. Bixby, Mott, Dr. Adams, Dupignac and others of the 'old guard' of amateurs present at the convention, even if they should not be delegates, as it is intended to make the meeting a regular reunion of the old amateur school of ball play."

I was then 57. I guess that made me "old guard."

The time was right for there to be two distinct organizations with two distinct objectives and although I had given up my involvement in such undertakings, I supported the idea.

JOSEPH BAINBRIDGE   Jones Clubs sent representatives to New York for the meeting that formed the National Association of Amateur Base Ball Players. That so many clubs attended was testimony to the idea that amateurism was still very much alive and still very desirable. The character of the meeting may be judged from the fact that such venerable clubs as the Knickerbocker, Gotham, and Eagle of New York, and the Excelsior, Enterprise, and Star of Brooklyn all sent representatives.

JAMES WHYTE DAVIS   I agreed to attend the organizational meeting as one of two official delegates from the Knickerbockers (Hinsdale was the other), but I had some concerns about whether an effective amateur organization was possible. I knew there would be objections from some amateur clubs to any rule which would cut off their supply of funds from gate money receipts which they used to defray organizational expenses.

On the other hand, however, if we didn't take action we would remain in the position of sharing the odium attached to the abuses of the professional game.

We had a good turnout for the meeting. Still I doubt if the organization would ever have gotten started without the Knickerbockers. This was not because of me, but because of what our club stood for. As far as I was concerned, we were still the standard for amateurism by which all clubs were measured.

JOSEPH BAINBRIDGE JONES   I had the honor of calling the meeting to order and briefly explaining the objectives of the gathering.

In honor of their position in the amateur game, I then nominated Jamie Davis of the Knickerbockers as temporary chairman of the convention. He accepted graciously as I knew he would.

JAMES WHYTE DAVIS   After names were placed before the convention, I appointed five delegates as the committee to draft a constitution and by-laws—Albro of the Fleetwood Club, Thatcher of the Olympic, Wood of the Champion, Bush of Harvard College, and, of course, Dr. Jones from the Excelsior Club, who I understood came prepared with written notes containing his ideas for the organization.

While the rest of us engaged in conversation and a little drink, the committee retired to another room to work out details. Attesting to the thoroughness of Dr. Jones' preparation, the committee returned in just half an hour with a workable draft of a constitution and by-laws of what they logically called The National Association of Amateur Base Ball Players.

JOSEPH BAINBRIDGE JONES   We agreed that the association would be composed of two delegates from each club. New clubs would be admitted to the organization upon application to a committee on nominations. This committee would ascertain the condition and character of each club to assure they lived up to the high standards of amateurism to which we all aspired. Each applicant club had to be composed of at least eighteen active members.

We all agreed that any member who was guilty of "conspiracy with any person or persons to cause by any contrivance the loss of a match game in which he is or may be one of the contestants for money, place, position, emolument or any consideration of any nature whatsoever would immediately lose the privilege of membership, and no new club would be admitted to membership which had among its members anyone who had been convicted of such action, and no match game could be played by any club which had any such person among its members, under penalty of forfeiture of membership." We also added the wording, "Any member belonging to this association behaving in an ungentlemanly manner, or rendering himself obnoxious to the association may, by a vote of two-thirds of the members present, be expelled."

So you can see we took seriously the sentiment that we were first and foremost gentlemen and that this sentiment would be at the heart of the association.

We then moved to the election of officers. There were three nominations for president — me, Mr. Davis, and Mr. Bush.

JAMES WHYTE DAVIS   For several reasons, I declined the nomination: I felt I had done my duty to the game of base ball in the various capacities in which I had served over the years; the demands being made on me as a stockbroker were increasing; I needed to spend more time with my sons and their families. These may have been rationalizations, though, because what was concerning me most was the direction in which the game itself was going, and even though this new association was a step in the right direction, I questioned whether it would prove to be successful in combating the ills of the game.

ARCHIBALD MCCLURE BUSH   After Dr. Jones and Mr. Davis declined the nomination, it fell to me to lead the organization over the next year.

The first order of business was to adopt a code of playing rules.

There followed quite a little skirmish of words between Mr. Edwards of the Champion Club of Jersey City and Mr. Sterling of the Stars.

To no one's surprise, at issue was whether or not clubs should be allowed to charge admission to games.

The word "professional" was spat out as if it were a swear word worthy of a mandated fine; "amateur" as if it were sacrosanct.

"If we take in money at the gate, we're professionals," went the case for no admission charges.

"We're professionals only if we pay players," went the counter.

Fraley Rogers from the Star Club was particularly incensed when the argument seemed to be turning against permitting charging for admission. "We will not be part of any organization that prohibits admission fees. We have sold tickets for years and will continue to do so as it is our only way of keeping afloat. If this group prohibits this, then we will not be a part of it. We cannot be."

It seemed as if this issue would destroy our amateur organization before it got started. Several representatives stood up as if to leave before cooler heads agreed that those clubs who wished to charge for admissions would be free to remain as members of the Association just so long as they were not using the money to pay the players.

JAMES WHYTE DAVIS   No one argued for paying the players. Amateurism after all was why we were there, but there was considerable discussion about who could be paid by clubs. Those who tended the fields? Cleaned the clubhouses? What if these people were club members who were paid? What if they were non-members?

We never came to any conclusions about these issues but one thing about which I'm sure, you can't maintain a brotherly feeling toward those you are employing.

It wasn't always thus. Can you imagine Alick saying to Doc, "Come on, old boy, cut the grass and we'll take up a collection among the members and pay you for your labors?"

ALBERT SPALDING   In an effort to establish a successful amateur association, the amateur clubs either didn't understand, refused to admit, or grossly underestimated the extent to which the game had already been transformed. There was no possibility of going back, and I think from the point of view of most base ball supporters, no desire to either.

It is always easier to criticize than do, always easier to complain than to make.

JAMES WHYTE DAVIS   Let me see how to put this as politely as I can. The Amateur Association of Base Ball Players was a mess from the beginning. To wit:

We met again for the expressed purpose of reviewing the existing code of playing rules. The convention was called for 8 P.M., but the absence of all the officers of the Association except our treasurer, William Thatcher, at that hour prevented the conducting of any business. Finally, Vice President Jewell showed up and called the meeting to order.

He informed us that the secretary of the Association, Mr. Uhthoff of Baltimore's Pastime Club, had not only resigned his position but also had been neglectful of his duties to such an extent that it would be difficult to conduct even preliminary business. Well, it quickly became evident that there weren't enough members present to constitute a quorum.

Before adjournment, however, several clubs that had applied to the secretary for probationary membership reported that they had received no reply. Other clubs complained that some of the official duties of the principal positions of the Association had been rather loosely attended to.

Clearly there were problems with the Amateur Association from the start and some of those problems were the same as those that did in the old National Association.

The next season we didn't even have a meeting. Some clubs thought there was no need to revise any rules. Others, given the mess at the last meeting, simply had no interest in getting together again. I must say, some of the Knicks felt the same way.

Still, Rogers, from the Staten Island Club, contacted me and suggested that we call another meeting in an attempt to reorganize.

"Jamie," he said, "there are still a number of other active clubs that had sent delegates to the last meeting — the Alerts of Seton Hall, the Excelsior of Brooklyn, the Silver of New York, the Olympic of Philadelphia, the college clubs of Harvard, Fordham, Manhattan, New Haven, and Brown, and of course your club. Surely there is enough reason to think we can re-organize."

"Can, or should?"

"Both."

"To what end?"

"A viable and permanent organization."

"I'm not convinced that's possible."

"We need to try and we need the Knickerbockers."

But did the Knickerbockers need the Amateur Association? Perhaps not. Nevertheless, I presented this idea at a club meeting, and although we weren't exactly optimistic about the prospects, we consented.

So three of the stronger amateur clubs got together — The Knicks, the Staten Island Club, and the Arlington Club — and we wrote up a circular which we sent to every amateur club in the country for which we could collect any information.

This is what we sent out:

> As amateur base ball playing has had an impetus given it this season, judging from the number of contests that have taken place throughout the country, and the reorganization of such time honored clubs as the Excelsior and Powhatan clubs of Brooklyn and others, and the great number of clubs in existence throughout the country, the undersigned ask your hearty

support and cooperation to bring about an amateur revival — one that will remind us of the "good old days of yore," and will at once create and awaken a lively interest in the hearts of all lovers of base ball, who enjoy the game for the game itself, and not for any greed of gain, etc.

The meeting, however, was poorly attended and of those present, most were from the younger amateur clubs. Little, if anything, was accomplished, and the meeting adjourned with little hope for the future of the organization.

HENRY CHADWICK   In order to establish a permanent organization, I felt there were three conditions that needed to be in place: It had to have a simple, but clear, code of rules; it had to keep its expenses light; and it had to have as its principal object that of advancing the best interests of the amateur class.

I continually reminded the amateurs that it was highly desirable that one code of playing regulations should govern the entire fraternity. We certainly didn't need two separate games of base ball. The only appreciable difference should be that one group was paid to play; the other not.

JAMES WHYTE DAVIS   The Professional Association appointed Harry Wright as a committee of one to meet with us to agree on one set of rules. One would think that would be an easy thing to accomplish, but nothing was easy in those days of jousting between the two groups.

HARRY WRIGHT   There was room for both amateurs and professionals. The amateurs, though, were at a critical juncture. They had to decide whether to adopt the professional code of playing rules — of course with such exceptions as applied to the status of the two classes — or to adopt a special code of their own.

Of even more importance, though, was the need to give a plain and unmistakable definition to the term "amateur." It was a well-known fact that dozens of so-called amateur clubs were paying players and accepting gate money. It was an insincere position that needed to be addressed, but their inability to form a permanent amateur organization rendered that impossible. Either out of stubbornness, stupidity, or inefficiency, they were floundering as the professionals were flourishing.

"You need to take the leadership," I told Jamie one day. "Get the Knicks behind a real organization. Clear up this mess once and for all."

He nodded wearily.

"If not from the Knicks, from whom?"

He nodded again. Still, they were the first among the many and had done so much to advance the game that I hated to see them give up the fight now.

Jamie stubbed out his cigar with enough force to break it in two. "I can't even convince some of our own Goddamned members to forego gate receipt games," he said.

I guess that said it all.

JAMES WHYTE DAVIS   Look, the writing was on the wall. It was time for us to stand up for what we claimed to be — pure amateurs in every sense of the word. And that meant no salaries, no hidden benefits, no paid admissions to games, no gate sharing, no shenanigans.

We were, if not the last of the pure amateurs, one of the damn select few, but the issues surrounding the gate money question were tearing the club apart.

The Olympian games were the occasions for the highest interest for all of Greece. A victory there made a man a hero for a year and distinguished for life. It carried joy to the hearts of his family. But the prize was a crown of olive leaves. There was no gate money at Olympia. Can you imagine a modern man being asked to play for olive leaves!

Of course, it wasn't just the players who were going in for the money. Almost always it was the keepers of public houses and the backers of men who were the fomenters of the whole affair. Their object was simply a share — a lion's share — of the gate money and the profit from the sale of liquor at their bars which was often a considerable amount.

To me the solution to these problems was simple. Gentlemen of all kinds should give up these contests for championships, leaving them to the professional gatherers of gate money, and enjoy games among themselves for their own sake.

There were, in fact, not two classes of base ball players, but three: the professionals, the true amateurs, and the hypocrites who claimed to be amateurs but who blurred the lines to such a degree that you couldn't find them with a goddamned magnifying glass the size of Manhattan Island.

I got on my high horse, and at a club meeting, once again waxed as eloquently as I could about the virtues of acting on what we claimed to be right.

"As far as I'm concerned, any of you who want to take money for playing can resign now. As far as I'm concerned, any of you who want this club to accept gate money can make a bee line for the door now. As far as I'm concerned, any of you who think we should compromise our principles can go straight to hell."

SAM KISSAM   Jamie's escalating rants and his holier-than-thou self-righteous act wore on some of the members, particularly the younger ones, but when it came down to it, no one put up much of a protest. We agreed to go our own way, which meant, among other things, that we would no longer be sending delegates to the Amateur Association meetings. This had its positive as well as negative repercussions. On one hand we were taking a stand for pure amateurism that everyone in the base ball fraternity could see. On the other hand, we were surrendering our ability to influence the future of the game. So be it. That was our decision and we were prepared to live with the consequences ... I think.

JAMES WHYTE DAVIS   The Knick-less Amateur Association was comprised of some 36 members from various states—hardly a representative sample when considered on a national level. More importantly, though, was the question of exactly who the hell were the amateurs anyway? Was the New York Club strictly amateur? Or the Hudson, or Nassau, or Confidence, or Mutual, all of which played on enclosed grounds and shared gate money?

In '74, Beach of the Princeton College Club called a meeting in New York. From everything I heard, the meeting was messy, disorganized, lacking in leadership, and attended by only a few members.

The purpose of the meeting was to consider revising the code of playing rules, but so much debate followed about the calling of "wides" that nothing else of substance was accomplished and the meeting broke up in disarray.

A separate movement then arose to organize a New York State Amateur Association similar to those in Massachusetts and Pennsylvania. The idea was to have the organization establish a code of rules for amateur clubs leading to a state championship pennant. Along with this they had the harebrained idea that they would legitimize the accepting of gate money by the members for competitions at State fairs and country town visits.

All I can say is, no, no, no, no. Gate money should not, is not, cannot be part of the amateur code no matter in what cloak it is wrapped.

HENRY CHADWICK   The biggest problem the amateurs were facing was the continued practice of revolving, which led to endless quarrels, disputes, and annoyances. What hippodroming was to the professional class, so was revolving to the amateur branch.

JAMES WHYTE DAVIS   One time we formally objected to the Gothams' use of Mr. Pinckney in a match against us while he was still a member of the Union Club.

Some clubs went to extraordinary lengths to deal with the problem. The Cincinnati Club even proffered charges of revolving against John Hatfield and then published the results of their hearing in a pamphlet, "Case of John. V.B. Hatfield before the Cincinnati Base Ball Club: Charges, Specifications and Testimony for the Prosecution and Defense." What was the result? Nothing whatsoever. Hatfield stayed with the club.

No, we didn't miss the Association, and no, revolving was not an issue with us. We played our games and for the most part, paid little or no attention to the goings-on of the Amateur Association or their members.

HENRY CHADWICK   Too many clubs didn't hesitate to strengthen (in reality weaken) their nines by accepting seceders from other clubs who were not legally eligible to play. The question needing clarification was, what constitutes the term "cease to be a member"? Is it when he had duly resigned from the other club and was not in arrears for dues, etc.? Or was it when he chose to join another club and left his former club without a "by your leave"? It wasn't unusual to find a player in Club A one week, in Club B the next, and in Club C the week after that, and so on.

Another issue among the amateur clubs was that relating to an amateur championship of the United States. There was considerable promotion of this idea, but in reality it was impossible. City, county, and state competitions were certainly possible, but a national championship would have involved more time and travel expenses than were even incurred by professional clubs.

The professional championship contests were certainly a necessity and as such they could be regulated to yield satisfactory results. Not so in amateur circles.

THOMAS MCKIERNAN   Here's a perfect example of the problems we were having. Morris Moore signed articles to play with our club — the Chatham Club — for the 1875 season in accordance with the rules of the Amateur Association. Well, he then proceeded to play in a match with the Flyaway Base Ball Club. As we were told, he was informed by some person in authority in the Flyaway Club that the signing of articles to play with us didn't amount to anything and he could play with them. If their interpretation of the rules was correct, what the hell was the use of the Association? It was nothing but a mockery.

JAMES WHYTE DAVIS   When Tommy McKiernan complained to me (and none too politely, I might add) about the Moore situation, I informed him (very politely, I might add) that the binding force of the articles is not worth the paper they were written on. Only the professional clubs can bind players to a contract for services.

"Bloody hell!"

"Precisely."

I also heard that Harry Beach played with the Oneidas of Orange one day and then a few days later played for the Staten Islands. The Islanders acknowledged this but he played for them anyway. What a flagrant disregard for the rules! And the thing is, the Staten Island Club had once been one of the most faithful to the amateur code.

Is there any question why we no longer participated in the Association?

C.W. BLODGETT   By 1876, most of the old clubs were either no longer operating, or as in the case of the Knicks, no longer participating in organizational meetings. We had a strong hope that a new era would be inaugurated in which our aim would be to return to the old time usages of the original amateur school of ball playing when crooked play and all the abuses incident to professionalism were unknown.

To that end, I tried to talk Jamie Davis into getting the Knicks to reconsider their absence, but to no avail. He was nothing if not inflexible. Then again, I'm not sure he was wrong, either.

JAMES WHYTE DAVIS    So, after a couple of sloppily run, semi-organized conventions, the Amateur Association withered away due to lack of interest. No surprises in that.

ASHLEY HYDE    I don't think there was any great mystery as to why both the old National Association of Base Ball Players and National Association of Amateur Base Ball Players fell apart while the professional association survived. It's simply that when you're playing for money, the organization and structure has to be there in order to turn a profit. When you're playing just for fun, well, there just really isn't any need for the same sort of organization.

---

## 104

# *Blurring the Lines*

ASHLEY HYDE    The situation was simply this: As much as the amateurs wanted nothing to do with the professionals and the professionals with the amateurs, there was little to distinguish the two.

JAMES WHYTE DAVIS    This was the condition of the game as I knew it to be. At least three clubs were paying their players salaries—the Athletics of Philadelphia, Forest City of Cleveland, and Mutuals of New York. Four others were organized as stock companies—the Boston, Chicago, Haymakers of Troy, and Olympic of Washington. Five professional clubs shared gate money with their players—Atlantic of Brooklyn, Eckford of Brooklyn, Forest City of Rockford, Kekiongas of Fort Wayne, and National of Washington.

Among the amateur clubs that were defraying the expenses of their organization by sharing gate money on tours, etc., were the Athletic and Stars of Brooklyn; Harvards of Boston; Yale of New Haven; Expert of Philadelphia; Primetime of Baltimore; Amateur of Chicago; Cincinnati; Lone Stars, Robert E. Lees, Southerns of New Orleans; and Eagles of Louisville.

So we were left among a select group of clubs that were not organized as stock companies, did not share gate money, or pay salaries. The clubs that I knew to be in this group were the Excelsiors, Harmonics, and Osceolas of Brooklyn, the Equity and Olympics of Philadelphia, and the Fleetwood of Tremont.

I may not have accounted for every club in the country but these are the ones of which I had any knowledge. Were any of the amateur clubs hiding receipts? All I can say is, not that I know of. We were a select but rapidly diminishing breed — amateurs both in spirit and actuality.

Some people took to calling us the "simon pures" (I hope they didn't mean that as an insult, I rather liked it), and those who shared gate receipts, the "half breeds."

CANDY CUMMINGS    Look, when I was on the Stars, we were taking gate money for our expenses and nothing more. The fact is it costs money to travel all over playing matches, and so, whenever there was gate money to be had, we damn well were not going to turn it down. In case anyone didn't know, they charge to ride trains and to stay in hotels. Where the grounds were not enclosed, and so, no gate money available, we paid our own expenses. Otherwise, our pockets were open.

HENRY CHADWICK    Putting aside the semi-professional business indulged in by most of the amateur clubs, it is interesting to note that time and again first-class professional nines were forced to succumb to the superior playing ability of the amateur nines. Take, for instance, the defeat of the Philadelphia, Athletic, Hartford, Atlantic, and New Haven teams by amateur nines, one of the closest contests being the Olympics of Patterson — the New Jersey amateur champions— and the professional Athletics which was marked by the remarkable score of 1–0 in a full nine-inning game.

JAMES WHYTE DAVIS    Amateurs? The Patterson Olympics were amateurs in name only. In reality they were liars.

JOHN WIDLEY    Our club, the Mutuals, was organized early in 1857 and had been playing ever since, and I must say, very successfully. We had a good side and won most of our matches. Of course we were proud of our record and didn't want to abandon the idea of playing to win, so what we decided to do was to create two divisions in our club. One played as a professional nine, the other strictly as an amateur side. Our professional nine played games against the likes of the Union, Eckford, and Forest City nines, while our amateur side played the Star and Atlantic clubs as well as the Harvard and Yale college sides.

It was quite a satisfactory arrangement and several other clubs followed suit. Those who wanted to maintain their membership and play for the simple fun of playing could do so, while those whose skills so merited could play highly competitive matches and get paid from gate receipts.

This does not mean the amateur side didn't play hard to win. Sometimes I think they played even harder. I remember one particular weekend when our professional side whitewashed the Chicago Club, 9–0, while our amateur side beat the Amateur Club of Chicago, 65–11. The competitive spirit will always come to the fore regardless of the level of competition.

JOHN O'BRIEN   I am a living example of how the two-level system of base ball worked. While still not 20 years old, I began playing catcher for the amateur Yeager Club in my hometown, Philadelphia. In fact, I was the catcher for our extraordinary contest with the Girard College nine that went 21 innings before we won 10 to 7.

It was my play in that game that led directly to my engagement with the Athletics, the representative professional team in my native city. Had they not seen me play as an amateur, who knows if I would ever have had the opportunity to pay for play? When they offered me a contract I was not about to turn it down. Who wouldn't play a game for money if they had the chance?

JAMES WHYTE DAVIS   When some clubs decided to allow amateurs and professionals within the same club, the press often referred to the professional players simply as "the players," and the amateurs as "the gentlemen."

ARCHIBALD MCCLURE BUSH   It wouldn't be far from the truth to say that the purest form of the game was being played by our college nines. It was in these matches that the admirers of the game looked for the most exciting contests. The *esprit de corps* and the natural rivalry between leading colleges trying to carry off the palm for their alma mater was the purest expression of the sport.

JAMES WHYTE DAVIS   I had the opportunity to watch a match between the professional Athletics and the amateur Harvards. Archie Bush led the Harvards in a valiant effort against the paid players, but eventually they lost 20 to 8. Could you expect Archie and his boys to defeat the likes of Wes Fisler and Al Reach? Certainly not in terms of runs scored, but I maintain the Harvards won in every other conceivable way. They were clearly superior in terms of the way they approached the game — with dignity and integrity. Reach and the others played as if the results were preordained and they couldn't wait to be done so they could move on to something more important.

The fact that Al Reach later formed a company to make bats and balls and earned a fortune in the process only underscores my point.

To this day, I have an article from *The Spirit of the Times* in which it wrote of a match between our club and the Stars: "It is true that amateurs cannot devote the same time to practice that men who make it a profession can spare; but the advantages of education and superior intelligence ought in very great measure to make up for this disadvantage."

Don't for a minute think that the public's interest was only in watching the professionals. The fact is that for some important matches, thousands of fans turned out for amateur games.

I remember once watching a match between the Stars of Brooklyn and the Resolutes of Elizabeth, New Jersey. When the Stars took an early lead, a spectator behind me (obviously a Resolute crank) started complaining loudly.

"What's Greathead doing in there at short stop? He's not the batsman that Laing is. They should be playing Laing."

Now, I knew William Greathead, and he was a fine lad and an earnest player and didn't deserve to hear these remarks. He was playing with all his heart and deserved nothing but admiration and respect.

Candy Cummings was the pitcher that day for the Stars, and I dare say anyone would have had difficulty in batting well against him. When the game got to 22 to 9 in favor of the Stars and Greathead hit a weak ball to the first baseman, this unrefined spectator shouted, "Greathead, you should go home and take up knitting."

I had all I could do to refrain from hurling my own insults at this man (I shall not call him a "gentleman"). After the match, I took Greathead out to a local tavern for a beer. I told him not to pay any heed to the insults. He said he never did but I don't believe him and I know he didn't play many more games all season.

My concern was that more and more amateur clubs were being driven to play only their best players as "first-class nine," leaving most of their members to be mere spectators.

What was happening was that while we had a division between amateur and professional clubs, the distinctions between us were becoming more blurred as time went on.

HENRY CHADWICK    Probably the most significant difference between the amateurs and the professionals was that the professionals came almost exclusively from the working classes, while the amateur clubs like the Knickerbockers remained clubs for men of what might be considered a higher social level. At least that's the way they saw it.

One thing which the professionals did which, to my way of thinking, was valuable, was that given the ongoing problems with the abuses being heaped on the umpires, they eventually decided to allow the clubs to pay for umpires.

JAMES WHYTE DAVIS    I saved this clipping from the *Brooklyn Eagle* because it seems to me to sum up very well the situation the game was in.

> In contrast to the charges of fraud and the sequences of quarrels, dissensions and conflicts which are now features of professional play, we turn with pleasure to the efforts of such organizations as the old Knickerbocker Club, and the Staten Island Base Ball and Cricket Association, to restore the lost prestige of reputable playing to the ball playing fraternity. The former club,

now in its thirtieth year of its existence, is marking its seasons play with
the most enjoyable contests each week....

I couldn't have said it better myself.

---

## 105

# *The Professionals Regroup*

HARRY WRIGHT    With the retreat of the Cincinnati club back to the ranks
of the amateurs, I moved on to the Boston Red Stockings.

Then one day while in New York looking for strong players to add to our
club, I ran into one of my old Knickerbocker colleagues (I'd rather not say
who) and he went on at some length about how the game of base ball was
"played out."

Not wanting to engage in an argument with the old gentleman, I nodded
polite agreement. This idea of "played out" seemed to be the general impression with all the "old boys" of our game who had long since passed their best
days on the playing fields.

The truth, however, is that the game was never healthier. Never had more
spectators attended matches. Never had more money been made in base ball
despite the fact that some trips had been cancelled and some clubs had been
obliged to suspend operations.

Just a few years earlier the admission fee to most matches was but ten
cents and, at best, with maybe one great match played each week. By the season of '75, we were getting half a dollar and first class matches were held every
fine day. The Boston Club announced receipts of $17,000 for their three-week
Western tour. The professional class was supported by organizations investing
an aggregate capital of some $200,000. Add to that the capital generated by bat
and ball factories, manufacturing houses for uniforms, shoes, belts, gloves, etc.,
and you have a very significant figure. Then, too, thousands of people were
earning a livelihood through manufacturing the implements and materials of
the game. A permanent industry had been established. A healthy and invigorating sport was provided for the masses, and an exciting series of contests were
staged for the people of leisure.

Played out? No, nothing like that.

There had never been a better time to organize a national association of
our own.It was clear that there could never again be a harmonious government
of the two groups under one administration. With a National Association of

Professional Ball Players we wouldn't again have to sit through the angry discussions as to which club was champion. We could also set up a court of appeals to settle the many requests which inevitably came up each season.

If amateurs, like my old friends on the Knickerbockers, wanted to hold on to their ideas of an idealized game, let them. We would be the future of the game and leave them as a curiosity, a quaint recollection of a time gone by, much as a museum displays its relics.

We formed the National Association of Base Ball Players with ten clubs— Mutual of New York, Athletic of Philadelphia, Olympic of Washington, White Stockings of Chicago, Red Stockings of Boston, Forest City of Cleveland, Kekionga of Fort Wayne, National of Washington, Forest City of Rockford, and Haymakers of Troy.

Our first game was in May. The Cleveland Forest Citys lost to the Fort Wayne Kekiongas 2 to 0.

I wasn't in Fort Wayne for the game but the report in the newspapers the next day called the match the "finest game of base ball ever witnessed in this country, the playing being throughout without precedent in the annals of base ball, the members of both clubs establishing beyond a doubt their reputation as among the most skilled ball players in the United States."

Exactly how a reporter in Fort Wayne, Indiana, considered himself qualified to label it the finest game ever played is beyond my ken, but at least the Professional Association seemed to be up and running with an appealing game. Our goal was to be able to name a championship team at the end of the season, although if that Fort Wayne reporter was to be believed, the outcome seemed inevitable.

Organized professional base ball had officially begun. Highly skilled players were in demand and were being paid accordingly.

I would have to say that first season was a success. We did, however, have a few issues that needed to be sorted out. Clubs played a different number of games; as many as 35, and as few as 27. This was mostly because even with the new improvements in the national railroad system, some of the Eastern clubs found it too financially difficult to make trips out west and vice versa. Another problem was that there was nothing to stop players from moving from one club to another, and frankly, too many of them did even though we put in a rule that a player couldn't play for another for 60 days.

It was far from a perfect start, but it wasn't bad, either.

SAM KISSAM    I don't know what induced me, but I got an itching to see a professional game. Maybe I just wanted to snicker at their playing, which may have been better than ours in some ways but was anything but the faultless skill they claimed. We had just finished losing a game against the Eagles when I made the suggestion to Richard Stevens that we go the next day over to Union Ball

Grounds to see a match between the Mutuals and the noted Haymakers of Troy. He thought the idea worthy of an early summer's afternoon.

The Mutual Club was well known to both of us. They had begun as an amateur club, but then they went all professional and moved to the enclosed Union Grounds in Brooklyn. At any rate, they were considered one of the strongest sides in the area. Richard knew someone who played for them, someone he rather disliked, so on Saturday we set out for the game, both eager to revel in our displeasure. The weather was fine and a big crowd was expected.

When we got near the grounds we could see that many of the potential spectators were in a state of agitation. I turned to a man with two youngsters in tow.

"What's all the bother?"

"Didn't you see the sign?" he said.

"Which one is that?"

"The tariff has been increased to fifty cents," he said in obvious disgust.

"Has it really?"

"After paying for the three of us to get all the way over here from the city I can't afford another $1.50 to get in. It's always been 25 cents before and now they want to double it! Who do they think's coming, the Astors?"

"That doesn't seem right," I said masking any inclination for joy I might have felt at the thought of the consternation the professional fraternity was brewing amongst the public.

"It's not right. Not right at all."

"You could always watch the Knickerbockers," I said.

"I want my boys to see real ball players," he said as he turned and headed back in the direction of the ferry.

He and hundreds of others stormed off in protest. The large crowd soon turned into a small crowd, some of whom were still grumbling as they entered the grounds.

"What do you think, Dick?" I said as we watched the retreating masses.

"I think we should see real ball players," he said.

"Do you suppose they're all 7 feet tall?"

"At least."

"And run as fast as greyhounds?"

"If not faster."

We paid the king's ransom and took our places among the mostly empty seats behind first base. By the announced time for the beginning of the game, the Mutuals were nowhere to be found. The spectators began to make their displeasure known. Not only had they paid twice what they had expected, but now they were being made to wait for the high and mighty Mutuals.

"Enjoy the sunshine." Dick said.

"I might as well as I have nothing else to do."

By the time the Mutuals finally showed up, many in the crowd had switched their allegiances to the Haymakers who had already been entertaining us for over an hour with their practices.

The Mutuals manager, Bob Ferguson, apologized to the crowd for their late arrival, but this did little to appease the agitated spectators.

Then came the game. The best I can say about it is that it was over in two hours. The Haymakers won 25 to 10. Total fielding errors: Haymakers 13, Mutuals 25.

Dick and I thoroughly enjoyed the match.

JAMES WHYTE DAVIS    There is a world of difference between playing a game on a warm Saturday afternoon and going to work. We played, the professionals worked, and no matter how you describe it or analyze it, therein lay a profound and fundamental difference.

So as to make the point very clear, here is all a club had to do to join the National Association of Professionals: a $10 entry fee.

What the clubs were playing for was the right to fly a pennant on a pole over their grounds.

HARRY WRIGHT    So when the Athletics won the championship that first year, what did they do with the pennant? They hung it in a Philadelphia tavern! It should have been in their club rooms. After all, to elevate the National Game, we had to earn the respect of all; and since the Athletics were champions—first legal and recognized champion of the United States—they would be looked up to as the exponents of what is right and wrong in base ball.

By the middle of July in our second season, we had raced to a 22–1 record so I took everyone out to an island off Boston for a ten-day break of hunting and fishing. When we returned we had to call a special meeting because the Troys, Nationals, and Olympics had dropped out of the Association. So we agreed that nine rather than five games would be played between all contending clubs. Near the end of October we beat the Eckfords 4–3 for our 39th win of the season and thus the championship. We clinched the championship the next season, too.

JAMES WHYTE DAVIS    The Wright brothers, Harry and George, set about to turn their Boston team into a dynasty. Dynasty! Now how is that good for the game? Open play where anyone can win is good for the game. Dynasties are only good for the inhabitants of the dynastic city.

Behind his back Harry was often referred to as the "bearded boy in bloomers."

I had the opportunity to lunch with the bearded boy one afternoon when the Red Stockings were sitting out a rainy day in New York.

"You'll lose control you know," I told him. "The club owners, the investors, they'll take over. Sooner or later they will. Money always takes charge. I think you know that."

"We're an association, an association of players not owners, so we'll always have the decisive voice."

He was wrong, of course, and as things turned out for the Association, what I said was exactly what happened.

DOC ADAMS    The Boston Nine released the season salaries of their players. Spalding, Barnes, the Wrights, $1800 each; White, $1500; Leonard, $1400; Schafer, $1200; Birdsall, $1000; Sweasy and O'Rourke, $800 each; Manning, $500: and Addy, $75 per month since being engaged. That's more than $9000 a season just for the club to pay its players.

By playing a boys' game, these players were paid exceedingly well and lived a comfortable life.

Compare that to the Five Points where there might be 75 people living in 12 rooms and paying about $4 a month for rent which was maybe a week's pay. In the back of the building were wooden hovels which rented for $3 a month. Many of these tenements did not have indoor plumbing or running water. Sewage collected in outhouses and rats were prevalent, carrying, and spreading disease, often to children. Almost two-thirds of New York City's deaths were children under age 5, mostly Irish.

And all this while the Professional Association was paying men almost $2000 to play games!

JAMES WHYTE DAVIS    The Red Stockings played a game utilizing ten men and ten innings, the extra man being a right short stop. Chadwick campaigned for that and for a while we played that way, as did a lot of the other clubs. Nine men, nine innings had worked perfectly well all those years. I was all for making the game better when and where we could, but that was an absolutely unnecessary experiment. Obviously I wasn't the only one to think so.

HENRY CHADWICK    In the summer of the 1874 season, we organized a base ball tour of England for a side composed of players from the Professional Association's Boston and Philadelphia clubs. The idea was simply to show off our game to the British. We arranged for a series of games in a number of cities as well as a cricket match against the Marlybone Club, in which we were allowed to use 18 players against their eleven since we "obviously neither understood nor could competently play *their* game." Only four of our players were familiar with cricket, but thanks to a timely downpour that halted the play, we technically won the match.

As the tour was concluding one paper called base ball "the cricket of the American continent," and opined: "The verdict of the spectators is almost universally against base ball as a competitor with our national game ... it has so many inherent defects."

HARRY WRIGHT   Our Association lasted but five years before it gave way to the National League. Nevertheless, it would be wrong to think we didn't contribute greatly to the development of the game. We established once and for all that professional clubs could survive, could turn a profit, and could pay a reasonable wage to its players.

JAMES WHYTE DAVIS   Here are two events that characterized the Professional Association in its brief and sordid life: John Radcliff was expelled from the Association for attempting to bribe umpire William McLean, and the Chicago White Sox committed 36 errors in a game with the Mutuals. And they were being paid to do that!

## 106

# Club Doings

JAMES WHYTE DAVIS   While the professionals were off running around the country making money, we continued to schedule practices and games within our membership.

At one point we were forced to vacate our old grounds at the Elysian Fields which had then become a sort of lumber yard no longer fit for ball playing. Instead we engaged the enclosed cricket field at the foot of Ninth Street in Hoboken. At a rental fee of $200 dollars it was relatively expensive for us, and to boot, we only had use of it on Fridays. It offered no shady place for spectators nor any accommodations for lady visitors, but it did have an excellent turfy field.

Some of our members had misgivings about the cost and lack of amenities, but I couldn't see any reasonable alternative. To subdue the strong feelings of those who were particularly upset about the problems for lady visitors, we agreed to erect a tent whenever necessary. We also arranged to practice on Mondays when the St. George Cricket Club was not using the field.

We also showed off our new uniforms consisting of blue barred stockings, blue striped shirts, and dark blue Knickerbockers, and white caps trimmed in blue.

I remember in '72 we played a series of lively games between the bachelors and the single men. I pitched for the bachelors and Walter Avery played second base. It was good to see him back with us. Then in May we put together a game between our newly organized first nine and a side of 15 other active members. It was what we called a "field" team with the extra players stationed in fact in the field and at right short stop. It was the largest turnout we had seen in about 5 or 6 years. Again, I pitched as my days of running about the field were coming to a close.

By the end of the second inning, we were already well behind.

"Look at them," said Avery. "Remind you of anyone?"

"Not that I can think of," I said.

"Us. Us when we were younger."

"We never looked that good. They start so much younger now. They learn the game at a younger age than we did. That's why they're so damn good."

"Get ready for a comeback," he said. "We'll show those whippersnappers a thing or two."

We showed them all right. We lost 58–14.

We played our annual game of the "old fellows" against the "boys." As usual, the youngsters on the club won but we gave them a good match before we lost 22–13. I pitched and accounted for three runs. So this old fellow still had something left.

"Not bad for an old man," said Sam.

"Speak for yourself."

"I would if I could catch my breath."

We also arranged games between our first and second nines, and match games with the Gothams. On several occasions we played by dividing the first nine up on the two sides. In one I remember both Sam Kissam and I played right short for our sides and had a little private bet going as to who would score the most runs. I won with three to Sam's one. Chadwick umpired most of these for us.

I can also recall a game with the Star Club of Brooklyn and their new amateur nine. In that game, I was stationed out in right field because Lyons wanted to do the pitching. I'll tell you one thing: Those Stars put together one hell of a side. By the fifth inning they were leading 28 to 5. We pulled up a little in the latter part of the game, but they were too much for us. They won 49 to 11. I accounted for but one of the 11.

After the game I was so tired and sore from all that running, I thought I'd sleep for a week — at least.

The next day one report in the papers said, "Never since the primitive days of the game has so complete a display of "muffinism" been witnessed ... of the Knickerbockers, the less said the better. A few good catches by Mortimer and Halstead, and good stops by Bacon hardly compensated for the uninterrupted run of errors which marked the first few innings. Davis, the excitable veteran, had little to do, but by his humorous remarks created much merriment among the spectators, of whom about 100 were present."

"Nothing to do," my behind! I ran around all afternoon.

When we played the Staten Island "Reds" I served as umpire and was very happy to stand still during the whole damn game. Our club scored 59 runs but still lost.

HERB WORTH   Forget the professional clubs, just about all the amateur sides in the area could beat the Knicks. About the only time a side of Knicker-bockers won a game was when they played against another side of Knickerbock-ers.

It seems to me there were three groups of ball clubs around: the professionals, the amateurs, and the Knicks.

SAM KISSAM   For a couple of years after we returned to the Elysian Fields, roughs were in the habit of gathering every evening and annoying the ball players. Finally the people who were in charge put an end to the shenanigans. Then the authorities put a stop to ball playing except by clubs having special permission from the city. So, the south field was reserved for the Knickerbocker, Eagle, and Social clubs, and the north field for the Gothams and the Columbia College Club.

I must say that was a big help to us as we could play our games undisturbed by the rowdy youths who were becoming a bigger problem with each passing year.

JAMES WHYTE DAVIS   In December I went to the club's annual dinner at a fine establishment down on East 12th Street. It was a well-attended meeting and the newer members like the Bacon brothers, Kirkland, Rodgers, Clarke, Brown, Thorn, and the lively Tams, treated me, Sam and a few of the others as the "grand old men" of the Knickerbockers, and yet it felt somehow strange to be thought of that way.

The young men, as young men are wont to do, displayed great enthusiasm for the coming season. "An amateur revival," they predicted. It was hard for me to see from where this prediction came if not from the unbridled optimism of youth. I was not as sanguine but I kept my opinions to myself as a good guest should.

As in the banquets of the old days, the evening was filled with speeches and songs, sentiments and toasts. A letter from Chadwick was read in which he offered commendation to the club and his thoughts on the proper aspects of the game, all of which I had heard before but they were met with great approval from the young members.

The literary event of the evening was the reading of a poetical effusion of "Young Jim's," which elicited hearty applause for its witty allusions to incidents in the club's past and to some of the individuals who were its members, particularly this old Jim. Of course, I was only 46 but the club and the game were made for younger men.

Doc Adams   I'm not sure why, but I suppose it was because I was so involved in making the balls in the early days that I continued to follow developments in that regard. At some point, the powers that be decided that the ball was too soft, so for a while they used cotton yarn. This did little more than evoke the anger of the fielders who claimed it was unsafe. The argument went that after a few innings of use the woolen-wound balls mellowed some, but those using cotton didn't.

Harry Wright led the loud charge against the cotton ball and it was soon dropped.

Incidentally, Harry and his brother George opened a sports store in New York, where they sold, among other things, base balls wound with wool. I guess they figured as long as they were going to make base ball their professions, they might as well make as much money as they could. And who could blame them?

James Whyte Davis   At our annual meeting in March of '73 I was again elected club president and Sam Kissam, treasurer. Two of our younger members were also elected to office — Frederick Tams, vice president, and Al Kirkland, secretary. I think we all realized it was critical that if we were to survive in the new era of base ball, we had to attract and involve new, younger members — members who met the membership standards for which our club had long been known. It wasn't always that easy either as some players who might otherwise have been candidates were attracted to the professional game and even those who weren't had scores of local clubs from which to choose. Nevertheless, we did manage to attract qualified new members like Fryat who had previously played for the Eurekas and H. A. Smith, once a stalwart of the Harvards.

It took a while, but we finally got our finances in order so that for the start of our 29th season we were able to put up a new clubhouse, complete with nice facilities for lady visitors. It was a fine day in May and the large turnout suggested that we were still a strong organization with a sustainable membership, constantly refreshed by new young men eager to play the game the Knickerbocker way.

We took advantage of the new holiday known as Decoration Day to play a match between our first and second nines, the latter winning 29–19. After the game we had a grand dinner reminiscent of some of those big affairs from the old days.

That June we played a cricket match against the Manhattan Cricket Club, eleven versus eleven. They may have been playing with their second eleven, but they were an experienced and savvy side and showed great spirit in meeting their base ball friends. A shower interrupted the proceeding at the end of the first innings, but we managed to get the match in before dark.

It was a remarkably close battle throughout and I am proud to say that although we lost, this old base ball player bowled well enough to take two wickets. All in all it was a good day for the amateur base ball players. They repaid the visit by engaging us later in the year in a game of base ball which we won by a very large margin. In this instance at least the base ball players were much better at cricket than the cricketers were at base ball.

We also played other games with the Veterans against the Youngsters and the Bachelors against the Benedicts. We also played a particularly fine game against the gentlemen and scholars of Yale.

There were quite a number of new amateur clubs being formed, and almost all wanted to play the Knickerbockers. I suppose in a way it gave them a certain sense of being accepted into the amateur fraternity. When we played against the Englewood Club, they said as much.

One day Sam said to me, "I read where they're playing base ball in China and Japan. Suppose they want to play us, too?"

"Doesn't everyone?"

I remember one particular match with the Manhattan Club when they came up short-handed. I was loaned to the Manhattans as their right short stop for the afternoon and got to watch my Knicks turn in a very pretty triple play by Stanton, Bucklin, and Dorsett.

As a sign of the times I received a note from an acquaintance who had moved up to Boston. He wrote that their club, the Beacon Club, which he described as about the only legitimate "Knickerbocker amateur club in the Hub," had recently retired from the field, having no opponents of their own class to play with semi-professionalism having gobbled up all the other so-called amateur clubs in the area.

I wrote back telling him we might not be too far behind.

Meanwhile the Amateur Association trudged on with Chadwick as chairman of the Rules Committee. I know he was doing his best, but despite continued requests to join, we continued to go it on our own.

Oh, I followed what was going on with other clubs a little — but just a little. I couldn't help getting a big kick out of the accounting published in the *Eagle* for the trip of the Cincinnatis to Hartford.

Expenses

| | |
|---|---|
| Board for 11 men at the City Hotel for three nights | $88.00 |
| Boy to carry bats from hotel to grounds | .50 |
| Hot mustard plaster for Williams' sore arm | .25 |
| Total expenses | $88.75 |

Receipts

| | |
|---|---|
| 250 paying spectators at 50 cents each | $125.00 |
| One-third of which belongs to the Reds | $41.66 |
| Total receipts | $41.66 |
| Total expenses | $88.75 |

So they lost $47.09 for the trip, but had they carried their own damn bats to the grounds they would have been better off. I guess you can't blame them, though, because those bats are heavy and anyway, one shouldn't expect a professional to have to do manual labor as that is apparently below their class.

The same column in the paper went on to say that the Excelsiors had passed a resolution "inviting the veteran Knickerbockers" to play them a game at Prospect Park, but since our secretary was out of time, no reply had yet been received. They opined that since Mr. Davis, the club president, was in town, he should be notified immediately and undoubtedly a game would be quickly arranged. Well and good, but then it added, "By all means let us have a good old fashioned legitimate amateur contest between nines of these two old organizations just for the novelty of the thing."

A novelty? Hogwash, pure and simple.

"Thousands of spectators would throng to the park to see it, and a large gathering of old ball tossers would be the result."

As I must have said a million times, we didn't play for the spectator's benefit, we played for our benefit. We weren't a goddamned side-show attraction.

SAM KISSAM   Up in New Haven, two professional base ball players were arrested on robbery charges. So much for the idea of the gentleman ball player.

ASHLEY HYDE   Reading the reports of ball games in the papers, one had to wonder exactly what was going on. For instance, at one point I read that "George Wright was given a life on a bad muff by Fisler," and that "Anson went out on a magnificent foul-fly catch by MvVey."

I can only assume by these descriptions that Mr. Fisler sacrificed his life in some kind of a muff for the benefit of Mr. Wright, and that Mr. Anson rode off on the back of some kind of active and offensive insect.

SAM KISSAM   We were regularly sent notices like this: "Amateur players desirous of becoming members of professional clubs next season are requested to send their names, home positions, terms of service, etc., to this office, in order that a private list of such applicants may be made up for reference, not necessarily for publication."

I don't know. Maybe if I were 25 years younger I might have been tempted to apply.

Jamie got angry with me one day when I didn't turn out for a match at which I was expected to play.

"What the hell is the matter with you?" he demanded when I saw him later in the week.

"Nothing's the matter. What do you mean?"

"You were supposed to be at the game Friday."

"Sorry, I was with the kids at the new carousel in Central Park. We didn't get back in time."

"Carousel? It's there every damn day. Why couldn't you have gone some other time?

"Have you seen it? It's driven by a mule under the platform."

"I don't give a damn about the mule. We were short a man."

"Well, I didn't want to be short a son."

"A goddamned mule!"

"Brown, long ears."

"Ought to be illegal."

Sometimes I just couldn't resist getting a rise from Jamie. They say you mellow with age and I suppose that's true, but with Jamie it was taking a long time. The truth was I had forgotten about that game but I didn't dare say that to him. To Jamie, forgetting a game was a mortal sin, punishable probably by eternal damnation in a hell without a decent ball ground.

On one day when we weren't scheduled to play we all trekked up to Madison Avenue and 27th Street to see P.T. Barnum's Great Roman Hippodrome.

As we were nearing the gigantic building, Jamie said, "Did you know that this is just about where the men who were the first Knicks actually played their games. This is where it all started. Then they put up a passenger depot for the New York Harlem Railroad. This is it, though. Somewhere right around here."

"The high holy ground, is it?"

"It used to all be open ground. Look at it now."

JAMES WHYTE DAVIS    For a while we had a flap going on about our Exchange. The crook William Tweed substituted false names on the new charter of incorporation for the New York Stock Exchange, so many of us brokers refused to accept the charter or to pay Tweed for getting it passed. It was quite a mess for a while and I had to miss a number of club meetings while everything was getting sorted out.

I asked Sam Kissam to take charge and look after things until I got back full time.

"Jamie, the world will still revolve whether you're busy or not."

"Really, I thought it was the sun that did the revolving."

"Read the papers. It's the latest thing."

Still, with so many new members, it was important that the club maintained strong leadership. It's one thing to have good players, but without leadership it wouldn't amount to a hill of beans.

In March of '74 we held our 29th annual meeting at which I was again elected club president. We had added a lot of new members but a few of us old timers such as me and Sam Kissam were still around to mentor the youngsters.

Once again we were set to occupy our grounds in Hoboken, which by then had been enclosed, and to open out thirtieth season in the second week in April. In any match games we might play that season, we would send out Sherwood, Wells, Halstead, Goodspeed, Smith, Buck, Kirkland, McKim, Hitchcock, and Brooks. These were all relatively new members, but with sufficient practice I felt they would be a side equal to any amateur ten in the metropolis. Halstead in particular was a rather gifted player. He had tendered his resignation the previous year, but with a little cajoling, I was able to lure him back into the fold. He played the tenth man, or right short stop position on our first nine.

Permit me to point out that on a day that we beat the Englewood Base Ball Club, at least 50 amateur sides played games that same day. Junior clubs, too, were very much alive and well. In fact the Junior Championship was played that summer between the Monitors of East New York and the Washingtons of Brooklyn with the Washingtons coming out on top, 5–3.

Later that summer the college championship was decided by matches between the Yale side and nines from Princeton and Harvard. As I recall, Yale won.

In September I sent out a notice to the local press stating my desire to get up a game of base ball in which none but veterans of not less than 40 years of age would take part. I was particularly interested in the over-40-year-old members of the Gothams, Eagles, Excelsiors, Putnams, and Empire nines. Dick Stevens, once a Knick, was the first to express interest.

Many of the over 40 set had retired from the game, some had moved away, and many had family responsibilities which took up much of their time. Still, I had hoped for a positive response. It took a while, but eventually we got something organized.

We scheduled a match on our grounds between nine of the Knickerbocker "Old boys" against a nine of old members of the various other clubs who were active in the season of '58.

"Still haven't learned, have you?" said Tom Van Cott of the Gothams.

"What's that?"

"You were too old then and more than too old now."

"We'll see."

"Having trouble getting low enough for the daisy cutters are you?"

"Not in this lifetime."

The assemblage included quite a few who had not seen a match for years. For that matter, quite a few of the veterans had handled neither bat nor ball for years either.

Me and Sam were still playing some, but others such as Alonzo Slote, well let's say he was rusty. Anyway, they beat us on the ball ground, but we easily won the match at knives and forks which took place afterwards at Duke's Hotel.

SAM KISSAM     I suppose it was little more than a novelty act along the lines of those put on by P.T. Barnum, but two base ball nines made up entirely of women began touring. They were simply known as the Blondes and the Brunettes. They were promoted as "selected troupes of girls of reputable character who have shown some degree of aptitude in ball playing." They played on a shrunken field with only 50 feet between the bases. And they played with lighter bats and smaller balls.

Let's face facts. The novelty of seeing 18 girls prettily attired in gymnastic dress was nothing more than that ... a novelty.

JAMES WHYTE DAVIS     The "boys in blue" of the old Excelsior Club of Brooklyn, against whom we had played some memorable games in years past, invited me to be a guest at the celebration of their 21st anniversary. They hosted a grand reunion dinner at Delmonico's. I was asked to prepare a speech and a song for the occasion and was happy to do so. Pearsall, Brainard, Whiting, Leggett, and many others were there. It was quite an occasion as we all reminisced about the old days and told stories, some of which had evolved considerably over the years. But no matter.

"I remember the first time we played you," said Joe Leggett. "You had Charlie DeBost, Harry Wright, Doc Adams, yourself. I think Fraley Niebuhr and Sam Kissam were on the club then, too."

"I remember."

"We beat you something awful."

"That I don't remember."

"Well, I guess at your age, memory becomes rather selective."

"Sure. I select to remember the truth."

"Do you remember it was in July of '58?"

"I remember that."

"We played at our grounds in Brooklyn?"

"Yes."

"And beat you 31 to 13."

"I don't remember that."

"Strange."

"You boys couldn't ever score 31 runs in a single contest."

"Unless we were playing the Knicks."

I gave a speech. Rather stirring if I don't say so myself. A little too long, maybe but we were all having such a good time reliving the late '50s that nobody complained ... at least not to me.

I ended up with a little song that started:

> You were always known as the boys in blue,
> Who caught the ball and ran and threw
> And played the game like lovers of the sport
> Even if against the Knicks you came up short.

Maybe I had a bit too much to drink, but I think I actually got a bit misty-eyed.

Their club still existed but only in name. In fact, the newer members were proposing to drop the "Base Ball" from their name and become strictly a social organization.

HENRY CHADWICK   As it was the Centennial year I offered the suggestion that the Excelsiors and the Knickerbockers present a series of amateur club contests as a feature of the campaign of 1876, both clubs to visit Philadelphia and play the old Olympic amateur club of that city.

SAM KISSAM   We talked about touring but that's about as far as it got.

One thing that did get around, though, was a widely reported story that in a game between the Brown Stockings and the Stars, at least twenty people said they saw Kraus of the Brown Stockings, who was acting as back stop, change the ball. That is, he threw in the live ball when his side was batting and a dead ball when the Stars were batting.

You know what? I stopped caring about all the cheating. We didn't cheat and that's all that mattered to us.

---

## 107

# *Chicanery on the Field*

HARRY WRIGHT   Say what you want about the effects of professionalism, but one thing was patently clear: the game on the field was getting better — a whole lot better. After all, if you're asking spectators to pay good money to watch, you had better play good ball.

SAM KISSAM   Yeah, the professionals played good ball. It would be ridiculous to deny them that, but they were also developing all manner of tricky plays and methods that in the old days we would have considered nothing short of unsportsmanlike.

JAMES WHYTE DAVIS   Stalling had become more than just a game-day irritant. It was becoming as infectious as the cholera. There were as many different ways of stalling as there were players for whom winning was the only thing that mattered. How could you prolong the game long enough for darkness to arrive and the umpire to call the game?

One way was to bring in change pitchers. What some clubs would do is to put a second pitcher in the long field, and then when they saw the need for a pitcher with a different style of delivery — say a slow pitcher for a swift one — they would switch positions. They could do this as many times as they saw fit either for the purposes of strategy, or to delay the game.

Then, too, there were the always popular fake injuries or substitutions. Substitutions weren't allowed unless one of the players became ill or injured, and then only if the opposing captain agreed.

The rule makers who replaced the likes of Doc and the others in the early years had their hands full trying to close all the loopholes that the professionals were prying open seemingly at every opportunity.

In the old days, we never tried to deceive an umpire by claiming to put a player out when we knew him safe, or to claim we had caught a ball fairly when we knew we hadn't, or to say we had touched a runner with the ball when such was not the case. As the game developed, though, the inclination to get away with whatever one could and to exploit the holes in the rules to the fullest became a popular pastime.

Sometimes players would attempt to distract a player with loud yells just as he was about to catch a ball or collide purposely with a fielder. I saw fielders "accidentally" trip runners, and coaches running down the line so as to decoy the pitcher into thinking he was the runner. When the umpire's attention was elsewhere, I saw runners cut corners at third, never touching the base on the way home. I saw players needlessly complaining about calls so as to try to gain an advantage the next time they were involved in a close play.

These and other acts of chicanery and out-and-out cheating should have, but as far as I know, never did elicit apologies.

---

# 108

# *Tinkering with the Rules*

JAMES WHYTE DAVIS   Every season the rules were tinkered with. It got so you'd just about have to read a damn book every March just to figure out how the hell we were going to play that season. It seems to me that we already had a pretty good set of rules and at some point we needed to just leave them alone. These rule changes were mostly made by the professionals but pretty much everyone followed them.

As per example, in 1874 a 6 x 3 rectangular box was set up for the batter. He had to remain in this little prison while hitting.

One particular rule I did applaud was that the professionals decided to prohibit a player from betting on his own team, and to withhold his pay if he bet on another team. What an idea!

HENRY CHADWICK    Base ball, like Charles Darwin claims mankind does, is always evolving.

Prior to the 1871 season the striker was free to call for the ball to be delivered wherever he thought he would have the best chance to strike it solidly. Then that year, the striker was restricted to calling only for either a high or a low pitch. In effect this meant that there were now two distinct strike zones. The high zone was between the waist and the shoulder, and the low zone between the waist and the knees. Of course this varied in both height and width according to the striker's size. Now whenever the striker took his position at the home base, the umpire was required to satisfy himself as best he could as to what constitutes the fair reach of a batsman.

The Association was rather specific in their delincation of the rules. For example, in order to accommodate players who might arrive late, they included a provision that substitutes would be permitted up until the fourth inning. Starting in the fifth inning, substitutions were only allowed in the game for injured players. If the opposing captain agreed, an injured player could have a substitute run the bases for him and still remain in the game. In such cases, the opposing captain would select a player from any extras who might be available who would then stand behind the home base and begin running as soon as the batsman for whom he was running struck the ball. Also, should an injured player leave the game, only to regain his spryness later, he could then reenter the game.

SAM KISSAM    The calling of balls and strikes was here to stay, and no one had a greater influence on exactly how they were to be called than Henry Chadwick. I watched him umpire a practice game up on the Cap — the Capoline ball grounds in Brooklyn as they were then called. He only umpired practice games there, claiming he became too interested in real games and altogether too nervous to act in a position requiring so much calmness and nerve.

It seems that every ball that went beyond the reach of a striker's bat, over his head, or too close to be struck at he called "wide." Once he gave a man his base on three successive wides. I noticed that when a ball was not "wide" but also not over the base, he did not call it, but simply counted it by passing a penny from one hand to the other until three such balls had been pitched when he would call "one ball," then he would count two more if similarly pitched — that is, not wide but not over the base or not at the height the striker called for. When the next third ball was pitched he would call "two balls." He did not count "wides" as called "balls."

At one point he called two "wides" and before another "wide" was called, he called "two balls" but before either a third "wide" was called or a third "ball," the ball was fairly hit. All balls which hit the striker's person he called "dead."

There continued to be differences in the way and manner of calling "wides" and "balls." We needed one set of playing rules for everyone. The Marylebone Cricket Club of London legislates for every cricket club throughout the world, but we had the Professional Association and the Amateur Association and we had the college clubs.

No wonder the public was often confused.

WALTER AVERY   Despite all the hoopla about the new rules, they weren't always enforced. In a game between the Red Stockings and the Olympics, a reporter for the *Clipper* was forced into duty as the umpire when nobody else was available. Now the reporter had lost a leg in the recent war and had to work the game by hopping around on his one leg. Then, as fate would have it, a foul ball smacked him on the leg and sent him sprawling. This annoyed him so much that for the rest of the game he called a ball for every ball that was not fair, thus sending 30 men to first on walks.

And they said the game was chaotic before we Knickerbockers solidified the rules!

WILLIAM TUCKER   One thing that for a long time characterized our grounds in the Elysian Fields is that unlike the grounds on which the professional clubs played, we didn't have an outfield fence and that meant that playing the field sometimes required that we ran seemingly forever to track down balls. I remember one particular game when I must have run a couple of miles by the fifth inning.

"I need a substitute," I said, panting like there wasn't enough air left on the planet.

"What, chasing a little ball?" said Charlie DeBost.

"I don't see you running your behind off."

"I'm too smart for that. That's why I'm a catcher."

"And I thought it was because you were too slow."

"You should become a professional. They only have to run as far as a little fence."

I didn't get a substitute, but I did get a courtesy runner, which at the time wasn't uncommon.

WALTER AVERY   The only professional I can remember who played after turning 40 was Nate Berkenstock, and he only got to bat four times. Of course, when he struck out three of those times, it didn't help the cause of us older men. This beautiful game that is so valuable for exercising the body shouldn't eliminate those of us who need the exercise most. At least that's the way I saw it.

I could no longer hit the ball as far as I once did, nor run to the bases as I had in my youth. I could no longer reach balls that once were easily within my grasp. I suppose had I wanted to I could have hired somebody to do all those things for me as in professional base ball, and then paid money to watch them do it, but I just couldn't bring myself to such a state. No, I continued to play on creaky knees and was much the better for it.

One day I even played two full games, since one of the younger players decided he had to leave the game early so that he could go uptown to see George Armstrong Custer, who was giving some kind of speech about military service. Such was the devotion of many of the younger set.

---

## 109

# *Availability of Goods*

DOC ADAMS   In a game between the professional White Stockings and Mutuals, the final score ended 9–0 in favor of the Mutuals. The fact that a club could play a complete game and not score a single run was mind-boggling and led to the term "being Chicagoed," meaning being held to no runs. The only way this was conceivable was if the game used dead balls. Whether the cranks preferred this I don't know, but there certainly was a trend to lower-scoring games.

The press portrayed these games as more exciting and somehow purer than the higher scoring games, but I always felt a close contest was exciting regardless of the score. Better yet was a well-played close game where the players played the scientific game, where batters did more than simply try to hit the ball as hard as possible without the slightest idea where it might be headed. This is simply child's play, and we had worked hard to move the game to one for grown men in which skill, not chance, was predominant.

HENRY CHADWICK   It became clear to me that a change in the composition of the ball was necessary. There had been just too great a catalogue of severe injuries arising from the use of an overly elastic and heavy ball. Accordingly, I campaigned for a rule limiting the use of rubber in the ball to an ounce and a half. My suggestion, however, was met with strenuous opposition from some clubs.

Two young ball players had recently been killed outright by being struck on the head by one of those elastic rubber balls— one in Chicago from a swiftly thrown ball and the other in New Hampshire from a batted ball. Players had sustained injuries in the form of blackened eyes, bruised faces, broken fingers, split hands and endless smaller injuries received from efforts to stop or catch swiftly thrown rubber balls.

Some were blaming the ball manufacturers, but they were simply supplying the market demand. What was needed was a change in the attitude of the public toward batting skills. It was up to the public to put a stop to the use of balls with two ounces and more of rubber by refusing to patronize the matches of clubs that used them.

SAM KISSAM   Harry Wright's Red Stockings promoted the use of a dead ball and some writers began to crusade for less rubber so the next year they changed the rules so that the balls had to be made out of some different kind of rubber. I don't know the details, but it seems to have done the trick.

SAM KISSAM   One day, Al Kirkland showed up with the strangest bat I had ever seen. He didn't say anything when he arrived. However, the first time he swung at a pitch, he missed the ball wildly, but the bat made a weird noise. After two more errant swings he returned to the sidelines and I asked him what was going on with his bat.

"Go ahead, take a swing with it," he said, handing me the new instrument.

So I took the bat and, making sure no one was within striking distance, took my usual swing. It was the oddest of feelings, like something was moving inside the bat.

Al smiled. "That's something, isn't it? It's the latest thing in base ball lumber."

"Does it have a mouse inside it or what?"

"Here, let me show you," he said, taking the bat back from me. "Up here at the large end, a hole was bored. It's length and size is precisely proportional to the length and weight of the bat."

"And what exactly is that supposed to do?" I asked.

"I was getting to that. Into the drilled out hole is a weight that fits closely but which can nevertheless slide freely. At the bottom end of the hole are pieces of cork that fit tight and are stationary."

I took the bat back and looked at the big end. "I don't see anything like a hole here." I said.

"That because it's been filled up perfectly with a plug. Go ahead, swing it again. You'll feel the weight shift."

I took another swing and did notice the shifting weight. "What's supposed to be the advantage if that?" I asked.

Al launched into a full-scale explanation. "First of all it gives the bat the full regulation size without the useless extra weight at the large end because that was removed by the boring. Now the movable weight can be either greater or less than that removed, depending of the desire of the batsman. The sliding weight is always where most needed in using the bat."

"What the devil is that supposed to mean?"

"Well, for example, when the bat is elevated for the stroke, the weight slides to the center where it gives the batsman more perfect control, and as the stroke is made, the weight slides toward the end, thereby greatly increasing the weight of the blow. The result is a much quicker and heavier blow can be given than with ordinary bats."

"Says who?"

"Lots of players who are using them, including James Wood of the White Stockings."

"You mean other players have fallen for this?"

"Lyman's self-adjusting bats they're called. Try it when you come to bat."

"No thanks. I saw how well it worked for you. I think I'll stick with my simple, solid white ash bat."

"You've got to keep up with the times."

"You keep up for me."

JAMES WHYTE DAVIS   Perhaps the popularity of the game can be seen in the availability of base ball goods. From any number of suppliers, you could buy a good dead ball for a dollar, ash bats for $2 per dozen, full polished willow bats for $6 per dozen. A pair of base ball shoes could be had for $2 and you could add safety shoe spikes complete with screws for $1.50 a dozen. Caps with corded seams could be found for 50 cents; and pants, either cotton or flannel, for $1. White cotton or flannel shirts with colored letters and shields were $2.

---

## 110

# *On Curvers and Long Throws*

DOC ADAMS   For some time there had been considerable speculation as to whether a pitcher could actually make a ball curve on a horizontal line. Some said it could, others said it was an optical illusion.

Walt Avery in particular was of the latter persuasion. "Doc, it's against the laws of physics. An object will continue in a straight line unless another force is acted on it and once a pitcher releases a ball, the only force acting on it is gravity and that pulls it down, not sideways."

"Unless there's metal in it and coachers have big magnets in their pockets."

"Seriously, you know it's not possible."

"I think Newton's *Principia* has something about that in it."

"A big base ball supporter was he?"

"A little-known fact."

"If you can prove there's such a thing as a ball curver, I'll eat the ball."

Well, I didn't, but a professor in Ohio did. What he did was use the straight line from the home plate to the first base on the Cincinnati grounds for a trail. It seems this line runs due north and south. Mid-way between the home plate and the first base he placed a portion of a paling fence, one end resting on the line and the other pointing toward the infield at right angles. Another section of fence was placed pointing in the other direction. That is, one section pointed due east and the other due west. Then at the south end a board was placed on the end on the line.

Bond, one of the Boston pitchers, then stood on the west side of the board and a little behind it such that he had to deliver the ball from the west side of the line. After a few failed attempts he managed to send the ball around the middle barrier, landing it on the same side it started from at the other end of the line. That the ball curved horizontally was shown beyond doubt and was clearly visible to the naked eye.

Some days later, Jamie, Walt, DeBost and I met for lunch. Naturally we had a great time as DeBost had arranged with the waiter to serve Walt pan-dowdy with a ball substituting for the apple.

"They do a good pan-dowdy here, don't you think? said DeBost.

"I've sometimes found it a bit leathery myself," said Jamie.

"See," I said. "When the ball leaves the hand of a pitcher with a spin, the motion of the ball through the air causes a compression of the air and leaves a vacuum behind, thus..."

"Oh, just shut up, Doc," said Walt with a big smile.

CHARLES DEBOST    They might have saved themselves the bother and asked me. I'd seen enough with my own eyes to make the point. In case anyone is interested, I can also assure them that it was possible to get a sail on the ball and make it rise.

HENRY CHADWICK    The art of spin pitching was definitely having an impact on the game, but it was really only effective when the pitcher had a catcher familiar with this type of delivery and expert enough to give him the necessary support. Pitchers like Cummings who knew how to do this imparted to the ball a rotary motion as it left his hand that it gave such a bias to the right or left that the catcher had to be on the alert to watch for the eccentric rebound in order to avoid passed balls.

Often the twist to the ball was more disadvantageous than it was effective because it made it exceedingly difficult for the catcher to judge accurately and, if hit, a troublesome ball for the fielder to catch.

Nevertheless, it undoubtedly made Cummings the number one pitchist of his day.

HARRY WRIGHT   One day in March we had a ball tossing competition. There had been some bets made that Johnny Hatfield could throw a base ball 127 yards clear. If he succeeded, he was to get a suit of clothing. In the betting, distance was the favorite. As I was the umpire, I measured off the ground. His first throw went 123 yards; the second, 129; the third, 132. As there was a slight breeze and some said it helped him, he agreed to throw the ball back in the opposite direction. His first throw was 127 yards, 1½ feet; the second, 127 yards, one foot; the third, 126 yards, for a total of 2,265 feet, six inches. As far as I know, this feat has not been equaled since.

WALTER AVERY   I know many players went to the gymnasium during the winter months for muscular training. For base ball? It is well known that an athlete wanting to excel in any game must be trained only to the extent that suits the requirement of that game. To train the same way for cricket, rowing, running, lacrosse, or base ball makes no sense.

What is necessary for a base ball player is only that exercise which makes him agile and quick of movement, and which trains the eyes to judge the ball, or the arms and chest to wield the bat, or the legs to run the bases. Lifting heavy weights is useless. So is swinging clubs and jumping rope. Work on the parallel bars, the trapeze, etc., was needless.

Exercise in short distance running is good, and all exercise such as skating which tends to strengthen the ankle muscles is good. I think the best exercise of all, though, is handball. It's a game that strengthens the hands, trains the sight, and builds endurance. A skillful handball player when he becomes accustomed to base ball will always excel in picking up hard hit ground balls.

# 111

# *Celebrating Davis*

SAM KISSAM   Well, the big KBBC event of 1875 was the fete for Jamie Davis. It would be a stretch to say that he was universally loved, but he certainly was respected by the members for the years of dedicated service he had invested in the well-being of our club.

DOC ADAMS    I was persuaded (it didn't take much) to go down to New York City on the occasion of Jamie's 25th anniversary with the Knickerbockers. I had been retired from my medical practice for ten years and living contentedly in Ridgefield, Connecticut, in the former home of Colonel Philip Burr Bradley.

By then Cornelia and I had two young daughters and two younger sons. Catherine was nine; Mary, seven; Francis, four; and Roger, one. They were the joys of my life.

I had served briefly in the State House of Representatives, and since 1871, as the first president of the Ridgefield Savings Bank. Later I was elected as the first treasurer of the Ridgefield Library. The current of my life had been very quiet and uniform, neither distinguished by any great successes, nor disturbed by serious reverses. I was content to consider myself one of the ordinary, everyday workers of the world, with no ambition to fill its high positions and had no reason to complain about the results of my labor.

Anyway, although I hadn't played any ball for some time, I agreed to take part in the Davis festivities.

SAM KISSAM    We thought it would be good to honor Jamie in some appropriate way, and what would be more appropriate than a game with some of his old friends? So we arranged to play a game in the afternoon and then retire to a gala dinner at Duke's.

WALTER AVERY    I had left the club some seven years earlier and hadn't played a lick since then, but the idea of all getting together again seemed like fun. To do it to honor Jamie just added to the enticement. Now I can't say I never had my run-ins with him, for he could be prickly at times (and I, of course, was always a saint) but he was such a staunch supporter of the club and a vigorous defender of amateurism.

I was sorry to hear that Charlie DeBost couldn't make it for he certainly would have added to the frivolity of the occasion as was his wont, but there were plenty of the old-timers to make a good game of it.

WILLIAM TUCKER    The weather that day was absolutely magnificent, undoubtedly the result of an insistent request to the Almighty put in by "Poor Old Davis," a name duly earned as a result of his frequent laments concerning the state of the game.

"Nobody respects us amateurs anymore."

"The game isn't what it used to be."

"What's to become of our beautiful game?"

Anyway, it was a beautiful late-September day, warm enough but with just a hint of the fall to come, complete with the faint aroma of burning leaves wafting slowly across the grounds. The grounds themselves were in tip-top order thanks to Mr. Giles, that gentlemanly professional of the St. George Cricket Club. Jamie, himself, wanting the event to celebrate his base ball birthday to be perfect, arranged for a carpeted tent for the ladies, a group that included his mother and daughter, and plenty of temporary seats for guests. Seats, I might add, that did not go wanting on this occasion.

Jamie was as excited as ever I saw him. He was, to be sure, a boy again. Everything turned out so propitious that his delight was spread across his face for all to see.

By 3 o'clock most of the old boys had gathered on the field, some of us decked out in uniforms we had not worn in years and on a few of us, the extra pounds we had accumulated made themselves more obvious than we would have wished. Others came wrapped up to guard against the "rheumaticks," as Rip Van Winkle says. Gray heads and gray beards were as evident as the turning leaves on the trees.

Appropriately, the first to go over and greet Jamie was Doc, whom I hadn't seen since he moved up to Connecticut years before. He looked fine, although I had been told he had not been in the best of health. He still looked as poised and controlled as ever. The beard was gone, but not the welcoming smile.

I saw Dick Stevens. I always liked Dick and was pleased to see him again. Then, much to my (pleasant) surprise, I saw Duncan Curry walk over to Jamie. Duncan, our first president, hadn't been a member for maybe the past twenty years, but his influence on the club was undeniable. I had seen him only a few times in recent years, and then in his capacity as an insurance man. He was in his early sixties and considerably bigger than in his playing days. He had his son with him whom he introduced to Jamie who then promptly asked him why he had never become a member of his father's club.

"I guess I was never much of one for base ball," the son said.

Jamie recoiled in mock horror as if he had just been told he was talking with a vampire.

"Duncan, you're a failure as a father, do you know that?"

Duncan laughed. "I tried, Jamie, I tried."

After he left Jamie, I asked Duncan if he was going to play in the game.

"I'm going to try, Will, I'm sure going to try."

Walt Avery was there, and Sam Kissam, and Fraley Niebuhr, and Talman, and Murray, and Dr. Anthony, and quite a few others.

There were representatives from other old clubs, too—Tryon of the old Eagles; Thorne, the old Empire pitcher; Johnny Grum of the Eckfords, the king of short stops in his day; J. Seaver Page of the Actives, who used to excel at second base; and Dick Oliver of the more modern Excelsior Club. And, many, many more, all of whom formally greeted Jamie out on the field, with the result that the game didn't begin for at least another hour. I suppose some of the spectators might have been getting anxious for the game, but no one said anything.

This was Jamie's day remember, and Jamie was always "too late," anyway. He didn't know the meaning of the words "on time."

Jamie organized the sides from those willing and able to play. On one side were the "Old Duffers," as he called us. I was to play left field, with Stanton in center and Murray in right. Avery was at his natural first base position, Purdy at second, Bensel at third. Talman manned short stop, and Dick Stevens was our pitcher. As far as I can remember, it was the first time I ever saw Doc at catcher, but apparently his situation was such that he wasn't about to do the running that playing the field would have required. We were playing ten men base ball, so Duncan Curry was in as right short stop.

The other side, Jamie called the "Youngsters," it being understood that was a relative term. Naturally, Jamie was the captain of the "Youngsters." He had Sam Kissam on his side, and he managed to rope in the two Kirklands to play center field and short stop, so naturally they had the advantage. Jamie would do the pitching. Henry Chadwick was the umpire.

Just as Jamie drew back his hand to deliver the first ball, his married daughter, Mrs. McClinton, stepped forward amid the cheers of the spectators and bound around his waist a belt of blue ribbon, on the front of which was embroidered in silver letters the name of the club, while from the left side descended two broad silk ribbons. On one were the words, "To Poor Old Davis," and on the other, "For his 25th ball birthday." Underneath in big letters was the word "Knickerbocker."

Everyone cheered as Jamie waved. His daughter kissed him on the cheek and then took the scarf back to her seat as the game began, or as the paper said the next day, "The old boys threw down their canes and went in to win."

The game, as one might expect, was played purely for fun. Given Jamie's obvious superiority in all aspects of the game, particularly his pitching, the Old Duffers could not manage a single run in the five-inning game, while Jamie, himself, accounted for three of the Youngsters' 21 runs. After five innings of huffing and puffing, the sun had sunk and the damps of evening had begun to settle in.

Poor Old Davis stopped the game and called out, "Come, get out of here you old fellows. Let the youngsters finish the game. It's getting cold and I ain't going to have you say you got sick on my account."

So us old men retired and let the younger members select sides and finish the game while we lounged and laughed on the sidelines.

WALTER AVERY   I never saw a more brilliant display of pitching in all my life. Jamie simply had no equal on his day.

DOC ADAMS   It was good to see everyone together again. Well, most everyone. Of course, Alick wasn't there, nor was Will Wheaton. I think it's fair to say that by dint of his stubborn will, Jamie had prodded and pushed, cajoled and commanded, and by so doing refused to let the organization wither away as some had long before suggested it would.

WILLIAM TUCKER    As soon as the game was over, carriages arrived and the ladies and the veterans were driven over to Duke's Hotel. Most of the youngsters walked, as well they should have.

At the hotel we all went into a private parlor where a sumptuous dinner was provided. I don't recall having seen Jamie's mother at any of our functions before, so I introduced myself to her. She was a lady through and through, and although I don't think she knew a base ball from a bread box, she certainly could appreciate the respect the game was showing for her son.

Jamie had two sons of his own but neither became involved with the club. I suppose I could have asked Jamie why, but I never did and he didn't talk about them much.

Anyway, the evening was a great success. Dr. Anthony presided and in a short but eloquent address, complimented Jamie on his long list of accomplishments.

DUNCAN CURRY    Most of us who played the game in those early days left it behind at some point. Family, work, and other activities took its place. Jamie, though, was quite an exception. Maybe when he was widowed at such a young age, he needed something to replace that void, or maybe he would have maintained his interest anyway. Who knows? Anyway, we were lucky to have him to carry on the name and the spirit of our club.

During the post-game festivities, I sat between Doc and Tuck.

"Like the old days, isn't it?" I said.

"Nothing's like the old, old days," said Tuck with a little laugh. "Remember when we had one ball between us and if we had two people watching, it was a crowd? You think the game's better now?"

"It's different," said Doc, "and it will be different yet in the years to come. It will always be different, always changing, always reflecting the times in which it's played. At least I can imagine it will."

"The thing I don't understand," said Tuck, "is how many people watch it. I mean there must be hundreds of thousands of people watching games on any given summer's day, and most of them paying for the privilege to boot. Remember playing up by Murray Hill, and over at Sunfish Pond? We had a hard time getting enough players to make a game, much less someone to watch."

"You should have stayed with making balls Doc," I said. "You'd be a wealthy man by now. Let's see, they're selling in the stores at $1.50 each and if there are say, conservatively, 10,000 games a week being played someplace and if each of them used 2 balls, that's $30,000..."

"Why didn't you tell me that 30 years ago?" he laughed.

"Thirty years ago I thought we were the only men interested in playing the game."

"What do you suppose Alick is doing right now?" said Tuck.

"Probably telling somebody he knows how to do something better than they do," I said.

"And he'd probably be right," Doc added.

It was good to be back together again, although in some ways it was bittersweet. We were older men looking back on our younger selves with a mixture of admiration and longing. We would never again play as we once did although men such as Jamie certainly tried their best to hold off the inevitable as long as possible.

DOC ADAMS    I, for one, was never much for re-living the past. I have no regrets. Life, as Shakespeare said, is made up of many different stages. In one stage I played base ball, but it was only one of several. At various times I was also a student, a physician, a state representative, a bank president. I was also a son, a husband, a father.

I worried a little about what would happen when Jamie had to give up base ball. Then again, the same thought arose about the club. Every organization needs a purpose, a sense of direction, and it needs leaders who are consonant with that purpose. I can't say I was familiar with the current club members other than Jamie and Sam, but from what I heard I didn't know where the new leaders would come from, and I wasn't sure the purpose was as clear as it once was.

Organizations, like people, go through stages, and like people, there comes the inevitable end. As wonderful as the evening honoring Jamie was, I couldn't help feeling that perhaps the club was nearer the end than the beginning.

WILLIAM TUCKER    Maybe the highlight of the evening was when Bill Taylor presented Jamie an elegant Morocco case on which was stamped in gold, "James Whyte Davis, Sept. 25th, 1875."

"This is from all of your fellow Knicks with admiration and gratitude," said Taylor.

Holding the box up for all to see, Jamie said, "Thank you very much. I appreciate it."

"Well, open it," said Taylor.

"Oh," he said, looking slightly sheepish, a look I might add, that did not often visit his face.

Jamie opened the hinged case carefully, as if something might jump out and bite him. Inside the velvet-lined box was an exquisite silver trophy in the form of a base ball and two crossed silver bats. "J.W. Davis. K.B.B.C." was engraved on each bat and the ball read: "Presented to James Whyte Davis on the Twenty Fifth Anniversary of his election as a member of the Knickerbocker Base Ball Club by his fellow members. 1850 Sept. 26 1875." Below this were the words "Never Too Late."

Jamie was clearly moved and for one of the few times in his life seemed at a loss for words. "Thank you all very much. Thank you. This is lovely," is about all he could get out.

"Well, sit down Jamie," Taylor joked. "You think you're the only speaker we've got tonight?"

We had all contributed to the impressive trophy but this is the first time I had seen it.

Many tributes followed. Thorne talked about pitching against Jamie and reminded us just how good a batsman he had been. Seaver Page, as was his wont, gave a particularly eloquent speech worthy of a politician.

FRALEY NIEBUHR   I told a couple of stories backing up the "too late" attribution. And every one of them true.

"Jamie, you'll be late for your funeral," I ended.

HENRY CHADWICK   I thought it would be appropriate to acknowledge some of the important early members of the club.

"For thirty years the Knickerbocker Base Ball of New York has played base ball at Hoboken according to the purest rules of amateurism and without missing a single season. For twenty-five of those years, Jamie has been an active member, first as an outstanding left fielder, then as the most serious of working members, afterwards as he is to this day, your worthy and esteemed president.

"On the 26th of September in 1850 he joined the leading base ball club in the country. At that time, the club included in its list of members, William Tucker, Charles Birney, Duncan Curry, Fraley Niebuhr, Ebenezer Dupignac, Doc Adams— all veterans of 1845; Charlie DeBost, Walter Avery, Eugene Plunkett, veterans of 1846; and Ladd, Murray, and Stevens of 1849. Poor Old Davis was of the corps of 1850, and after him came Kissam, Eager, McLaughlin — now General McLaughlin — Beloni, Taylor, Slote, Wenman and Thomas, all of whom joined between 1850 and 1859.

"Many of you are here today and know of the achievements of our honoree. Those of you who don't should make an effort to learn, for the Knickerbockers did and do stand for the highest principles of sportsmanship and fair play and he has been among the foremost advocates of these principles."

SAM KISSAM   I don't think most of the younger members knew much about the old days and probably took Jamie for granted. It seems like he had always been there.

I'm afraid I got a little overly sentimental as I got up and recalled those glorious old days. Actually I was misty-eyed because I didn't think we'd see their likes again. I was happy and sad at the same time.

DOC ADAMS   "You young men of the club," I said, when it was my turn to speak, "have but one man to thank for the fact that the club is still here for you today, and that man is James Whyte Davis. His service to the club cannot be matched to anyone here. He has dedicated his life to the Knickerbockers and we are all the better for it. When it came time to modify our stance, Jamie said 'no.' When it came time to compromise, Jamie said 'no.' When it came time to give up, Jamie said 'no.' I am pleased to call him a friend. Base ball is lucky to have him as a friend."

Everything I said, I believed to be true. Naturally over the years I had my share of differences with him. The issue of refusing admission of colored clubs to the Association comes to mind. But this was an evening to celebrate his accomplishments, and celebrate we did.

SAM KISSAM    As memento of the occasion, Mr. Chadwick gave him a copy of *The Umpire's Guide.*

At the end of the speechifying, Jamie got up and thanked everybody, and then thanked them again and then looked up at the old club banner that was hanging at the far end of the hall. It was familiar to all of us as we were used seeing it flying on the pole on game days. It was a triangular pennant with a "K" in a circle.

"You know what I'd really like," he said. "I'd love to have that banner. It would mean a lot to me."

It was something of a brash request, but no one was about to deny Jamie on this night. The banner was taken down and handed to him. Shortly after that, the party concluded.

JAMES WHYTE DAVIS    It was, of course, a wonderful day, but it had its melancholy aspect, too, for I knew — I think we all did — that this would be the last time we would all be together. And so it was.

## 112

# *A New Approach*

JAMES WHYTE DAVIS   When in 1875 the Professional Association came tumbling down like a house of cards, there were many causes. Take your pick: domination by one team (Boston), financial instability, lack of central authority, gambling. Probably all of these and maybe more. The Boston payroll alone was said to be more than $20,000 and only seven of the 13 member clubs managed to complete their full season.

ALBERT SPALDING   It seems to me that what was wrong with the Professional Association was that the game needed to be in the hands of businessmen who could conduct the details of managing men, administering discipline, arranging schedules, and finding ways and means of financing a team.

WILLIAM HULBERT   I never played the game myself, but as a businessman, I believed that the game itself, if properly administered, would not only provide profits for its investors, but also generate more business for concerns in the cities in which teams were located. To that end, I was instrumental in organizing the National League of Professional Base Ball Clubs.

We assessed each club $100 per year for administrative expenses and began with eight clubs located in Chicago, Cincinnati, Boston, Philadelphia, St. Louis, Louisville, Hartford, and New York. We established a standard gate receipt agreement, paid our umpires $5 a game, set the admission price at 50 cents with an allowance for a surcharge for covered seats, forbade Sunday games and encouraged a ban on the selling of alcohol on the grounds. In other words, we were organized in a way that the old Professional Association never was.

We arranged for a regular schedule with each club playing every other club ten times during the season.

The most important thing, though, was that unlike the old Professional Association, the National League was an organization of teams, not players.

SAM KISSAM   The new National League was of little interest to us. We continued to play our games as we had been doing for 31 years, and we weren't alone. A number of the old clubs had reorganized.

Professionals? What professionals?

JAMES WHYTE DAVIS   Among the many mistakes made by the National League was setting a tariff of 50 cents admission to their match games. Club managers either didn't realize or didn't care that we were in the midst of an era of "retrenchment," and that the first thing many people cut down on was expenses for entertainment. Why they thought people would pay half a dollar to see a ball match when for the same sum they could see the Centennial Exposition is beyond me. Is there any wonder that some clubs went bankrupt?

Even worse, though, was how many of the idiot club managers condoned the dishonesty of well-known suspected players and trusted the stringency of their own rules to prevent fraudulent play. Since the integrity of the whole damn professional fraternity was in question, no wonder it led to a loss of patronage.

It looked to me as if the professionals were cutting their own idiotic throats.

Changes in the professional National League occurred every season. The stability that the league had hoped for was proving difficult to achieve. Following the first season, the New York and Philadelphia clubs were ousted from the league because they were unable to complete the schedule as agreed. The next season the Hartford Dark Blues operated out of Brooklyn while the Louisville club was involved in a huge gambling scandal. For the next season they added the Indianapolis Blues, and the Providence and Milwaukee Grays. For the '79 season they lost the Indianapolis Blues and Milwaukee Grays, but added the Buffalo Bisons, Syracuse Star and Troy Trojans. Neither the Syracuse nor the Troy clubs managed to complete the season. The Syracuse Star then folded, but the Trojans reorganized and fielded a team the following season during which the league added the Brooklyn Bridegrooms and the Worchester Worchesters. The next year they threw out the new Cincinnati Red Stockings (because it violated two league rules: the team's ballpark marketed beer, and they refused to close their ballpark on Sundays) but added the Detroit Wolverines.

And so it went.

WILLIAM HULBERT   With the destruction of the Union and Capitoline grounds, the Polo Grounds seemed the logical location for professional ball. Ironically, New York, the great seat of base ball development, was one of the last cities to have its own National League professional nine. We would have had one earlier but for the fact that the Polo Grounds could not be controlled by such a club because the Polo Association needed the field two days a week for its own matches. I could envision a time, though, when the requirements of the grounds as a money investment would cause it to be given over entirely to base ball and cricket at the expense of polo.

The patrons of base ball were hungry for professional contests.

HENRY CHADWICK   It was not impossible for the professionals to restore confidence in their game, but it was something they themselves had to address.

Given the assurance of a legitimate trial of skill between two rival nines with a reasonable tariff of admission, a return to the old days of large crowds would certainly follow.

The key to this, though, was the word "legitimate." When I asked the League directors why they threw out the Philadelphia Club for alleged dishonest practices and then, with glaring inconsistency, re-engaged some of the most marked men, the reply was: "We thought it best to forgive them their crooked ways and to trust that the stringency of our League laws will make them play straight this season." The folly of this line of action led to nothing but more crooked work than we had ever seen before.

The League clubs were growling at the falling off of patronage and wondered why when the answer was plain and palpable to ordinary observers—lack of confidence in the honesty of some players. People by the thousands took the trouble to go out to Prospect Park or Elysian Fields to see legitimate contests between amateur nines like the Knickerbockers while a pitiful 50 or so attended the contests at the Union Grounds.

In 1876 it was reported that not a single National League team received sufficient gate money receipts in Philadelphia, Brooklyn, or Hartford to pay hotel and traveling expenses, while the Athletic and Mutual Clubs announced their inability to complete their return trips to clubs in the western cities.

Clubs were forced to cut their admission prices to 25 cents and lower the salaries of most players.

The lessons were clear, but would the teams listen?

---

# 113

# *Suspicions*

JAMES WHYTE DAVIS   While the National League staggered on, we opened the centennial season on a chilly day in April. Mr. Giles had the field in excellent order for us and a good practice game was had.

There was a considerable fuss made about the selection of nines for a series of so-called amateur matches between picked nines of Brooklyn and New York. The fuss, naturally, was about gate sharing. Certain clubs had approached Cammeyer for the use of the Union Grounds and he agreed. If they had wanted a real amateur competition, they would have arranged to play at Prospect Park, not in Cammeyer's playpen.

The true amateur clubs were now down to a handful of what the papers had taken to calling the "minority class of city clubs."

I don't know this for a fact, but I had suspicions about some other clubs such as the Hudson of Brooklyn and the Confidence of New Rochelle. The Hudsons claim they never shared gate money. Nevertheless, they played so often on the enclosed Capitoline and Union Grounds that it was natural to assume they were sharing in the receipts. Why else would they play there? And why was it that clubs like the Confidence were seldom or ever seen playing on the free fields?They protested their innocence, but I thinketh they protested too much.

We, of course, continued to play at Hoboken. In Manhattan, Central Park was devoted to the exclusive use of public school boys. Prospect Park in Brooklyn was different, however. Owing to an enlightened Brooklyn Park Commission, they created extensive ball fields open to all reputable amateur clubs there on which 20 games might be played at the same time. Field No. 1 was reserved for the playing of match games by amateur clubs having a special reputation for excellence. Permits were granted to those clubs upon the written requests. In some ways, Brooklyn was far ahead of New York.

We ended the season of '76 on a brisk and breezy October election day. We all voted early and then went to our grounds in Hoboken where in the morning we played a match of the Marrieds against the Singles. We followed that with dinner in the club house and then in the afternoon played the Veterans against the Youngsters, and thus our final game of the season.

For the first time in a game I tried out my new curved delivery. I thought I'd save it for Al Kirkland. When he came to bat, I threw two balls as hard as I could but off the base. Then on the third pitch, I tried the curver, a pitch I had been working on my own for weeks. Lo and behold, it actually worked, curving away from Al as he stood dumbfounded and watched it sail by.

"Well, I'll be a son of a buck," he said.

"Who said you can't teach a new trick to an old dog?" said Sam Kissam.

I stood there smiling the smug smile of a younger man.

For the season of '78, there were said to be about 20 co-operative gate-money clubs. We, on the other hand, played not only our regular practice matches, but also scheduled contests with the Nameless and Staten Island clubs and a number of college and school nines, including those of the Columbia, Stevens, Rutgers, New York and Polytechnic schools.

For our 33rd consecutive season, so-called improvements to the grounds had been undertaken by the Stevens Institute Club, but they had started too late in the spring to level and extend the field, so it looked as if the field wouldn't be completely restored until the end of the season.

"Where are the Knickerbockers?" some people asked.

Where were we? We were meeting at the St. George Cricket Club grounds every Monday and Friday doing what we always did.

# 114

# *Changes*

HENRY CHADWICK   One thing that was changing very rapidly was the use of defensive articles. Well, to put it more precisely, the *idea* of defensive articles. Case in point: the use of the catcher's mask. Mr. Thayer of the Harvard College Club invented a steel mask for protecting his face. It was constructed of upright bars about an inch apart, and stood out from the face 3 or 4 inches. Thayer's invention worked well to protect him from dangerous hits in the face when playing close up behind the bat. The fact is, the wire mask was something all catchers who faced swift pitching should have worn. It was light, simple and sure protection.

Wisely the amateur catchers quickly adopted this valuable invention. Why the professional catchers took so long to adopt it was due probably to lacking the moral courage to face the music of the fire of raillery from the crowd, which the wearing of the mask frequently elicited. Plucky enough to face the dangerous fire of balls from the swift pitcher, they trembled before the remarks of the small boys in the crowd, and preferred to run the risk of broken cheek bones, dislocated jaws, smashed noses or blackened eyes, than stand the chaff of the assembled fools.

This is but another example of the amateurs being ahead of the professionals.

Lots of other changes were in the wind, too. The order of batting, for example. Often what happened was that when a base runner accounted for the last out of an inning, the next inning would see the batter who followed that runner in the batting order leading off. This was the rule as adopted by the National Association in 1857. Under this rule, the fourth batsman might force the third man out at second base, and in the next inning take his strike over again. Then in 1878, we required that a new inning would be led off by the batter following the last one to have completed his at bat.

It was becoming apparent, too, that more and more pitchers were throwing from the height of their shoulder, or in some cases, even higher. This was leading to dangerous pitches delivered towards the head of batsmen. It was just as apparent that bases on balls was not a sufficient deterrent, so we empowered the umpires to assess fines ranging from $10 to $50, if in the opinion of the umpire, the pitcher was deliberately trying to hit a batter. The problem was, of course, that it was nigh impossible for the umpire to know the pitcher's intention, so the problem continued.

Another change was that in 1881 the pitcher was moved back another five feet. He then stood at fifty feet.

We also experimented with using square bats. These in their widest part — from corner to corner at its end — were not wider than the round bat. The four sides extended only to the handle. It was just as if a round bat had been planed off on four sides. The idea of changing the form from the round to the four-sided was to enable the batsman to place the ball better.

These were tried at an exhibition game, but unluckily, the groundskeeper only provided three of the new four-sided bats and as these were all broken before the game was finished, the contest did not present a fair opportunity for testing the merits of the new sticks and the idea was dropped.

JAMES WHYTE DAVIS    The world was a-changin'. We got the telephone, the electric light, milk in bottles. Boss Tweed was arrested and then died in jail. An express train made the trip from New York to San Francisco in 83 hours. George Armstrong Custer's Seventh Cavalry were massacred at Little Big Horn.

Our club was changing, too. Younger players were agitating for all sorts of things, most of which involved money.

As my playing days were drawing to a close, I couldn't help the reflecting impulse that comes so naturally in older age. Looking back it seemed as if it were only yesterday that we were playing out by Sunfish Pond. I was growing nostalgic for those days. I guess I was just getting old.

HENRY CHADWICK    I know Jamie and some of the old guard saw the progress of the game as a downhill slide, but I for one did not. It's simply too easy to edit our memories such that the past was ever better than the present.

ASHLEY HYDE    Some thirty years earlier, the Knickerbockers made some material changes and improvements in the old game of town ball. The members of the old club, or those remaining, still held it in dear memory and the organization was still kept up, but for the most part they had settled down into sober, dignified citizens who gathered, however, each year at an annual banquet. Many, of course, were missing from the original roster — a portion scattered to all parts of the world, and still more gathered to their fathers. A quarter of a century and more effects many changes.

---

# 115

# *Old-Timers*

JAMES WHYTE DAVIS    I hadn't completely given up base ball. As late as 1878 I agreed to participate in a match between the veteran Atlantics and a picked nine of old New York players at Washington Park. Interestingly enough, Charlie DeBost was there. I hadn't seen Charlie in quite some time.

He showed me a letter he had received a few years earlier from Alick Cartwright in response to a letter he had sent Alick.

"He's in Honolulu," Charlie said as if that was the strangest thing in the world. But knowing Alick, I wouldn't have been surprised had it come from the moon.

In the letter he mentioned his good feelings for Fraley, Charlie Birney, Walt Avery, Tuck, Duncan, me, and a few of the old boys. He made particular note of "old Charlie" and his knack for grand and lofty tumbling and his ability to strike the ball.

> Dear old Knickerbockers, I hope the club is still kept up, and that I shall someday meet again with them on the pleasant fields of Hoboken. Charlie, I have in my possession the original ball with which we used to play on Murray Hill. Many is the pleasant chase I have had after it on Mountain and Prairie, and many an equally pleasant one on the sunny plains of Hawaii. Sometimes I have thought of sending it home to be played for by the Clubs, but I cannot bear to part with it, it is so linked in with cherished home memories.

Alick was never shy about a little embroidering of reality when it suited him, but still I could easily picture him throwing a ball to an Indian as he crossed the plains.

> Some time ago I wrote to Dr. Adams, but have received no answer — please ask him if he received my letter and once on a time I heard that a lithograph of the old members of the Knickerbockers was to be published. Was it ever done, or if not, is it possible still to have it done? It would be interesting as a memorial of the first Base Ball club of N.Y., truly the first, for the old New York Club never had a regular organization. I will give $100 — or $200 if necessary towards its publication — my mother, residing in Brooklyn has my portrait as <u>I used to was</u>.

We did have that one old lithograph, but I guess Alick never saw it.

> I will soon send you a carte de visite as I am, and I tell you Charlie that (as they say in California) I am not the man I was in '49, though I am still hale and hearty, I feel the want of exercise and a bracing climate. I have resided here now over 15 years and have not been off this island for the past 12 years. I am so fearfully seasick when I go on the water, that it deters me from traveling.

I just couldn't imagine Alick being stopped by anything as trivial as an upset stomach.

> You were kind enough to ask about my fortunes. Although by no means rich, I am independent and occupy an excellent position in society. I have

every reason to be satisfied and grateful, *and I am*. I have a few spare thousands in Uncle Sam's bosum (6% Bonds, Gold), my health is excellent and always has been — my children as good as most, and my wife is too good for me. Why should I not be content — but above all this, Charlie boy, "I am sound on the goose."

I wish you would write to me again and ask Fraley Niebuhr, Dr. Adams and others to do so. Please send photographs of all old friends that are obtainable.

Good bye, Charlie. God Bless you. I send "Aloha" to you and any Sandwich Islander you will meet will translate that for you.

I made a note to myself to write to Alick but I don't think I ever did.

CHARLIE DEBOST   Hearing from Ol' Alick brought back memories — good ones, too, but much like him, I was never one to spend much time looking back.

JAMES WHYTE DAVIS   I had occasion during the early summer of '79 to have a conversation with Ed Russell of the old Excelsiors. It seems they were putting together a reunion game of Brooklyn ballists for a game at Prospect Park. According to Ed, all the players were to be veterans of '59, and the game would be "the largest gathering of old ball players known to the history of the game."

"Is that so?"

"We've got agreements to play from players, all of whom were on Brooklyn Club nines in existence in 1859, including the Pastimes, Excelsiors, Putnams, Eckfords, Atlantics, Stars and Charter Oaks."

"Never heard of any of them."

"Before your time, were they?"

"Apparently."

"We're going to play by the rules of '59 too, when bound catches of fair balls were legal, and no balls were called on the pitchers. Neither will strikes be called on the batsmen unless they strike at the ball. And, we're going to play with an old regulation ten-inch ball weighing five and a half ounces with plenty of rubber in it. No over running of first base will be allowed either. Dr. Jones is going to umpire and see to it that all the old rules are obeyed."

"Let me tell you something, Ed," I said. "I could raise a nine of the old Knicks, Gothams, Eagles, Empires, and Morrisania Unions of 1859 which would knock spots out of any Brooklyn nine from that time."

ED RUSSELL   Jamie was great on talk of that kind, but I told him I'd be willing to bet a century on being able to put together a side of Brooklyn vets in the field who would send the New Yorkers home about as badly a whipped crowd as ever left the city of churches.

JAMES WHYTE DAVIS   I had in mind a side made up of me, DeBost, and Welling from our club; Thorne, Miller, and Cuyler of the Empires; and a few others I knew were still around.

"You don't seriously think that side could compete with a Brooklyn nine with Brown and Grum from the Eckfords, and..."

Talk like this had become common fare among the old players. Sometimes the games were actually organized, but more often than not there was more talk than action. I guess that's what happens when you get older — more talk than action.

Once we arranged for a match between the old Excelsiors with Leggett, Brainard, Pearsall and others against a Knick side with me, Stevens, Kissam, and even Doc who agreed to come down for the occasion.

I don't know what was a bigger inducement, the games or the dinners that followed.

It seems that, in some circles at least, there was more interest in the old boys' game than the young boys'. I wonder why that was?

---

## 116

# *New Amateurs*

HENRY CHADWICK   Championship contests were particularly popular, including county and college championships, which were beginning to assume as much prominence as the annual rowing contests between Harvard and Yale.

JAMES WHYTE DAVIS   The Nameless and Star clubs, along with a few other Brooklyn clubs got together to form the Long Island Amateur Association. They barred all players from the association who played for money. However, they did admit players who had once been professionals but wanted to return to amateur status. One of the stated objectives of the association was to play the Knickerbockers. By this time (1879), the reality was that we weren't playing much against outside clubs. Hell, we weren't playing much at all.

HENRY CHADWICK   We decided to organize a club of journalistic base ballists — the Press Base Ball Club. If nothing else, it demonstrated just how far the game had come because we had writers from the *Eagle, Herald, Times, Tribune, World, Sun, Brooklyn Sunday Sun, Clipper, Forest and Stream, Frank Leslie's,* etc. — all of whom either covered base ball or had a strong interest in the game.

We believed ourselves to be strong enough to give the best amateur nines a good fight — the regular amateur clubs, not the gate-money semi-professionals. We arranged to play games at Prospect Park in Brooklyn and Central Park in New York and scheduled matches against the Excelsiors, the reorganized old Stars, and the Knickerbockers. We also arranged visits to Princeton and New Haven to receive — or give lessons to — the College nines of those cities, and to Boston to play Harvard, and to Philadelphia to meet the Olympics.

JAMES WHYTE DAVIS    The Stock Exchange decided to form its own nine. In fact, they put together a pretty fair side as among those working at the Exchange were two or three players of the old Harvard and Yale nines. We organized matches against them, and I must say in defense of my colleagues that these gentlemen played according to the old Excelsior and Knickerbocker spirit. Although I didn't participate in the matches, I was proud of both sides.

## 117

# *And Then There Was One*

JAMES WHYTE DAVIS    There was a developing rift between some of the younger players and the handful of veterans like me and Sam who were still hanging on. I suppose it was a direct result of surviving long enough to have old members. Let's face it, most clubs didn't have this problem because they were long out of existence before such tensions could arise.

AL KIRKLAND    There were days when a few of the older members were playing with us younger members. For the most part, we would be making swift and accurate throws, fine running catches, and all those kind of things while the older men could only play the regular old fashioned muffin game.

It came down to this: Either we had to assign one day for the exclusive use of the veterans, or the younger members would lose interest in the club. Look, the old men came out for the healthful pleasure and exercise and they had no interest in playing anything but their own practice games in which they chose up sides. Well and good, but this needed to be done on one day, while letting us have the other day. This way we could raise a good nine to play regular club matches and the veterans could have a day when they could have their own fun all to themselves, without having the annoyance of playing side by side with better players.

SAM KISSAM    The divisions within the club were obvious to anyone who cared to look. We had young members and we had old members and the aims of the two were rather different. I suppose the young members' interest in competitive matches was natural, and had we been able to play as we once did, undoubtedly we would have wanted to do the same. But we weren't, and we didn't.

I knew what Jamie's reaction would be even before Al Kirkland suggested splitting our two-day-a-week schedule. He wanted no part of it.

"We're either one club, or we're no club," he said.

The writing on the wall was clear.

JAMES WHYTE DAVIS   We all know there is a tendency to think that the yesterdays were always better than the todays and that the tomorrows will be worse still. So be it. Nevertheless, I remember when players greeted players with a hearty welcome and enjoyed every incident and feature of the game to the utmost. I remember when no ill-feeling was engendered by reason of defeat. I remember when each nine under their captain's leadership gave a round of cheers at the conclusion of a match. I remember when a representative of the unsuccessful nine presented the game ball to the victorious nine accompanied by words of encouragement and praise and when the captain of the victors received it with an appropriate and graceful speech. I remember when the banquet board was spread with the choicest viands in honor of the visitors, and when the features of the day's game were pleasantly discussed, toasts offered, songs sung, speeches made.

We were of one brotherhood, fighting for a common cause, namely that of promoting a game which is beyond question the noblest and grandest of all pastimes.

To the active player of the late '70s, these and similar sentiments probably sounded like the highly tinted, soul-bewitching tales of the Arabian Nights. But strange as it may have appeared to them, my memories were not of myths.

Anyway, these were the perspectives of this "old, played-out, base ballist."

AL KIRKLAND   No one wanted to insult Jamie, but at the same time we had heard his "good old days" litany so many times that it was growing so tiresome that I know some members went out of their way to avoid him whenever possible.

JAMES WHYTE DAVIS   In '79 Sam announced his retirement from the club.

"You're leaving me alone with the young boys," I said.

"Jamie, you know as well as I do that the club is barely hanging on."

"More the reason to stay."

"We're playing fewer and fewer games. Hell, we're hardly ever even practicing anymore."

"You're making me the last of the Mohicans."

"Someone has to be."

"One by one you've all abandoned the ship"

"The analogy is appropriate."

"Stick around."

"Besides, as my waist expands, my batting declines, and my waist ain't getting any smaller."

"That I understand."

"I am so busy these days with the brokerage and the Stock Exchange..."

So we presented Sam with a silver ball.

SAM KISSAM    These presentations, of which by then we had many, I always found awkward.

"Presented to Samuel H. Kissam by a fellow member to commemorate his twenty-fifth anniversary of membership in the Knickerbocker Base Ball Club. And as a remembrance of an unbroken and warm friendship on 1854, the green fields of Hoboken 1879. And also attesting his many sacrifices and kindnesses which will be cherished forever, by your loving and grateful friends. God be with you."

JAMES WHYTE DAVIS    And then there was one.

# PART THIRTEEN: THE END 1880–1882

## 118

# *Final Days*

JAMES WHYTE DAVIS    I read in the *New York Times* where someone wrote "our experience with the national game of base ball has been sufficiently thorough to convince us that it was in the beginning a sport unworthy of men, and that it is now, in its fully developed state, unworthy of gentlemen."

Unworthy of men! To this absurdity I can only say ... well, what I want to say is probably not fit for print.

AL KIRKLAND    On September 27, 1880, we had another event celebrating Jamie's long tenure with the club. This one marked the thirtieth anniversary of his membership. We had another reunion of some of the older ball-tossers. It was looking as if this was becoming an annual event.

We started practice for the season '81 in late April. Although the weather was cloudy and threatening worse, for a couple of hours we enjoyed a lively practice game of "one-two-three." Owing to the chilly weather, most of our older members did not turn out.

I particularly remember our first game that year. As Jamie was wont to remind us, it was our thirty-sixth successive season of ball play at Hoboken. It was a beautiful day in May and we faced the Stevens Institute freshman nine at the St. George Cricket Grounds. The freshmen's team included six players who were on the regular Stevens nine.

We started well but were never able to catch up and they went on to win 12 to 2.

We were a young nine, but we were Knickerbockers and that still counted for something. Jamie, Sam and the other older members weren't playing with us any longer, but they still occasionally turned out for our practices.

SAM KISSAM    Someone sent me a copy of *The Philadelphia Record* in which they insisted in calling the Olympic Club of that city "the oldest base ball organization in existence." Horsefeathers! They did not begin to play base ball until 1859. Previous to that time they were a "town ball" club, a very different game from base ball. We were a base ball club in 1845.

JAMES WHYTE DAVIS    It seemed to me the omens were all around.

One club hired the pugilist, John L. Sullivan, for a day. They said they didn't expect he'd play well, but they did expect him to significantly increase the gate money take. That being the case, I could well imagine we'd see Mr. Sullivan as a side show at many other base ball matches.

Maybe Sullivan would turn up at the Sunday school picnic of some enterprising congregation where he would sing a hymn. Of course, Mr. Sullivan can't sing, but he can't play base ball either and that didn't stop club managers.

As if that wasn't enough, the board of directors of the National League of Professional Base Ball Clubs met in secret session to try Richard Higham, one of the league's umpires, on the charge of crookedness preferred against him by the president of the Detroit Club. Higham himself was present at the formal trial. Apparently the charges were based on letters written by Higham to gamblers advising them to bet on certain games in which he umpired. As a result of the trial, the League directors expelled him from the League.

The League indicated it would have preferred to inflict greater penalties, but under the law there was nothing more they could do. Need I say more?

The professionals decided that when a game was prevented by rain from being finished, the local club would not refund either tickets or money. They claimed that when a person entered a ground, he took the same chances that the club did of being disappointed by the interposition of nature. In other words, the professionals would keep the money whether they played or not and the hell with the spectators.

The Nameless Club, the worthy successors of the old Excelsiors, put on an amateur minstrel entertainment at the Waverly Theater in Brooklyn and managed to attract a crowded and fashionable house. Were we destined to become black-faced entertainers?

When Dan McDonald, a long-time member of the Brooklyn Atlantics, died of consumption I noticed that I was going to almost as many funerals as games. Funny how that happens.

Although we don't often realize it at the time, all endings are beginnings. I had been a member of the Knickerbocker Base Ball Club for 30 years. I had enjoyed thousands of hours on the practice field. I had played scores of match games. I had gotten my share of hits, muffed my share of balls, had more than my share of laughs and a few tears.

Nothing is worse than trying to hang on where you are no longer wanted. Oh, nobody said as much, but it was clear that if the club were to continue, it would have to do so with the leadership of younger men. That's what happens in any organization — the torch keeps getting passed down to new leaders — and that's what should happen.

And so I resigned. I was looking forward to doing some traveling and perhaps engaging in some new activities. My sons and daughter were grown, married, and living with their families. There was nothing to keep me tied down any longer.

I had seen the game develop from a boy's game played for exercise and fun, to a man's game played for prizes and profits. I had seen a game played by a handful of devotees become a game played by thousands, maybe millions.

Through it all, though, I am proud to say that we, the gentlemen of the Knickerbockers, maintained our integrity and played the game with the honor it was due. Not many other clubs could make that claim. Maybe none.

AL KIRKLAND   I tried to talk Jamie out of resigning, but in all honesty, my heart wasn't in it. He knew the time had come. I knew the time had come, too, but out of respect and consideration for him, I made the token effort.

"I appreciate the sentiment, Al, but my mind's pretty well made up."

That left the door open just a little. Did he really want me to talk him out of it?

"What are you going to do, Jamie," I asked. "Without the club, what are you going to do?"

"Don't you think I have anything in my life other than base ball?"

"Well..."

"I'm going to see the world."

"It's big."

"Part of it, anyway."

"Bring base ball to the unwashed masses?"

"They already have it."

"Al, I don't know the club anymore. It's ... different now, and I don't fit in. I'll leave it to you."

I know he really didn't want to go, but I know he knew he couldn't stay either. It was a difficult situation and although he fought hard not to show it, I could tell how emotional he was. He was walking away from something he truly loved. And no, "loved" is not too strong a word.

"You'll always be welcome, you know."

JAMES WHYTE DAVIS   But I knew I wouldn't be. Not really.

AL KIRKLAND   So we said goodbye to Jamie and vowed to carry on. It wasn't the same, though. Nobody could remember a time when Jamie wasn't around. It was like losing a member of the family.

CHARLES DEBOST   Jamie tried to put on a good front, but I could tell he was hurt. I think the reality is that he was gently pushed aside by the younger members, but he insisted he had enough of the old club and couldn't wait to leave.

"I should have done it years earlier," he said.

"The only thing you should have done earlier was to learn to hit the curver better."

"You can't play forever. You know that."

"You could still lead the club without playing."

"Could but won't."
"Stubborn to the last."
"It's not the same anymore, the game."
"Of course it's not, you idiot. Nothing is."
"Meet me for dinner tomorrow night?"
"Sorry old boy. I've got a business meeting."
"Maybe some other time."
"Sure."

SAM KISSAM    See, the thing is, Jamie didn't have a lot of interests outside of base ball. I'm not sure he had a lot of friends outside of the game either, and he wasn't exactly what you would call a dedicated family man.

I told him we'd get together regularly, and we did for a while, but as time went on, I saw less and less of him. I suspect that's the way those things always go.

JAMES WHYTE DAVIS    That spring I retired from my brokerage activities. I was 56, too young for the rocker, but too old to play ball. So, all at once, the club was gone, and the job was gone, and I was restless.

In May I boarded a train for an extended Western tour, seeing the sights along the way and going as far as San Francisco. It was in that beautiful place that I found the Knickerbocker Base Ball Club of San Francisco, the most successful and famous club in the city.

I went to see one of their games and afterwards talked to some of the players. As an "original Knickerbocker" (that's how I was introduced to the other players) I was treated as visiting royalty. I learned that their club, named for us, was formed in 1860 and had been playing ever since. I was also told that some of them had been playing the game there as early as 1850 and wondered if Alick, who had arrived there the year before, was responsible. I can readily believe he was.

After I returned home, the restless spirit was still with me, so I made plans for a trip to Europe. I wanted to see some of the great sights that continent had to offer. On the first day of July, I boarded the good steamship Circassia for the grand adventure.

When all 500 of us had secured berths, the anchor weighed, and the sails hoisted, the big steamer pushed out into the New York harbor and set course across the Atlantic. Some of the passengers were crying, some singing, some dancing. Soon we were speeding rapidly through the beautiful blue sea. Wonderful suppers were laid out every night.

After tea one afternoon, someone proposed we get up a concert for that night. When volunteers to perform were solicited, I agreed to do a little song.

I thought I would do one of the little ditties I had written some years earlier for one of our Knickerbocker dinners. I went to my cabin to find the old notebook in which I had scribbled the lyrics. Seeing the words again brought back fond memories of happy times.

> We were never diggers, butchers, or dockers
> We were gentlemen all, us Knickerbockers
> We didn't lie, cheat or shame
> We didn't play at tit-for-tat
> Or ask for pelf for the game
> For we were always gentlemen at the bat.
>
> We were not for guile, deceit, or bags of tricks
> Not us, not the always honorable Knicks
> We didn't play for outright praise
> We never played the game like that
> Or sought out scoundrelly ways
> For we were always gentlemen at the bat.

A collection was taken up for the Lifeboat Fund and everyone was in a felicitous and generous mood. I performed my song as if I was back with Doc and the boys and was received with charitable applause for my effort if not my talent.

When all the performances were concluded, a man who appeared familiar approached me. Still, I couldn't quite place him.

"Mr. Davis," he said, "I'm Ashley Hyde. I've seen you play so many times at the Elysian Fields. I just wanted to say hello and tell you how much I enjoyed your song. Particularly since I knew who you were singing about."

"Yes, now I remember seeing you at games."

Over the ship's best lager, we struck up a conversation that lasted well into the night.

"I always enjoyed those afternoons," he said. "There was something both exciting and relaxing at the same time. I don't know how to explain it really."

"Are you a player yourself?"

Pointing at his stiff leg he said, "I couldn't. I can't run."

"That never stopped Charlie DeBost."

"I mean really can't run."

"You know, I never understood cranks. Playing the game I understand; watching someone else play is quite another story."

"It's no different than any other entertainment, I suppose."

"Then why not go see *The Black Crook*?"

"I did — all 5½ hours, which for me was about 5 too long."

"That all?"

"But a good match of base ball ... well, caring is the entertainment."

"So who do you care about now?"

"What do you mean?"

"Let me guess. Cap Anson and Chicago, or Harry Wright and..."

"I know it's funny, but I've never been interested in the professional game."

"Not a gambler?"

"I've always enjoyed more the game you played. Somehow just knowing that there was nothing at stake — no money, I mean — just the game for the sake of the game..."

"But as you say, you care, then certainly you must care who wins."

"Didn't you?"

"Of course, but if we didn't, well anyway we had fun in the playing."

"And I in the watching."

Ashley Hyde was a true crank in the same way I was a true player. And so for the remainder of the twelve-day journey we re-lived the old days with Doc, and Charlie, and Fraley, and Tuck, and Sam, and the rest. The memories were good and the time went by fast. He was going back to London to visit family and watch a cricket match or two and I on to the continent. We said we'd keep in touch when we were both back in New York, but we never did.

Life is a one-way street and as much as you might want, you can't go back.

---

## 119

# *A Quiet End*

HENRY CHADWICK    This was the base ball situation in the area at the dawn of the season of 1882: The professional Metropolitan Club had tried to gain admission to the professional league but was unsuccessful. Nevertheless, the club was set to play games at the Polo Grounds, having made great improvements to that facility. It was being claimed that the Mets had secured some of the best ball players in the country. In Brooklyn, the Atlantics were also preparing to put a strong nine on the field.

An alliance known as the American College Association was to be composed of clubs from Harvard, Yale, Princeton, Brown, Amherst, and Dartmouth. There was talk that the Williams College nine had wanted to join in, but faculty refused to allow it. Other college clubs including nines from Manhattan College, St. John's, and Fordham were still around and were planning to compete against other amateur clubs.

Members of the Long Island Amateur Association were set to play Saturday afternoons on the parade grounds at Prospect Park. There were still some clubs playing for sport and exercise — Nameless, Commercial, Putnam, Dauntless, and Polytechnic School. The New York Stock Exchange was also getting ready to put two strong nines on the field at Prospect Park.

Nowhere to be seen were the Knickerbockers.

DOC ADAMS   It wasn't long after Jamie left that the members decided it was time to put the club quietly to rest. I suspect Jamie saw this coming and that played a large part in his decision to resign. He didn't want to be around for the funeral.

Base ball had moved on and interest in the amateur game had waned. As I understand it, there weren't many members who were at the meeting where the decision was made. I guess that in itself said it all. Without fanfare or much press coverage, the papers of incorporation were returned to the state, and just that simply, the venerable Knickerbocker Base Ball Club of New York was no more.

Never mind. The club lives forever in the game that it reformed, nurtured, and saw to maturity. It was time for other clubs and other men to take over.

AL KIRKLAND   It wasn't so much a decision as a lack of one. We were getting fewer and fewer members at our practices and meetings, and no one really came forward with the initiative to revitalize the old club. It was more like it just died in its sleep one night without many people taking notice.

I can't say I wasn't disappointed, but by the same token, I hadn't the inclination to try to be the savior. Everything in its time I suppose. The KBBC had its time. Now it was another time.

ASHLEY HYDE   I credit the end of the Knicks as much to the loss of leadership as to anything else. With Doc Adams long gone and with Davis ending his interest, there was simply no one to pick up the responsibility. To the membership, too many other things came first. Cartwright, Tucker, Wheaton, and the other pioneers may have invented it, Doc Adams may have given it respectability, Jamie Davis may have kept it alive, but there was no one to take it from there.

HENRY CHADWICK   They played one more season after Jamie left and then with nary a whisper, they quietly disbanded. No big pronouncements, no ceremonies.

They didn't invent the game as some have claimed, but they did give it an enduring form, they did nurture it through its difficult years, and they did set a standard for fair play, honesty, and integrity that brought credit to both their organization and the game itself.

In reality, they helped foster a game that became bigger than them. The Knickerbockers sustained it until it was ready to go out into the world on its own.

The game will, of course, go on and develop new rules and methods of playing, but there will always be a place for the amateur game as espoused by the Knickerbockers. Wherever there are empty lots and sunny weather, boys will gather to play for fun. A few, a very few, may eventually play for money, but most will play for the other values the game offers. They will play without knowledge of the Knickerbockers and that is truly a shame.

JAMES WHYTE DAVIS    Did we leave base ball, or did base ball leave us?

WILLIAM TUCKER    When you come right down to it, we weren't the first to play the game, and we weren't the best to play the game, but we were first the best.

DUNCAN CURRY    It was progress they said. The way the game changed was progress and progress was inevitable they said, and the mark of a good action is that in retrospect it seems inevitable. And so it was.

DOC ADAMS    It is a fine thing to watch the creation of a hero before your eyes. Heroes are the stuff of sports: without a hero there is no story; without the truly exceptional performer, the narrative loses its fizz. The world has a hunger for heroes and it is that hunger that created the Harry Wrights, and the Al Spaldings, and professional base ball as an integral part of the continuity of American culture. Like the country it reflects, base ball adjusts with the times, just as it marks the times and reminds of a time that was good.

# Epilogue

## In Which We Return to the Beginning and Then Move On

HOWARD BURMAN   Alick Cartwright remained in Hawaii where he was appointed chief engineer of the Fire Department of the City of Honolulu. He was also very active in numerous civic activities including, most prominently, founding the Honolulu Library and Reading Room and serving as its president from 1886 to 1892. He was an advisor to the queen and served as executor of her Last Will & Testament. He was also appointed consul to Peru, and served on the organizing committee for Honolulu's Centennial Celebration of American Independence.

Albert Spalding's world tour in 1888 saw the Chicago White Stockings and an All-American team arrive in Honolulu for an exhibition. According to reports, however, their ship was delayed and the players didn't arrive until early on a Sunday. In his 1911 book, *America's National Game,* Spalding wrote: "The American game had at that point, nearly a quarter of a century ago, taken strong hold of the popular heart at Honolulu. Here was the home of Alexander J. Cartwright, founder of the first Base Ball club ever organized — Father of the famed Knickerbockers. Many Americans were there who had played the game at home, and the natives were also developing some skill at the pastime.... Everybody wanted to witness the game; but alas, it was Sunday. We were to leave late that evening; therefore it was Sunday or never. Petitions came flooding in upon me for a Sunday game. I at once made an investigation, which satisfied me that the missionaries who were looking after the moral welfare of the natives had closed the doors against Sunday entertainments good and tight. There was no doubt about it; Sunday ball was as taboo in Honolulu as had been a whole lot of things when the heathens were in full control of their island."

Cartwright died on July 12, 1892, apparently of an "illness in his throat that worsened."

Duncan Curry remained in his Brooklyn home until his death on April 18, 1894. In part his obituary in *The New York Times* read, "Mr. Curry was the first President of the first baseball club ever organized in this country, the famous old Knickerbocker Baseball Club founded in 1845." His Brooklyn Green-Wood Cemetery marker proclaims him the "Father of Baseball."

William Wheaton died in his Oakland, California, home on September 11, 1888, at 75. He had served as president of the Society of California Pioneers, a member of the Vigilance Committee of San Francisco, register of the Land Office, and president of the Bar Association. An obituary noted that "Mr. Wheaton came to California from New York, his native state, as a master of his own ship in 1849."

It is worth noting that Wheaton completely disappears from the Knickerbocker records in the summer of 1846. Randall Brown, writing in *The National Pastime*, wonders if, as a member of the 7th Regiment, Wheaton might have been mobilized for the Mexican War. Neither Curry, nor Adams, nor Cartwright, though, mentions him in their accounts, leading to the speculation that there may have been hard feelings involved.

Fraley Niebuhr's obituary in *The New York Times* mentions that he was "formerly a member of the Knickerbocker Baseball Club." He had been in failing health for several years and died at his home in Brooklyn in December 1901 at 82.

Until his retirement in 1895, Sam Kissam was considered one of the powers of the New York financial district. After a long illness, he died at 84 in 1915.

Charles DeBost died in Brooklyn in July 1912. The epitaph on his Green-Wood Cemetery headstone reads, "The strife is over, the battle done, the victory of life is won."

Walter Avery's obituary claims he was the last living member of the original Knickerbocker Baseball Club. And so he was. He died on June 10, 1904, at the age of 90.

After attending two opening-day games in April 1908, Henry Chadwick came down with a cold that developed into pneumonia. He was 83 when he died. In his will he wrote, "I remind Albert G. Spalding of his promise to me that a monument shall be erected over my grave in Greenwood Cemetery." Spalding kept his promise writing in his *Guide*, "It will not be too ornate, showy or ostentatious, but a simple and solid affair in keeping with the life of the man whose virtues it marks." The erected monument includes bronze replicas of crossed bats, a glove, and a catcher's mask. On top is a granite baseball and the four corners of his plot are marked by stone bases.

Doc Adams maintained his interest in the game all his life. Even in his seventies, he could sometimes be found playing in games with his sons and other younger men in his neighborhood. According to his son Roger, he could even then "astonish all the boys with his batting. He remained active in body and mind until his death at the age of eighty-four, January 3rd, 1899."

Poor Old Davis spent his last years living alone in a small Manhattan apartment with little contact with his family or old base ball playing friends. He had asked in the 1893 letter to Edward Talcott, an owner of the New York Giants, that money be collected for his headstone as a tribute to his role in the development of baseball. He suggested ten cents from each contributor. For whatever reason or reasons, those who remembered him failed to contribute and on a cold February Day in 1899 he was lowered into an unmarked grave where he remains to this day wrapped in whatever is left of his cherished Knickerbocker pennant.

In 2005, Lelands.com, an auction site for sports and Americana memorabilia, offered the following:

> One of the most important baseball trophies extant. Sterling silver trophy given to James Whyte Davis in 1875 to commemorate his 25th year with the New York Knickerbocker Baseball Club, the first ever organized baseball team. This is one of the oldest baseball trophies known, given to one of the earliest ballplayers. It comes in its original case, a hinged hard-shell display with "James Whyte Davis Sept. 26, 1875" stamped on top. The case is a velvet lined presentation box and in VG condition. The exquisite silver trophy inside is in the form of a baseball and has two silver bats lying in front of it. The award presentation took place at a banquet following baseball's first old-timers' game, between the Knicks of 1850 (known as the "Veterans"; the team included Daniel Luscious Adams, the catcher and founding father) and players from the 1860 squad, the "Youngs." Davis pitched for them. "J. W. Davis. K.B.B.C" is engraved on each of the bats and the ball reads: "Presented to James Whyte Davis on the Twenty Fifth Anniversary of his election as a member of the Knickerbocker Base Ball Club by his fellow members. 1850 Sept. 26 1875. Never 'Too Late.'" Davis had two nicknames: "The Fiend" and "Too Late." The names were as a result of his protesting at not being included in a game after arriving a few minutes late. James Whyte Davis was born in New York in 1826. He eventually chose the profession of stockbroker after deciding he did not wish to be part of his father's trade as a shipmaster but it was baseball that made him tick. He loved it with an almost unmatched passion and this passion led him to the Knickerbocker Base Ball Club. Just before the team reached its 10th anniversary in 1855 they unveiled their first banner on their clubhouse at Elysian Fields in Hoboken, New Jersey. The banner was taken home by Davis and it remained draped over his dresser. The original seller of this trophy discovered it in the attic of her husband's uncle in New Jersey in 1877, after his uncle had died. All we know about him is that he was in his 80s and that he had been an enormous fan of baseball who had grown up in the area in the early 1900s. The woman who found it has had it in storage ever since, but she wants its new owner to be someone who truly appreciates baseball history as well as someone who understands just how important this trophy is. If that describes you, then we need to go no further.

The trophy was sold for $105,850.71.

In 1938 the Baseball Hall of Fame began electing "Pioneers." These were individuals deemed to have made a significant off-the-field impact on the development of the sport. Cartwright and Chadwick were the first two admitted as Pioneers. In 1953 Harry Wright joined them. So, of the original Knickerbockers, only Cartwright is in the Hall of Fame. Doc and Jamie, for all of their contributions to the game of baseball, are, and probably always will be, ignored by all but the most serious of baseball historians.

It has been said that only the first step is difficult. The Knickerbockers took that first organizational step. Undoubtedly baseball would have survived without the Knickerbockers, but would it have been the game we know today? Likely not.